WODEHOUSE
IS THE BEST
MEDICINE

P. G. WODEHOUSE

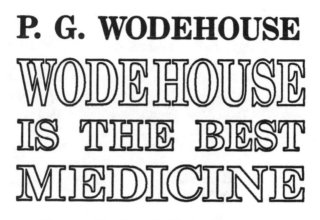

WODEHOUSE IS THE BEST MEDICINE

Foreword by Lendon H. Smith, M.D.
Preface by D. R. Bensen

BARNES
&NOBLE
BOOKS
NEW YORK

CONTENTS

FOREWORD
R̩: P. G. W.

I gravitated to the practice of pediatrics partly because I have a short attention span. It's easier to get children's medical histories, which are necessarily shorter than those of adults, especially those old enough to have trouble remembering whether the appendix came out in 1921 or 1931. It is all too easy for me to lose track of those, but pediatrics is a delight if you have a short attention span and you want to laugh and have fun: Examining the three-month-old who laughs and smiles at anyone; tricking the three-year-old into enjoying the exam as you pull a quarter out of his ear; and scaring the eight-year-old who likes to be scared (a little).

It's not a slam at P. G. Wodehouse's stories to say that part of their appeal for me is their comparative brevity—they don't strain my limited attention span as a novel would. This is not to say that they're simple. I am a slow, plodding reader and over the years I have learned that I can get most of a story line if I read the first sentence of every paragraph. You can't do that with Wodehouse—each one of his stories is an intricate weave of interconnected fibers, unexpected interactions and sudden appearances, all of them absolutely necessary to the final effect.

The Reader's Digest has a venerable department called "Laughter Is the Best Medicine," and that is the idea behind The Laugh Clinic, a program of "humor as healer" seminars I have been associated with for the last few years. When we laugh, the endorphins (our own private morphine-like substance) in our brain flow and make us feel good. The late Norman Cousins told in *Anatomy of an Illness* how he beat a debilitating, usually fatal illness with heavy doses of the Marx Brothers and other funny movies. Cousins found that if he laughed for ten minutes he would have two hours of pain-free sleep, and wonder of wonders, his blood sedimentation rate (a test of inflammation) would drop by about 10 or 12 percent.

I am trying to get the world to stop every hour on the hour and laugh, uproariously. Not little "tee-hees" but real guffaws: "Ho-ho." We do not need to actually find something funny before we laugh: just laugh for ten seconds every hour, and we will be healthier. If you think free-floating laughing is too silly, just read a little Wodehouse every hour for a few minutes. Your endorphins will flow, and you will be a better, healthier person for it. Can we get Public Broadcasting to read Wodehouse on the air every night? It might do wonders for the pledge drives.

When I give a lecture I start with a joke. One reason is that it is a kind of intelligence test for the audience, and gives me an idea of the direction the talk should take. If they don't laugh right away, I give them the basic "facts-and-get-out" lecture, called "This Is the Only Way to Rear Your Child." If they give me a few guffaws, I will get a lot deeper and more complex, going into the philosophical aspects of medical treatment (well laced with doctor jokes). But the big reason I get the audience to laugh is to get them to like me. If they like me, they will agree with most everything I say, and they will also be in a mood to buy my books at the end of the talk.

Wodehouse does the same thing (and sold a lot more books than I have). He gets us laughing with the first scene-setting paragraph. E.g., " ...the idea of having a Fat Uncles Sweepstake at the Drones Club had long been in Freddie Widgeon's mind, such as it was." Right from the start, the endorphins kick in. You cannot laugh and be depressed. You cannot laugh and get an ulcer. And you cannot read P. G. Wodehouse and not laugh.

The recommended dosage for Wodehouse is as many stories at a sitting as you feel like. There are no reported adverse side effects.

Lendon H. Smith, M.D.

PREFACE
Dr. Wodehouse

Unlike Fu Manchu, we know what kind of doctor P. G. Wodehouse was.
Doctor of Letters (D. Litt.) is what the University of Oxford granted him in
the summer of 1939. The degree was honorary, which was a good thing, as it
would have been pretty slow work for him to be earning the regular kind at
the age of fifty-eight. The Public Orator, Dr. Cyril Bailey, embellished the
occasion with an address in Latin, hailing Wodehouse as (in translation): "a
magic writer, than whom none is more expert to delight men's spirits and
get them laughing."

As Dr. Smith has just pointed out, delighting men's (and women's and
children's, of course) spirits and getting them laughing is better than drugs
for a lot of ailments and for promoting general good health, so Dr.
Wodehouse is right up there with Kildare and Welby.

These eleven (or doctor's dozen) stories show Wodehouse at his therapeutic
best, not only providing heroic doses of laughter but dealing fearlessly and
candidly with what we might call the cutting edge of medicine if it didn't
sound silly. Jeeves's hangover cure in "Jeeves Takes Charge" is as much a
medical breakthrough as any wonder drug, and the expose of chronic-patient
culture in "Romance at Droitgate Spa" is searing journalism worthy of
Geraldo Rivera or anyhow public television. Never before has the influence
of broken bones on painting and patronage been depicted as it has in "The
Spot of Art," and the aspiring hypnotic therapist need look no further than
"Sleepy Time" for the dangers and benefits of the technique. The difficulties
of giving up smoking and overeating are among the hottest health topics
today, and "The Man Who Gave Up Smoking" and "The Fat of the Land"
examine them from a markedly original standpoint.

Homeopathic medicine, with its doctrine of "like cures like," is practiced
rudely but effectively by Bobbie Wickham in "Mr. Potter Takes a Rest
Cure," in which the cure for stress is *lots* more stress. Mental health, speech
impediment and medical ethics are also dealt with, the volume as a whole
therefore covering as many areas as any issue of *The New England Journal
of Medicine* and providing more laughs.

An Exalted Personage in England, Exalted enough so that we prefer not
to mention her name (Mum's the word), is said to have told a guest that she
habitually kept a volume of Wodehouse on her bedside table. "Very good
reading when you're ill, Ma'am," the guest said. "*And* when you're well," the
Personage said firmly.

So, reader, hale or frail, read on. Dr. Wodehouse is always ready for a
house call.

D. R. Bensen

Romance at Droitgate Spa

It has been rightly said—and it is a fact on which we pride ourselves—that in the bar-parlour of the Anglers' Rest distinctions of class are unknown. Double Best Ports hobnob on terms of the easiest affability with humble Ginger Ales, and I myself have heard a Draught Beer in a Pewter call a Half Bottle of Champagne "old chap" and be addressed in turn as "old fellow." Once inside that enchanted room, we are all brothers, all equals, from the highest to the lowest.

It was with distress and embarrassment, therefore, that we had watched the Plain Vichy snubbing the friendly overtures of a meek little Milk and Soda, high-hatting him so coldly and persistently that in the end he gave it up and slunk out. Soon afterwards the Vichy also left, explaining that his doctor had warned him not to be out of bed after ten o'clock at night, and as the door closed behind him we settled down to discuss the unfortunate affair. The Small Bass who had introduced the two men to one another scratched his head ruefully.

"I can't understand it," he said. "I thought they'd have got on so well together. Twin souls, I thought they'd have been."

Mr. Mulliner stirred his hot scotch and lemon.

"What made you think that?"

"Well, they've both just had operations, and they both like talking about them."

"Ah," said Mr. Mulliner, "but what you are forgetting is that while one has been operated on for duodenal ulcer, the other has merely had his tonsils removed."

"What difference would that make?"

"Every difference. There is no sphere of life in which class-consciousness is so rampant as among invalids. The ancient Spartans, I believe, were a little standoffish towards their Helots, but not so standoffish as the man who has been out in Switzerland taking insulin for his diabetes towards the man who is simply undergoing treatment from the village doctor for an ingrowing toenail. This is particularly so, of course, in those places where invalids collect in gangs—Bournemouth, for example, or Buxton, or Droitgate Spa. In such resorts the atmosphere is almost unbelievably clique-y. The old aristocracy, the topnotchers with maladies that get written up in the medical journals, keep themselves to themselves pretty rigidly, I can assure you, and have a very short way with the smaller fry."

Mention of Droitgate Spa (said Mr. Mulliner, having ordered a second hot scotch and lemon) recalls to my mind the romance of my distant connection Frederick Fitch-Fitch, whose uncle, Major General Sir Aylmer Bastable, lived there. It was at Droitgate Spa that the story had its setting, and I have always thought it one that throws a very interesting light on conditions in the class of the community of which we have been speaking.

Frederick at that time was a young man of pleasing manners and exterior who supported life on a small private income, the capital of which was held in trust for him by his uncle, Sir Aylmer; and it was his great desire to induce the other to release this capital, so that he could go into the antique business.

For that was where Frederick's heart was. He wanted to buy a half interest in some good Olde Shoppe in the Bond Street neighbourhoode and start selling walnutte tables and things. So every once in a while he would journey down to Droitgate Spa and plead for the stuff, but every time he did so he went away with his dreams shattered. For circumstances had unfortunately so ordered themselves as to make this uncle of his a warped, soured uncle.

Major General Sir Aylmer Bastable, you see, had an unpleasant shock on coming to settle in Droitgate Spa. The head of a fine old family and the possessor of a distinguished military record, he had expected upon his arrival to be received with open arms by the best people and welcomed immediately into the inner set. But when it was discovered that all he had wrong with him was the gout in the right foot, he found himself cold-shouldered by the men who mattered and thrust back on the society of the asthma patients and the fellows with slight liver trouble.

This naturally soured his disposition a good deal, and his ill humour reacted upon his nephew. Every time Freddie came asking for capital to invest in antique shoppes, he found his uncle smarting from a snub from some swell whom the doctors had twice given up for dead, and so in no mood to part.

And then one day a more serious issue forced itself onto the agenda paper. At a charity matinée Freddie for the first time set eyes on Annabel Purvis. She was the assistant of The Great Boloni, a conjurer who had been engaged to perform at the entertainment, her duties being to skip downstage from time to time, hand him a bowl of goldfish, beam at the audience, do a sort of dance step, and skip back again. And with such winsome grace did she do this that Freddie fell in love at first sight.

It is not necessary for me to describe in detail how my distant connection contrived to make the girl's acquaintance, nor need I take you step by step through his courtship. Suffice it to say that during the cheese and celery course of a luncheon à deux some few weeks later Freddie proposed and was accepted. So now it became even more imperative than before that he induce his uncle to release his capital.

It was with a certain uneasiness that he travelled down to Droitgate Spa, for he was fully alive to the fact that the interview might prove a disagreeable one. However, his great love bore him on, and he made the journey and was shown into the room where the old man sat nursing a gouty foot.

"Hullo-ullo-ullo, Uncle!" he cried, for it was always his policy on these occasions to be buoyant till thrown out. "Good morning, good morning, good morning."

"Gaw!" said Sir Aylmer, with a sort of long, shuddering sigh. "It's you, is it?"

And he muttered something which Freddie did not quite catch, though he was able to detect the words "last straw."

"Well," he went on, "what do you want?"

"Oh, I just looked in," said Freddie. "How's everything?"

"Rotten," replied Sir Aylmer. "I've just lost my nurse."

"Dead?"

"Worse. Married. The clothheaded girl has gone off and got spliced to one of the *canaille*—a chap who's never had so much as athlete's foot. She must be crazy."

"Still, one sees her point of view."

"No, one doesn't."

"I mean," said Freddie, who felt strongly on this subject, "it's love that makes the world go round."

"It isn't anything of the kind," said Sir Aylmer. Like so many fine old soldiers, he was inclined to be a little literal-minded. "I never heard such dashed silly nonsense in my life. What makes the world go round is ... Well, I've forgotten at the moment, but it certainly isn't love. How the deuce could it?"

"Oh, right ho. I see what you mean," said Freddie. "But put it another way. Love conquers all. Love's all right, take it from me."

The old man looked at him sharply.

"Are you in love?"

"Madly."

"Of all the young cuckoos! And I suppose you've come to ask for money to get married on?"

"Not at all. I just dropped round to see how you were. Still, as the subject has happened to crop up—"

Sir Aylmer brooded for a moment, snorting in an undertone. "Who's the girl?" he demanded.

Freddie coughed, and fumbled with his collar. The crux of the situation, he realised, had now been reached. He had feared from the first that this was where the good old snag might conceivably sidle into the picture. For his Annabel was of humble station, and he knew how rigid were his relative's views on the importance of birth. No bigger snob ever swallowed a salicylate pill.

"Well, as a matter of fact," he said, "she's a conjurer's stooge."

"A *what?*"

"A conjurer's assistant, don't you know. I saw her first at a charity matinée. She was abetting a bloke called The Great Boloni."

"In what sense, abetting?"

"Well, she stood there upstage, don't you know, and every now and then she would skip downstage, hand this chap a bowl of goldfish or something, beam at the audience, do a sort of dance step and skip back again. You know the kind of thing."

A dark frown had come into Sir Aylmer's face.

"I do," he said grimly. "So! My only nephew has been ensnared by a bally, beaming goldfish-handler! Ha!"

"I wouldn't call it ensnared exactly," said Freddie deferentially.

"I would," said Sir Aylmer. "Get out of here."

"Right," said Freddie, and caught the 2:35 express back to London. And it was during the journey that an idea flashed upon him.

The last of the Fitch-Fitches was not a great student of literature, but he occasionally dipped into a magazine; and everybody who has ever dipped into a magazine has read a story about a hardhearted old man who won't accept the hero's girl at any price, so what do they do but plant her on him without telling him who she is and, by Jove, he falls under her spell completely and then they tear off their whiskers and there they are. There was a story of this nature in the magazine which Freddie had purchased at the newsstand at Droitgate Spa station, and as he read it, he remembered what his uncle had told him about his nurse handing in her portfolio.

By the time the train checked in at Paddington, his plans were fully formed.

"Listen," he said to Annabel Purvis, who had met him at the terminus, and Annabel said, "What?"

"Listen," said Freddie, and Annabel again said "What?"

"Listen," said Freddie, clasping her arm tenderly and steering her off in the direction of the refreshment room, where it was his intention to have a quick one. "To a certain extent I am compelled to admit that my expedition has been a washout... "

Annabel caught her breath sharply.

"No blessing?"

"No blessing."

"And no money?"

"No money. The old boy ran entirely true to stable form. He listened to what I had to say, snorted in an unpleasant manner and threw me out. The old routine. But what I'm working round to is that the skies are still bright and the bluebird on the job. I have a scheme. Could you be a nurse?"

"I used to nurse my uncle Joe."

"Then you shall nurse my uncle Aylmer. The present incumbent, he tells me, has just tuned out, and he needs a successor. I will phone him that I am despatching immediately a red-hot nurse whom he will find just the same as Mother makes, and you shall go down to Droitgate Spa and ingratiate yourself."

"But how?"

"Why, cluster round him. Smooth his pillow. Bring him cooling drinks. Coo to him, and give him the old oil. Tell him you are of gentle birth, if that's the expression I want. And when the time is ripe, when you have twined yourself about his heart and he looks upon you as a daughter, shoot me a wire and I'll come down and fall in love with you and he will give his consent, blessing and the stuff. I guarantee this plan. It works."

So Annabel went to Droitgate Spa, and about three weeks later a telegram arrived for Freddie, running as follows:

HAVE INGRATIATED SELF   COME AT ONCE   LOVE AND KISSES ANNABEL

Within an hour of its arrival, Freddie was on his way to Podagra Lodge, his uncle's residence.

He found Sir Aylmer in his study. Annabel was sitting by his side, reading aloud to him from a recently published monograph on certain obscure ailments of the medulla oblongata. For the old man, though a mere gout patient, had pathetic aspirations towards higher things. There was a cooling drink on the table, and as Freddie entered the girl paused in her reading to smooth her employer's pillow.

"Gaw!" said Sir Aylmer. "You again?"

"Here I am," said Freddie.

"Well, by an extraordinary chance, I'm glad to see you. Leave us for a moment, Miss Purvis. I wish to speak to my nephew here, such as he is, on a serious and private matter. Did you notice that girl?" he said, as the door closed.

"I did, indeed."

"Pretty."

"An eyeful."

"And as good," said Sir Aylmer, "as she is beautiful. You should see her smooth pillows. And what a cooling drink she mixes! Excellent family, too, I understand. Her father is a colonel. Or, rather, was. He's dead."

"Ah well, all flesh is as grass."

"No, it isn't. It's nothing of the kind. The two things are entirely different. I've seen flesh and I've seen grass. No resemblance whatever. However, that is not the point at issue. What I wanted to say was that if you were not a damned fool, that's the sort of girl you would be in love with."

"I am."

"A damned fool?"

"No. In love with that girl."

"What! You have fallen in love with Miss Purvis? Already?"

"I have."

"Well, that's the quickest thing I ever saw. What about your beaming goldfish?"

"Oh, that's all over. A mere passing boyish fancy."

Sir Aylmer took a deep swig at his cooling drink, and regarded him in silence for a moment.

"Well," he said at length, breathing heavily, "if that's the airy, casual way in which you treat life's most sacred emotions, the sooner you are safely married and settled down, the better. If you're allowed to run around loose much longer, indulging those boyish fancies of yours, I foresee the breach-of-promise case of the century. However, I'm not saying I'm not relieved. I am relieved. I suppose she wore tights, this goldfish girl?"

"Pink."

"Disgusting. Thank God it's all over. Very good, then. You are free, I understand, to have a pop at Miss Purvis. Do you propose to do so?"

"I do."

"Excellent. You get that sweet, refined, most-suitable-in-all-respects girl to marry you, and I'll hand over that money of yours, every penny of it."

"I will start at once."

"Heaven speed your wooing." said Sir Aylmer.

And ten minutes later Freddie was able to inform his uncle that his whirlwind courtship had been successful, and Sir Aylmer said that when he had asked heaven to speed his wooing he had had no notion that it would speed it to quite that extent. He congratulated Freddie warmly and said he hoped that he appreciated his good fortune, and Freddie said he certainly did, because his love was like a red, red rose, and Sir Aylmer said, No, she wasn't, and when Freddie added that he was walking on air Sir Aylmer said he couldn't be, the thing was physically impossible.

However, he gave his blessing and promised to release Freddie's capital as soon as the necessary papers were drawn up, and Freddie went back to London to see his lawyer about this.

His mood, as the train sped through the quiet countryside, was one of perfect tranquillity and happiness. It seemed to him that his troubles were now definitely ended. He looked down the vista of the years and saw nothing but joy and sunshine. If somebody had told Frederick Fitch-Fitch at that moment that even now a V-shaped depression was coming along which would shortly blacken the skies and lower the general temperature to freezing point, he would not have believed him.

Nor when, two days later, as he sat in his club, he was informed that a Mr. Rackstraw was waiting to see him in the small smoking room, did he have an inkling that here was the V-shaped depression in person. His heart was still light as he went down the passage, wondering idly, for the name was unfamiliar to him, who this Mr. Rackstraw might be. He entered the room, and found there a tall, thin man with pointed black moustaches who was pacing up and down, nervously taking rabbits out of his top hat as he walked.

"Mr. Rackstraw?"

His visitor spun round, dropping a rabbit. He gazed at Freddie piercingly. He had bright, glittering, sinister eyes.

"That is my name. Mortimer Rackstraw."

Freddie's mind had flown back to the charity matinée at which he had first seen Annabel, and he recognised the fellow now.

"The Great Boloni, surely?"

"I call myself that professionally. So you are Mr. Fitch? So *you* are Mr. Fitch? Ha! Fiend!"

"Eh?"

"I am not mistaken? You are Frederick Fitch?"

"Frederick Fitch-Fitch."

"I beg your pardon. In that case, I should have said 'Fiend! Fiend!' "

He produced a pack of cards and asked Freddie to take one —any one—and memorise it and put it back. Freddie did so absently. He was considerably fogged. He could make nothing of all this.

"How do you mean—Fiend-Fiend?" he asked.

The other sneered unpleasantly.

"Cad!" he said, twirling his moustache.

"Cad?" said Freddie, mystified.

"Yes, sir. Cad. You have stolen the girl I love."

"I don't understand."

"Then you must be a perfect ass. It's quite simple, isn't it? I can't put it any plainer, can I? I say you have stolen ... Well, look here," said Mortimer Rackstraw. "Suppose this top hat is me. This rabbit," he went on, producing it from the lining, "is the girl I love. You come along and, presto, the rabbit vanishes."

"It's up your sleeve."

"It is not up my sleeve. And if it were, if I had a thousand sleeves and rabbits up every one of them, that would not alter the fact that you have treacherously robbed me of Annabel Purvis."

Freddie began to see daylight. He was able to appreciate the other's emotion.

"So you love Annabel too?"

"I do."

"I don't wonder. Nice girl, what? I see, I see. You worshipped her in secret, never telling your love ... "

"I did tell my love. We were engaged."

"Engaged?"

"Certainly. And this morning I get a letter from her saying that it's all off, because she has changed her mind and is going to marry you. She has thrown me over."

"Oh, ah? Well, I'm frightfully sorry—deepest sympathy, and all that—but I don't see what's to be done about it, what?"

"I do. There still remains—revenge."

"Oh, I say, dash it! You aren't going to be stuffy about it?"

"I am going to be stuffy about it. For the moment you triumph. But do not imagine that this is the end. You have not heard the last of me. Not by any means. You may have stolen the woman I love with your underhanded chicanery, but I'll fix you."

"How?"

"Never mind how. You will find out how quite soon enough. A nasty jolt you're going to get, my good fiend, and almost immediately. As sure," said Mortimer Rackstraw, illustrating by drawing one from Freddie's back hair, "as eggs are eggs. I wish you a very good afternoon."

He took up his top hat, which in his emotion he had allowed to fall to the ground, brushed it on his coat sleeve, extracted from it a cage of lovebirds and strode out.

A moment later he returned, bowed a few times to right and left and was gone again.

To say that Freddie did not feel a little uneasy as the result of this scene would be untrue. There had been something in the confident manner in which the other had spoken of revenging himself that he had not at all liked. The words had had a sinister ring, and all through the rest of the day he pondered thoughtfully, wondering what a man so trained in the art of having things up his sleeve might have up it now. It was in meditative mood that he dined, and only on the following morning did his equanimity return to him.

Able, now that he had slept on it, to review the disturbing conversation in its proper perspective, he came to the conclusion that the fellow's threats had been mere bluff. What, after all, he asked himself, could this conjurer do? It was not as if they had been living in the Middle Ages, when chaps of that sort used to put spells on you and change you into things.

No, he decided, it was mere bluff, and with his complacency completely restored had just lighted a cigarette and fallen to dreaming of the girl he loved, when a telegram was brought to him.

It ran as follows:

COME AT ONCE   ALL LOST   RUIN STARES FACE   LOVE AND KISSES   ANNABEL

Half an hour later, he was in the train, speeding towards Droitgate Spa.

It had been Freddie's intention, on entering the train, to devote the journey to earnest meditation. But, as always happens when one wishes to concentrate and brood during a railway journey, he found himself closeted with a talkative fellow-traveller.

The one who interrupted Freddie's thoughts was a flabby, puffy man of middle age, wearing a red waistcoat, brown shoes, a morning coat and a bowler hat. With such a Grade A bounder, even had his mind been at rest, Freddie would have had little in common, and he sat chafing while the prismatic fellow prattled on. Nearly an hour passed before he was freed from the infliction of the other's conversation, but eventually the man's head began to nod, and presently he was snoring and Freddie was able to give himself up to his reverie.

His thoughts became less and less agreeable as the train rolled on. And what rendered his mental distress so particularly acute was the lack of informative detail in Annabel's telegram. It seemed to him to offer so wide a field for uncomfortable speculation.

"All lost," for instance. A man could do a lot of thinking about a phrase like that. And "Ruin stares face." Why, he asked himself, did ruin stare face? While commending Annabel's thriftiness in keeping the thing down to twelve words, he could not help wishing that she could have brought herself to spring another twopence and be more lucid.

But of one thing he felt certain. All this had something to do with his recent visitor. Behind that mystic telegram he seemed to see the hand of Mortimer Rackstraw, that hand whose quickness deceived the eye, and he knew that in lightly dismissing the other as a negligible force he had been too sanguine.

By the time he reached Podagra Lodge, the nervous strain had become almost intolerable. As he rang the bell, he was quivering like some jelly set before a diet patient, and the sight of Annabel's face as she opened the door did nothing to alleviate his perturbation. The girl was obviously all of a twitter.

"Oh, Freddie!" she cried. "The worst has happened."

Freddie gulped.

"Rackstraw?"

"Yes," said Annabel. "But how did you know about him?"

"He came to see me, bubbling over a good deal with veiled menaces and what not," explained Freddie. He frowned and eyed her closely. "Why didn't you tell me you had been engaged to that bird?"

"I didn't think you would be interested. It was just a passing girlish fancy."

"You're sure? You didn't really love this blighted prestidigitator?"

"No, no. I was dazzled for a while, as any girl might have been, when he sawed me in half, but then you came along and I saw that I had been mistaken and that you were the only man in the world for me."

"Good egg," said Freddie, relieved.

He kissed her fondly and, as he did so, there came to his ears the sound of rhythmic hammering from somewhere below.

"What's that?" he asked.

Annabel wrung her hands.

"It's Mortimer!"

"Is he here?"

"Yes. He arrived on the one-fifteen. I locked him in the cellar."

"Why?"

"To stop him going to the Pump Room."

"Why shouldn't he go to the Pump Room?"

"Because Sir Aylmer has gone there to listen to the band, and they must not meet. If they do, we are lost. Mortimer has hatched a fearful plot."

Freddie's heart seemed to buckle under within him. He had tried to be optimistic, but all along he had known that Mortimer Rackstraw would hatch some fearful plot. He could have put his shirt on it. A born hatcher.

"What plot?"

Annabel wrung her hands again.

"He means to introduce Sir Aylmer to my uncle Joe. He wired to him to come to Droitgate Spa. He had arranged to meet him at the Pump Room, and then he was going to introduce him to Sir Aylmer."

Freddie was a little fogged. It did not seem to him much of a plot.

"Now that I can never be his, all he wants is to make himself unpleasant and prevent our marriage. And he knows that Sir Aylmer will never consent to your marrying me if he finds out that I have an uncle like Uncle Joe."

Freddie ceased to be fogged. He saw the whole devilish scheme now—a scheme worthy of the subtle brain that could put the ace of spades back in the pack, shuffle, cut three times, and then produce it from the inside of a lemon.

"Is he so frightful?" he quavered.

"Look," said Annabel simply. She took a photograph from her bosom and extended it towards him with a trembling hand. "That is Uncle Joe, taken in the masonic regalia of a Grand Exalted Periwinkle of the Mystic Order of Whelks."

Freddie glanced at the photograph and started back with a hoarse cry. Annabel nodded sadly.

"Yes," she said. "That is how he takes most people. The only faint hope I have is that he won't have been able to come. But if he has— "

"He has," cried Freddie, who had been fighting for breath. "We travelled down in the train together."

"What!"

"Yes. He must be waiting at the Pump Room now."

"And at any moment Mortimer will break his way out of the cellar. The door is not strong. What shall we do?"

"There is only one thing left to do. I have all the papers..."

"You have no time to read now."

"The legal papers, the ones my uncle has to sign in order to release my money. There is just a chance that if I rush to the Pump Room I may get him to put his name on the dotted line before the worst happens."

"Then rush," cried Annabel.

"I will," said Freddie.

He kissed her quickly, grabbed his hat, and was off the mark like a jack rabbit.

A man who is endeavouring to lower the record for the distance between Podagra Lodge, which is in Arterio-Sclerosis Avenue, and the Droitgate Spa Pump Room has little leisure for thinking, but Freddie managed to put in a certain amount as his feet skimmed the pavement. And the trend of his thought was such as to give renewed vigour to his legs. He could scarcely have moved more rapidly if he had been a character in a two-reel film with the police after him.

And there was need for speed. Beyond a question, Annabel had been right when she had said that Sir Aylmer would never consent to their union if he found out that she had an uncle like her uncle Joe. Uncle Joe would get right in amongst him. Let them but meet, and nothing was more certain than that the haughty old man would veto the proposed nuptials.

A final burst of speed took him panting up the Pump Room steps and into the rotunda where all that was best and most refined in Droitgate Spa was accustomed to assemble of an afternoon and listen to the band. He saw Sir Aylmer in a distant seat and hurried towards him.

"Gaw!" said Sir Aylmer. "You?"

Freddie could only nod.

"Well, stop puffing like that and sit down," said Sir Aylmer. "They're just going to play 'Poet and Peasant.' "

Freddie recovered his breath.

"Uncle— " he began. But it was too late. Even as he spoke, there was a crash of brass and Sir Aylmer's face assumed that reverent, doughlike expression of attention so familiar in the rotundas of cure resorts.

"Sh," he said.

Of all the uncounted millions who in their time have listened to bands playing "Poet and Peasant," few can ever have listened with such a restless impatience as did Frederick Fitch-Fitch on this occasion. Time was flying. Every second was precious. At any moment disaster might befall. And the band went on playing as if it had taken on a life job. It seemed to him an eternity before the final oom-pom-pa.

"Uncle," he cried, as the echoes died away.

"Sh," said Sir Aylmer testily, and Freddie, with a dull despair, perceived that they were going to get an encore.

Of all the far-flung myriads who year in and year out have listened to bands playing the "Overture" to *Raymond*, few can ever have chafed as did Frederick Fitch-Fitch now. This suspense was unmanning him, this delay was torture. He took the papers and a fountain pen from his pocket and toyed with them nervously. He wondered dully as he sat there how the opera *Raymond* had ever managed to get itself performed, if the "Overture" was as long as this. They must have rushed it through in the last five minutes of the evening as the audience groped for its hats and wraps.

But there is an end to all things, even to the "Overture" from *Raymond.* Just as the weariest river winds somewhere safe to sea, so does this "Overture" eventually finish. And when it did, when the last notes faded into silence and the conductor stood bowing and smiling with that cool assumption, common to all conductors, that it is they and not the perspiring orchestra who have been doing the work, he started again.

"Uncle," he said, "may I trouble you for a moment... These papers."

Sir Aylmer cocked an eye at the documents.

"What papers are those?"

"The ones you have to sign, releasing my capital."

"Oh, those," said Sir Aylmer genially. The music had plainly mellowed him. "Of course, yes. Certainly, certainly. Give me... "

He broke off, and Freddie saw that he was looking at a distinguished, silvery-haired man with thin, refined features, who was sauntering by.

"Afternoon, Rumbelow," he said.

There was an unmistakable note of obsequiousness in Sir Aylmer's voice. His face had become pink, and he was shuffling his feet and twiddling his fingers. The man to whom he had spoken paused and looked down. Seeing who it was that had accosted him, he raised a silvery eyebrow. His manner was undisguisedly supercilious.

"Ah, Bastable," he said distantly.

A duller man than Sir Aylmer Bastable could not have failed

to detect the cold hauteur in his voice. Freddie saw the flush on his uncle's face deepen. Sir Aylmer mumbled something about hoping that the distinguished-looking man was feeling better today.

"Worse," replied the other curtly. "Much worse. The doctors are baffled. Mine is a very complicated case." He paused for a moment, and his delicately chiselled lip curled in a sneer. "And how is the gout, Bastable? Gout! Ha, ha!"

Without waiting for a reply, he passed on and joined a group that stood chatting close by. Sir Aylmer choked down a mortified oath.

"Snob!" he muttered. "Thinks he's everybody just because he's got telangiecstasis. I don't see what's so wonderful about having telangiecstasis. Anybody could have... What on earth are you doing? What the devil's all this you're waving under my nose? Papers? Papers? I don't want any papers. Take them away, sir!"

And before Freddie could burst into the impassioned plea which trembled on his lips, a commotion in the doorway distracted his attention. His heart missed a beat, and he sat there, frozen.

On the threshold stood Mortimer Rackstraw. He was making some enquiry of an attendant, and Freddie could guess only too well what the enquiry was. Mortimer Rackstraw was asking which of those present was Major General Sir Aylmer Bastable. Attached to his arm, obviously pleading with him and appealing to his better self, Annabel Purvis gazed up into his face with tear-filled eyes.

A moment later, the conjurer strode up, still towing the girl. He halted before Sir Aylmer and threw Annabel aside like a soiled glove. His face was cold and hard and remorseless. With one hand he was juggling mechanically with two billiard balls and a bouquet of roses.

"Sir Aylmer Bastable?"

"Yes."

"I forbid the banns."

"What banns?"

"Their banns," said Mortimer Rackstraw, removing from his lips the hand with which he had been coldly curling his moustache and jerking it in the direction of Annabel and Freddie, who stood clasped in each other's arms, waiting for they knew not what.

"They're not up yet," said Annabel.

The conjurer seemed a little taken aback.

"Oh?" he said. "Well, when they are, I forbid them. And so will you, Sir Aylmer, when you hear all."

Sir Aylmer puffed.

"Who is this tight bounder?" he asked irritably.

Mortimer Rackstraw shook his head and took the two of clubs from it.

"A bounder, maybe," he said, "but not tight. I have come here, Sir Aylmer, in a spirit of altruism to warn you that if you allow your nephew to marry this girl the grand old name of Bastable will be mud."

Sir Aylmer started.

"Mud?"

"Mud. She comes from the very dregs of society."

"I don't," cried Annabel.

"Of course she doesn't," cried Freddie.

"Certainly she does not," assented Sir Aylmer warmly. "She told me herself that her father was a colonel."

Mortimer Rackstraw uttered a short, sneering laugh and took an egg from his left elbow.

"She did, eh? Did she add that he was a colonel in the Salvation Army?"

"What!"

"And that before he saw the light he was a Silver Ring bookie, known to all the heads as Rat-Faced Rupert, the Bermondsey Twister?"

"Good God!"

Sir Aylmer turned to the girl with an awful frown.

"Is this true?"

"Of course it's true," said Mortimer Rackstraw. "And if you want further proof of her unfitness to be your nephew's bride, just take a look at her uncle Joe, who is now entering left-centre."

And Freddie, listless now and without hope, saw that his companion of the train was advancing towards them. He heard Sir Aylmer gasp and was aware that Annabel had stiffened in his arms. He was not surprised. The sun, filtering through the glass of the rotunda, lit up the man's flabby puffiness, his morning coat, his red waistcoat and his brown shoes, and rarely, if ever, thought Freddie, could the sun of Droitgate Spa have shone on a more ghastly outsider.

There was nothing, however, in the newcomer's demeanour to suggest that he felt himself out of place in these refined surroundings. His manner had self-confidence. He sauntered up and without *gêne* slapped the conjurer on the back and patted Annabel on the shoulder.

" 'Ullo, Mort. 'Ullo, Annie, my dear."

Sir Aylmer, who had blinked, staggered and finally recovered himself, spoke in a voice of thunder.

"You, sir! Is this true?"

"What's that, old cock?"

"Are you this girl's uncle?"

"That's right."

"Gaw!" said Sir Aylmer.

He would have spoken further, but at this point the band burst into "Pomp and Circumstance" and conversation was temporarily suspended. When it became possible once more for the human voice to make itself heard, it was Annabel's Uncle Joe who took the floor. He had recognised Freddie.

"Why, I've met you," he said. "We travelled down in the train together. Who's this young feller, Annie, that's huggin' and squeezin' you?"

"He is the man I am going to marry," said Annabel.

"He is not the man you are going to marry," said Sir Aylmer.

"Yes, I am the man she is going to marry," said Freddie.

"No, you're not the man she is going to marry," said Mortimer Rackstraw.

Annabel's Uncle Joe seemed puzzled. He appeared not to know what to make of this conflict of opinion.

"Well, settle it among yourselves," he said genially. "All I know is that whoever does marry you, Annie, is going to get a good wife."

"That's me," said Freddie.

"No, it isn't," said Sir Aylmer.

"Yes, it is," said Annabel.

"No, it's not," said Mortimer Rackstraw.

"Because I'm sure no man," proceeded Uncle Joe, "ever had a better niece. I've never forgotten the way you used to come and smooth my pillow and bring me cooling drinks when I was in the hospital."

There was the sound of a sharp intake of breath. Sir Aylmer, who was saying, "It isn't, it isn't, it isn't," had broken off abruptly.

"Hospital?" he said. "Were you ever in a hospital?"

Mr. Boffin laughed indulgently.

"Was I ever in a hospital! That's a good 'un. That would make the boys on the medical council giggle. Ask them at St. Luke's if Joe Boffin was ever in a hospital. Ask them at St. Christopher's. Why, I've spent most of my life in hospitals. Started as a child with Congenital Pyloric Hypertrophy of the Stomach and never looked back."

Sir Aylmer was trembling violently. A look of awe had come into his face, the look which a small boy wears when he sees a heavyweight champion of the world.

"Did you say your name was Joe Boffin?"

"That's right."

"Not *the* Joe Boffin? Not the man there was that interview with in the Christmas number of *The Lancet?*"

"That's me."

Sir Aylmer started forward impulsively.

"May I shake your hand?"

"Put it there."

"I am proud to meet you, Mr. Boffin. I am one of your greatest admirers."

"Nice of you to say so, ol' man."

"Your career has been an inspiration to me. Is it really true that you have Thrombosis of the Heart *and* Vesicular Emphysema of the Lungs?"

"That's right."

"And that your temperature once went up to 107.5?"

"Twice. When I had Hyperpyrexia."

Sir Aylmer sighed.

"The best I've ever done is 102.2."

Joe Boffin patted him on the back.

"Well, that's not bad," he said. "Not bad at all."

"Excuse me," said a well-bred voice.

It was the distinguished-looking man with the silvery hair who had approached them, the man Sir Aylmer had addressed as Rumbelow. His manner was diffident. Behind him stood an eager group, staring and twiddling their fingers.

"Excuse me, my dear Bastable, for intruding on a private conversation, but I fancied... and my friends fancied... "

"We all fancied," said the group.

"That we overheard the name Boffin. Can it be, sir, that you are Mr. *Joseph* Boffin?"

"That's right."

"Boffin of St. Luke's?"

"That's right."

The silvery-haired man seemed overcome by a sudden shyness. He giggled nervously.

"Then may we say—my friends and I—how much... We felt we would just like... Unwarrantable intrusion, of course, but we are all such great admirers... I suppose you have to go through a good deal of this sort of thing, Mr. Boffin... people coming up to you, I mean, and... perfect strangers, I mean to say... "

"Quite all right, old man, quite all right. Always glad to meet the fans."

"Then may I introduce myself? I am Lord Rumbelow. These are my friends, the Duke of Mull, the Marquis of Peckham, Lord Percy... "

" 'Ow are you, 'ow are you? Come and join us, boys. My niece, Miss Purvis."

"Charmed."

"The young chap she's going to marry."

"How do you do?"

"And his uncle, Sir Aylmer Bastable."

All heads were turned towards the Major General. Lord Rumbelow spoke in an awed voice.

"Is this really so, Bastable? Your nephew is actually going to marry Mr. Boffin's niece? I congratulate you, my dear fellow. A most signal honor." A touch of embarrassment came into his manner. He coughed. "We were just talking about you, oddly enough, Bastable, my friends and I. Saying what a pity it was that we saw so little of you. And we were wondering—it was the Duke's suggestion—if you would care to become a member of a little club we have—quite a small affair—rather exclusive, we like to feel —the Twelve Jolly Stretcher Cases... "

"My dear Rumbelow!"

"We have felt for a long time that our company was incomplete without you. So you will join us? Capital, capital! Perhaps you will look in there tonight? Mr. Boffin, of couse," he went on deprecatingly, "would, I am afraid, hardly condescend to allow himself to be entertained by so humble a little circle. Otherwise—"

Joe Boffin slapped him affably on the back.

"My dear feller, I'd be delighted. There's nothing stuck-up about me."

"Well, really! I hardly know what to say... "

"We can't all be Joe Boffins. That's the way I look at it."

"The true democratic spirit."

"Why, I was best man at a chap's wedding last week, and all he'd got was emotional dermatitis."

"Amazing! Then you and Sir Aylmer will be with us tonight? Delightful. We can give you a bottle of lung tonic which I think you will appreciate. We pride ourselves on our cellar."

A babble of happy chatter had broken out, almost drowning the band, which was now playing the "Overture" to *William Tell*, and Mr. Boffin, opening his waistcoat, was showing the Duke of Mull the scar left by his first operation. Sir Aylmer, watching them with a throbbing heart, was dizzily aware of a fountain pen being thrust into his hand.

"Eh?" he said. "What? What's this? What, what?"

"The papers," said Freddie. "The merry old documents in the case. You sign here, where my thumb is."

"Eh? What? Eh? Ah yes, to be sure. Yes, yes, yes," said Sir Aylmer, absently affixing his signature.

"Thank you, Uncle, a thousand— "

"Quite, quite. But don't bother me now, my boy. Busy. Got a lot to talk about to these friends of mine. Take the girl away and give her a sulphur water."

And, brushing aside Mortimer Rackstraw, who was offering him a pack of cards, he joined the group about Joe Boffin. Freddie clasped Annabel in a fond embrace. Mortimer Rackstraw stood glaring for a moment, twisting his moustache. Then he took the flags of all nations from Annabel's back hair and with a despairing gesture strode from the room.

Jeeves Takes Charge

————— • —————

Now, touching this business of old Jeeves—my man, you know —how do we stand? Lots of people think I'm much too dependent on him. My Aunt Agatha, in fact, has even gone so far as to call him my keeper. Well, what I say is: Why not? The man's a genius. From the collar upward he stands alone. I gave up trying to run my own affairs within a week of his coming to me. That was about half a dozen years ago, directly after the rather rummy business of Florence Craye, my Uncle Willoughby's book, and Edwin, the Boy Scout.

The thing really began when I got back to Easeby, my uncle's place in Shropshire. I was spending a week or so there, as I generally did in the summer; and I had had to break my visit to come back to London to get a new valet. I had found Meadowes, the fellow I had taken to Easeby with me, sneaking my silk socks, a thing no bloke of spirit could stick at any price. It transpiring, moreover, that he had looted a lot of other things here and there about the place, I was reluctantly compelled to hand the misguided blighter the mitten and go to London to ask the registry office to dig up another specimen for my approval. They sent me Jeeves.

I shall always remember the morning he came. It so happened that the night before I had been present at a rather cheery little supper, and I was feeling pretty rocky. On top of this I was trying to read a book Florence Craye had given me. She had been one of the house-party at Easeby, and two or three days before I left we had got engaged. I was due back at the end of the week, and I knew she would expect me to have finished the book by then. You see, she was particularly keen on boosting me up a bit nearer her own plane of intellect. She was a girl with a wonderful profile, but steeped to the gills in serious purpose. I can't give you a better idea of the way things stood than by telling you that the book she'd given me to read was called *Types of Ethical Theory*, and that when I opened it at random I struck a page:—

> *The postulate or common understanding involved in speech is certainly co-extensive, in the obligation it carries, with the social organism of which language is the instrument, and the ends of which it is an effort to subserve.*

All perfectly true, no doubt; but not the sort of thing to spring on a lad with a morning head.

I was doing my best to skim through this bright little volume when the bell rang. I crawled off the sofa and opened the door. A kind of darkish sort of respectful Johnnie stood without.

"I was sent by the agency, sir," he said. "I was given to understand that you required a valet."

I'd have preferred an undertaker; but I told him to stagger in, and he floated noiselessly through the doorway like a healing zephyr. That impressed me from the start. Meadowes had had flat feet and used to clump. This fellow didn't seem to have any feet at all. He just streamed in. He had a grave, sympathetic face, as if he, too, knew what it was to sup with the lads.

"Excuse me, sir," he said gently.

Then he seemed to flicker, and wasn't there any longer. I heard him moving about in the kitchen, and presently he came back with a glass on a tray.

"If you would drink this, sir," he said, with a kind of bedside manner, rather like the royal doctor shooting the bracer into the sick prince. "It is a little preparation of my own invention. It is the Worcester sauce that gives it its colour. The raw egg makes it nutritious. The red pepper gives it its bite. Gentlemen have told me they have found it extremely invigorating after a late evening."

I would have clutched at anything that looked like a life-line that morning. I swallowed the stuff. For a moment I felt as if somebody had touched off a bomb inside the old bean and was strolling down my throat with a lighted torch, and then everything seemed suddenly to get all right. The sun shone in through the window; birds twittered in the tree-tops; and, generally speaking, hope dawned once more.

"You're engaged!" I said, as soon as I could say anything.

I perceived clearly that this cove was one of the world's workers, the sort no home should be without.

"Thank you, sir. My name is Jeeves."

"You can start in at once?"

"Immediately, sir."

"Because I'm due down at Easeby, in Shropshire, the day after to-morrow."

"Very good, sir." He looked past me at the mantelpiece. "That is an excellent likeness of Lady Florence Craye, sir. It is two years since I saw her ladyship. I was at one time in Lord Worplesdon's employment. I tendered my resignation because I could not see eye to eye with his lordship in his desire to dine in dress trousers, a flannel shirt, and a shooting coat."

He couldn't tell me anything I didn't know about the old boy's eccentricity. This Lord Worplesdon was Florence's father. He was the old buster who, a few years later, came down to breakfast one morning, lifted the first cover he saw, said "Eggs! Eggs! Eggs! Damn all eggs!" in an overwrought sort of voice, and instantly legged it for France, never to return to the bosom of his family. This, mind you, being a bit of luck for the bosom of the family, for old Worplesdon had the worst temper in the county.

I had known the family ever since I was a kid, and from boyhood up this old boy had put the fear of death into me. Time, the great healer, could never remove from my memory the occasion when he found me—then a stripling of fifteen—smoking one of his special cigars in the stables. He got after me with a hunting-crop just at the moment when I was beginning to realise that what I wanted most on earth was solitude and repose, and chased me more than a mile across difficult country. If there was a flaw, so to speak, in the pure joy of being engaged to Florence, it was the fact that she rather took after her father, and one was never certain when she might erupt. She had a wonderful profile, though.

"Lady Florence and I are engaged, Jeeves," I said.

"Indeed, sir?"

You know, there was a kind of rummy something about his manner. Perfectly all right and all that, but not what you'd call chirpy. It somehow gave me the impression that he wasn't keen on Florence. Well, of course, it wasn't my business. I supposed that while he had been valeting old Worplesdon she must have trodden on his toes in some way. Florence was a dear girl, and, seen sideways, most awfully good-looking; but if she had a fault it was a tendency to be a bit imperious with the domestic staff.

At this point in the proceedings there was another ring at the front door. Jeeves shimmered out and came back with a telegram. I opened it. It ran:

RETURN IMMEDIATELY. EXTREMELY URGENT. CATCH FIRST TRAIN. FLORENCE.

"Rum!" I said.

"Sir?"

"Oh, nothing!"

It shows how little I knew Jeeves in those days that I didn't go a bit deeper into the matter with him. Nowadays I would never dream of reading a rummy communication without asking him what he thought of it. And this one was devilish odd. What I mean is, Florence knew I was going back to Easeby the day after to-morrow, anyway; so why the hurry call? Something must have happened, of course; but I couldn't see what on earth it could be.

"Jeeves," I said, "we shall be going down to Easeby this afternoon. Can you manage it?"

"Certainly, sir."

"You can get your packing done and all that?"

"Without any difficulty, sir. Which suit will you wear for the journey?"

"This one."

I had on a rather sprightly young check that morning, to which I was a good deal attached; I fancied it, in fact, more than a little. It was perhaps rather sudden till you got used to it, but nevertheless, an extremely sound effort, which many lads at the club and elsewhere had admired unrestrainedly.

"Very good, sir."

Again there was that kind of rummy something in his manner. It was the way he said it, don't you know. He didn't like the suit. I pulled myself together to assert myself. Sonething seemed to tell me that, unless I was jolly careful and nipped this lad in the bud, he would be starting to boss me. He had the aspect of a distinctly resolute blighter.

Well, I wasn't going to have any of that sort of thing, by Jove! I'd seen so many cases of fellows who had become perfect slaves to their valets. I remember poor old Aubrey Fothergill telling me —with absolute tears in his eyes, poor chap!—one night at the club, that he had been compelled to give up a favourite pair of brown shoes simply because Meekyn, his man, disapproved of them. You have to keep these fellows in their place, don't you know. You have to work the good old iron-hand-in-the-velvet-glove wheeze. If you give them a what's-its-name, they take a thingummy.

"Don't you like this suit, Jeeves?" I said coldly.

"Oh, yes, sir."

"Well, what don't you like about it?"

"It is a very nice suit, sir."

"Well, what's wrong with it? Out with it, dash it!"

"If I might make the suggestion, sir, a simple brown or blue, with a hint of some quiet twill— "

"What absolute rot!"

"Very good, sir."

"Perfectly blithering, my dear man!"

"As you say, sir."

I felt as if I had stepped on the place where the last stair ought to have been, but wasn't. I felt defiant, if you know what I mean, and there didn't seem anything to defy.

"All right, then," I said.

"Yes, sir."

And then he went away to collect his kit, while I started in again on *Types of Ethical Theory* and took a stab at a chapter headed "Idiopsychological Ethics."

Most of the way down in the train that afternoon, I was wondering what could be up at the other end. I simply couldn't see what could have happened. Easeby wasn't one of those country houses you read about in the society novels, where young girls are lured on to play baccarat and then skinned to the bone of their jewellery, and so on. The house-party I had left had consisted entirely of law-abiding birds like myself.

Besides, my uncle wouldn't have let anything of that kind go on in his house. He was a rather stiff, precise sort of old boy, who liked a quiet life. He was just finishing a history of the family or something, which he had been working on for the last year, and didn't stir much from the library. He was rather a good instance of what they say about its being a good scheme for a fellow to sow his wild oats. I'd been told that in his youth Uncle Willoughby had been a bit of a rounder. You would never have thought it to look at him now.

When I got to the house, Oakshott, the butler, told me that Florence was in her room, watching her maid pack. Apparently there was a dance on at a house about twenty miles away that night,

and she was motoring over with some of the Easeby lot and would
be away some nights. Oakshott said she had told him to tell her
the moment I arrived; so I trickled into the smoking-room and
waited, and presently in she came. A glance showed me that she
was perturbed, and even peeved. Her eyes had a goggly look, and
altogether she appeared considerably pipped.

"Darling!" I said, and attempted the good old embrace; but she
side-stepped like a bantam weight.

"Don't!"

"What's the matter?"

"Everything's the matter! Bertie, you remember asking me,
when you left, to make myself pleasant to your uncle?"

"Yes."

The idea being, of course, that as at that time I was more or
less dependent on Uncle Willoughby I couldn't very well marry
without his approval. And though I knew he wouldn't have any
objection to Florence, having known her father since they were
at Oxford together, I hadn't wanted to take any chances; so I had
told her to make an effort to fascinate the old boy.

"You told me it would please him particularly if I asked him to
read me some of his history of the family."

"Wasn't he pleased?"

"He was delighted. He finished writing the thing yesterday
afternoon, and read me nearly all of it last night. I have never
had such a shock in my life. The book in an outrage. It is impossible. It is horrible!"

"But, dash it, the family weren't so bad as all that."

"It is not a history of the family at all. Your uncle had written
his reminiscences! He calls them *Recollections of a Long Life*!"

I began to understand. As I say, Uncle Willoughby had been
somewhat on the tabasco side as a young man, and it began to
look as if he might have turned out something pretty fruity if he
had started recollecting his long life.

"If half of what he has written is true," said Florence, "your uncle's youth must have been perfectly appalling. The moment we began to read he plunged straight into a most scandalous story of how he and my father were thrown out of a music-hall in 1887!"

"Why?"

"I decline to tell you why."

It must have been something pretty bad. It took a lot to make them chuck people out of music-halls in 1887.

"Your uncle specifically states that father had drunk a quart and a half of champagne before beginning the evening," she went on. "The book is full of stories like that. There is a dreadful one about Lord Emsworth."

"Lord Emsworth? Not the one we knew? Not the one at Blandings?"

A most respectable old Johnnie, don't you know. Doesn't do a thing nowadays but dig in the garden with a spud.

"The very same. That is what makes the book so unspeakable. It is full of stories about people one knows who are the essence of propriety to-day, but who seem to have behaved, when they were in London in the 'eighties, in a manner that would not have been tolerated in the fo'c'sle of a whaler. Your uncle seems to remember everything disgraceful that happened to anybody when he was in his early twenties. There is a story about Sir Stanley Gervase-Gervase at Rosherville Gardens which is ghastly in its perfection of detail. It seems that Sir Stanley—but I can't tell you!"

"Have a dash!"

"No!"

"Oh, well, I shouldn't worry. No publisher will print the book if it's as bad as all that."

"On the contrary, your uncle told me that all negotiations are settled with Riggs and Ballinger, and he's sending off the manuscript to-morrow for immediate publication. They make a special thing of that sort of book. They published Lady Carnaby's

Memories of Eighty Interesting Years."

"I read 'em!"

"Well, then, when I tell you that Lady Carnaby's Memories are simply not to be compared with your uncle's Recollections, you will understand my state of mind. And father appears in nearly every story in the book! I am horrified at the things he did when he was a young man!"

"What's to be done?"

"The manuscript must be intercepted before it reaches Riggs and Ballinger, and destroyed!"

I sat up.

This sounded rather sporting.

"How are you going to do it?" I inquired.

"How can I do it? Didn't I tell you the parcel goes off to-morrow? I am going to the Murgatroyds' dance to-night and shall not be back till Monday. You must do it. That is why I telegraphed to you."

"What!"

She gave me a look.

"Do you mean to say you refuse to help me, Bertie?"

"No; but—I say!"

"It's quite simple."

"But even if I— What I mean is— Of course, anything I can do —but—if you know what I mean— "

"You say you want to marry me, Bertie?"

"Yes, of course; but still— "

For a moment she looked exactly like her old father.

"I will never marry you if those Recollections are published."

"But, Florence, old thing!"

"I mean it. You may look on it as a test, Bertie. If you have the resource and courage to carry this thing through, I will take it as evidence that you are not the vapid and shiftless person most people think you. If you fail, I shall know that your Aunt Agatha was right when she called you a spineless invertebrate and advised me strongly not to marry you, It will be perfectly simple for you to intercept the manuscript, Bertie. It only requires a little resolution."

"But suppose Uncle Willoughby catches me at it? He'd cut me off with a bob."

"If you care more for your uncle's money than for me—"

"No, no! Rather not!"

"Very well, then. The parcel containing the manuscript will, of course, be placed on the hall table to-morrow for Oakshott to take to the village with the letters. All you have to do is to take it away and destroy it. Then your uncle will think it has been lost in the post."

It sounded thin to me.

"Hasn't he got a copy of it?"

"No; it has not been typed. He is sending the manuscript just as he wrote it."

"But he could write it over again."

"As if he would have the energy!"

"But—"

"If you are going to do nothing but make absurd objections, Bertie—"

"I was only pointing things out."

"Well, don't! Once and for all, will you do me this quite simple act of kindness?"

The way she put it gave me an idea.

"Why not get Edwin to do it? Keep it in the family, kind of, don't you know. Besides, it would be a boon to the kid."

A jolly bright idea it seemed to me. Edwin was her young brother, who was spending his holidays at Easeby. He was a ferret-faced kid, whom I had disliked since birth. As a matter of fact, talking of Recollections and Memories, it was young blighted Edwin who, nine years before, had led his father to where I was smoking his cigar and caused all the unpleasantness. He was fourteen now and had just joined the Boy Scouts. He was one of those thorough kids, and took his responsibilities pretty seriously. He was always in a sort of fever because he was dropping behind schedule with his daily acts of kindness. However hard he tried, he'd fall behind; and then you would find him prowling about the house, setting such a clip to try and catch up with himself that Easeby was rapidly becoming a perfect hell for man and beast.

The idea didn't seem to strike Florence.

"I shall do nothing of the kind, Bertie. I wonder you can't appreciate the compliment I am paying you—trusting you like this."

"Oh, I see that all right, but what I mean is, Edwin would do it so much better than I would. These Boy Scouts are up to all sorts of dodges. They spoor, don't you know, and take cover and creep about, and what not."

"Bertie, will you or will you not do this perfectly trivial thing for me? If not, say so now, and let us end this farce of pretending that you care a snap of the fingers for me."

"Dear old soul, I love you devotedly!"

"Then will you or will you not—"

"Oh, all right," I said. "All right! All right! All right!"

And then I tottered forth to think it over. I met Jeeves in the passage just outside.

"I beg your pardon, sir. I was endeavouring to find you."

"What's the matter?"

"I felt that I should tell you, sir, that somebody has been putting black polish on our brown walking shoes."

"What! Who? Why?"

"I could not say, sir."

"Can anything be done with them?"

"Nothing, sir."

"Damn!"

"Very good, sir."

I've often wondered since then how these murderer fellows manage to keep in shape while they're contemplating their next effort. I had a much simpler sort of job on hand, and the thought of it rattled me to such an extent in the night watches that I was a perfect wreck next day. Dark circles under the eyes—I give you my word! I had to call on Jeeves to rally round with one of those life-savers of his.

From breakfast on I felt like a bag-snatcher at a railway station. I had to hang about waiting for the parcel to be put on the hall table, and it wasn't put. Uncle Willoughby was a fixture in the library, adding the finishing touches to the great work, I supposed, and the more I thought the thing over the less I liked it. The chances against my pulling it off seemed about three to two, and the thought of what would happen if I didn't gave me cold shivers down the spine. Uncle Willoughby was a pretty mild sort of old boy, as a rule, but I've known him to cut up rough, and, by Jove, he was scheduled to extend himself if he caught me trying to get away with his life work.

It wasn't till nearly four that he toddled out of the library with the parcel under his arm, put it on the table, and toddled off again. I was hiding a bit to the south-east at the moment, behind a suit of armour. I bounded out and legged it for the table. Then I nipped upstairs to hide the swag. I charged in like a mustang and nearly stubbed my toe on young blighted Edwin, the Boy Scout. He was standing at the chest of drawers, confound him, messing about with my ties.

"Hallo!" he said.

"What are you doing here?"

"I'm tidying your room. It's my last Saturday's act of kindness."

"Last Saturday's."

"I'm five days behind. I was six till last night, but I polished your shoes."

"Was it you—"

"Yes. Did you see them? I just happened to think of it. I was in here, looking round. Mr. Berkeley had this room while you were away. He left this morning. I thought perhaps he might have left something in it that I could have sent on. I've often done acts of kindness that way."

"You must be a comfort to one and all!"

It became more and more apparent to me that this infernal kid must somehow be turned out eftsoons or right speedily. I had hidden the parcel behind my back, and I didn't think he had seen it; but I wanted to get at that chest of drawers quick, before anyone else came along.

"I shouldn't bother about tidying the room," I said.

"I like tidying it. It's not a bit of trouble—really."

"But it's quite tidy now."

"Not so tidy as I shall make it."

This was getting perfectly rotten. I didn't want to murder the kid, and yet there didn't seem any other way of shifting him. I pressed down the mental accelerator. The old lemon throbbed fiercely. I got an idea.

"There's something much kinder than that which you could do," I said. "You see that box of cigars? Take it down to the smoking-room and snip off the ends for me. That would save me no end of trouble. Stagger along, laddie."

He seemed a bit doubtful; but he staggered. I shoved the parcel into a drawer, locked it, trousered the key, and felt better. I might be a chump, but, dash it, I could out-general a mere kid with a face like a ferret. I went downstairs again. Just as I was passing the smoking-room door out curveted Edwin. It seemed to me that if he wanted to do a real act of kindness he would commit suicide.

"I'm snipping them," he said.

"Snip on! Snip on!"

"Do you like them snipped much, or only a bit?"

"Medium."

"All right. I'll be getting on, then."
"I should."
And we parted.

Fellows who know all about that sort of thing—detectives, and so on—will tell you that the most difficult thing in the world is to get rid of the body. I remember, as a kid, having to learn by heart a poem about a bird by the name of Eugene Aram, who had the deuce of a job in this respect. All I can recall of the actual poetry is the bit that goes:

> *Tum-tum, tum-tum, tum-tumty-tum,*
> *I slew him, tum-tum tum!*

But I recollect that the poor blighter spent much of his valuable time dumping the corpse into ponds and burying it, and what not, only to have it pop out at him again. It was about an hour after I had shoved the parcel into the drawer when I realised that I had let myself in for just the same sort of thing.

Florence had talked in an airy sort of way about destroying the manuscript; but when one came down to it, how the deuce can a chap destroy a great chunky mass of paper in somebody else's house in the middle of summer? I couldn't ask to have a fire in my bedroom, with the thermometer in the eighties. And if I didn't burn the thing, how else could I get rid of it? Fellows on the battlefield eat dispatches to keep them from falling into the hands of the enemy, but it would have taken me a year to eat Uncle Willoughby's Recollections.

I'm bound to say the problem absolutely baffled me. The only thing seemed to be to leave the parcel in the drawer and hope for the best.

I don't know whether you have ever experienced it, but it's a dashed unpleasant thing having a crime on one's conscience. Towards the end of the day the mere sight of the drawer began to depress me. I found myself getting all on edge; and once when Uncle Willoughby trickled silently into the smoking-room when I was alone there and spoke to me before I knew he was there, I broke the record for the sitting high jump.

I was wondering all the time when Uncle Willoughby would sit up and take notice. I didn't think he would have time to suspect that anything had gone wrong till Saturday morning, when he would be expecting, of course, to get the acknowledgment of the manuscript from the publishers. But early on Friday evening he came out of the library as I was passing and asked me to step in. He was looking considerably rattled.

"Bertie," he said—he always spoke in a precise sort of pompous kind of way— "an exceedingly disturbing thing had happened. As you know, I dispatched the manuscript of my book to Messrs. Riggs and Ballinger, the publishers, yesterday afternoon. It should have reached them by the first post this morning. Why I should have been uneasy I cannot say, but my mind was not altogether at rest respecting the safety of the parcel. I therefore telephoned to Messrs. Riggs and Ballinger a few moments back to make inquiries. To my consternation they informed me that they were not yet in receipt of my manuscript."

"Very rum!"

"I recollect distinctly placing it myself on the hall table in good time to be taken to the village. But here is a sinister thing. I have spoken to Oakshott, who took the rest of the letters to the post office, and he cannot recall seeing it there. He is, indeed, unswerving in his assertions that when he went to the hall to collect the letters there was no parcel among them."

"Sounds funny!"

"Bertie, shall I tell you what I suspect?"

"What's that?"

"The suspicion will no doubt sound to you incredible, but it alone seems to fit the facts as we know them. I incline to the belief that the parcel has been stolen."

"Oh, I say! Surely not!"

"Wait! Hear me out. Though I have said nothing to you before, or to anyone else, concerning the matter, the fact remains that during the past few weeks a number of objects—some valuable, others not—have disappeared in this house. The conclusion to which one is irresistibly impelled is that we have a kleptomaniac in our midst. It is a peculiarity of kleptomania, as you are no doubt aware, that the subject is unable to differentiate between the intrinsic values of objects. He will purloin an old coat as readily as a diamond ring, or a tobacco pipe costing but a few shillings with the same eagerness as a purse of gold. The fact that this manuscript of mine could be of no possible value to any outside person convinces me that— "

"But, uncle, one moment; I know all about those things that were stolen. It was Meadowes, my man, who pinched them. I caught him snaffling my silk socks. Right in the act, by Jove!"

He was tremendously impressed.

"You amaze me, Bertie! Send for the man at once and question him."

"But he isn't here. You see, directly I found that he was a sock-sneaker I gave him the boot. That's why I went to London—to get a new man."

"Then, if the man Meadowes is no longer in the house it could not be he who purloined my manuscript. The whole thing is inexplicable."

After which we brooded for a bit. Uncle Willoughby pottered about the room, registering baffledness, while I sat sucking at a cigarette, feeling rather like a chappie I'd once read about in a book, who murdered another cove and hid the body under the dining-room table, and then had to be the life and soul of a dinner party, with it there all the time. My guilty secret oppressed me to such an extent that after a while I couldn't stick it any longer.

I lit another cigarette and started for a stroll in the grounds, by way of cooling off.

It was one of those still evenings you get in the summer, when you can hear a snail clear its throat a mile away. The sun was sinking over the hills and the gnats were fooling about all over the place, and everything smelled rather topping—what with the falling dew and so on—and I was just beginning to feel a little soothed by the peace of it all when suddenly I heard my name spoken.

"It's about Bertie."

It was the loathsome voice of young blighted Edwin! For a moment I couldn't locate it. Then I realised that it came from the library. My stroll had taken me within a few yards of the open window.

I had often wondered how those Johnnies in books did it—I mean the fellows with whom it was the work of a moment to do about a dozen things that ought to have taken them about ten minutes. But, as a matter of fact, it was the work of a moment with me to chuck away my cigarette, swear a bit, leap about ten yards, dive into a bush that stood near the library window, and stand there with my ears flapping. I was as certain as I've ever been of anything that all sorts of rotten things were in the offing.

"About Bertie?" I heard Uncle Willoughby say.

"About Bertie and your parcel. I heard you talking to him just now. I believe he's got it."

When I tell you that just as I heard these frightful words a fairly substantial beetle of sorts dropped from the bush down the back of my neck, and I couldn't even stir to squash the same, you will understand that I felt pretty rotten. Everything seemed against me.

"What do you mean, boy? I was discussing the disappearance of my manuscript with Bertie only a moment back, and he professed himself as perplexed by the mystery as myself."

"Well, I was in his room yesterday afternoon, doing him an act of kindness, and he came in with a parcel. I could see it, though he tried to keep it behind his back. And then he asked me to go to the smoking-room and snip some cigars for him; and about two minutes afterwards he came down—and he wasn't carrying anything. So it must be in his room."

I understand they deliberately teach these dashed Boy Scouts to cultivate their powers of observation and deduction and what not. Devilish thoughtless and inconsiderate of them, I call it. Look at the trouble it causes.

"It sounds incredible," said Uncle Willoughby, thereby bucking me up a trifle.

"Shall I go and look in his room?" asked young blighted Edwin. "I'm sure the parcel's there."

"But what could be his motive for perpetrating this extraordinary theft?"

"Perhaps he's a—what you said just now."

"A kleptomaniac? Impossible!"

"It might have been Bertie who took all those things from the very start," suggested the little brute hopefully. "He may be like Raffles."

"Raffles?"

"He's a chap in a book who went about pinching things."

"I cannot believe that Bertie would—ah—go about pinching things."

"Well, I'm sure he's got the parcel. I'll tell you what you might do. You might say that Mr. Berkeley wired that he had left something here. He had Bertie's room, you know. You might say you wanted to look for it."

"That would be possible. I— "

I didn't wait to hear any more. Things were getting too hot. I sneaked softly out of my bush and raced for the front door. I sprinted up to my room and made for the drawer where I had put the parcel. And then I found I hadn't the key. It wasn't for the deuce of a time that I recollected I had shifted it to my evening trousers the night before and must have forgotten to take it out again.

Where the dickens were my evening things? I had looked all over the place before I remembered that Jeeves must have taken them away to brush. To leap at the bell and ring it was with me the work of a moment. I had just rung it when there was a footstep outside, and in came Uncle Willoughby.

"Oh, Bertie," he said, without a blush, "I have—ah—received a telegram from Berkeley, who occupied this room in your absence, asking me to forward him his—er—his cigarette-case, which it would appear, he inadvertently omitted to take with him when he left the house. I cannot find it downstairs; and it has, therefore, occurred to me that he may have left it in this room. I will —er—just take a look round."

It was one of the most disgusting spectacles I've ever seen —this white-haired old man, who should have been thinking of the hereafter, standing there lying like an actor.

"I haven't seen it anywhere," I said.

"Nevertheless, I will search. I must—ah—spare no effort."

"I should have seen it if it had been here—what?"

"It may have escaped your notice. It is—er—possibly in one of the drawers."

He began to nose about. He pulled out drawer after drawer, pottering round like an old bloodhound, and babbling from time to time about Berkeley and his cigarette-case in a way that struck me as perfectly ghastly. I just stood there, losing weight every moment.

Then he came to the drawer where the parcel was "This appears to be locked," he said, rattling the handle.

"Yes; I shouldn't bother about that one. It—it's—er—locked, and all that sort of thing."

"You have not the key?"

A soft, respectful voice spoke behind me.

"I fancy, sir, that this must be the key you require. It was in the pocket of your evening trousers."

It was Jeeves. He had shimmered in, carrying my evening things, and was standing there holding out the key. I could have massacred the man.

"Thank you," said my uncle.

"Not at all, sir."

The next moment Uncle Willoughby had opened the drawer. I shut my eyes.

"No," said Uncle Willoughby, "there is nothing here. The drawer is empty. Thank you, Bertie. I hope I have not disturbed you. I fancy—er—Berkeley must have taken his case with him after all."

When he had gone I shut the door carefully. Then I turned to Jeeves. The man was putting my evening things out on a chair.

"Er—Jeeves!"

"Sir?"

"Oh, nothing."

It was deuced difficult to know how to begin.

"Er—Jeeves!"

"Sir?"

"Did you—Was there—Have you by chance—"

"I removed the parcel this morning, sir."

"Oh—ah—why?"

"I considered it more prudent, sir."

I mused for a while.

"Of course, I suppose all this seems tolerably rummy to you, Jeeves?"

"Not at all, sir. I chanced to overhear you and Lady Florence speaking of the matter the other evening, sir."

"Did you, by Jove?"

"Yes, sir."

"Well—er—Jeeves, I think that, on the whole, if you were to —as it were—freeze on to that parcel until we get back to London— "

"Exactly, sir."

"And then we might—er—so to speak—chuck it away somewhere—what?"

"Precisely, sir.

"I'll leave it in your hands."

"Entirely, sir."

"You know, Jeeves, you're by way of being rather a topper."

"I endeavour to give satisfaction, sir."

"One in a million, by Jove!"

"It is very kind of you to say so, sir."

"Well, that's about all, then, I think."

"Very good, sir."

Florence came back on Monday. I didn't see her till we were all having tea in the hall. It wasn't till the crowd had cleared away a bit that we got a chance of having a word together.

"Well, Bertie?" she said.

"It's all right."

"You have destroyed the manuscript?"

"Not exactly; but—"

"What do you mean?"

"I mean I haven't absolutely—"

"Bertie, your manner is furtive!"

"It's all right. It's this way—"

And I was just going to explain how things stood when out of the library came leaping Uncle Willoughby, looking as braced as a two-year-old. The old boy was a changed man.

"A most remarkable thing, Bertie! I have just been speaking with Mr. Riggs on the telephone, and he tells me he received my manuscript by the first post this morning. I cannot imagine what can have caused the delay. Our postal facilities are extremely inadequate in the rural districts. I shall write to head-quarters about it. It is unsufferable if valuable parcels are to be delayed in this fashion."

I happened to be looking at Florence's profile at the moment, and at this juncture she swung round and gave me a look that went right through me like a knife. Uncle Willoughby meandered back to the library, and there was a silence that you could have dug bits out of with a spoon.

"I can't understand it," I said at last. "I can't understand it, by Jove!"

"I can. I can understand it perfectly, Bertie. Your heart failed you. Rather than risk offending your uncle you—"

"No, no! Absolutely!"

"You preferred to lose me rather than risk losing the money. Perhaps you did not think I meant what I said. I meant every word. Our engagement is ended."

"But—I say!"

"Not another word!"

"But, Florence, old thing!"

"I do not wish to hear any more. I see now that your Aunt Agatha was perfectly right. I consider that I have had a very lucky escape. There was a time when I thought that, with patience, you might be moulded into something worth while. I see now that you are impossible!"

And she popped off, leaving me to pick up the pieces. When I had collected the débris to some extent I went to my room and rang for Jeeves. He came in looking as if nothing had happened or was ever going to happen. He was the calmest thing in captivity.

"Jeeves!" I yelled. "Jeeves, that parcel has arrived in London!"

"Yes, sir?"

"Did you send it?"

"Yes, sir. I acted for the best, sir. I think that both you and Lady

Florence overestimated the danger of people being offended at being mentioned in Sir Willoughby's Recollections. It has been my experience, sir, that the normal person enjoys seeing his or her name in print, irrespective of what is said about them. I have an aunt, sir, who a few years ago was a martyr to swollen limbs. She tried Walkinshaw's Supreme Ointment and obtained considerable relief—so much so that she sent them an unsolicited testimonial. Her pride at seeing her photograph in the daily papers in connection with descriptions of her lower limbs before taking, which were nothing less then revolting, was so intense that it led me to believe that publicity, of whatever sort, is what nearly everybody desires. Moreover, if you have ever studied psychology, sir, you will know that respectable old gentlemen are by no means averse to having it advertised that they were extremely wild in their youth. I have an uncle— "

I cursed his aunts and his uncles and him and all the rest of the family.

"Do you know that Lady Florence has broken off her engagement with me?"

"Indeed, sir?"

Not a bit of sympathy! I might have been telling him it was a fine day.

"You're sacked!"

"Very good, sir."

He coughed gently.

"As I am no longer in your employment, sir, I can speak freely without appearing to take a liberty. In my opinion you and Lady Florence were quite unsuitably matched. Her ladyship is of a highly determined and arbitrary temperament, quite opposed to your own. I was in Lord Worplesdon's service for nearly a year, during which time I had ample opportunities of studying her ladyship. The opinion of the servants' hall was far from favourable to her. Her ladyship's temper caused a good deal of adverse comment among us. It was at times quite impossible. You would not have been happy, sir!"

"Get out!"

"I think you would also have found her educational methods a little trying, sir. I have glanced at the book her ladyship gave you —it has been lying on your table since our arrival—and it is, in my opinion, quite unsuitable. You would not have enjoyed it. And I have it from her ladyship's own maid, who happened to overhear a conversation between her ladyship and one of the gentlemen staying here—Mr. Maxwell, who is employed in an editorial capacity by one of the reviews—that it was her intention to start you almost immediately upon Nietzsche. You would not enjoy Nietzshe, sir. He is fundamentally unsound."

"Get out!"

"Very good, sir."

It's rummy how sleeping on a thing often makes you feel quite different about it. It's happened to me over and over again. Somehow or other, when I woke next morning the old heart didn't feel half so broken as it had done. It was a perfectly topping day, and there was something about the way the sun came in at the window and the row the birds were kicking up in the ivy that made me half wonder whether Jeeves wasn't right. After all, though she had a wonderful profile, was it such a catch being engaged to Florence Craye as the casual observer might imagine? Wasn't there something in what Jeeves had said about her character? I began to realise that my ideal wife was something quite different, something a lot more clinging and drooping and prattling, and what not.

I had got as far as this in thinking the thing out when that *Types of Ethical Theory* caught my eye. I opened it, and I give you my honest word this was what hit me:

Of the two antithetic terms in the Greek philosophy one only was real and self-subsisting; and that one was Ideal Thought as opposed to that which it has to penetrate and mould. The other, corresponding to our Nature, was in itself phenomenal, unreal, without any permanent footing, having no predicates that held true for two moments together; in short, redeemed from negation only by including indwelling realities appearing through.

Well—I mean to say—what? And Nietzsche, from all accounts, a lot worse than that!

"Jeeves," I said, when he came in with my morning tea, "I've been thinking it over. You're engaged again."

"Thank you, sir."

I sucked down a cheerful mouthful. A great respect for this bloke's judgment began to soak through me.

"Oh, Jeeves," I said; "about that check suit."

"Yes, sir?"

"Is it really a frost?"

"A trifle too bizarre, sir, in my opinion."

"But lots of fellows have asked me who my tailor is."

"Doubtless in order to avoid him, sir."

"He's supposed to be one of the best men in London."

"I am saying nothing against his moral character, sir."

I hesitated a bit. I had a feeling that I was passing into this chappie's clutches, and that if I gave in now I should become just like poor old Aubrey Fothergill, unable to call my soul my own. On the other hand, this was obviously a cove of rare intelligence, and it would be a comfort in a lot of ways to have him doing the thinking for me. I made up my mind.

"All right, Jeeves," I said. "You know! Give the bally thing away to somebody!"

He looked down at me like a father gazing tenderly at the wayward child.

"Thank you, sir. I gave it to the under-gardener last night. A little more tea, sir?"

The Man Who Gave Up Smoking

In a mixed assemblage like the little group of serious thinkers which gathers nightly in the bar-parlour of the Anglers' Rest it is hardly to be expected that there will invariably prevail an unbroken harmony. We are all men of spirit: and when men of spirit, with opinions of their own, get together, disputes are bound to arise. Frequently, therefore, even in this peaceful haven, you will hear voices raised, tables banged, and tenor Permit-me-to-inform-you-sir's competing with baritone And-jolly-well-permit-me-to-inform-*you*'s. I have known fists to be shaken and on one occasion the word "fathead" to be used.

Fortunately, Mr. Mulliner is always there, ready with the soothing magic of his personality to calm the storm before things have gone too far. Tonight, as I entered the room, I found him in the act of intervening between a flushed Lemon Squash and a scowling Tankard of Ale who had fallen foul of one another in the corner by the window.

"Gentlemen, gentlemen," he was saying in his suave, ambassadorial way, "what is all the trouble about?"

The Tankard of Ale pointed the stem of his pipe accusingly at his adversary. One could see that he was deeply stirred.

"He's talking Rot about smoking."

"I am talking sense."

"I didn't hear any."

"I said that smoking was dangerous to the health. And it is."

"It isn't."

"It is. I can prove it from my own personal experience. I was once," said the Lemon Squash, "a smoker myself, and the vile habit reduced me to a physical wreck. My cheeks sagged, my eyes became bleary, my whole face gaunt, yellow and hideously lined. It was giving up smoking that brought about the change."

"What change?" asked the Tankard.

The Lemon Squash, who seemed to have taken offence at something, rose and, walking stiffly to the door, disappeared into the night. Mr. Mulliner gave a little sigh of relief.

"I am glad he has left us," he said. "Smoking is a subject on which I hold strong views. I look upon tobacco as life's outstanding boon, and it annoys me to hear these faddists abusing it. And how foolish their arguments are, how easily refuted. They come to me and tell me that if they place two drops of nicotine on the tongue of a dog the animal dies instantly: and when I ask them if they ever tried the childishly simple device of not placing nicotine on the dog's tongue, they have nothing to reply. They are non-plussed. They go away mumbling something about never having thought of that."

He puffed at his cigar in silence for a few moments. His genial face had grown grave.

"If you ask my opinion, gentlemen," he resumed, "I say it is not only foolish for a man to give up smoking—it is not safe. Such an action wakes the fiend that sleeps in all of us. To give up smoking is to become a menace to the community. I shall not readily forget what happened in the case of my nephew Ignatius. Mercifully, the thing had a happy ending, but..."

Those of you (said Mr. Mulliner) who move in artistic circles are possibly familiar with the name and work of my nephew Ignatius. He is a portrait-painter of steadily growing reputation. At the time of which I speak, however, he was not so well-known as he is to-day, and consequently had intervals of leisure between commissions. These he occupied in playing the ukulele and proposing marriage to Hermione, the beautiful daughter of Herbert J. Rossiter and Mrs. Rossiter, of 3 Scantlebury Square, Kensington. Scantlebury Square was only just round the corner from his studio, and it was his practice, when he had a moment to spare, to pop across, propose to Hermione, get rejected, pop back again, play a bar or two on the ukulele, and then light a pipe, put his feet on the mantelpiece, and wonder what it was about him that appeared to make him distasteful to this lovely girl.

It could not be that she scorned his honest poverty. His income was most satisfactory.

It could not be said that she had heard something damaging about his past. His past was blameless.

It could not be that she objected to his looks for, like all the Mulliners, his personal appearance was engaging and even—from certain angles—fascinating. Besides, a girl who had been brought up in a home containing a father who was one of Kensington's leading gargoyles and a couple of sub-humans like her brother Cyprian and her brother George would scarcely be an exacting judge of male beauty. Cyprian was pale and thin and wrote art-criticism for the weekly papers, and George was stout and pink and did no work of any kind, having developed at an early age considerable skill in the way of touching friends and acquaintances alike for small loans.

The thought occurred to Ignatius that one of these two might be able to give him some inside information on the problem. They were often in Hermione's society, and it was quite likely that she might have happened to mention at one time or another what it was about him that caused her so repeatedly to hand the mitten to a good man's love. He called upon Cyprian at his flat and put the thing to him squarely. Cyprian listened attentively, stroking his left side-whisker with a lean hand.

"Ah?" said Cyprian. "One senses, does one, a reluctance on the girl's part to entertain one's suggestions of marriage?"

"One does," replied Ignatius.

"One wonders why one is unable to make progress?"

"One does."

"One asks oneself what is the reason?"

"One does—repeatedly."

"Well, if one really desires to hear the truth," said Cyprian, stroking his right whisker, "I happen to know that Hermione objects to you because you remind her of my brother George."

Ignatius staggered back, appalled, and an animal cry escaped his lips.

"Remind her of George?"

"That's what she says."

"But I can't be like George. It isn't humanly possible for anybody to be like George."

"One merely repeats what one has heard."

Ignatius staggered from the room and, tottering into the Fulham Road, made for the Goat and Bottle to purchase a restorative. And the first person he saw in the saloon-bar was George, taking his elevenses.

"What ho!" said George. "What ho, what ho, what ho!"

He looked pinker and stouter than ever, and the theory that he could possibly resemble this distressing object was so distasteful to Ignatius that he decided to get a second opinion.

"George," he said, "have you any idea why it is that your sister Hermione spurns my suit?"

"Certainly," said George.

"You have? Then why is it?"

George drained his glass.

"You ask me why?"

"Yes."

"You want to know the reason?"

"I do."

"Well, then, first and foremost," said George, "can you lend me a quid till Wednesday week without fail?"

"No, I can't."

"Nor ten bob?"

"Nor ten bob. Kindly stick to the subject and tell me why your sister will not look at me."

"I will," said George. "Not only have you a mean and parsimonious disposition, but she says you remind her of my brother Cyprian."

Ignatius staggered and would have fallen had he not placed a foot on the brass rail.

"I remind her of Cyprian?"

"That's what she says."

With bowed head Ignatius left the saloon-bar and returned to his studio to meditate. He was stricken to the core. He had asked for inside information and he had got it, but nobody was going to make him like it.

He was not only stricken to the core, but utterly bewildered. That a man—stretching the possibilities a little—might resemble George Rossiter was intelligible. He could also understand that a man—assuming that Nature had played a scurvy trick upon him—might conceivably be like Cyprian. But how could anyone be like both of them and live?

He took pencil and paper and devoted himself to making a list in parallel columns of the qualities and characteristics of the brothers. When he had finished, he scanned it carefully. This is what he found he had written:

GEORGE	CYPRIAN
Face like pig	*Face like camel*
Pimples	*Whiskers*
Confirmed sponger	*Writes art-criticism*
Says "What ho!"	*Says "One senses"*
Slaps back	*Has nasty, dry snigger*

Eats too much	*Fruitarian*
Tells funny stories	*Recites poetry*
Clammy hands	*Bony hands*

He frowned. The mystery was still unsolved. And then he came to the last item.

GEORGE	CYPRIAN
Heavy smoker	*Heavy smoker*

A spasm ran through Ignatius Mulliner. Here, at last, was a common factor. Was it possible...? Could it be...?

It seemed the only solution, and yet Ignatius fought against it. His love for Hermione was the lodestar of his life, but next to it, beaten only by a short head, came his love for his pipe. Had he really to choose between the two?

Could he make the sacrifice?

He wavered.

And then he saw the eleven photographs of Hermione Rossiter gazing at him from the mantelpiece, and it seemed to him that they smiled encouragingly. He hesitated no longer. With a soft sigh such as might have proceeded from some loving father on the steppes of Russia when compelled, in order to ensure his own safety, to throw his children out of the back of the sleigh to the pursuing wolf-pack, he took the pipe from his mouth, collected his other pipes, his tobacco and his cigars, wrapped them in a neat parcel and, summoning the charwoman who cleaned his studio, gave her the consignment to take home to her husband, an estimable man of the name of Perkins who, being of straitened means, smoked, as a rule, only what he could pick up in the street.

Ignatius Mulliner had made the great decision.

As those of you who have tried it are aware, the deadly effects of giving up smoking rarely make themselves felt immediately in their full virulence. The process is gradual. In the first stage, indeed, the patient not only suffers no discomfort but goes about inflated by a sort of gaseous spiritual pride. All through the morning of the following day, Ignatius, as he walked abroad, found himself regarding such fellow-members of the community as had pipes and cigarettes in their mouths with a pitying disdain. He felt like some saint purified and purged of the grosser emotions by a life of asceticism. He longed to tell these people all about pyridine and the intense irritation it causes to the throats and other mucous surfaces of those who inhale the tobacco smoke in which it lurks. He wanted to buttonhole men sucking at their cigars and inform them that tobacco contains an appreciable quantity of the gas known as carbon monoxide, which, entering into direct combination with the colouring matter of the blood, forms so stable a compound as to render the corpuscles incapable of carrying oxygen to the tissues. He yearned to make it clear to them that smoking was simply a habit which with a little exercise of the will-power a man could give up at a moment's notice, whenever he pleased.

It was only after he had returned to his studio to put the finishing touches to his Academy picture that the second stage set in.

Having consumed an artist's lunch consisting of two sardines, the remnants of a knuckle of ham, and a bottle of beer, he found stealing over him, as his stomach got onto the fact that the meal was not to be topped off by a soothing pipe, a kind of vague sense of emptiness and bereavement akin to that experienced by the historian Gibbon on completing his *Decline and Fall of the Roman Empire.* Its symptoms were an inability to work and a dim feeling of oppression, as if he had just lost some dear friend. Life seemed somehow to have been robbed of all motive. He wandered about the studio, haunted by a sensation that he was leaving undone something that he ought to be doing. From time to time he blew little bubbles, and once or twice his teeth clicked, as if he were trying to close them on something that was not there.

A twilight sadness had him in its grip. He took up his ukulele, an instrument to which, as I have said, he was greatly addicted, and played "Ol' Man River" for awhile. But the melancholy still lingered. And now, it seemed to him, he had discovered its cause. What was wrong was the fact that he was not doing enough good in the world.

Look at it this way, he felt. The world is a sad, grey place, and we are put into it to promote as far as we can the happiness of others. If we concentrate on our own selfish pleasures, what do we find? We find that they speedily pall. We weary of gnawing knuckles of ham. The ukulele loses its fascination. Of course, if we could sit down and put our feet up and set a match to the good old pipe, that would be a different matter. But we no longer smoke, and so all that is left to us is the doing of good to others. By three o'clock, in short, Ignatius Mulliner had reached the third stage, the glutinously sentimental. It caused him to grab his hat, and sent him trotting round to Scantlebury Square.

But his object was not, as it usually was when he went to Scantlebury Square, to propose to Hermione Rossiter. He had a more unselfish motive. For some time past, by hints dropped and tentative remarks thrown out, he had been made aware that Mrs. Rossiter greatly desired him to paint her daughter's portrait: and until now he had always turned to these remarks and hints a deaf ear. Mrs. Rossiter's mother's heart wanted, he knew, to get the portrait for nothing: and, while love is love and all that, he had the artist's dislike for not collecting all that was coming to him. Ignatius Mulliner, the man, might entertain the idea of pleasing the girl he worshipped by painting her on the nod, but Ignatius Mulliner, the artist, had his schedule of prices. And until to-day it was the second Ignatius Mulliner who had said the deciding word.

This afternoon, however, everything was changed. In a short but moving speech he informed Hermione's mother that the one wish of his life was to paint her daughter's portrait; that for so great a privilege he would not dream of charging a fee; and that if she would call at the studio on the morrow, bringing Hermione with her, he would put the job in hand right away.

In fact, he very nearly offered to paint another portrait of Mrs. Rossiter herself, in evening dress with her Belgian griffon. He contrived, however, to hold the fatal words back: and it was perhaps the recollections of this belated prudence which gave him, as he stood on the pavement outside the house after the interview, a sense of having failed to be as altruistic as he might have been.

Stricken with remorse, he decided to look up good old Cyprian and ask him to come to the studio to-morrow and criticize his Academy picture. After that, he would find dear old George and press a little money on him. Ten minutes later, he was in Cyprian's sitting-room.

"One wishes what?" asked Cyprian incredulously.

"One wishes," repeated Ignatius, "that you would come round to-morrow morning and have a look at one's Academy picture and give one a hint or two about it."

"Is one really serious?" cried Cyprian, his eyes beginning to gleam. It was seldom that he received invitations of this kind. He had, indeed, been thrown out of more studios for butting in and giving artists a hint or two about their pictures than any other art-critic in Chelsea.

"One is perfectly serious," Ignatius assured him. "One feels that an opinion from an expert will be invaluable."

"Then one will be there at eleven sharp," said Cyprian, "without fail."

Ignatius wrung his hand warmly, and hurried off to the Goat and Bottle to find George.

"George," he said, "George, my dear old chap, I passed a sleepless night last night, wondering if you had all the money you require. The fear that you might have run short seemed to go through me like a knife. Call on me for as much as you need."

George's face was partially obscured by a tankard. At these words, his eyes, bulging above the pewter, took on a sudden expression of acute horror. He lowered the tankard, ashen to the lips, and raised his right hand.

"This," he said in a shaking voice, "is the end. From this moment I will go off the stuff. Yes, you have seen George Plimsoll Rossiter drink his last mild-and-bitter. I am not a nervous man, but I know when I'm licked. And when it comes to a fellow's ears going... "

Ignatius patted his arm affectionately.

"Your ears have not gone, George," he said. "They are still there."

And so, indeed, they were, as large and red as ever. But George was not to be comforted.

"I mean when a fellow thinks he hears things....I give you my honest word, old man—I solemnly assure you that I could have sworn I heard you voluntarily offer me money."

"But I did."

"You did?"

"Certainly."

"You mean you definitely—literally—without any sort of prompting on my part—without my so much as saying a word to indicate that I could do with a small loan till Friday week —absolutely, positively offered to lend me money?"

"I did."

George drew a deep breath and took up his tankard again.

"All this modern, advanced stuff you read about miracles not happening," he said severely, "is dashed poppycock. I disapprove of it. I resent it keenly. About how much?" he went on, pawing adoringly at Ignatius's sleeve. "To about what, as it were, extent would you be prepared to go? A quid?"

Ignatius raised his eyebrows.

"A quid is not much, George," he said with quiet reproach.

George made little gurgling noises.

"A fiver?"

Ignatius shook his head. The movement was a silent rebuke.

"Correct this petty, cheese-paring spirit, George," he urged. "Be big and broad. Think spaciously."

"Not—a tenner?"

"I was about to suggest fifteen pounds," said Ignatius. "If you are sure that will be enough."

"What ho!"

"You're positive you can manage with that? I know how many expenses you have."

"What ho!"

"Very well, then. If you can get along with fifteen pounds, come round to my studio to-morrow morning and we'll fix it up."

And, glowing with fervour, Ignatius slapped George's back in a hearty sort of way and withdrew.

"Something attempted, something done," he said to himself, as he climbed into bed some hours later, "has earned a night's repose."

Like so many men who live intensely and work with their brains, my nephew Ignatius was a heavy sleeper. Generally, after waking to a new day, he spent a considerable time lying on his back in a sort of coma, not stirring till lured from his couch by the soft, appealing smell of frying bacon. On the following morning, however, he was conscious, directly he opened his eyes, of a strange alertness. He was keyed up to quite an extraordinary extent. He had, in short, reached the stage when the patient becomes a little nervous.

Yes, he felt, analysing his emotions, he was distinctly nervous. The noise of the cat stamping about in the passage outside caused him exquisite discomfort. He was just about to shout to Mrs.

Perkins, his charwoman, to stop the creature, when she rapped suddenly on the panel to inform him that his shaving-water lay without: and at the sound he immediately shot straight up to the ceiling in a cocoon of sheets and blankets, turned three complete somersaults in mid-air, and came down, quivering like a frightened mustang, in the middle of the floor. His heart was entangled with his tonsils, his eyes had worked round to the back of their sockets, and he wondered dazedly how many human souls besides himself had survived the bomb-explosion.

Reason returning to her throne, his next impulse was to cry quietly. Remembering after a while that he was a Mulliner, he checked the unmanly tears and, creeping to the bathroom, took a cold shower and felt a little better. A hearty breakfast assisted the cure, and he was almost himself again, when the discovery that there was not a pipe or a shred of tobacco in the place plunged him once more into an inky gloom.

For a long time Ignatius Mulliner sat with his face in his hands, while all the sorrows of the world seemed to rise before him. And then, abruptly, his mood changed again. A moment before, he had been pitying the human race with an intensity that racked him almost unendurably. Now, the realization surged over him that he didn't care a hoot about the human race. The only emotion the human race evoked in him was an intense dislike. He burned with an irritable loathing for all created things. If the cat had been present, he would have kicked it. If Mrs. Perkins had entered, he would have struck her with a mahl-stick. But the cat had gone off to restore its tissues in the dust-bin, and Mrs. Perkins was in the kitchen singing hymns. Ignatius Mulliner boiled with baffled fury. Here he was, with all this concentrated hatred stored up within him, and not a living thing in sight on which to expend it. That, he told himself with a mirthless laugh, was the way things happened.

And just then the door opened, and there, looking like a camel arriving at an oasis, was Cyprian.

"Ah, my dear fellow," said Cyprian. "May one enter?"

"Come right in," said Ignatius.

At the sight of this art-critic, who not only wore short side-whiskers but also one of those black stocks which go twice round the neck and add from forty to fifty per cent to the loathsomeness of the wearer's appearance, a strange, febrile excitement had gripped Ignatius Mulliner. He felt like a tiger at the Zoo who sees the keeper approaching with the luncheon-tray. He licked his lips slowly and gazed earnestly at the visitor. From a hook on the wall beside him there hung a richly inlaid Damascus dagger. He took it down and tested its point with the ball of his thumb.

Cyprian had turned his back, and was examining the Academy picture through a black-rimmed monocle. He moved his head about and peered between his fingers and made funny art-critic noises.

"Ye-e-s," said Cyprian. " 'Myes. Ha! H'm. Hrrmph! The thing has rhythm, undoubted rhythm, and, to an extent, certain inevitable curves. And yet can one conscientiously say that one altogether likes it? One fears one cannot."

"No?" said Ignatius.

"No," said Cyprian. He toyed with his left whisker. He seemed to be massaging it for purposes of his own. "One quite inevitably senses at a glance that the patine lacks vitality."

"Yes?" said Ignatius.

"Yes," said Cyprian. He toyed with the whisker again. It was too early to judge whether he was improving it at all. He shut his eyes, opened them, half closed them once more, drew back his head, fiddled with his fingers, and expelled his breath with a hissing sound, as if he were grooming a horse. "Beyond a question one senses in the patine a lack of vitality. And vitality must never be sacrificed. The artist should use his palette as an orchestra. He should put on his colours as a great conductor uses his instruments. There must be significant form. The colour must have a flatness, a gravity, shall I say an aroma? The figure must be placed on the canvas in a manner not only harmonious but awake. Only so can a picture quite too exquisitely live. And, as regards the patine ... "

He broke off. He had had more to say about the patine, but he had heard immediately behind him an odd, stealthy shuffling sound not unlike that made by a leopard of the jungle when stalking its prey. Spinning round, he saw Ignatius Mulliner advancing upon him. The artist's lips were curled back over his teeth in a hideous set smile. His eyes glittered. And poised in his right hand he held a Damascus dagger, which, Cyprian noticed, was richly inlaid.

An art-critic who makes a habit of going round the studios of Chelsea and speaking his mind to men who are finishing their Academy pictures gets into the way of thinking swiftly. Otherwise, he would not quite too exquisitely live through a single visit. To cast a glance at the door and note that it was closed and that his host was between him and it was with Cyprian Rossiter the work of a moment; to dart behind the easel the work of another. And with the easel as a basis the two men for some tense minutes played a silent game of round-and-round-the-mulberry-bush. It was in the middle of the twelfth lap that Cyprian received a flesh wound in the upper arm.

On another man this might have had the effect of causing him to falter, lose his head, and become an easy prey to the pursuer. But Cyprian had the advantage of having been through this sort of thing before. Only a day or two ago, one of England's leading animal-painters had chivvied him for nearly an hour in a fruitless endeavour to get at him with a short bludgeon tipped with lead.

He kept cool. In the face of danger, his footwork, always impressive, took on a new agility. And finally, when Ignatius tripped over a loose mat, he seized his opportunity like the strategist which every art-critic has to be if he mixes with artists, and dodged nimbly into a small cupboard near the model-throne.

Ignatius recovered his balance just too late. By the time he had disentangled himself from the mat, leaped at the cupboard door and started to tug at the handle, Cyprian was tugging at it from the other side, and, strive though he might, Ignatius could not dislodge him.

Presently, he gave up the struggle and, moving moodily away, picked up his ukulele and played "Ol' Man River" for awhile. He was just feeling his way cautiously through that rather tricky "He don't say nuffin', He must know somefin' " bit, when the door opened once more and there stood George.

"What ho!" said George.

"Ah!" said Ignatius.

"What do you mean, Ah?"

"Just 'Ah!' " said Ignatius.

"I've come for that money."

"Ah?"

"That twenty quid or whatever it was that you very decently promised me yesterday. And, lying in bed this morning, the thought crossed my mind: Why not make it twenty-five? A nice round sum," argued George.

"Ah!"

"You keep saying 'Ah!' " said George. "Why do you say 'Ah!'?"

Ignatius drew himself up haughtily.

"This is my studio, paid for with my own money, and I shall say 'Ah!' in it just as often as I please."

"Of course," agreed George hurriedly. "Of course, my dear old chap, of course, of course. Hullo!" He looked down. "Shoelace undone. Dangerous. Might trip a fellow. Excuse me a moment."

He stooped: and as Ignatius gazed at his spacious trouser-seat, the thought came to him that in the special circumstances there was but one thing to be done. He waggled his right leg for a moment to limber it up, backed up a pace or two and crept forward.

Mrs. Rossiter, meanwhile, accompanied by her daughter Hermione, had left Scantlebury Square and, though a trifle short in the wind, had covered the distance between it and the studio in quite good time. But the effort had told upon her, and half-way up the stairs she was compelled to halt for a short rest. It was as she stood there, puffing slightly like a seal after diving for fish, that something seemed to shoot past her in the darkness.

"What was that?" she exclaimed.

"I thought I saw something, too," said Hermione.

"Some heavy, moving object."

"Yes," said Hermione. "Perhaps we had better go up and ask Mr. Mulliner if he has been dropping things downstairs."

They made their way to the studio. Ignatius was standing on one leg, rubbing the toes of his right foot. Your artist is proverbially a dreamy, absent-minded man, and he had realized too late that he was wearing bedroom slippers. Despite the fact, however, that he was in considerable pain, his expression was not unhappy. He had the air of a man who is conscious of having done the right thing.

"Good morning, Mr. Mulliner," said Mrs. Rossiter.

"Good morning, Mr. Mulliner," said Hermione.

"Good morning," said Ignatius, looking at them with deep loathing. It amazed him that he had ever felt attracted by this girl. Until this moment, his animosity had been directed wholly against the male members of her family: but now that she stood before him he realized that the real outstanding Rossiter gumboil was this Hermione. The brief flicker of *joie-de-vivre* which had followed his interview with George had died away, leaving his mood blacker than ever. One scarcely likes to think what might have happened, had Hermione selected that moment to tie her shoelace.

"Well, here we are," said Mrs. Rossiter.

At this point, unseen by them, the cupboard door began to open noiselessly. A pale face peeped out. The next instant, there was a cloud of dust, a whirring noise, and the sound of footsteps descending the stairs three at a time.

Mrs. Rossiter put a hand to her heart and panted.

"What was that?"

"It was a little blurred," said Hermione, "but I think it was Cyprian."

Ignatius uttered a passionate cry and dashed to the head of the stairs.

"Gone!"

He came back, his face contorted, muttering to himself. Mrs. Rossiter looked at him keenly. It seemed plain to her that all that was wanted here was a couple of doctors with fountain-pens to sign the necessary certificate, but she was not dismayed. After all, she reasoned with not a little shrewd sense, a gibbering artist is just as good as a sane artist, provided he makes no charge for painting portraits.

"Well, Mr. Mulliner," she said cheerily, dismissing from her mind the problem, which had been puzzling her a little, of why her son Cyprian had been in this studio behaving like the Scotch Express, "Hermione has nothing to do this morning, so, if you are free, now would be a good time for the first sitting."

Ignatius came out of his reverie.

"Sitting?"

"For the portrait."

"What portrait?"

"Hermione's portrait."

"You wish me to paint Miss Rossiter's portrait?"

"Why, you said you would—only last night."

"Did I?" Ignatius passed a hand across his forehead. "Perhaps I did. Very well. Kindly step to the desk and write out a cheque for fifty pounds. You have your book with you?"

"Fifty—what?"

"Guineas," said Ignatius. "A hundred guineas. I always require a deposit before I start work."

"But last night you said you would paint her for nothing."

"I said I would paint her for nothing?"

"Yes."

A dim recollection of having behaved in the fatuous manner described came to Ignatius.

"Well, and suppose I did," he said warmly. "Can't you women ever understand when a man is kidding you? Have you no sense of humour? Must you always take every light quip literally? If you want a portrait of Miss Rossiter, you will jolly well pay for it in the usual manner. The thing that beats me is why do you want a portrait of a girl who not only has most unattractive features but is also a dull yellow in colour. Furthermore, she flickers. As I look at her, she definitely flickers round the edges. Her face is sallow and unwholesome. Her eyes have no sparkle of intelligence. Her ears stick out and her chin goes in. To sum up, her whole appearance gives me an indefinable pain in the neck: and, if you hold me to my promise, I shall charge extra for moral and intellectual damage and wear and tear caused by having to sit opposite her and look at her."

With these words, Ignatius Mulliner turned and began to rummage in a drawer for his pipe. But the drawer contained no pipe.

"What!" cried Mrs. Rossiter.

"You heard," said Ignatius.

"My smelling-salts!" gasped Mrs. Rossiter.

Ignatius ran his hand along the mantelpiece. He opened two cupboards and looked under the settee. But he found no pipe.

The Mulliners are by nature a courteous family: and, seeing Mrs. Rossiter sniffing and gulping there, a belated sense of having been less tactful than he might have been came to Ignatius.

"It is possible," he said, "that my recent remarks may have caused you pain. If so, I am sorry. My excuse must be that they came from a full heart. I am fed to the tonsils with the human race and look on the entire Rossiter family as perhaps its darkest blots. I cannot see the Rossiter family. There seems to be no market for them. All I require of the Rossiters is their blood. I nearly got Cyprian with a dagger, but he was too quick for me. If he fails as a critic, there is always a future for him as a Russian dancer. However, I had decidedly better luck with George. I gave him the juiciest kick I have ever administered to human frame. If he had been shot from a gun he couldn't have gone out quicker. Probably he passed you on the stairs?"

"So *that* was what passed us!" said Hermione, interested. "I remember thinking at the time that there was a whiff of George."

Mrs. Rossiter was staring, aghast.

"You kicked my son?"

"As squarely in the seat of the pants, madam," said Ignatius with modest pride, "as if I had been practising for weeks."

"My stricken child!" cried Mrs. Rossiter. And, hastening from the room, she ran down the stairs in quest of the remains. A boy's best friend is his mother.

In the studio she had left, Hermione was gazing at Ignatius, in her eyes a look he had never seen there before.

"I had no idea you were so eloquent, Mr. Mulliner," she said, breaking the silence. "What a vivid description that was that you gave of me. Quite a prose poem."

Ignatius made a deprecating gesture.

"Oh, well," he said.

"Do you really think I am like that?"

"I do."

"Yellow?"

"Greeny yellow."

"And my eyes...?" She hesitated for a word.

"They are not unlike blue oysters," said Ignatius, prompting her, "which have been dead some time."

"In fact, you don't admire my looks?"

"Far from it."

She was saying something, but he had ceased to listen. Quite suddenly he had remembered that about a couple of weeks ago, at a little party which he had given in the studio, he had dropped a half-smoked cigar behind the bureau. And as no charwoman is allowed by the rules of her union to sweep under bureaux, it might—nay, must—still be there. With feverish haste he dragged the bureau out. It was.

Ignatius Mulliner sighed an ecstatic sigh. Chewed and mangled, covered with dust and bitten by mice, this object between his fingers was nevertheless a cigar—a genuine, smokeable cigar, containing the regulation eight per cent of carbon monoxide. He struck a match and the next moment he had begun to puff.

And, as he did so, the milk of human kindness surged back into his soul like a vast tidal wave. As swiftly as a rabbit, handled by a competent conjurer, changes into a bouquet, a bowl of goldfish or the grand old flag, Ignatius Mulliner changed into a thing of sweetness and light, with charity towards all, with malice towards none. The pyridine played about his mucous surfaces, and he welcomed it like a long-lost brother. He felt gay, happy, exhilarated.

He looked at Hermione, standing there with her eyes sparkling and her beautiful face ashine, and he realized that he had been all wrong about her. So far from being a gumboil, she was the loveliest thing that had ever breathed the perfumed air of Kensington.

And then, chilling his ecstasy and stopping his heart in the middle of a beat, came the recollection of what he had said about her appearance. He felt pale and boneless. If ever a man had dished himself properly, that man, he felt, was Ignatius Mulliner. And he did not mean maybe.

She was looking at him, and the expression on her face seemed somehow to suggest that she was waiting for something.

"Well?" she said.

"I beg your pardon?" said Ignatius.

She pouted.

"Well, aren't you going to—er—?"

"What?"

"Well, fold me in your arms and all that sort of thing," said Hermione, blushing prettily.

Ignatius tottered.

"Who, me?"

"Yes, you."

"Fold you in my arms?"

"Yes."

"But—er—do you want me to?"

"Certainly."

"I mean... after all I said... "

She stared at him in amazement.

"Haven't you been listening to what I've been telling you?" she cried.

"I'm sorry." Ignatius stammered. "Good deal on my mind just now. Must have missed it. What did you say?"

"I said that, if you really think I look like that, you do not love me, as I had always supposed, for my beauty, but for my intellect. And if you knew how I have always longed to be loved for my intellect!"

Ignatius put down his cigar and breathed deeply.

"Let me get this right," he said. "Will you marry me?"

"Of course I will. You always attracted me strangely, Ignatius, but I thought you looked upon me as a mere doll."

He picked up his cigar, took a puff, laid it down again, took a step forward, extended his arms, and folded her in them. And for a space they stood there, clasped together, murmuring those broken words that lovers know so well. Then gently disengaging her, he went back to the cigar and took another invigorating puff.

"Besides," she said, "how could a girl help but love a man who could lift my brother George right down a whole flight of stairs with a single kick?"

Ignatius's face clouded.

"George! That reminds me. Cyprian said you said I was like George."

"Oh! I didn't mean him to repeat that."

"Well, he did," said Ignatius moodily, "and the thought was agony."

"But I only meant that you and George were both always playing the ukulele. And I hate ukuleles."

Ignatius's face cleared.

"I will give mine to the poor this afternoon. And, touching Cyprian... George said you said I reminded you of him."

She hastened to soothe him.

"It's only the way you dress. You both wear such horrid sloppy clothes."

Ignatius folded her in his arms once more.

"You shall take me this very instant to the best tailor in London," he said. "Give me a minute to put my boots on, and I'll be with you. You don't mind if I just step in at my tobacconist's for a moment on the way? I have a large order for him."

Sleepy Time

———— • ————

In his office on the premises of Popgood and Grooly, publishers of the Book Beautiful, Madison Avenue, New York, Cyril Grooly, the firm's junior partner, was practicing putts into a tooth glass and doing rather badly even for one with a twenty-four handicap, when Patricia Binstead, Mr. Popgood's secretary, entered, and dropping his putter he folded her in a close embrace. This was not because all American publishers are warmhearted, impulsive men and she a very attractive girl, but because they had recently become betrothed. On his return from his summer vacation at Paradise Valley, due to begin this afternoon, they would step along to some convenient church and become man, if you can call someone with a twenty-four handicap a man, and wife.

"A social visit?" he asked, the embrace concluded. "Or business?"

"Business. Popgood had to go out to see a man about subsidiary rights, and Count Dracula has blown in. Well, when I say Count Dracula, I speak loosely. He just looks like him. His name is Professor Pepperidge Farmer, and he's come to sign his contract."

"He writes books?"

"He's written one. He calls it *Hypnotism as a Device to Uncover the Unconscious Drives and Mechanism in an Effort to Analyze the Functions Involved Which Give Rise to Emotional Conflicts in the Waking State*, but the title's going to be changed to *Sleepy Time*. Popgood thinks it's snappier."

"Much snappier."

"Shall I send him in?"

"Do so, queen of my soul."

"And Popgood says, Be sure not to go above two hundred dollars for the advance," said Patricia, and a few moments later the visitor made his appearance.

It was an appearance, as Patricia had hinted, of a nature to chill the spine. Sinister was the adjective that automatically sprang to the lips of those who met Professor Pepperidge Farmer for the first time. His face was gaunt and lined and grim, and as his burning eyes bored into Cyril's the young publisher was conscious of a feeling of relief that this encounter was not taking place down a dark alley or in some lonely spot in the country. But a man used to mingling with American authors, few of whom look like anything on earth, is not readily intimidated and he greeted him with his customary easy courtesy.

"Come right in," he said. "You've caught me just in time. I'm off to Paradise Valley this afternoon."

"A golfing holiday?" said the Professor, eyeing the putter.

"Yes, I'm looking forward to getting some golf."

"How is your game?"

"Horrible," Cyril was obliged to confess. "Mine is a sad and peculiar case. I have the theory of golf at my fingertips, but once out in the middle I do nothing but foozle."

"You should keep your head down."

"So Tommy Armour tells me, but up it comes."

"That's life."

"Or shall we say hell?"

"If you prefer it."

"It seems the *mot juste*. But now to business. Miss Binstead tells me you have come to sign your contract. I have it here. It all appears to be in order except that the amount of the advance has not been decided on."

"And what are your views on that?"

"I was thinking of a hundred dollars. You see," said Cyril, falling smoothly into his stride, "a book like yours always involves a serious risk for the publisher owing to the absence of the Sex Motif, which renders it impossible for him to put a nude female of impressive vital statistics on the jacket and no hope of getting banned in Boston. Add the growing cost of paper and the ever-increasing demands of printers, compositors, binders and... why are you waving your hands like that?"

"I have French blood in me. On my mother's side."

"Well, I wish you wouldn't. You're making me sleepy."

"Oh, am I? How very interesting. Yes, I can see that your eyes are closing. You are becoming drowsy. You are falling asleep... you are falling asleep... asleep... asleep... asleep..."

It was getting on for lunch time when Cyril awoke. When he did so, he found that the recent gargoyle was no longer with him. Odd, he felt, that the fellow should have gone before they settled the amount of his advance, but no doubt he had remembered some appointment elsewhere. Dismissing him from his mind, Cyril resumed his putting and soon after lunch he left for Paradise Valley.

On the subject of Paradise Valley the public-relations representative of the Paradise Hotel has expressed himself very frankly. It is, he says in his illustrated booklet, a dream world of breathtaking beauty, and its noble scenery, its wide-open spaces, its soft mountain breezes and sun-drenched pleasaunces impart to the jaded city worker a new vim and vigour and fill him so full of red corpuscles that before a day has elasped in these delightful surroundings he is conscious of a *je ne sais quoi* and a *bien être* and goes about with his chin up and both feet on the ground, feeling as if he had just come back from the cleaner's. And, what is more, only a step from the hotel lies the Squashy Hollow golf course, of whose amenities residents can avail themselves on payment of a greens fee.

What, however, the booklet omits to mention is that the Squashy Hollow course is one of the most difficult in the country. It was constructed by an exiled Scot who, probably from some deep-seated grudge against the human race, has modeled the eighteen holes on the nastiest and most repellent of his native land, so that after negotiating—say—the Alps at Prestwick the pleasure-seeker finds himself confronted by the Stationmaster's Garden at St. Andrew's, with the Eden and the Redan just around the corner.

The type of golfer it attracts, therefore, is the one with high ideals and an implicit confidence in his ability to overcome the toughest obstacles; the sort who plays in amateur championships and mutters to himself "Why this strange weakness?" if he shoots worse than a seventy-five, and one look at it gave Cyril that uncomfortable feeling known to scientists as the heebie-jeebies. He had entered for the medal contest which was to take place tomorrow, for he always entered for medal contests, never being able to forget that he had once shot a ninety-eight and that this, if repeated, would with his handicap give him a sporting chance of success. But the prospect of performing in front of all these hardened experts created in him the illusion that caterpillars to the number of about fifty-seven were parading up and down his spinal cord. He shrank from exposing himself to their bleak, contemptuous stares. His emotions when he did would, he knew, be similar in almost every respect to those of a mongrel which had been rash enough to wander into some fashionable kennel show.

As, then, he sat on the porch of the Paradise Hotel on the morning before the contest, he was so far from being filled with *bien être* that he could not even achieve *je ne sais quoi*, and at this moment the seal was set on his despondency by the sight of Agnes Flack.

Agnes Flack was a large young woman who, on the first day of his arrival, had discovered that he was a partner in a publishing firm and had immediately begun to speak of a novel which she had written and would be glad to have his opinion of when he had a little time to spare. And experience had taught him that when large young women write novels they were either squashily sentimental or so Chatterleyesque that it would be necessary to print them on asbestos, and he had spent much of his leisure avoiding her. She seemed now to be coming in his direction, so rising hastily he made on winged feet for the bar. Entering it at a rapid gallop, he collided with a solid body, and this proved on inspection to be none other that Professor Pepperidge Farmer, looking more sinister than ever in Bermuda shorts, a shirt like a Turner sunset and a Panama hat with a pink ribbon round it.

He stood amazed. There was, of course, no reason why the other should not have been there, for the hotel was open to all whose purses were equal to the tariff, but somehow he seemed out of place, like a ghoul at a garden party or a vampire bat at a picnic.

"You!" he exclaimed. "What ever became of you that morning?"

"You allude to our previous meeting?" said the Professor. "I saw you had dozed off, so I tiptoed out without disturbing you. I thought it would be better to resume our acquaintance in these more agreeable surroundings. For if you are thinking that my presence here is due to one of those coincidences which are so strained and inartistic, you are wrong. I came in the hope that I might be able to do something to improve your golf game. I feel I owe you a great deal."

"You do? Why?"

"We can go into that some other time. Tell me, how is the golf going? Any improvement?"

If he had hoped to receive confidences, he could not have put the question at a better moment. Cyril did not habitually bare his soul to comparative strangers, but now he found himself unable to resist the urge. It was as though the Professor's query had drawn a cork and brought all his doubts and fears and inhibitions foaming out like ginger pop from a ginger-pop bottle. As far as reticence was concerned, he might have been on a psychoanalyst's couch at twenty-five dollars the half hour. In burning words he spoke of the coming medal contest, stressing his qualms and the growing coldness of his feet, and the Professor listened attentively, clicking a sympathetic tongue from time to time. It was plain that, though he looked like something Charles Addams might have thought up when in the throes of a hangover, if Mr. Addams does ever have hangovers, he had a feeling heart.

"I'm paired with a fellow called Sidney McMurdo, who they tell me is the club champion, and I fear his scorn. It's going to take me a least a hundred and fifteen shots for the round, and on each of those hundred and fifteen shots Sidney McMurdo will look at me as if I were something slimy and obscene that had crawled out from under a flat stone. I shall feel like a crippled leper, and so," said Cyril, concluding his remarks, "I have decided to take my name off the list of entrants. Call me weak if you will, but I can't face it."

The Professor patted him on the shoulder in a fatherly manner and was about to speak, but before he could do so, Cyril heard his name paged and was told that he was wanted on the telephone. It was some little time before he returned, and when he did the dullest eye could see that something had occurred to ruffle him. He found Professor Farmer sipping a lemon squash, and when the Professor asked him if he would care for one of the same, he thundered out a violent no.

"Blast and damn all lemon squashes!" he cried vehemently. "Do you know who that was on the phone? It was Popgood, my senior partner. And do you know what he said? He wanted to know what had gotten into me to make me sign a contract giving you five thousand dollars advance on that book of yours. He said you must have hypnotized me."

A smile, probably intended to be gentle, but conveying the impression that he was suffering from some internal disorder, played over the Professor's face.

"Of course I did, my dear fellow. It was one of the ordinary business precautions an author has to take. The only way to get a

decent advance from a publisher is to hypnotize him. That was
what I referring to when I said I owed you a great deal. But for
you I should never have been able to afford a holiday at a place
like Paradise Valley where even the simplest lemon squash sets
you back a prince's ransom. Was Popgood annoyed?"

"He was."

"Too bad. He should have been rejoicing to think that his money
had been instrumental in bringing a little sunshine into a fellow
creature's life. But let us forget him and return to this matter of
your golfing problems."

He had said the one thing capable of diverting Cyril's thoughts
from his incandescent partner. No twenty-four-handicap man is
ever deaf to such an appeal.

"You told me you had the theory of the game at your fingertips.
Is that so? Your reading has been wide?"

"I've read every golf book that has been written."

"You mentioned Tommy Armour. Have you studied his
preachings?"

"I know them by heart."

"But lack of confidence prevents you putting them into practice?"

"I suppose that's it."

"Then the solution is simple. I must hypnotize you again. You
should still be under the influence, but the effects may have worn
off and it's best to be on the safe side. I will instill into you the
conviction that you can knock spots off the proudest McMurdo.
When you take club in hand, it will be with the certainty that your
ball is going to travel from Point A to Point B by the shortest route
and will meet with no misadventures on the way. Whose game
would you prefer yours to resemble? Arnold Palmer's? Gary
Player's? Jack Nicklaus's? Palmer's is the one I would recommend.
Those spectaular finishes of his. You agree? Palmer's it shall be,
then. So away we go. Your eyes are closing. You are feeling drowsy.
You are falling asleep... asleep... asleep..."

Paradise Valley was at its best the next day, its scenery just as noble, its mountain breezes just as soft, its spaces fully as wide and open as the public-relations man's booklet had claimed them to be, and Cyril, as he stood beside the first tee of the Squashy Hollow course awaiting Sidney McMurdo's arrival, was feeling, as he confided to the caddy master when picking up his clubs, like a million dollars. He would indeed scarcely have been exaggerating if he made it two million. His chin was up, both his feet were on the ground, and the red corpuscles of which the booklet had spoken coursed through his body like students rioting in Saigon, Moscow, Cairo, Panama and other centers. Professor Farmer, in assuring him that he would become as confident as Arnold Palmer, had understated it. He was as confident as Arnold Palmer, Gary Player, Ken Venturi, Jack Nicklaus and Julius Boros all rolled into one.

He had not been waiting long when he beheld a vast expanse of man approaching and presumed that this must be his partner for the round. He gave him a sunny smile.

"Mr. McMurdo? How do you do? Nice day. Very pleasant, those soft mountain breezes."

The newcomer's only response was a bronchial sound such as might have been produced by an elephant taking its foot out of a swamp in a teak forest. Sidney McMurdo was in a dark and sullen mood. On the previous night, Agnes Flack, his fiancée, had broken their engagement, owing to a trifling disagreement they had had about the novel she had written. He had said it was a lot of prune juice and advised her to burn it without delay, and she had said it was not, either, a lot of prune juice, adding that she never wanted to see or speak to him again, and this had affected him adversely. It always annoyed him when Agnes Flack broke their engagement, because it made him overswing, particularly off the tee.

He did so now, having won the honour, and was pained to see

that his ball, which he had intended to go due north, was traveling
nor'-nor'-east. And as he stood scowling after it, Cyril spoke.

"I wonder if you noticed what you did wrong there, Mr.
McMurdo," he said in the friendliest way. " Your backswing was
too long. Length of backswing does not have as much effect on
distance as many believe. You should swing back only just as far
as you can without losing control of the club. Control is all-
important. I always take my driver to about the horizontal position on the backswing. Watch me now."

And so saying, Cyril with effortless grace drove two hundred
and eighty yards straight down the fairway.

"See what I mean?" he said.

It was on the fourth green, after he had done an eagle, that he
spoke again. Sidney McMurdo had had some difficulty in getting
out of a sand trap, and he hastened to give him the benefit of his
advice. There was nothing in it for him except the glow that comes
from doing an act of kindness, but it distressed him to see a quite
promising player like McMurdo making mistakes of which a wiser
head could so easily cure him.

"You did not allow for the texture of the sand," he said. "Your
sand shot should differ with the texture of the sand. If it is wet,
hard or shallow, your clubhead will not cut into it as deeply as
it would into soft and shifting sand. If the sand is soft, try to dig
into it about two inches behind the ball, but when it is hard, penetrate it about one and a half inches behind the ball. And since firm
sand will slow down your club considerably, be sure to give your
swing a full follow-through."

The game proceeded. On the twelfth Cyril warned his partner
to be careful to remember to bend the knees slightly for greater
flexibility throughout the swing, though—on the sixteenth—he
warned against bending them too much, as this often led to topping. When both had holed out at the eighteenth, he had a word
of counsel to give on the subject of putting.

"Successful putting, Sidney," he said, for he felt that they might now consider themselves on first-name terms, "depends largely on the mental attitude. Confidence is everything. Never let anxiety make you tense. Never for an instant harbor the thought that your shot may miss. When I sank that last fifty-foot putt, I *knew* it was going in. My mind was filled with a picture of the ball following a proper line to the hole, and it is that sort of picture I should like to encourage in you. Well, it has been a most pleasant round. We must have another soon. I shot a sixty-two, did I not? I thought so, I was quite on my game today, quite on my game."

Sidney McMurdo's eyebrows, always beetling, were beetling still more darkly as he watched Cyril walking away with elastic tread. He turned to a friend who had just come up.

"Who is that fellow?" he asked hoarsely.

"His name's Grooly," said the friend. "One of the summer visitors."

"What's his handicap?"

"I can tell you that, for I was looking at the board this morning. It's twenty-four."

"Air!" cried Sidney McMurdo, clutching his throat. "Give me air!"

Cyril, meanwhile, had rounded the clubhouse and was approaching the practice green that lay behind it. Someone large and female was engaged there in polishing her chip shots, and as he paused to watch he stood astounded at her virtuosity. A chip shot, he was aware, having read his Johnny Farrell, is a crisp hit with the clubhead stopping at the ball and not following through. "Open your stance," says the venerable Farrell. "Place your weight on the left foot and hit down at the ball," and this was precisely what this substantial female was doing. Each ball she struck dropped on the green like a poached egg, and as she advanced to pick them up he saw that she was Agnes Flack.

A loud gasp escaped Cyril. The dream world of breathtaking

beauty pirouetted before his eyes as if Arthur Murray were teaching it dancing in a hurry. He was conscious of strange, tumultuous emotions stirring within him. Then the mists cleared, and gazing at Agnes Flack he knew that there before him stood his destined mate. A novelist she might be, and no doubt as ghastly a novelist as ever set finger to typewriter key, but what of that? Quite possibly she would grow out of it in time, and in any case he felt that as a man who went about shooting sixty-twos in medal contests he owed it to himself to link his lot with a golfer of her caliber. Theirs would be the ideal union.

In a situation like this no publisher hesitates. A moment later, Cyril was on the green, his arms as far around Agnes Flack as they would go.

"Old girl," he said. "You're a grand bit of work!"

Two courses were open Agnes Flack. She could draw herself to her full height, say "Sir!" and strike this clinging vine with her number seven iron, or, remembering that Cyril was a publisher and that she had a top copy and two carbons of a novel in her suitcase, she could cooperate and accept his addresses. She chose the latter alternative, and when Cyril suggested that they should spend the honeymoon in Scotland, playing all the famous courses there, she said that that would suit her perfectly. If, as she plighted her troth, a thought of Sidney McMurdo came into her mind, it was merely the renewed conviction that he was an oaf and a fathead, temperamentally incapable of recognizing good literature when it was handed to him on a skewer.

These passionate scenes take it out of a man, and it is not surprising that Cyril's first move on leaving Agnes Flack should have been in the direction of the bar. Arriving there, he found Professor Farmer steeping himself, as was his custom, in lemon squashes. The warm weather engendered thirst, and since he had come to the Paradise Hotel the straw had seldom left his lips.

"Ah, Cyril, if you don't mind me calling you Cyril, though you will be the first to admit that it's a hell of a name," said the Professor, "how did everything come out?"

"Quite satisfactorily, Pepperidge. The returns are not all in, but I think I must have won the medal. I shot a sixty-two, which, subtracting my handicap, gives me a thirty-eight. I doubt if anyone will do better than thirty-eight"

"Most unlikely."

"Thirty-four under par takes a lot of beating."

"Quite a good deal. I congratulate you."

"And that's not all. I'm engaged to the most wonderful girl."

"Really? I congratulate you again. Who is she?"

"Her name is Agnes Flack."

The Professor started, dislodging a drop of lemon squash from his lower lip.

"Agnes Flack?"

"Yes."

"You couldn't be mistaken in the name?"

"No."

"H'm!"

"Why do you say h'm?"

"I was thinking of Sidney McMurdo."

"How does he get into the act?"

"He is—or was—betrothed to Agnes Flack, and I am told he has rather a short way with men who get engaged to his fiancée, even if technically ex. Do you know a publisher called Pickering?"

"Harold Pickering? I've met him."

"He got engaged to Agnes Flack, and it was only by butting Sidney McMurdo in the stomach with his head and disappearing over the horizon that he was able to avoid being torn by the latter into little pieces. But for his ready resource he would have become converted into, as one might say, a sort of publishing hash, though, of course, McMurdo might simply have jumped on him with spiked shoes."

It was Cyril's turn to say h'm, and he said it with a good deal of thoughtful fervor. He had parted so recently from Sidney McMurdo that he had not had time to erase from his mental retina what might be called the over-all picture of him. The massive bulk of Sidney McMurdo rose before his eyes, as did the other's rippling muscles. The discovery that in addition to possessing the physique of a gorilla he had also that animal's easily aroused temper was not one calculated to induce a restful peace of mind. Given the choice between annoying Sidney McMurdo and stirring up a nest of hornets with a fountain pen, he would unhesitatingly have cast his vote for the hornets.

And it was as he sat trying to think what was to be done for the best that the door flew open and the bar became full of McMurdo. He seemed to permeate its every nook and cranny. Nor had Professor Farmer erred in predicting that his mood would be edgy. His eyes blazed, his ears wiggled and a clicking sound like the manipulation of castanets by a Spanish dancer told that he was gnashing his teeth. Except that he was not beating his chest with both fists, he resembled in every respect the gorilla to which Cyril had mentally compared him.

"Ha!" he said, sighting Cyril.

"Oh, hullo, Sidney."

"Less of the Sidney!" snarled McMurdo. "I don't want a man of your kidney calling me Sidney," he went on, rather surprisingly dropping into poetry. "Agnes Flack tells me she is engaged to you."

Cyril replied nervously that there had been some infomal conversation along those lines.

"She says you hugged her."

"Only a little."

"And kissed her."

"In the most respectful manner."

"In other words, you have sneaked behind my back like a slithery serpent and stolen from me the woman I love. Perhaps if you have a moment to spare, you will step outside."

Cyril did not wish to step outside, but it seemed that there was no alternative. He preceded Sidney McMurdo through the door, and was surprised on reaching the wide-open spaces to find that Professor Farmer had joined the party. The Professor was regarding Sidney with that penetrating gaze of his which made him look like Boris Karloff on one of his bad mornings.

"Might I ask you to look me in the eye for a moment, Mr. McMurdo," he said. "Thank you. Yes, as I thought. You are drowsy. Your eyes are closing. You are falling asleep."

"No, I'm not."

"Yes, you are."

"By Jove, I believe you're right," said Sidney McMurdo, sinking slowly into a conveniently placed deck chair. "Yes, I think I'll take a nap."

The Professor continued to weave arabesques in the air with his hands, and suddenly Sidney McMurdo sat up. His eye rested on Cyril, but it was no longer the flaming eye it had been. Almost affectionate it seemed, and when he spoke his voice was mild.

"Mr. Grooly."

"I have been thinking it over, Mr. Grooly, and I have reached a decision, which, though painful, I am sure is right. It is wrong to think only of self. There are times when a man must make the great sacrifice no matter what distress it causes him. You love Agnes Flack, Agnes loves you, and I must not come between you. Take her, Mr. Grooly. I yield her to you, yield her freely. It breaks my heart, but her happiness is all that matters. Take her, Grooly, and if a broken man's blessing is of any use to you, I give it without reserve. I think I'll go to the bar and have a gin and tonic," said Sidney McMurdo, and proceeded to do so.

"A very happy conclusion to your afternoon's activities," said

Professor Farmer as the swing door closed behind him. "I often say that there is nothing like hypnotism for straightening out these little difficulties. I thought McMurdo's speech of renunciation was very well phrased, didn't you? In perfect taste. Well, as you will now no longer have need of my services, I suppose I had better dehypnotise you. It will not be painful, just a momentary twinge," said the Professor, blowing a lemon-squash-charged breath in Cyril's face, and Cyril was aware of an odd feeling of having been hit by an atom bomb while making a descent in an express elevator. He found himself a little puzzled by his companion's choice of the expression "momentary twinge," but he had not the leisure to go into what was after all a side issue. With the removal of the hypnotic spell there had come to him the realization of the unfortunate position in which he had placed himself, and he uttered a sharp "Oh, golly!"

"I beg your pardon?" said the Professor.

"Listen," said Cyril, and his voice shook like a jelly in a high wind. "Does it count if you ask a girl to marry you when you're hypnotised?"

"You are speaking of Miss Flack?"

"Yes, I proposed to her on the practice green, carried away by the superexcellence of her chip shots, and I can't stand the sight of her. And, what's more, in about three weeks I'm supposed to be marrying someone else. You remember Patricia Binstead, the girl who showed you into my office?"

"Very vividly."

"She holds the copyright. What am I to do? You couldn't go and hypnotise Agnes Flack and instill her, as you call it, with the idea that I'm the world's leading louse, could you?"

"My dear fellow, nothing easier."

"Then do it without an instant's delay," said Cyril. "Tell her I'm scratch and pretended to have a twenty-four handicap in order to win the medal. Tell her I'm sober only at the rarest intervals.

Tell her I'm a Communist spy and my name's really Groolinsky. Tell her I've two wives already. But you'll know what to say."

He waited breathlessly for the Professor's return.

"Well?" he cried.

"All washed up, my dear Cyril. I left her reunited to McMurdo. She says she wouldn't marry you if you were the last publisher on earth and wouldn't let you sponsor her novel if you begged her on bended knees. She says she is going to let Simon and Schuster have it, and she hopes that will be a lesson to you."

Cyril drew a deep breath.

"Pepperidge, you're wonderful!"

"One does one's best," said the Professor modestly. "Well, now that the happy ending has been achieved, how about returning to the bar? I'll buy you a lemon squash."

"Do you really like that stuff?"

"I love it."

It was on the tip of Cyril's tongue to say that one would have thought he was a man who would be more likely to share Count Dracula's preference for human blood when thirsty, but he refrained from putting the thought into words. It might, he felt, be lacking in tact, and after all, why criticise a man for looking like something out of a horror film if his heart was so patently of the purest gold. It is the heart that matters, not the features, however unshuffled.

"I'm with you," he said. "A lemon squash would be most refreshing."

"They serve a very good lemon squash here."

"Probably made from contented lemons."

"I shouldn't wonder," said the Professor.

He smiled a hideous smile. It had just occurred to him that if he hypnotised the waiter, he would be spared the necessity of disbursing money, always a consideration to a man of slender means.

The Spot of Art

——— • ———

I was lunching at my Aunt Dahlia's, and despite the fact that
Anatole, her outstanding cook, had rather excelled himself in the
matter of the bill-of-fare, I'm bound to say the food was more or
less turning to ashes in my mouth. You see, I had some bad news
to break to her—always a prospect that takes the edge off the appetite. She wouldn't be pleased, I knew, and when not pleased Aunt
Dahlia, having spent most of her youth in the hunting-field, has
a crispish way of expressing herself.

However, I supposed I had better have a dash at it and get it over.

"Aunt Dahlia," I said, facing the issue squarely.

"Hullo?"

"You know that cruise of yours?"

"Yes."

"That yachting-cruise you are planning?"

"Yes."

"That jolly cruise in your yacht in the Mediterranean to which
you so kindly invited me and to which I have been looking forward with such keen anticipation?"

"Get on, fathead, what about it?"

"I swallowed a chunk of *cotelette-supreme-aux-choux-fleurs* and
slipped her the distressing info'.

"I'm frightfully sorry, Aunt Dahlia," I said, "but I shan't be able
to come."

As I had foreseen, she goggled.

"What!"

"I'm afraid not."

"You poor, miserable hell-hound, what do you mean, you won't be able to come?"

"Well, I won't."

"Why not?"

"Matters of the most extreme urgency render my presence in the Metropolis imperative."

She sniffed.

"I suppose what you really mean is that you're hanging round some unfortunate girl again?"

I didn't like the way she put it, but I admit I was stunned by her penetration, if that's the word I want. I mean the sort of thing detectives have.

"Yes, Aunt Dahlia," I said, "you have guessed my secret. I do indeed love."

"Who is she?"

"A Miss Pendlebury. Christian name, Gwladys. She spells it with a 'w.' "

"With a 'g,' you mean."

"With a 'w' *and* a 'g.' "

"Not Gwladys?"

"That's it."

The relative uttered a yowl.

"You sit there and tell me you haven't enough sense to steer clear of a girl who calls herself Gwladys? Listen, Bertie," said Aunt Dahlia earnestly, "I'm an older woman than you are—well, you know what I mean—and I can tell you a thing or two. And one of them is that no good can come of association with anything labelled Gwladys or Ysobel or Ethyl or Mabelle or Kathryn. But particularly Gwladys. What sort of girl is she?"

"Slightly divine."

"She isn't that female I saw driving you at sixty miles p.h. in the Park the other day. In a red two-seater?"

"She did drive me in the Park the other day. I thought it rather a hopeful sign. And her Widgeon Seven is red."

Aunt Dahlia looked relieved.

"Oh well, then, she'll probably break your silly fat neck before she can get you to the altar. That's some consolation. Where did you meet her?"

"At a party in Chelsea. She's an artist."

"Ye gods!"

"And swings a jolly fine brush, let me tell you. She's painted a portrait of me. Jeeves and I hung it up in the flat this morning. I have an idea Jeeves doesn't like it."

"Well, if it's anything like you I don't see why he should. An artist! Calls herself Gwladys! And drives a car in the sort of way Segrave would if he were pressed for time." She brooded awhile. "Well, it's all very sad, but I can't see why you won't come on the yacht."

I explained.

"It would be madness to leave the metrop. at this juncture," I said. "You know what girls are. They forget the absent face. And I'm not at all easy in my mind about a certain cove of the name of Lucius Pim. Apart from the fact that he's an artist, too, which forms a bond, his hair waves. One must never discount wavy hair, Aunt Dahlia. Moreover, this bloke is one of those strong, masterful men. He treats Gwladys as if she were less than the dust beneath his taxi wheels. He criticizes her hats and says nasty things about her chiaroscuro. For some reason, I've often noticed, this always seems to fascinate girls, and it has sometimes occurred to me that, being myself more the parfait gentle knight, if you know what I mean, I am in grave danger of getting the short end. Taking all these things into consideration, then, I cannot breeze off to the Mediterranean, leaving this Pim a clear field. You must see that?"

Aunt Dahlia laughed. Rather a nasty laugh. Scorn in its *timbre*, or so it seemed to me.

"I shouldn't worry," she said. "You don't suppose for a moment that Jeeves will sanction the match?"

I was stung.

"Do you imply, Aunt Dahlia," I said—and I can't remember if I rapped the table with the handle of my fork or not, but I rather think I did— "that I allow Jeeves to boss me to the extent of stopping me marrying somebody I want to marry?"

"Well, he stopped you wearing a moustache, didn't he? And purple socks. And soft-fronted shirts with dress-clothes."

"That is a different matter altogether."

"Well, I'm prepared to make a small bet with you, Bertie. Jeeves will stop this match."

"What absolute rot!"

"And if he doesn't like that portrait, he will get rid of it."

"I never heard such dashed nonsense in my life."

"And finally, you wretched, pie-faced wambler, he will present you on board my yacht at the appointed hour. I don't know how he will do it, but you will be there, all complete with yachting-cap and spare pair of socks."

"Let us change the subject, Aunt Dahlia," I said coldly.

Being a good deal stirred up by the attitude of the flesh-and-blood at the luncheon table, I had to go for a bit of a walk in the Park after leaving, to soothe the nervous system. By about four-thirty the ganglions had ceased to vibrate, and I returned to the flat. Jeeves was in the sitting-room, looking at the portrait.

I felt a trifle embarrassed in the man's presence, because just before leaving I had informed him of my intention to scratch the yacht-trip, and he had taken it on the chin a bit. You see, he had been looking forward to it rather. From the moment I had accepted the invitation, there had been a sort of nautical glitter in his eye, and I'm not sure I hadn't heard him trolling chanties in the kitchen. I think some ancestor of his must have been one of Nelson's tars or something, for he has always had the urge of the salt sea in his blood. I have noticed him on liners, when we were going to

America, striding the deck with a sailorly roll and giving the distinct impression of being just about to heave the main-brace or splice the binnacle.

So, though I had explained my reasons, taking the man fully into my confidence and concealing nothing, I knew that he was distinctly peeved; and my first act, on entering, was to do the cheery a bit. I joined him in front of the portrait.

"Looks good, Jeeves, what?"

"Yes, sir."

"Nothing like a spot of art for brightening the home."

"No, sir."

"Seems to lend the room a certain—what shall I say—"

"Yes, sir."

The responses were all right, but his manner was far from hearty, and I decided to tackle him squarely. I mean, dash it. I mean, I don't know if you have ever had your portrait painted, but if you have you will understand my feelings. The spectacle of one's portrait hanging on the wall creates in one a sort of paternal fondness for the thing: and what you demand from the outside public is approval and enthusiasm—not the curling lip, the twitching nostril, and the kind of supercilious look which you see in the eye of a dead mackerel. Especially is this so when the artist is a girl for whom you have conceived sentiments deeper and warmer than those of ordinary friendship.

"Jeeves," I said, "you don't like this spot of art."

"Oh, yes, sir."

"No. Subterfuge is useless. I can read you like a book. For some reason this spot of art fails to appeal to you. What do you object to about it?"

"Is not the colour-scheme a trifle bright, sir?"

"I had not observed it, Jeeves. Anything else?"

"Well, in my opinion, sir, Miss Pendlebury has given you a somewhat too hungry expression."

"Hungry?"

"A little like that of a dog regarding a distant bone, sir."

I checked the fellow.

"There is no resemblance whatever, Jeeves, to a dog regarding a distant bone. The look to which you allude is wistful and denotes Soul."

"I see, sir."

I proceeded to another subject.

"Miss Pendlebury said she might look in this afternoon to inspect the portrait. Did she turn up?"

"Yes, sir."

"But has left?"

"Yes, sir."

"You mean she's gone, what?"

"Precisely, sir."

"She didn't say anything about coming back, I suppose?"

"No, sir. I received the impression that it was not Miss Pendlebury's intention to return. She was a little upset, sir, and expressed a desire to go to her studio and rest."

"Upset? What was she upset about?"

"The accident, sir."

I didn't actually clutch the brow, but I did a bit of mental brow-clutching, as it were.

"Don't tell me she had an accident!"

"Yes, sir."

"What sort of accident?"

"Automobile, sir."

"Was she hurt?"

"No, sir. Only the gentleman."

"What gentleman?"

"Miss Pendlebury had the misfortune to run over a gentleman in her car almost immediately opposite this building. He sustained a slight fracture of the leg."

"Too bad! But Miss Pendlebury is all right?"

"Physically, sir, her condition appeared to be satisfactory. She was suffering a certain distress of mind."

"Of course, with her beautiful, sympathetic nature. Naturally. It's a hard world for a girl, Jeeves, with fellows flinging themselves under the wheels of her car in one long, unending stream. It must have been a great shock to her. What became of the chump?"

"The gentleman, sir?"

"Yes."

"He is in your spare bedroom, sir."

"What!"

"Yes, sir."

"In my spare bedroom?"

"Yes, sir. It was Miss Pendlebury's desire that he should be taken there. She instructed me to telegraph to the gentleman's sister, sir, who is in Paris, advising her of the accident. I also summoned a medical man, who gave it as his opinion that the patient should remain for the time being *in statu quo*.

"You mean, the corpse is on the premises for an indefinite visit?"

"Yes, sir."

"Jeeves, this is a bit thick!"

"Yes, sir."

And I meant it, dash it. I mean to say, a girl can be pretty heftily divine and ensnare the heart and what not, but she's no right to turn a fellow's flat into a morgue. I'm bound to say that for a moment passion ebbed a trifle.

"Well, I suppose I'd better go and introduce myself to the blighter. After all, I am his host. Has he a name?"

"Mr. Pim, sir."

"Pim!"

"Yes, sir. And the young lady addressed him as Lucius. It was owing to the fact that he was on his way here to examine the portrait which she had painted that Mr. Pim happened to be in the roadway at the moment when Miss Pendlebury turned the corner."

I headed for the spare bedroom. I was perturbed to a degree. I don't know if you have ever loved and been handicapped in your wooing by a wavy-haired rival, but one of the things you don't want in such circs. is the rival parking himself on the premises with a broken leg. Apart from anything else, the advantage the position gives him is obviously terrific. There he is, sitting up and toying with a grape and looking pale and interesting, the object of the girl's pity and concern, and where do you get off, bounding about the place in morning costume and spats and with the rude flush of health on the cheek? It seemed to me that things were beginning to look pretty mouldy.

I found Lucius Pim lying in bed, draped in a suit of my pyjamas, smoking one of my cigarettes, and reading a detective story. He waved the cigarette at me in what I considered a dashed patronising manner.

"Ah, Wooster!" he said.

"Not so much of the 'Ah, Wooster!' " I replied brusquely. "How soon can you be moved?"

"In a week or so, I fancy."

"In a week!"

"Or so. For the moment, the doctor insists on perfect quiet and repose. So forgive me, old man, for asking you not to raise your voice. A hushed whisper is the stuff to give the troops. And now, Wooster, about this accident. We must come to an understanding."

"Are you sure you can't be moved?"

"Quite. The doctor said so."

"I think we ought to get a second opinion."

"Useless, my dear fellow. He was most emphatic, and evidently a man who knew his job. Don't worry about my not being comfortable here. I shall be quite all right. I like this bed. And now, to return to the subject of the accident. My sister will be arriving to-morrow. She will be greatly upset. I am her favourite brother."

"You are?"

"I am."

"How many of you are there?"

"Six."

"And you're her favourite?"

"I am."

It seemed to me that the other five must be pretty fairly sub-human, but I didn't say so. We Woosters can curb the tongue.

"She married a bird named Slingsby. Slingsby's Superb Soups. He rolls in money. But do you think I can get him to lend a trifle from time to time to a needy brother-in-law?" said Lucius Pim bitterly. "No, sir! However, that is neither here nor there. The point is that my sister loves me devotedly: and, this being the case, she might try to prosecute and persecute and generally bite pieces out of poor little Gwladys if she knew that it was she who was driving the car that laid me out. She must never know, Wooster. I appeal to you as a man of honour to keep your mouth shut."

"Naturally."

"I'm glad you grasp the point so readily, Wooster. You are not the fool people take you for."

"Who takes me for a fool?"

The Pim raised his eyebrows slightly.

"Don't people?" he said. "Well, well. Anyway, that's settled. Unless I can think of something better I shall tell my sister that I was knocked down by a car which drove on without stopping and I didn't get its number. And now perhaps you had better leave me. The doctor made a point of quiet and repose. Moreover, I want to go on with this story. The villain has just dropped a cobra down the heroine's chimney, and I must be at her side. It is impossible not to be thrilled by Edgar Wallace. I'll ring if I want anything."

I headed for the sitting-room. I found Jeeves there, staring at the portrait in rather a marked manner, as if it hurt him.

"Jeeves," I said, "Mr. Pim appears to be a fixture."

"Yes, sir."

"For the nonce, at any rate. And to-morrow we shall have his sister, Mrs. Slingsby, of Slingsby's Superb Soups, in our midst."

"Yes, sir. I telegraphed to Mrs. Slingsby shortly before four. Assuming her to have been at her hotel in Paris at the moment of the telegram's delivery, she will no doubt take a boat early to-morrow afternoon, reaching Dover—or, should she prefer the alternative route, Folkestone—in time to begin the railway journey at an hour which will enable her to arrive in London at about seven. She will possibly proceed first to her London residence—"

"Yes, Jeeves," I said, "Yes. A gripping story, full of action and human interest. You must have it set to music some time and sing it. Meanwhile, get this into your head. It is imperative that Mrs. Slingsby does not learn that it was Miss Pendlebury who broke her brother in two places. I shall require you, therefore, to approach Mr. Pim before she arrives, ascertain exactly what tale he intends to tell, and be prepared to back it up in every particular."

"Very good, sir."

"And now, Jeeves, what of Miss Pendlebury?"

"Sir?"

"She's sure to call to make enquiries."

"Yes, sir."

"Well, she mustn't find me here. You know all about women, Jeeves?"

"Yes, sir."

"Then tell me this. Am I not right in supposing that if Miss Pendlebury is in a position to go into the sick-room, take a long look at the interesting invalid, and then pop out, with the memory of that look fresh in her mind, and get a square sight of me lounging about in sponge-bag trousers, she will draw damaging comparisons? You see what I mean? Look on this picture and on that—the one romantic, the other not... Eh?"

"Very true, sir. It is a point which I had intended to bring to your attention. An invalid undoubtedly exercises a powerful appeal to the motherliness which exists in every woman's heart, sir. Invalids seem to stir their deepest feelings. The poet Scott has put the matter neatly in the lines— 'Oh, Woman in our hours of ease uncertain, coy, and hard to please. . .When pain and anguish rack the brow—' "

I held up a hand.

"At some other time, Jeeves," I said, "I shall be delighted to hear you speak your piece, but just now I am not in the mood. The position being as I have outlined, I propose to clear out early to-morrow morning and not to reappear until nightfall. I shall take the car and dash down to Brighton for the day."

"Very good, sir."

"It is better so, is it not, Jeeves?"

"Indubitably, sir."

"I think so, too. The sea breezes will tone up my system, which sadly needs a dollop of toning. I leave you in charge of the old home."

"Very good, sir."

"Convey my regrets and sympathy to Miss Pendlebury and tell her I have been called away on business."

"Yes, sir."

"Should the Slingsby require refreshment, feed her in moderation."

"Very good, sir."

"And, in poisoning Mr. Pim's soup, don't use arsenic, which is readily detected. Go to a good chemist and get something that leaves no traces."

I sighed, and cocked an eye at the portrait.

"All this is very wonky, Jeeves."

"Yes, sir."

"When that portrait was painted, I was a happy man."

"Yes, sir."

"Ah, well, Jeeves!"

"Very true, sir."

And we left it at that.

It was lateish when I got back on the following evening. What with a bit of ozone-sniffing, a good dinner, and a nice run home in the moonlight with the old car going as sweet as a nut, I was feeling in pretty good shape once more. In fact, coming through Purley, I went so far as to sing a trifle. The spirit of the Woosters is a buoyant spirit, and optimism had begun to reign again in the W. bosom.

The way I looked at it was, I saw I had been mistaken in assuming that a girl must necessarily love a fellow just because he has broken a leg. At first, no doubt, Gwladys Pendlebury would feel strangely drawn to the Pim when she saw him lying there a more or less total loss. But it would not be long before other reflections crept in. She would ask herself if she were wise in trusting her life's happiness to a man who hadn't enough sense to leap out of the way when he saw a car coming. She would tell herself that, if this sort of thing had happened once, who knew that it might not go on happening again and again all down the long years. And she would recoil from a married life which consisted entirely of going to hospitals and taking her husband fruit. She would realise how much better off she would be, teamed up with a fellow like Bertram Wooster, who, whatever his faults, at least walked on the pavement and looked up and down a street before he crossed it.

It was in excellent spirits, accordingly, that I put the car in the garage, and it was with a merry Tra-la on my lips that I let myself into the flat as Big Ben began to strike eleven. I rang the bell and presently, as if he had divined my wishes, Jeeves came in with siphon and decanter.

"Home again, Jeeves," I said, mixing a spot.

"Yes, sir."

"What has been happening in my absence? Did Miss Pendlebury call?"

"Yes, sir. At about two o'clock."

"And left?"

"At about six, sir."

I didn't like this so much. A four-hour visit struck me as a bit sinister. However, there was nothing to be done about it.

"And Mrs. Slingsby?"

"She arrived shortly after eight and left at ten, sir."

"Ah? Agitated?"

"Yes, sir. Particularly when she left. She was very desirous of seeing you, sir."

"Seeing me?"

"Yes, sir."

"Wanted to thank me brokenly, I suppose, for so courteously allowing her favourite brother a place to have his game legs in. Eh?"

"Possibly, sir. On the other hand, she alluded to you in terms suggestive of disapprobation, sir."

"She—what?"

" 'Feckless idiot' was one of the expressions she employed, sir."

"Feckless idiot?"

"Yes, sir."

I couldn't make it out. I simply couldn't see what the woman had based her judgment on. My Aunt Agatha has frequently said that sort of thing about me, but she has known me from a boy.

"I must look into this, Jeeves. Is Mr. Pim asleep?"

"No, sir. He rang the bell a moment ago to enquire if we had not a better brand of cigarette in the flat."

"He did, did he?"

"Yes, sir."

"The accident doesn't seem to have affected his nerve."

"No, sir."

"I found Lucius Pim sitting propped up among the pillows, reading his detective story.

"Ah, Wooster," he said. "Welcome home. I say, in case you were worrying, it's all right about the cobra. The hero had got at it without the villain's knowledge and extracted its poison-fangs. With the result that when it fell down the chimney and started trying to bite the heroine its efforts were null and void. I doubt if a cobra has ever felt so silly."

"Never mind about cobras."

"It's no good saying 'Never mind about cobras,' " said Lucius Pim in a gentle, rebuking sort of voice. "You've jolly well *got* to mind about cobras, if they haven't had their poison-fangs extracted. Ask anyone. By the way, my sister looked in. She wants to have a word with you."

"And I want to have a word with her."

" 'Two minds with but a single thought.' What she wants to talk to you about is this accident of mine. You remember that story I was to tell her? About the car driving on? Well, the understanding was, if you recollect, that I was only going to tell it if I couldn't think of something better. Fortunately, I thought of something much better. It came to me in a flash as I lay in bed looking at the ceiling. You see, that driving-on story was thin. People don't knock fellows down and break their legs and go driving on. The thing wouldn't have held water for a minute. So I told her you did it."

"What!"

"I said it was you who did it in your car. Much more likely. Makes the whole thing neat and well-rounded. I knew you would approve. At all costs we have got to keep it from her that I was outed by Gwladys. I made it as easy for you as I could, saying that you were a bit pickled at the time and so not to be blamed for what you did. Some fellows wouldn't have thought of that. Still," said Lucius

Pim with a sigh, "I'm afraid she's not any too pleased with you."

"She isn't, isn't she?"

"No, she is not. And I strongly recommend you, if you want anything like a pleasant interview to-morrow, to sweeten her a bit overnight."

"How do you mean, sweeten her?"

"I'd suggest you sent her some flowers. It would be a graceful gesture. Roses are her favourites. Shoot her in a few roses —Number Three, Hill Street is the address—and it may make all the difference. I think it is my duty to inform you, old man, that my sister Beatrice is rather a tough egg, when roused. My brother-in-law is due back from New York at any moment, and the danger, as I see it, is that Beatrice, unless sweetened, will get at him and make him bring actions against you for torts and malfeasances and what not and get thumping damages. He isn't over-fond of me and, left to himself, would rather approve than otherwise of people who broke my legs: but he's crazy about Beatrice and will do anything she asks him to. So my advice is, Gather ye rose-buds, while ye may and bung them in to Number Three, Hill Street. Otherwise, the case of Slingsby *v.* Wooster will be on the calendar before you can say What-ho."

I gave the fellow a look. Lost on him, of course.

"It's a pity you didn't think of all that before," I said. And it wasn't so much the actual words, if you know what I mean, as the way I said it.

"I thought of it all right," said Lucius Pim. "But, as we were both agreed that at all costs— "

"Oh, all right," I said. "All right, all right."

"You aren't annoyed?" said Lucius Pim, looking at me with a touch of surprise.

"Oh, no!"

"Splendid," said Lucius Pim, relieved. "I knew you would feel that I had done the only possible thing. It would have been awful if Beatrice had found out about Gwladys. I daresay you have noticed, Wooster, that when women find themselves in a position to take a running kick at one of their own sex they are twice as rough on her as they would be on a man. Now, you, being of the male persuasion, will find everything made nice and smooth for you. A quart of assorted roses, a few smiles, a tactful word or two, and she'll have melted before you know where you are. Play your cards properly, and you and Beatrice will be laughing merrily and having a game of Round and Round the Mulberry Bush together in about five minutes. Better not let Slingsby's Soups catch you at it, however. He's very jealous where Beatrice is concerned. And now you'll forgive me, old chap, if I send you away. The doctor says I ought not to talk too much for a day or two. Besides, it's time for bye-bye."

The more I thought it over, the better that idea of sending those roses looked. Lucius Pim was not a man I was fond of—in fact, if I had had to choose between him and a cockroach as a companion for a walking-tour, the cockroach would have had it by a short head—but there was no doubt that he had outlined the right policy. His advice was good, and I decided to follow it. Rising next morning at ten-fifteen, I swallowed a strengthening breakfast and legged it off to that flower-shop in Piccadilly. I couldn't leave the thing to Jeeves. It was essentially a mission that demanded the personal touch. I laid out a couple of quid on a sizeable bouquet, sent it with my card to Hill Street, and then looked in at the Drones for a brief refresher. It is a thing I don't often do in the morning, but this threatened to be rather a special morning.

It was about noon when I got back to the flat. I went into the sitting-room and tried to adjust the mind to the coming interview. It had to be faced, of course, but it wasn't any good my telling myself that it was going to be one of those jolly scenes the memory of which cheer you up as you sit toasting your toes at the fire in your old age. I stood or fell by the roses. If they sweetened the

Slingsby, all would be well. If they failed to sweeten her, Bertram was undoubtedly for it.

The clock ticked on, but she did not come. A late riser, I took it, and was slightly encouraged by the reflection. My experience of women has been that the earlier they leave the hay the more vicious specimens they are apt to be. My Aunt Agatha, for instance, is always up with the lark, and look at her.

Still, you couldn't be sure that this rule always worked, and after a while the suspense began to get in amongst me a bit. To divert the mind, I fetched the old putter out of its bag, and began to practise putts into a glass. After all, even if the Slingsby turned out to be all that I had pictured her in my gloomier moments, I should have improved my close-to-the-hole work on the green and be that much up, at any rate.

It was while I was shaping for a rather tricky shot that the front-door bell went.

I picked up the glass and shoved the putter behind the settee. It struck me that if the woman found me engaged on what you might call a frivolous pursuit she might take it to indicate lack of remorse and proper feeling. I straightened the collar, pulled down the waistcoat, and managed to fasten on the face a sort of sad half-smile which was welcoming without being actually jovial. It looked all right in the mirror, and I held it as the door opened.

"Mr. Slingsby," announced Jeeves.

And, having spoken these words, he closed the door and left us alone together.

For quite a time there wasn't anything in the way of chit-chat. The shock of expecting Mrs. Slingsby and finding myself confronted by something entirely different—in fact, not the same thing at all —seemed to have affected the vocal chords. And the visitor didn't appear to be disposed to make light conversation himself. He stood there looking strong and silent. I suppose you have to be like that if you want to manufacture anything in the nature of a really convincing soup.

Slingsby's Superb Soups was a Roman Emperor-looking sort of bird, with keen, penetrating eyes and one of those jutting chins. The eyes seemed to be fixed on me in a dashed unpleasant stare and, unless I was mistaken, he was grinding his teeth a trifle. For some reason he appeared to have taken a strong dislike to me at sight, and I'm bound to say this rather puzzled me. I don't pretend to have one of those Fascinating Personalities which you get from studying the booklets advertised in the back pages of the magazines, but I couldn't recall another case in the whole of my career where a single glimpse of the old map had been enough to make anyone look as if he wanted to foam at the mouth. Usually, when people meet me for the first time, they don't seem to know I'm there.

However, I exerted myself to play the host.

"Mr. Slingsby?"

"That is my name."

"Just got back from America?"

"I landed this morning."

"Sooner than you were expected, what?"

"So I imagine."

"Very glad to see you."

"You will not be long."

I took time off to do a bit of gulping. I saw now what had happened. This bloke had been home, seen his wife, heard the story of the accident, and had hastened round to the flat to slip it across me. Evidently those roses had not sweetened the female of the species. The only thing to do now seemed to be to take a stab at sweetening the male.

"Have a drink?" I said.

"No!"

"A cigarette?"

"No!"

"A chair?"

"No!"

I went into the silence once more. These non-drinking, non-smoking non-sitters are hard birds to handle.

"Don't grin at me, sir!"

I shot a glance at myself in the mirror, and saw what he meant. The sad half-smile *had* slopped over a bit. I adjusted it, and there was another pause.

"Now, sir," said the Superb Souper. "To business. I think I need scarcely tell you why I am here."

"No. Of course. Absolutely. It's about that little matter—"

He gave a snort which nearly upset a vase on the mantelpiece.

"Little matter? So you consider it a little matter, do you?"

"Well—"

"Let me tell you, sir, that when I find that during my absence from the country a man has been annoying my wife with his importunities I regard it as anything but a little matter. And I shall endeavour," said the Souper, the eyes gleaming a trifle brighter as he rubbed his hands together in a hideous, menacing way, "to make you see the thing in the same light."

I couldn't make head or tail of this. I simply couldn't follow him. The lemon began to swim.

"Eh?" I said. "Your wife?"

"You heard me."

"There must be some mistake."

"There is. You made it."

"But I don't know your wife."

"Ha!"

"I've never even met her."

"Tchah!"

"Honestly, I haven't."

"Bah!"

He drank me in for a moment.

"Do you deny you sent her flowers?"

I felt the heart turn a double somersault. I began to catch his drift.

"Flowers!" he proceeded. "Roses, sir. Great, fat, beastly roses. Enough of them to sink a ship. Your card was attached to them by a small pin—"

His voice died away in a sort of gurgle, and I saw that he was staring at something behind me. I spun round, and there, in the doorway—I hadn't seen it open, because during the last spasm of dialogue I had been backing cautiously towards it—there in the doorway stood a female. One glance was enough to tell me who she was. No woman could look so like Lucius Pim who hadn't the misfortune to be related to him. It was Sister Beatrice, the tough egg. I saw all. She had left home before the flowers had arrived: she had sneaked, unsweetened, into the flat, while I was fortifying the system at the Drones: and here she was.

"Er—" I said.

"Alexander!" said the female.

"Goo!" said the Souper. Or it may have been "Coo."

Whatever it was, it was in the nature of a battle-cry or slogan of war. The Souper's worst suspicions had obviously been confirmed. His eyes shone with a strange light. His chin pushed itself out another couple of inches. He clenched and unclenched his fingers once or twice, as if to make sure that they were working properly, and could be relied on to do a good, clean job of strangling. Then, once more observing "Coo!" (or "Goo!"), he sprang forward, trod on the golf-ball I had been practising putting with, and took one of the finest tosses I have ever witnessed. The purler of a lifetime. For a moment the air seemed to be full of arms and legs, and then, with a thud that nearly dislocated the flat, he made a forced landing against the wall.

And, feeling I had had about all I wanted, I oiled from the room and was in the act of grabbing my hat from the rack in the hall, when Jeeves appeared.

"I fancied I heard a noise, sir," said Jeeves.

"Quite possibly," I said. "It was Mr. Slingsby."

"Sir?"

"Mr. Slingsby practising Russian dances," I explained. "I rather think he has fractured an assortment of limbs. Better go in and see."

"Very good, sir."

"If he is the wreck I imagine, put him in my room and send for the doctor. The flat is filling up nicely with the various units of the Pim family and its connections, eh, Jeeves?"

"Yes, sir."

"I think the supply is about exhausted, but should any aunts or uncles by marriage come along and break their limbs, bed them out on the Chesterfield."

"Very good, sir."

"I, personally, Jeeves," I said, opening the front door and pausing on the threshold, "am off to Paris. I will wire you the address. Notify me in due course when the place is free from Pims and completely purged of Slingsbys, and I will return. Oh, and Jeeves."

"Sir?"

"Spare no effort to mollify these birds. They think—at least, Slingsby (female) thinks, and what she thinks to-day he will think to-morrow—that it was I who ran over Mr. Pim in my car. Endeavour during my absence to sweeten them."

"Very good, sir."

"And now perhaps you had better be going in and viewing the body. I shall proceed to the Drones, where I shall lunch, subsequently catching the two o'clock train at Charing Cross. Meet me there with an assortment of luggage."

It was a matter of three weeks or so before Jeeves sent me the

All Clear signal. I spent the time pottering pretty perturbedly about Paris and environs. It is a city I am fairly fond of, but I was glad to be able to return to the old home. I hopped on to a passing aeroplane and a couple of hours later was bowling through Croydon on my way to the centre of things. It was somewhere down in the Sloane Square neighbourhood that I first caught sight of the posters.

A traffic block had occurred, and I was glancing idly this way and that, when suddenly my eye was caught by something that looked familiar. And then I saw what it was.

Pasted on a blank wall and measuring about a hundred feet each way was an enormous poster, mostly red and blue. At the top of it were the words:—

SLINGSBY'S SUPERB SOUPS

and at the bottom:—

SUCCULENT AND STRENGTHENING

And in between, me. Yes, dash it, Bertram Wooster in person. A reproduction of the Pendlebury portrait, perfect in every detail.

It was the sort of thing to make a fellow's eyes flicker, and mine flickered. You might say a mist seemed to roll before them. Then it lifted, and I was able to get a good long look before the traffic moved on.

Of all the absolutely foul sights I have ever seen, this took the biscuit with ridiculous ease. The thing was a bally libel on the Wooster face, and yet it was as unmistakable as if it had had my name under it. I saw now what Jeeves had meant when he said that the portrait had given me a hungry look. In the poster this look had become one of bestial greed. There I sat absolutely slavering through a monocle about six inches in circumference at a plateful of soup, looking as if I hadn't had a meal for weeks. The whole thing seemed to take one straight away into a different and a dreadful world.

I woke from a species of trance or coma to find myself at the door of the block of flats. To buzz upstairs and charge into the home was with me the work of a moment.

Jeeves came shimmering down the hall, the respectful beam of welcome on his face.

"I am glad to see you back, sir."

"Never mind about that," I yipped. "What about—?"

"The posters, sir? I was wondering if you might have observed them."

"I observed them!"

"Striking, sir?"

"Very striking. Now, perhaps you'll kindly explain—"

"You instructed me, if you recollect, sir, to spare no effort to mollify Mr. Slingsby."

"Yes, but—"

"It proved a somewhat difficult task, sir. For some time Mr. Slingsby, on the advice and owing to the persuasion of Mrs. Slingsby, appeared to be resolved to institute an action in law against you—a procedure which I knew you would find most distasteful."

"Yes, but—"

"And then, the first day he was able to leave his bed, he observed the portrait, and it seemed to me judicious to point out to him its possibilities as an advertising medium. He readily fell in with the suggestion and, on my assurance that, should he abandon the projected action in law, you would willingly permit the use of the portrait, he entered into negotiations with Miss Pendlebury for the purchase of the copyright."

"Oh? Well, I hope she's got something out of it, at any rate?"

"Yes, sir. Mr. Pim, acting as Miss Pendlebury's agent, drove, I understand, an extremely satisfactory bargain."

"He acted as her agent, eh?"

"Yes, sir. In his capacity as fiancé to the young lady, sir."

"Fiancé!"

"Yes, sir."

It shows how the sight of that poster had got into my ribs when I state that, instead of being laid out cold by this announcement, I merely said "Ha!" or "Ho!" or it may have been "H'm". After the poster, nothing seemed to matter.

"After that poster, Jeeves," I said, "nothing seems to matter."

"No, sir?"

"No, Jeeves. A woman has tossed my heart lightly away, but what of it?"

"Exactly, sir."

"The voice of Love seemed to call to me, but it was a wrong number. Is that going to crush me?"

"No, sir."

"No, Jeeves. It is not. But what does matter is this ghastly business of my face being spread from end to end of the Metropolis with the eyes fixed on a plate of Slingsby's Superb Soup. I must leave London. The lads at the Drones will kid me without ceasing."

"Yes, sir. And Mrs. Spenser Gregson—"

I paled visibly. I hadn't thought of Aunt Agatha and what she might have to say about letting down the family prestige.

"You don't mean to say she has been ringing up?"

"Several times daily, sir."

"Jeeves, flight is the only resource."

"Yes, sir."

"Back to Paris, what?"

"I should not recommend the move, sir. The posters are, I understand, shortly to appear in that city also, advertising the *Bouillon Suprême*. Mr. Slingsby's products command a large sale in France. The sight would be painful for you, sir."

"Then where?"

"If I might make a suggestion, sir, why not adhere to your

original intention of cruising in Mrs. Travers' yacht in the Mediterranean? On the yacht you would be free from the annoyance of these advertising displays."

The man seemed to me to be drivelling.

"But the yacht started weeks ago. It may be anywhere by now."

"No, sir. The cruise was postponed for a month owing to the illness of Mr. Travers' chef, Anatole, who contracted influenza. Mr. Travers refused to sail without him."

"You mean they haven't started?"

"Not yet, sir. The yacht sails from Southampton on Tuesday next."

"Why, then, dash it, nothing could be sweeter."

"No, sir."

"Ring up Aunt Dahlia and tell her we'll be there."

"I ventured to take the liberty of doing so a few moments before you arrived, sir."

"You did?"

"Yes, sir. I thought it probable that the plan would meet with your approval."

"It does! I've wished all along I was going on that cruise."

"I, too, sir. It should be extremely pleasant."

"The tang of salt breezes, Jeeves."

"Yes, sir."

"The moonlight on the water!"

"Precisely, sir."

"The gentle heaving of the waves!"

"Exactly, sir."

I felt absolutely in the pink. Gwladys—pah! The posters—bah! That was the way I looked at it.

"Yo-ho-ho, Jeeves!" I said, giving the trousers a bit of a hitch.

"Yes, sir."

"In fact, I will go further. Yo-ho-ho and a bottle of rum!"

"Very good, sir. I will bring it immediately."

Mulliner's Buck-U-Uppo

———— • ————

The village Choral Society had been giving a performance of Gilbert and Sullivan's "Sorcerer" in aid of the Church Organ Fund; and, as we sat in the window of the Anglers' Rest, smoking our pipes, the audience came streaming past us down the little street. Snatches of song floated to our ears, and Mr. Mulliner began to croon in unison.

" 'Ah, me! I was a pa-ale you-oung curate then!' " chanted Mr. Mulliner in the rather snuffling voice in which the amateur singer seems to find it necessary to render the old songs.

"Remarkable," he said, resuming his natural tones, "how fashions change, even in clergymen. There are very few pale young curates nowadays."

"True," I agreed. "Most of them are beefy young fellows who rowed for their colleges. I don't believe I have ever seen a pale young curate."

"You never met my nephew Augustine, I think?"

"Never."

"The description in the song would have fitted him perfectly. You will want to hear all about my nephew Augustine."

At the time of which I am speaking (said Mr. Mulliner) my nephew Augustine was a curate, and very young and extremely pale. As a boy he had completely outgrown his strength, and I rather think that at his Theological College some of the wilder spirits must have bullied him; for when he went to Lower Briskett-in-the-Midden to assist the vicar, the Rev. Stanley Brandon, in his cure of souls, he was as meek and mild a young man as you could meet

115

in a day's journey. He had flaxen hair, weak blue eyes, and the general demeanor of a saintly but timid codfish. Precisely, in short, the sort of young curate who seems to have been so common in the eighties, or whenever it was that Gilbert wrote "The Sorcerer."

The personality of his immediate superior did little or nothing to help him overcome his native diffidence. The Rev. Stanley Brandon was a huge and sinewy man of violent temper, whose red face and glittering eyes might well have intimidated the toughest curate. The Rev. Stanley had been a heavyweight boxer at Cambridge, and I gather from Augustine that he seemed to be always on the point of introducing into debates on parish matters the methods which made him so successful in the roped ring. I remember Augustine telling me that once, on the occasion when he had ventured to oppose the other's views in the matter of decorating the church for the Harvest Festival, he thought for a moment that the vicar was going to drop him with a right hook to the chin. It was some quite trivial point that had come up—a question as to whether the pumpkin would look better in the apse or the clerestory, if I recollect rightly—but for several seconds it seemed as if blood was about to be shed.

Such was the Rev. Stanley Brandon. And yet it was to the daughter of this formidable man that Augustine Mulliner had permitted himself to lose his heart. Truly, Cupid makes heroes of us all.

Jane was a very nice girl, and just as fond of Augustine as he was of her. But, as each lacked the nerve to go to the girl's father and put him abreast of the position of affairs, they were forced to meet surreptitiously. This jarred upon Augustine, who, like all the Mulliners, loved the truth and hated any form of deception. And one evening, as they paced beside the laurels at the bottom of the vicarage garden, he rebelled.

"My dearest," said Augustine, "I can no longer brook this secrecy. I shall go into the house immediately and ask your father for your hand."

Jane paled and clung to his arm. She knew so well that it was not her hand but her father's foot which he would receive if he carried out this mad scheme.

"No, no, Augustine! You must not!"

"But, darling, it is the only straightforward course."

"But not tonight. I beg of you, not tonight."

"Why not?"

"Because father is in a very bad temper. He has just had a letter from the bishop, rebuking him for wearing too many orphreys on his chasuble, and it has upset him terribly. You see, he and the bishop were at school together, and father can never forget it. He said at dinner that if old Boko Bickerton thought he was going to order him about he would jolly well show him."

"And the bishop comes here tomorrow for the Confirmation services!" gasped Augustine.

"Yes. And I'm afraid they will quarrel. It's such a pity father hasn't some other bishop over him. He always remembers that he once hit this one in the eye for pouring ink on his collar, and this lowers his respect for his spiritual authority. So you won't go in and tell him tonight, will you?"

"I will not," Augustine assured her with a slight shiver.

"And you will be sure to put your feet in hot mustard and water when you get home? The dew has made the grass so wet."

"I will indeed, dearest."

"You are not strong, you know."

"No, I am not strong."

"You ought to take some really good tonic."

"Perhaps I ought. Good night, Jane."

"Good night, Augustine."

The lovers parted. Jane slipped back into the vicarage, and Augustine made his way to his cozy rooms in the High Street. And the first thing he noticed on entering was a parcel on the table, and beside it a letter.

He opened it listlessly, his thoughts far away.
"My dear Augustine."

He turned to the last page and glanced at the signature. The letter was from his Aunt Angela, the wife of my brother, Wilfred Mulliner. You may remember that I once told you the story of how these two came together. If so, you will recall that my brother Wilfred was the eminent chemical researcher who had invented, among other specifics, such world-famous preparations as Mulliner's Raven Gypsy Face Cream and the Mulliner Snow of the Mountains Lotion. He and Augustine had never been particularly intimate, but between Augustine and his aunt there had always existed a warm friendship.

My dear Augustine (wrote Angela Mulliner),

I have been thinking so much about you lately, and I cannot forget that, when I saw you last, you seemed very fragile and deficient in vitamins. I do hope you take care of yourself.

I have been feeling for some time that you ought to take a tonic, and by a lucky chance Wilfred has just invented one which he tells me is the finest thing he has ever done. It is called Buck-U-Uppo, and acts directly on the red corpuscles. It is not yet on the market, but I have managed to smuggle a sample bottle from Wilfred's laboratory, and I want you to try it at once. I am sure it is just what you need.

Your affectionate aunt,
Angela Mulliner.

P.S.—You take a tablespoonful before going to bed, and another just before breakfast.

Augustine was not an unduly superstitious young man, but the coincidence of this tonic arriving so soon after Jane had told him that a tonic was what he needed affected him deeply. It seemed to him that this thing must have been meant. He shook the bottle, uncorked it, and, pouring out a liberal tablespoonful, shut his eyes and swallowed it.

The medicine, he was glad to find, was not unpleasant to the taste. It had a slightly pungent flavor, rather like old boot soles beaten up in sherry. Having taken the dose, he read for a while in a book of theological essays, and then went to bed.

And as his feet slipped between the sheets, he was annoyed to find that Mrs. Wardle, his housekeeper, had once more forgotten his hot-water bottle.

"Oh, dash!" said Augustine.

He was thoroughly upset. He had told the woman over and over again that he suffered from cold feet and could not get to sleep unless the dogs were properly warmed up. He sprang out of bed and went to the head of the stairs.

"Mrs. Wardle!" he cried.

There was no reply.

"Mrs. Wardle!" bellowed Augustine in a voice that rattled the windowpanes like a strong nor'easter. Until tonight he had always been very much afraid of his housekeeper and had both walked and talked softly in her presence. But now he was conscious of a strange new fortitude. His head was singing a little, and he felt equal to a dozen Mrs. Wardles.

Shuffling footsteps made themselves heard.

"Well, what is it now?" asked a querulous voice.

Augustine snorted.

"I'll tell you what it is now," he roared. "How many times have I told you always to put a hot-water bottle in my bed? You've forgotten it again, you old cloth-head!"

Mrs. Wardle peered up, astounded and militant.

"Mr. Mulliner, I am not accustomed— "

"Shut up!" thundered Augustine. "What I want from you is less backchat and more hot-water bottles. Bring it up at once, or I leave tomorrow. Let me endeavour to get it into your concrete skull that you aren't the only person letting rooms in this village. Any more lip and I walk straight round the corner, where I'll be appreciated. Hot-water bottle ho! And look slippy about it."

"Yes, Mr. Mulliner. Certainly, Mr. Mulliner. In one moment, Mr. Mulliner."

"Action! Action!" boomed Augustine. "Show some speed. Put a little snap into it."

"Yes, yes, most decidedly, Mr. Mulliner," replied the chastened voice from below.

An hour later, as he was dropping off to sleep, a thought crept into Augustine's mind. Had he not been a little brusque with Mrs. Wardle? Had there not been in his manner something a shade abrupt—almost rude? Yes, he decided regretfully, there had. He lit a candle and reached for the diary which lay on the table at his bedside.

He made an entry.

The meek shall inherit the earth. Am I sufficiently meek? I wonder. This evening, when reproaching Mrs. Wardle, my worthy housekeeper, for omitting to place a hot-water bottle in my bed, I spoke quite crossly. The provocation was severe, but still I was surely to blame for allowing my passions to run riot. Mem: Must guard agst this.

But when he woke next morning, different feelings prevailed. He took his antebreakfast dose of Buck-U-Uppo; and looking at the entry in the diary, could scarcely believe that it was he who had written it. "Quite cross?" Of course he had been quite cross. Wouldn't anybody be quite cross who was for ever being persecuted by beetle-wits who forgot hot-water bottles?

Erasing the words with one strong dash of a thick-leaded pencil, he scribbled in the margin a hasty "Mashed potatoes! Served the old idiot right!" and went down to breakfast.

He felt most amazingly fit. Undoubtedly, in asserting that this tonic of his acted forcefully upon the red corpuscles, his Uncle Wilfred had been right. Until that moment Augustine had never supposed that he had any red corpuscles; but now, as he sat waiting for Mrs. Wardle to bring him his fried egg, he could feel them dancing about all over him. They seemed to be forming rowdy parties and sliding down his spine. His eyes sparkled, and from sheer joy of living he sang a few bars from the hymn for those of riper years at sea.

He was still singing when Mrs. Wardle entered with a dish.

"What's this?" demanded Augustine, eyeing it dangerously.

"A nice fried egg, sir."

"And what, pray, do you mean by nice? It may be an amiable egg. It may be a civil, well-meaning egg. But if you think it is fit for human consumption, adjust that impression. Go back to your kitchen, woman; select another; and remember this time that you are a cook, not an incinerating machine. Between an egg that is fried and an egg that is cremated there is a wide and substantial difference. This difference, if you wish to retain me as a lodger in these far too expensive rooms, you will endeavour to appreciate."

The glowing sense of well-being with which Augustine had begun the day did not diminish with the passage of time. It seemed, indeed, to increase. So full of effervescing energy did the young man feel that, departing from his usual custom of spending the morning crouched over the fire, he picked up his hat, stuck it at a rakish angle on his head, and sallied out for a healthy tramp across the fields.

It was while he was returning, flushed and rosy, that he observed a sight which is rare in the country districts of England—the spectacle of a bishop running. It is not often in a place like Lower Briskett-in-the-Midden that you see a bishop at all; and when you do he is either riding in a stately car or pacing at a dignified walk. This one was sprinting like a Derby winner, and Augustine paused to drink in the sight.

The bishop was a large, burly bishop, built for endurance rather than speed; but he was making excellent going. He flashed past Augustine in a whirl of flying gaiters; and then, proving himself thereby no mere specialist but a versatile all-round athlete, suddenly dived for a tree and climbed rapidly into its branches. His motive, Augustine readily divined, was to elude a rough, hairy dog which was toiling in his wake. The dog reached the tree a moment after his quarry had climbed it, and stood there, barking.

Augustine strolled up.

"Having a little trouble with the dumb friend, bish?" he asked genially.

The bishop peered down from his eyrie.

"Young man," he said, "save me!"

"Right most indubitably ho!" replied Augustine. "Leave it to me."

Until today he had always been terrified of dogs, but now he did not hesitate. Almost quicker than words can tell, he picked up a stone, discharged it at the animal, and whooped cheerily as it got home with a thud. The dog, knowing when he had had enough, removed himself at some forty-five m.p.h.; and the bishop, descending cautiously, clasped Augustine's hand in his.

"My preserver!" said the bishop.

"Don't give it another thought," said Augustine cheerily. "Always glad to do a pal a good turn. We clergymen must stick together."

"I thought he had me for a minute."

"Quite a nasty customer. Full of rude energy."

The bishop nodded.

"His eye was not dim, nor his natural force abated. Deuteronomy xxiv. 7," he agreed. "I wonder if you can direct me to the vicarage? I fear I have come a little out of my way."

"I'll take you there."

"Thank you. Perhaps it would be as well if you did not come

in. I have a serious matter to discuss with old Pieface—I mean, with the Rev. Stanley Brandon."

"I have a serious matter to discuss with his daughter. I'll just hang about the garden."

"You are a very excellent young man," said the bishop, as they walked along. "You are a curate, eh?"

"At present. But," said Augustine, tapping his companion on the chest, "just watch my smoke. That's all I ask you to do—just watch my smoke."

"I will. You should rise to great heights—to the very top of the tree."

"Like you did just now, eh? Ha, ha!"

"Ha, ha!" said the bishop. "You young rogue!"

He poked Augustine in the ribs.

"Ha, ha, ha!" said Augustine.

He slapped the bishop on the back.

"But all joking aside," said the bishop as they entered the vicarage grounds, "I really shall keep my eye on you and see that you receive the swift preferment which your talents and character deserve. I say to you, my dear young friend, speaking seriously and weighing my words, that the way you picked that dog off with that stone was the smoothest thing I ever saw. And I am a man who always tells the strict truth."

"Great is truth and mighty above all things. Esdras iv. 41," said Augustine.

He turned away and strolled toward the laurel bushes, which were his customary meeting place with Jane. The bishop went on to the front door and rang the bell.

Although they had made no definite appointment, Augustine was surprised when the minutes passed and no Jane appeared. He did not know that she had been told by her father to entertain the bishop's wife that morning, and show her the sights of Lower

Briskett-in-the-Midden. He waited some quarter of an hour with growing impatience, and was about to leave when suddenly from the house there came to his ears the sound of voices raised angrily.

He stopped. The voices appeared to proceed from a room on the ground floor facing the garden.

Running lightly over the turf, Augustine paused outside the window and listened. The window was open at the bottom, and he could hear quite distinctly.

The vicar was speaking in a voice that vibrated through the room.

"Is that so?" said the vicar.

"Yes, it is!" said the bishop.

"Ha, ha!"

"Ha, ha! to you, and see how you like it!" rejoined the bishop with spirit.

Augustine drew a step closer. It was plain that Jane's fears had been justified and that there was a serious problem afoot between these two old schoolfellows. He peeped in. The vicar, his hands behind his coattails, was striding up and down the carpet, while the bishop, his back to the fireplace, glared defiance at him from the hearth-rug.

"Who ever told you you were an authority on chasubles?" demanded the vicar.

"That's all right who told me," rejoined the bishop.

"I don't believe you know what a chasuble is."

"Is that so?"

"Well, what is it, then?"

"It's a circular cloak hanging from the shoulders, elaborately embroidered with a pattern and orphreys. And you can argue as much as you like, young Pieface, but you can't get away from the fact that there are too many orphreys on yours. And what I'm telling you is that you've jolly well got to switch off a few of those orphreys or you'll get it in the neck."

The vicar's eyes glittered furiously.

"Is that so?" he said. "Well, I just won't, so there! And it's like your cheek coming here and trying to high-hat me. You seem to have forgotten that I knew you when you were an inky-faced kid at school, and that, if I liked, I could tell the world one or two things about you which would probably amuse it."

"My past is an open book."

"Is it?" The vicar laughed malevolently. "Who put the white mouse in the French master's desk?"

The bishop started.

"Who put the jam in the dormitory prefect's bed?" he retorted.

"Who couldn't keep his collar clean?"

"Who used to wear a dickey?" The bishop's wonderful organ-like voice, whose softest whisper could be heard throughout a vast cathedral, rang out in tones of thunder. "Who was sick at the house supper?"

The vicar quivered from head to foot. His rubicund face turned a deeper crimson.

"You know jolly well," he said, in shaking accents, "that there was something wrong with the turkey. Might have upset anyone."

"The only thing wrong with the turkey was that you ate too much of it. If you had paid as much attention to developing your soul as you did to developing your tummy, you might by now," said the bishop, "have risen to my own eminence."

"Oh, might I?"

"No, perhaps I am wrong. You never had the brain."

The vicar uttered another discordant laugh.

"Brain is good! We know all about your eminence, as you call it, and how you rose to that eminence."

"What do you mean?"

"You are a bishop. How you became one we will not inquire."

"What do you mean?"

"What I say. We will not inquire."

"Why don't you inquire?"

"Because," said the vicar, "it is better not!"

The bishop's self-control left him. His face contorted with fury, he took a step forward. And simultaneously Augustine sprang lightly into the room.

"Now, now, now!" said Augustine. "Now, now, now, now, now!"

The two men stood transfixed. They stared at the intruder dumbly.

"Come, come!" said Augustine.

The vicar was the first to recover. He glowered at Augustine.

"What do you mean by jumping through my window?" he thundered. "Are you a curate or a harlequin?"

Augustine met his gaze with an unfaltering eye.

"I am a curate," he replied, with a dignity that well became him. "And, as a curate, I cannot stand by and see two superiors of the cloth, who are moreover old schoolfellows, forgetting themselves. It isn't right. Absolutely not right, my dear old superiors of the cloth."

The vicar bit his lip. The bishop bowed his head.

"Listen," proceeded Augustine, placing a hand on the shoulder of each. "I hate to see you two dear good chaps quarreling like this."

"He started it," said the vicar sullenly.

"Never mind who started it." Augustine silenced the bishop with a curt gesture as he made to speak. "Be sensible, my dear fellows. Respect the decencies of debate. Exercise a little good-humored give-and-take. You say," he went on, turning to the bishop, "that our good friend here has too many orphreys on his chasuble?"

"I do. And I stick to it."

"Yes, yes, yes. But what," said Augustine soothingly, "are a few orphreys between friends? Reflect! You and our worthy vicar here were at school together. You are bound by the sacred ties of the old Alma Mater. With him you sported on the green. With him you shared a crib and threw inked darts in the hour supposed to be devoted to the study of French. Do these things mean nothing to you? Do these memories touch no chord?" He turned appealingly from one to the other. "Vicar! Bish!"

The vicar had moved away and was wiping his eyes. The bishop fumbled for a pocket handkerchief. There was a silence.

"Sorry, Pieface," said the bishop, in a choking voice.

"Shouldn't have spoken as I did, Boko," mumbled the vicar.

"If you want to know what I think," said the bishop, "you are right in attributing your indisposition at the house supper to something wrong with the turkey. I recollect saying at the time that the bird should never have been served in such a condition."

"And when you put that white mouse in the French master's desk," said the vicar, "you performed one of the noblest services to humanity of which there is any record. They ought to have made you a bishop on the spot."

"Pieface!"

"Boko!"

The two men clasped hands.

"Splendid!" said Augustine. "Everything hotsy-totsy now?"

"Quite, quite," said the vicar.

"As far as I am concerned, completely hotsy-totsy," said the bishop. He turned to his old friend solicitously. "You will continue to wear all the orphreys you want—will you not, Pieface?"

"No, no. I see now that I was wrong. From now on, Boko, I abandon orphreys altogether."

"But, Pieface— "

"It's all right," the vicar assured him. "I can take them or leave them alone."

"Splendid fellow!" The bishop coughed to hide his emotion, and there was another silence. "I think, perhaps," he went on, after a pause, "I should be leaving you now, my dear chap, and going in search of my wife. She is with your daughter, I believe, somewhere in the village."

"They are coming up the drive now."

"Ah, yes, I see them. A charming girl, your daughter."

Augustine clapped him on the shoulder.

"Bish," he exclaimed, "you said a mouthful. She is the dearest, sweetest girl in the whole world. And I should be glad, vicar, if you would give your consent to our immediate union. I love Jane with a good man's fervor, and I am happy to inform you that my sentiments are returned. Assure us, therefore, of your own approval, and I will go at once and have the banns put up."

The vicar leaped as though he had been stung. Like so many vicars, he had a poor opinion of curates, and he had always regarded Augustine as rather below than above the general norm or level of the despised class.

"What!" he cried.

"A most excellent idea," said the bishop, beaming. "A very happy notion, I call it."

"My daughter!" The vicar seemed dazed. "My daughter marry a curate!"

"You were a curate once yourself, Pieface."

"Yes, but not a curate like that."

"No!" said the bishop. You were not. Nor was I. Better for us both had we been. This young man, I would have you know, is the most outstandingly excellent young man I have ever encountered. Are you aware that scarcely an hour ago he saved me with the most consummate address from a large shaggy dog with black spots and a kink in his tail? I was sorely pressed, Pieface, when this young man came up and, with a readiness of resource and an accuracy of aim which it would be impossible to overpraise, got that dog in the short ribs with a rock and sent him flying."

The vicar seemed to be struggling with some powerful emotion. His eyes had widened.

"A dog with black spots?"

"Very black spots. But no blacker, I fear, than the heart they hid."

"And he really plugged him in the short ribs?"

"As far as I could see, squarely in the short ribs."

The vicar held out his hand.

"Mulliner," he said, "I was not aware of this. In the light of the facts which have just been drawn to my attention, I have no hesitation in saying that my objections are removed. I have had it in for that dog since the second Sunday before Septuagesima, when he pinned me by the ankle as I paced beside the river composing a sermon on Certain Alarming Manifestations of the So-called Modern Spirit. Take Jane. I give my consent freely. And may she be as happy as any girl with such a husband ought to be."

A few more affecting words were exchanged, and then the bishop and Augustine left the house. The bishop was silent and thoughtful.

"I owe you a great deal, Mulliner," he said at length.

"Oh, I don't know," said Augustine. "Would you say that?"

"A very great deal. You saved me from a terrible disaster. Had you not leaped through that window at that precise juncture and intervened, I really believe I should have pasted my dear old friend Brandon in the eye. I was sorely exasperated."

"Our good vicar can be trying at times," agreed Augustine.

"My fist was already clenched, and I was just hauling off for the swing when you checked me. What the result would have been, had you not exhibited a tact and discretion beyond your years, I do not like to think. I might have been unfrocked." He shivered at the thought, though the weather was mild. "I could never have shown my face at the Athenaeum again. But, tut, tut!" went on the bishop, patting Augustine on the shoulder, "let us not dwell on what might have been. Speak to me of yourself. The vicar's charming daughter—you really love her?"

"I do, indeed."

The bishop's face had grown grave.

"Think well, Mulliner," he said. "Marriage is a serious affair. Do not plunge into it without due reflection. I myself am a hus-

band, and, though singularly blessed in the possession of a
devoted helpmeet, cannot but feel sometimes that a man is better
off as a bachelor. Women, Mulliner, are odd."

"True," said Augustine.

"My own dear wife is the best of women. And, as I never weary
of saying, a good woman is a wondrous creature, cleaving to the
right and the good under all change; lovely in youthful comeliness,
lovely all her life in comeliness of heart. And yet— "

"And yet?" said Augustine.

The bishop mused for a moment. He wriggled a little with an
expression of pain, and scratched himself between the shoulder
blades.

"Well, I'll tell you," said the bishop. "It is a warm and pleasant
day today, is it not?"

"Exceptionally clement," said Augustine.

"A fair, sunny day, made gracious by a temperate westerly
breeze. And yet, Mulliner, if you will credit my statement, my wife
insisted on my putting on my thick winter woollies this morning.
Truly," sighed the bishop, "as a jewel of gold in a swine's snout,
so is a fair woman which is without discretion. Proverbs xi. 21."

"Twenty-two," corrected Augustine.

"I should have said twenty-two. They are made of thick flannel,
and I have an exceptionally sensitive skin. Oblige me, my dear
fellow, by rubbing me in the small of the back with the ferrule
of your stick. I think it will ease the irritation."

"But, my poor dear old bish," said Augustine sympathetically,
"this must not be."

The bishop shook his head ruefully.

"You would not speak so hardily, Mulliner, if you knew my wife.
There is no appeal from her decrees."

"Nonsense," cried Augustine cheerily. He looked through the
trees to where the lady bishopess, escorted by Jane, was examining

a lobelia through her lorgnette with just the right blend of cordiality and condescension. "I'll fix that for you in a second."

The bishop clutched at his arm.

"My boy! What are you going to do?"

"I'm just going to have a word with your wife and put the matter to her as a reasonable woman. Thick winter woollies on a day like this! Absurd!" said Augustine. "Preposterous! I never heard such rot."

The bishop gazed after him with a laden heart. Already he had come to love this young man like a son; and to see him charging so lightheartedly into the very jaws of destruction afflicted him with a deep and poignant sadness. He knew what his wife was like when even the highest in the land attempted to thwart her; and this brave lad was but a curate. In another moment she would be looking at him through her lorgnette; and England was littered with the shriveled remains of curates at whom the lady bishopess had looked through her lorgnette. He had seen them wilt like salted slugs at the episcopal breakfast table.

He held his breath. Augustine had reached the lady bishopess, and the lady bishopess was even now raising her lorgnette.

The bishop shut his eyes and turned away. And then—years afterwards, it seemed to him—a cheery voice hailed him; and, turning, he perceived Augustine bounding back through the trees.

"It's all right, bish," said Augustine.

"All—all right?" faltered the bishop.

"Yes. She says you can go and change into the thin cashmere."

The bishop reeled.

"But—but—but what did you say to her? What arguments did you employ?"

"Oh, I just pointed out what a warm day it was and jollied her along a bit— "

"Jollied her along a bit!"

"And she agreed in the most friendly and cordial manner. She has asked me to call at the Palace one of these days."

The bishop seized Augustine's hand.

"My boy," he said in a broken voice, "you shall do more than call at the Palace. You shall come and live at the Palace. Become my secretary, Mulliner, and name your own salary. If you intend to marry, you will require an increased stipend. Become my secretary, boy, and never leave my side. I have needed somebody like you for years."

It was late in the afternoon when Augustine returned to his rooms, for he had been invited to lunch at the vicarage and had been the life and soul of the cheery little party.

"A letter for you, sir," said Mrs. Wardle obsequiously.

Augustine took the letter.

"I am sorry to say that I shall be leaving you shortly, Mrs. Wardle."

"Oh, sir! If there's anything I can do—"

"Oh, it's not that. The fact is, the bishop has made me his secretary, and I shall have to shift my toothbrush and spats to the Palace, you see."

"Well, fancy that, sir! Why, you'll be a bishop yourself one of these days."

"Possibly," said Augustine. "Possibly. And now let me read this."

He opened the letter. A thoughtful frown appeared on his face as he read.

My dear Augustine,

I am writing in some haste to tell you that the impulsiveness of your aunt has led to a rather serious mistake.

She tells me that she dispatched to you yesterday by parcel post a sample bottle of my new Buck-U-Uppo, which she obtained without my knowledge from my laboratory. Had she mentioned what she was intending to do, I could have prevented a very unfortunate occurrence.

Mulliner's Buck-U-Uppo is of two grades or qualities—the A and the B. The A is a mild, but strengthening, tonic designed for human invalids. The B, on the other hand, is purely for circulation in the animal kingdom, and was invented to fill a long-felt want throughout our Indian possessions.

As you are doubtless aware, the favorite pastime of the Indian Maharajahs is the hunting of the tiger of the jungle from the backs of elephants; and it has happened frequently in the past that hunts have been spoiled by the failure of the elephant to see eye to eye with its owner in the matter of what constitutes sport.

Too often elephants, on sighting the tiger, have turned and galloped home; and it was to correct this tendency on their part that I invented Mulliner's Buck-U-Uppo "B." One teaspoonful of the Buck-U-Uppo "B" administered in the morning bran mash will cause the most timid elephant to trumpet loudly and charge the fiercest tiger without a qualm.

Abstain, therefore, from taking any of the contents of the bottle you now possess,

> *And believe me,*
> *Your affectionate uncle,*
> *Wilfred Mulliner.*

Augustine remained for some time in deep thought after perusing this communication. Then, rising, he whistled a few bars of the psalm appointed for the twenty-sixth of June and left the room.

Half an hour later a telegraphic message was speeding over the wires.

It ran as follows:

Wilfred Mulliner,
   The Gables,
      Lesser Lossingham,
         Salop.

Letter received. Send immediately, C.O.D., three cases of the "B." "Blessed shall be thy basket and thy store." Deuteronomy *xxviii. 5.*

Augustine.

Without the Option

———————— • ————————

The evidence was all in. The machinery of the law had worked without a hitch. And the beak, having adjusted a pair of pince-nez which looked as though they were going to do a nose dive any moment, coughed like a pained sheep and slipped us the bad news. "The prisoner, Wooster," he said—and who can paint the shame and agony of Bertram at hearing himself so described?—"will pay a fine of five pounds."

"Oh, rather! I said. "Absolutely! Like a shot!"

I was dashed glad to get the thing settled at such a reasonable figure. I gazed across what they call the sea of faces till I picked up Jeeves, sitting at the back. Stout fellow, he had come to see the young master through his hour of trial.

"I say, Jeeves," I sang out, "have you got a fiver? I'm a bit short."

"Silence!" bellowed some officious blighter.

"It's all right," I said; "just arranging the financial details. Got the stuff, Jeeves?"

"Yes, sir."

"Good egg!"

"Are you a friend of the prisoner?" asked the beak.

"I am in Mr. Wooster's employment, Your Worship, in the capacity of gentleman's personal gentleman."

"Then pay the fine to the clerk."

"Very good, Your Worship."

The beak gave a coldish nod in my direction, as much as to say that they might now strike the fetters from my wrists; and having hitched up the pince-nez once more, proceeded to hand poor old

Sippy one of the nastiest looks ever seen in Bosher Street Police Court.

"The case of the prisoner Leon Trotzky—which," he said, giving Sippy the eye again, "I am strongly inclined to think an assumed and fictitious name—is more serious. He has been convicted of a wanton and violent assault upon the police. The evidence of the officer has proved that the prisoner struck him in the abdomen, causing severe internal pain, and in other ways interfered with him in the execution of his duties. I am aware that on the night following the annual aquatic contest between the Universities of Oxford and Cambridge a certain licence is traditionally granted by the authorities, but aggravated acts of ruffianly hooliganism like that of the prisoner Trotzky cannot be overlooked or palliated. He will serve a sentence of thirty days in the Second Division without the option of a fine."

"No, I say—here—hi—dash it all!" protested poor old Sippy.

"Silence!" bellowed the officious blighter.

"Next case," said the beak. And that was that.

The whole affair was most unfortunate. Memory is a trifle blurred; but as far as I can piece together the facts, what happened was more or less this:

Abstemious cove though I am as a general thing, there is one night in the year when, putting all other engagements aside, I am rather apt to let myself go a bit and renew my lost youth, as it were. The night to which I allude is the one following the annual aquatic contest between the Universities of Oxford and Cambridge; or, putting it another way, Boat-Race Night. Then, if ever, you will see Bertram under the influence. And on this occasion, I freely admit, I had been doing myself rather juicily, with the result that when I ran into old Sippy opposite the Empire I was in quite fairly bonhomous mood. This being so, it cut me to the quick to perceive that Sippy, generally the brightest of revellers, was far from being his usual sunny self. He had the air of a man with a secret sorrow.

"Bertie," he said as we strolled along toward Picadilly Circus, "the heart bowed down by weight of woe to weakest hope will cling." Sippy is by way of being an author, though mainly dependent for the necessaries of life on subsidies from an old aunt who lives in the country, and his conversation often takes a literary turn. "But the trouble is that I have no hope to cling to, weak or otherwise. I am up against it, Bertie."

"In what way, laddie?"

"I've got to go to-morrow and spend three weeks with some absolutely dud—I will go no further—some positively scaly friends of my Aunt Vera. She has fixed the thing up, and may a nephew's curse blister every bulb in her garden."

"Who are these hounds of hell?" I asked.

"Some people named Pringle. I haven't seen them since I was ten, but I remember them at that time striking me as England's premier warts."

"Tough luck. No wonder you've lost your morale."

"The world," said Sippy, "is very grey. How can I shake off this awful depression?"

It was then that I got one of those bright ideas one does get round about 11:30 on Boat-Race night.

"What you want, old man," I said, "is a policeman's helmet."

"Do I, Bertie?"

"If I were you, I'd just step straight across the street and get that one over there."

"But there's a policeman inside it. You can see him distinctly."

"What does that matter?" I said. I simply couldn't follow his reasoning.

Sippy stood for a moment in thought.

"I believe you're absolutely right," he said at last. "Funny I never thought of it before. You really recommend me to get that helmet?"

"I do, indeed."

"Then I will," said Sippy, brightening up in the most remarkable manner.

So there you have the posish, and you can see why, as I left the dock a free man, remorse gnawed at my vitals. In his twenty-fifth year, with life opening out before him and all that sort of thing, Oliver Randolph Sipperley had become a jailbird, and it was all my own fault. It was I who had dragged that fine spirit down into the mire, so to speak, and the question now arose, What could I do to atone?

Obviously the first move must be to get in touch with Sippy and see if he had any last messages and what not. I pushed about a bit, making inquiries, and presently found myself in a little dark room with whitewashed walls and a wooden bench. Sippy was sitting on the bench with his head in his hands.

"How are you, old lad?" I asked in a hushed, bedside voice.

"I'm a ruined man," said Sippy, looking like a poached egg.

"Oh, come," I said, "it's not so bad as all that. I mean to say, you had the swift intelligence to give a false name. There won't be anything about you in the papers."

"I'm not worrying about the papers. What's bothering me is, how can I go and spend three weeks with the Pringles, starting to-day, when I've got to sit in a prison cell with a ball and chain on my ankle?"

"But you said you didn't want to go."

"It isn't a question of wanting, fathead. I've got to go. If I don't my aunt will find out where I am. And if she finds out that I am doing thirty days, without the option, in the lowest dungeon beneath the castle moat—well, where shall I get off?"

I saw his point.

"This is not a thing we can settle for ourselves," I said gravely.

"We must put our trust in a higher power. Jeeves is the man we must consult."

And having collected a few of the necessary data, I shook his hand, patted him on the back and tooled off home to Jeeves.

"Jeeves," I said, when I had climbed outside the pick-me-up which he had thoughtfully prepared against my coming, "I've got something to tell you; something important; something that vitally affects one whom you have always regarded with—one whom you have always looked upon—one whom you have—well, to cut a long story short, as I'm not feeling quite myself—Mr. Sipperley."

"Yes, sir?"

"Jeeves, Mr. Souperley is in the sip."

"Sir?"

"I mean, Mr. Sipperley is in the soup."

"Indeed, sir?"

"And all owing to me. It was I who, in a moment of mistaken kindness, wishing only to cheer him up and give him something to occupy his mind, recommended to him to pinch that policeman's helmet."

"Is that so, sir?"

"Do you mind not intoning the responses, Jeeves?" I said. "This is a most complicated story for a man with a headache to have to tell, and if you interrupt you'll make me lose the thread. As a favour to me, therefore, don't do it. Just nod every now and then to show that you're following me."

I closed my eyes and marshalled the facts.

"To start with then, Jeeves, you may or may not know that Mr. Sipperley is practically dependent on his Aunt Vera."

"Would that be Miss Sipperley of the Paddock, Beckley-on-the-Moor, in Yorkshire, sir?"

"Yes. Don't tell me you know her!"

"Not personally, sir. But I have a cousin residing in the village who has some slight acquaintance with Miss Sipperley. He has described her to me as an imperious and quick-tempered old lady. ... But I beg your pardon, sir, I should have nodded."

"Quite right, you should have nodded. Yes, Jeeves, you should have nodded. But it's too late now."

I nodded myself. I hadn't had my eight hours the night before, and what you might call a lethargy was showing a tendency to steal over me from time to time.

"Yes, sir?" said Jeeves.

"Oh—ah—yes," I said, giving myself a bit of a hitch up. "Where had I got to?"

"You were saying that Mr. Sipperley is practically dependent upon Miss Sipperley, sir."

"Was I?"

"You were, sir."

"You're perfectly right; so I was. Well, then, you can readily understand, Jeeves, that he has got to take jolly good care to keep in with her. You get that?"

Jeeves nodded.

"Now mark this closely: The other day she wrote to old Sippy, telling him to come down and sing at her village concert. It was equivalent to a royal command, if you see what I mean, so Sippy couldn't refuse in so many words. But he had sung at her village concert once before and had got the bird in no uncertain manner, so he wasn't playing any return dates. You follow so far, Jeeves?"

Jeeves nodded.

"So what did he do, Jeeves? He did what seemed to him at the moment a rather brainy thing. He told her that, though he would have been delighted to sing at her village concert, by a most unfortunate chance an editor had commissioned him to write a series of articles on the colleges of Cambridge and he was obliged to pop down there at once and would be away for quite three weeks. All clear up to now?"

Jeeves inclined the coco-nut.

"Whereupon, Jeeves, Miss Sipperley wrote back, saying that she quite realised that work must come before pleasure—pleasure being her loose way of describing the act of singing songs at the Beckley-on-the-Moor concert and getting the laugh from the local toughs; but that, if he was going to Cambridge, he must certainly stay with her friends, the Pringles, at their house just outside the town. And she dropped them a line telling them to expect him on the twenty-eighth, and they dropped another line saying right-ho, and the thing was settled. And now Mr. Sipperley is in the jug, and what will be the ultimate outcome or upshot? Jeeves, it is a problem worthy of your great intellect. I rely on you."

"I will do my best to justify your confidence, sir."

"Carry on, then. And meanwhile pull down the blinds and bring a couple more cushions and heave that small chair this way so that I can put my feet up, and then go away and brood and let me hear from you in—say, a couple of hours, or maybe three. And if anybody calls and wants to see me, inform them that I am dead."

"Dead, sir?"

"Dead. You won't be so far wrong."

It must have been well toward evening when I woke up with a crick in my neck but otherwise somewhat refreshed. I pressed the bell.

"I looked in twice, sir," said Jeeves, "but on each occasion you were asleep and I did not like to disturb you."

"The right spirit, Jeeves....Well?"

"I have been giving close thought to the little problem which you indicated, sir, and I can see only one solution."

"One is enough. What do you suggest?"

"That you go to Cambridge in Mr. Sipperley's place, sir."

I stared at the man. Certainly I was feeling a good deal better than I had been a few hours before; but I was far from being in a fit condition to have rot like this talked to me.

"Jeeves," I said sternly, "pull yourself together. This is mere babble from the sickbed."

"I fear I can suggest no other plan of action, sir, which will extricate Mr. Sipperley from his dilemma."

"But think! Reflect! Why, even I, in spite of having had a disturbed night and a most painful morning with the minions of the law, can see that the scheme is a loony one. To put the finger on only one leak in the thing, it isn't me these people want to see; it's Mr. Sipperley. They don't know me from Adam."

"So much the better, sir. For what I am suggesting is that you go off to Cambridge, affecting actually to be Mr. Sipperley."

This was too much.

"Jeeves," I said, and I'm not half sure there weren't tears in my eyes, "surely you can see for yourself that this is pure banana-oil. It is not like you to come into the presence of a sick man and gibber."

"I think the plan I have suggested would be practicable, sir. While you were sleeping, I was able to have a few words with Mr. Sipperley, and he informed me that Professor and Mrs. Pringle have not set eyes upon him since he was a lad of ten."

"No, that's true. He told me that. But even so, they would be sure to ask him questions about my aunt—or rather his aunt. Where would I be then?"

"Mr. Sipperley was kind enough to give me a few facts respecting Miss Sipperley, sir, which I jotted down. With these, added to what my cousin has told me of the lady's habits, I think you would be in a position to answer any ordinary question."

There is something dashed insidious about Jeeves. Time and again since we first came together he has stunned me with some apparently drivelling suggestion or scheme or ruse or plan of campaign, and after about five minutes has convinced me that it is not only sound but fruity. It took nearly a quarter of an hour to reason me into this particular one, it being considerably the weirdest to date; but he did it. I was holding out pretty firmly, when he suddenly clinched the whole thing.

"I would certainly suggest, sir," he said, "that you left London as soon as possible and remained hid for some little time in some retreat where you would not be likely to be found."

"Eh? Why?"

"During the last hour Mrs. Spenser Gregson has been on the telephone three times, sir, endeavouring to get into communication with you."

"Aunt Agatha!" I cried, paling beneath my tan.

"Yes, sir. I gathered from her remarks that she had been reading in the evening paper a report of this morning's proceedings in the police court."

I hopped from the chair like a jack rabbit of the prairie. If Aunt Agatha was out with her hatchet, a move was most certainly indicated.

"Jeeves," I said, "this is a time for deeds, not words. Pack—and that right speedily."

"I have packed, sir."

"Find out when there is a train for Cambridge."

"There is one in forty minutes, sir."

"Call a taxi."

"A taxi is at the door, sir."

"Good!" I said. "Then lead me to it."

The Maison Pringle was quite a bit of a way out of Cambridge, a mile or two down the Trumpington Road; and when I arrived everybody was dressing for dinner. So it wasn't till I had shoved on the evening raiment and got down to the drawing-room that I met the gang.

"Hullo-ullo!" I said, taking a deep breath and floating in.

I tried to speak in a clear and ringing voice, but I wasn't feeling my chirpiest. It is always a nervous job for a diffident and unassuming bloke to visit a strange house for the first time; and it doesn't make the thing any better when he goes there pretending to be another fellow. I was conscious of a rather pronounced sinking feeling, which the appearance of the Pringles did nothing to allay.

Sippy had described them as England's premier warts, and it looked to me as if he might be about right. Professor Pringle was a thinnish, baldish, dyspeptic-lookingish cove with an eye like a haddock, while Mrs. Pringle's aspect was that of one who had had bad news round about the year 1900 and never really got over it. And I was just staggering under the impact of these two when I was introduced to a couple of ancient females with shawls all over them.

"No doubt you remember my mother?" said Professor Pringle mournfully, indicating Exhibit A.

"Oh—ah!" I said, achieving a bit of a beam.

"And my aunt," sighed the prof, as if things were getting worse and worse.

"Well, well, well!" I said, shooting another beam in the direction of Exhibit B.

"They were saying only this morning that they remembered you," groaned the prof, abandoning all hope.

There was a pause. The whole strength of the company gazed at me like a family group out of one of Edgar Allan Poe's less cheery yarns, and I felt my *joie de vivre* dying at the roots.

"I remember Oliver," said Exhibit A. She heaved a sigh. "He was such a pretty child. What a pity! What a pity!"

Tactful, of course, and calculated to put the guest completely at his ease.

"I remember Oliver," said Exhibit B, looking at me in much the same way as the Bosher Street beak had looked at Sippy before putting on the black cap. "Nasty little boy! He teased my cat."

"Aunt Jane's memory is wonderful, considering that she will be eighty-seven next birthday," whispered Mrs. Pringle with mournful pride.

"What did you say?" asked the Exhibit suspiciously.

"I said your memory was wonderful."

"Ah!" The dear old creature gave me another glare. I could see that no beautiful friendship was to be looked for by Bertram in this quarter. "He chased my Tibby all over the garden, shooting arrows at her from a bow."

At this moment a cat strolled out from under the sofa and made for me with its tail up. Cats always do take to me, which made it all the sadder that I should be so saddled with Sippy's criminal record. I stopped to tickle it under the ear, such being my invariable policy, and the Exhibit uttered a piercing cry.

"Stop him! Stop him!"

She leaped forward, moving uncommonly well for one of her years, and having scooped up the cat, stood eyeing me with bitter defiance, as if daring me to start anything. Most unpleasant.

"I like cats," I said feebly.

It didn't go. The sympathy of the audience was not with me. And conversation was at what you might call a low ebb, when the door opened and a girl came in.

"My daughter Heloise," said the prof moodily, as if he hated to admit it.

I turned to mitt the female, and stood there with my hand out, gaping. I can't remember when I've had such a nasty shock.

I suppose everybody has had the experience of suddenly meeting somebody who reminded them frightfully of some fearful person. I mean to say, by way of an example, once when I was golfing in Scotland I saw a woman come into the hotel who was the living image of my Aunt Agatha. Probably a very decent sort, if I had only waited to see, but I didn't wait. I legged it that evening, utterly unable to stand the spectacle. And on another occasion I was driven out of a thoroughly festive night club because the head waiter reminded me of my Uncle Percy.

Well, Heloise Pringle, in the most ghastly way, resembled Honoria Glossop.

I think I may have told you before about this Glossop scourge. She was the daughter of Sir Roderick Glossop, the loony doctor, and I had been engaged to her for about three weeks, much against my wishes, when the old boy most fortunately got the idea that I was off my rocker and put the bee on the proceedings. Since then the mere thought of her had been enough to make me start out of my sleep with a loud cry. And this girl was exactly like her.

"Er—how are you?" I said.

"How do you do?"

Her voice put the lid on it. It might have been Honoria herself talking. Honoria Glossop has a voice like a lion tamer making some authoritative announcement to one of the troupe, and so had this girl. I backed away convulsively and sprang into the air as my foot stubbed itself against something squashy. A sharp yowl rent the air, followed by an indignant cry, and I turned to see Aunt Jane, on all fours, trying to put things right with the cat, which had gone to earth under the sofa. She gave me a look, and I could see that her worst fears had been realised.

At this juncture dinner was announced—not before I was ready for it.

"Jeeves," I said, when I got him alone that night, "I am no faint-heart, but I am inclined to think that this binge is going to prove a shade above the odds."

"You are not enjoying your visit, sir?"

"I am not, Jeeves. Have you seen Miss Pringle?"

"Yes, sir, from a distance."

"The best way to see her. Did you observe her keenly?"

"Yes, sir."

"Did she remind you of anybody?"

"She appeared to me to bear a remarkable likeness to her cousin, Miss Glossop, sir."

"Her cousin! You don't mean to say she's Honoria Glossop's cousin!"

"Yes, sir. Mrs. Pringle was a Miss Blatherwick—the younger of two sisters, the elder of whom married Sir Roderick Glossop."

"Great Scott! That accounts for the resemblance."

"Yes, sir."

"And what a resemblance, Jeeves! She even talks like Miss Glossop."

"Indeed, sir? I have not yet heard Miss Pringle speak."

"You have missed little. And what it amounts to, Jeeves, is that, though nothing will induce me to let old Sippy down, I can see that this visit is going to try me high. At a pinch, I could stand the prof and wife. I could even make the effort of a lifetime and bear up against Aunt Jane. But to expect a man to mix daily with the girl Heloise—and to do it, what is more, on lemonade, which is all there was to drink at dinner—is to ask too much of him. What shall I do, Jeeves?"

"I think that you should avoid Miss Pringle's society as much as possible."

"The same great thought had occurred to me," I said.

It is all very well, though, to talk airily about avoiding a female's society; but when you are living in the same house with her, and she doesn't want to avoid you, it takes a bit of doing. It is a peculiar thing in life that the people you most particularly want to edge away from always seem to cluster round like a poultice. I hadn't been twenty-four hours in the place before I perceived that I was going to see a lot of this pestilence.

She was one of those girls you're always meeting on the stairs and in passages. I couldn't go into a room without seeing her drift in a minute later. And if I walked in the garden she was sure to leap out at me from a laurel bush or the onion bed or something.

By about the tenth day I had begun to feel absolutely haunted.

"Jeeves," I said, "I have begun to feel absolutely haunted."

"Sir?"

"This woman dogs me. I never seem to get a moment to myself. Old Sippy was supposed to come here to make a study of the Cambridge colleges, and she took me round about fifty-seven this morning. This afternoon I went to sit in the garden, and she popped up through a trap and was in my midst. This evening she cornered me in the morning-room. It's getting so that, when I have a bath, I wouldn't be a bit surprised to find her nestling in the soap dish."

"Extremely trying, sir."

"Dashed so. Have you any remedy to suggest?"

"Not at the moment, sir. Miss Pringle does appear to be distinctly interested in you, sir. She was asking me questions this morning respecting your mode of life in London."

"What?"

"Yes, sir."

I stared at the man in horror. A ghastly thought had struck me. I quivered like an aspen.

At lunch that day a curious thing had happened. We had just finished mangling the cutlets and I was sitting back in my chair, taking a bit of an easy before being allotted my slab of boiled pudding, when, happening to look up, I caught the girl Heloise's eye fixed on me in what seemed to me a rather rummy manner. I didn't think much about it at the time, because boiled pudding is a thing you have to give your undivided attention to if you want to do yourself justice; but now, recalling the episode in the light of Jeeves's words, the full sinister meaning of the thing seemed to come home to me.

Even at the moment, something about that look had struck me as oddly familiar, and now I suddenly saw why. It had been the identical look which I had observed in the eye of Honoria Glossop in the days immediately preceding our engagement—the look of a tigress that has marked down its prey.

"Jeeves, do you know what I think?"

"Sir?"

I gulped slightly.

"Jeeves," I said, "listen attentively. I don't want to give the impression that I consider myself one of those deadly coves who exercise an irresistible fascination over one and all and can't meet a girl without wrecking her peace of mind in the first half-minute. As a matter of fact, it's rather the other way with me, for girls on entering my presence are mostly inclined to give me the raised eyebrow and the twitching upper lip. Nobody, therefore, can say that I am a man who's likely to take alarm unnecessarily. You admit that, don't you?"

"Yes, sir."

"Nevertheless, Jeeves, it is a known scientific fact that there is a particular style of female that does seem strangely attracted to the sort of fellow I am."

"Very true, sir."

"I mean to say, I know perfectly well that I've got, roughly speaking, half the amount of brain a normal bloke ought to possess. And when a girl comes along who has about twice the regular allowance, she too often makes a bee line for me with the love light in her eyes. I don't know how to account for it, but it is so."

"It may be Nature's provision for maintaining the balance of the species, sir."

"Very possibly. Anyway, it has happened to me over and over again. It was what happened in the case of Honoria Glossop. She was notoriously one of the brainiest women of her year at Girton, and she just gathered me in like a bull pup swallowing a piece of steak."

"Miss Pringle, I am informed, sir, was an even more brilliant scholar than Miss Glossop."

"Well, there you are! Jeeves, she looks at me."

"Yes, sir?"

"I keep meeting her on the stairs and in passages."

"Indeed, sir?"

"She recommends me books to read, to improve my mind."

"Highly suggestive, sir."

"And at breakfast this morning, when I was eating a sausage, she told me I shouldn't, as modern medical science held that a four-inch sausage contained as many germs as a dead rat. The maternal touch, you understand; fussing over my health."

"I think we may regard that, sir, as practically conclusive."

I sank into a chair, thoroughly pipped.

"What's to be done, Jeeves?"

"We must think, sir."

"You think. I haven't the machinery."

"I will most certainly devote my very best attention to the matter, sir, and will endeavour to give satisfaction."

Well, that was something. But I was ill at ease. Yes, there is no getting away from it, Bertram was ill at ease.

Next morning we visited sixty-three more Cambridge colleges, and after lunch I said I was going to my room to lie down. After staying there for half an hour to give the coast time to clear, I shoved a book and smoking materials in my pocket, and climbing out of a window, shinned down a convenient water-pipe into the garden. My objective was the summer-house, where it seemed to me that a man might put in a quiet hour or so without interruption.

It was extremely jolly in the garden. The sun was shining, the crocuses were all to the mustard and there wasn't a sign of Heloise Pringle anywhere. The cat was fooling about on the lawn, so I chirruped to it and it gave a low gargle and came trotting up. I had just got it in my arms and was scratching it under the ear when there was a loud shriek from above, and there was Aunt Jane half out of the window. Dashed disturbing.

"Oh, right-ho," I said.

I dropped the cat, which galloped off into the bushes, and dismissing the idea of bunging a brick at the aged relative, went on my way, heading for the shrubbery. Once safely hidden there, I worked round till I got to the summer-house. And, believe me, I had hardly got my first cigarette nicely under way when a shadow fell on my book and there was young Sticketh-Closer-Than-a-Brother in person.

"So there you are," she said.

She seated herself by my side, and with a sort of gruesome playfulness jerked the gasper out of the holder and heaved it through the door.

"You're always smoking," she said, a lot too much like a lovingly chiding young bride for my comfort. "I wish you wouldn't. It's so bad for you. And you ought not to be sitting out here without your light overcoat. You want someone to look after you."

"I've got Jeeves."

She frowned a bit.

"I don't like him," she said.

"Eh? Why not?"

"I don't know. I wish you would get rid of him."

My flesh absolutely crept. And I'll tell you why. One of the first things Honoria Glossop had done after we had become engaged was to tell me she didn't like Jeeves and wanted him shot out. The realisation that this girl resembled Honoria not only in body but in blackness of soul made me go all faint.

"What are you reading?"

She picked up my book and frowned again. The thing was one I had brought down from the old flat in London, to glance at in the train—a fairly zippy effort in the detective line called *The Trail of Blood*. She turned the pages with a nasty sneer.

"I can't understand you liking nonsense of this—" She stopped suddenly. "Good gracious!"

"What's the matter?"

"Do you know Bertie Wooster?"

And then I saw that my name was scrawled right across the title page, and my heart did three back somersaults.

"Oh—er—well—that is to say—well, slightly."

"He must be a perfect horror. I'm surprised that you can make a friend of him. Apart from anything else, the man is practically an imbecile. He was engaged to my Cousin Honoria at one time, and it was broken off because he was next door to insane. You should hear my Uncle Roderick talk about him!"

I wasn't keen.

"Do you see much of him?"

"A goodish bit."

"I saw in the paper the other day that he was fined for making a disgraceful disturbance in the street."

"Yes, I saw that."

She gazed at me in a foul, motherly way.

"He can't be a good influence for you," she said. "I do wish you would drop him. Will you?"

"Well— " I began. And at this point old Cuthbert, the cat, having presumably found it a bit slow by himself in the bushes, wandered in with a matey expression on his face and jumped on my lap. I welcomed him with a good deal of cordiality. Though but a cat, he did make a sort of third at this party; and he afforded a good excuse for changing the conversation.

"Jolly birds, cats," I said.

She wasn't having any.

"Will you drop Bertie Wooster?" she said, absolutely ignoring the cat *motif.*

"It would be so difficult."

"Nonsense! It only needs a little will power. The man surely can't be so interesting a companion as all that. Uncle Roderick says he is an invertebrate waster."

I could have mentioned a few things that I thought Uncle Roderick was, but my lips were sealed, so to speak.

"You have changed a great deal since we last met," said the Pringle disease reproachfully. She bent forward and began to scratch the cat under the other ear. "Do you remember, when we were children together, you used to say that you would do anything for me?"

"Did I?"

"I remember once you cried because I was cross and wouldn't let you kiss me."

I didn't believe it at the time, and I don't believe it now. Sippy is in many ways a good deal of a chump, but surely even at the age of ten he cannot have been such a priceless ass as that. I think the girl was lying, but that didn't make the position of affairs any better. I edged away a couple of inches and sat staring before me, the old brow beginning to get slightly bedewed.

And then suddenly—well, you know how it is, I mean. I suppose everyone has had that ghastly feeling at one time or another of being urged by some overwhelming force to do some absolutely blithering act. You get it every now and then when you're in a crowded theatre, and something seems to be egging you on to shout "Fire!" and see what happens. Or you're talking to someone and all at once you feel, "Now, suppose I suddenly biffed this bird in the eye!"

Well, what I'm driving at is this, at this juncture, with her shoulder squashing against mine and her back hair tickling my nose, a perfectly loony impulse came sweeping over me to kiss her.

"No, really?" I croaked.

"Have you forgotten?"

She lifted the old onion and her eyes looked straight into mine. I could feel myself skidding. I shut my eyes. And then from the doorway there spoke the most beautiful voice I had ever heard in my life:

"Give me that cat!"

I opened my eyes. There was good old Aunt Jane, that queen of her sex, standing before me, glaring at me as if I were a vivisectionist and she had surprised me in the middle of an experiment. How this pearl among women had tracked me down I don't know, but there she stood, bless her dear, intelligent old soul, like the rescue party in the last reel of a motion picture.

I didn't wait. The spell was broken and I legged it. As I went, I heard that lovely voice again.

"He shot arrows at my Tibby from a bow," said this most deserving and excellent octogenarian.

For the next few days all was peace. I saw comparatively little of Heloise. I found the strategic value of that water-pipe outside my window beyond praise. I seldom left the house now by any other route. It seemed to me that, if only the luck held like this, I might after all be able to stick this visit out for the full term of the sentence.

But meanwhile, as they say in the movies—

The whole family appeared to be present and correct as I came down to the drawing-room a couple of nights later. The Prof, Mrs. Prof, the two Exhibits and the girl Heloise were scattered about at intervals. The cat slept on the rug, the canary in its cage. There was nothing, in short, to indicate that this was not just one of our ordinary evenings.

"Well, well, well!" I said cheerily. "Hullo-ullo-ullo!"

I always like to make something in the nature of an entrance speech, it seeming to me to lend a chummy tone to the proceedings.

The girl Heloise looked at me reproachfully.

"Where have you been all day?" she asked.

"I went to my room after lunch."

"You weren't there at five."

"No. After putting in a spell of work on the good old colleges

I went for a stroll. Fellow must have exercise if he means to keep fit."

"*Mens sana in corpore sano,*" observed the prof.

"I shouldn't wonder," I said cordially.

At this point, when everything was going as sweet as a nut and I was feeling on top of my form, Mrs. Pringle suddenly soaked me on the base of the skull with a sandbag. Not actually, I don't mean. No, no. I speak figuratively, as it were.

"Roderick is very late," she said.

You may think it strange that the sound of that name should have sloshed into my nerve centres like a half-brick. But, take it from me, to a man who has had any dealings with Sir Roderick Glossop there is only one Roderick in the world—and that is one too many.

"Roderick?" I gurgled.

"My brother-in-law, Sir Roderick Glossop, comes to Cambridge to-night," said the prof. "He lectures at St. Luke's to-morrow. He is coming here to dinner."

And while I stood there, feeling like the hero when he discovers that he is trapped in the den of the Secret Nine, the door opened.

"Sir Roderick Glossop," announced the maid or some such person, and in he came.

One of the things that get this old crumb so generally disliked among the better element of the community is the fact that he has a head like the dome of St. Paul's and eyebrows that want bobbing or shingling to reduce them to anything like reasonable size. It is a nasty experience to see this bald and bushy bloke advancing on you when you haven't prepared the strategic railways in your rear.

As he came into the room I backed behind a sofa and commended my soul to God. I didn't need to have my hand read to know that trouble was coming to me through a dark man.

He didn't spot me at first. He shook hands with the prof and wife, kissed Heloise and waggled his head at the Exhibits.

"I fear I am somewhat late," he said. "A slight accident on the road, affecting what my chauffeur termed the— "

And then he saw me lurking on the outskirts and gave a startled grunt, as if I hurt him a good deal internally.

"This— " began the prof, waving in my direction.

"I am already acquainted with Mr. Wooster."

"This," went on the prof, "is Miss Sipperley's nephew, Oliver. You remember Miss Sipperley?"

"What do you mean?" barked Sir Roderick. Having had so much to do with loonies has given him a rather sharp and authoritative manner on occasion. "This is that wretched young man, Bertram Wooster. What is all this nonsense about Olivers and Sipperleys?"

The prof was eyeing me with some natural surprise. So were the others. I beamed a bit weakly.

"Well, as a matter of fact— " I said.

The prof was wrestling with the situation. You could hear his brain buzzing.

"He said he was Oliver Sipperley," he moaned.

"Come here!" bellowed Sir Roderick. "Am I to understand that you have inflicted yourself on this household under the pretence of being the nephew of an old friend?"

It seemed a pretty accurate description of the facts.

"Well—er—yes," I said.

Sir Roderick shot an eye at me. It entered the body somewhere about the top stud, roamed around inside for a bit and went out at the back.

"Insane! Quite insane, as I knew from the first moment I saw him."

"What did he say?" asked Aunt Jane.

"Roderick says this young man is insane," roared the prof.

"Ah!" said Aunt Jane, nodding. "I thought so. He climbs down water-pipes."

"Does what?"

"I've seen him—ah, many a time!"

Sir Roderick snorted violently.

"He ought to be under proper restraint. It is abominable that a person in his mental condition should be permitted to roam the world at large. The next stage may quite easily be homicidal."

It seemed to me that, even at the expense of giving old Sippy away, I must be cleared of this frightful charge. After all, Sippy's number was up anyway.

"Let me explain," I said. "Sippy asked me to come here."

"What do you mean?"

"He couldn't come himself, because he was jugged for biffing a cop on Boat-Race Night."

Well, it wasn't easy to make them get the hang of the story, and even when I'd done it it didn't seem to make them any chummier towards me. A certain coldness about expresses it, and when dinner was announced I counted myself out and pushed off rapidly to my room. I could have done with a bit of dinner, but the atmosphere didn't seem just right.

"Jeeves," I said, having shot in and pressed the bell, "we're sunk."

"Sir?"

"Hell's foundations are quivering and the game is up."

He listened attentively.

"The contingency was one always to have been anticipated as a possibility, sir. It only remains to take the obvious step."

"What's that?"

"Go and see Miss Sipperley, sir."

"What on earth for?"

"I think it would be judicious to apprise her of the facts yourself, sir, instead of allowing her to hear of them through the medium of a letter from Professor Pringle. That is to say, if you are still anxious to do all in your power to assist Mr. Sipperley."

"I can't let Sippy down. If you think it's any good—"

"We can but try it, sir. I have an idea, sir, that we may find Miss Sipperley disposed to look leniently upon Mr. Sipperley's misdemeanour."

"What makes you think that?"

"It is just a feeling that I have, sir."

"Well, if you think it would be worth trying— How do we get there?"

"The distance is about a hundred and fifty miles, sir. Our best plan would be to hire a car."

"Get it at once," I said.

The idea of being a hundred and fifty miles away from Heloise Pringle, not to mention Aunt Jane and Sir Roderick Glossop, sounded about as good to me as anything I had ever heard.

The Paddock, Beckley-on-the-Moor, was about a couple of parasangs from the village, and I set out for it next morning, after partaking of a hearty breakfast at the local inn, practically without a tremor. I suppose when a fellow has been through it as I had in the last two weeks his system becomes hardened. After all, I felt, whatever this aunt of Sippy's might be like, she wasn't Sir Roderick Glossop, so I was that much on velvet from the start.

The Paddock was one of those medium-sized houses with a goodish bit of very tidy garden and a carefully rolled gravel drive curving past a shrubbery that looked as if it had just come back from the dry cleaner—the sort of house you take one look at and say to yourself, "Somebody's aunt lives there." I pushed up on the drive, and as I turned the bend I observed in the middle distance a woman messing about by a flower-bed with a trowel in her hand. If this wasn't the female I was after, I was very much mistaken, so I halted, cleared the throat and gave tongue.

"Miss Sipperley?"

She had had her back to me, and at the sound of my voice she executed a sort of leap or bound, not unlike a barefoot dancer who steps on a tin-tack halfway through the Vision of Salome. She came to earth and goggled at me in a rather goofy manner. A large, stout female with a reddish face.

"Hope I didn't startle you," I said.

"Who are you?"

"My name's Wooster. I'm a pal of your nephew, Oliver."

Her breathing had become more regular.

"Oh?" she said. "When I heard your voice I thought you were someone else."

"No, that's who I am. I came up here to tell you about Oliver."

"What about him?"

I hesitated. Now that we were approaching what you might call the nub, or crux, of the situation, a good deal of my breezy confidence seemed to have slipped from me.

"Well, it's rather a painful tale, I must warn you."

"Oliver isn't ill? He hasn't had an accident?"

She spoke anxiously, and I was pleased at this evidence of human feeling. I decided to shoot the works with no more delay.

"Oh, no, he isn't ill," I said; "and as regards having accidents, it depends on what you call an accident. He's in chokey."

"In what?"

"In prison."

"In prison!"

"It was entirely my fault. We were strolling along on Boat-Race Night and I advised him to pinch a policeman's helmet."

"I don't understand."

"Well, he seemed depressed, don't you know; and rightly or wrongly, I thought it might cheer him up if he stepped across the street and collared a policeman's helmet. He thought it a good idea, too, so he started doing it, and the man made a fuss and Oliver sloshed him."

"Sloshed him?"

"Biffed him—smote him a blow—in the stomach."

"My nephew Oliver hit a policeman in the stomach?"

"Absolutely in the stomach. And next morning the beak sent him to the bastille for thirty days without the option."

I was looking at her a bit anxiously all this while to see how she was taking the thing, and at this moment her face seemed suddenly to split in half. For an instant she appeared to be all mouth, and then she was staggering about the grass, shouting with laughter and waving the trowel madly.

It seemed to me a bit of luck for her that Sir Roderick Glossop wasn't on the spot. He would have been sitting on her head and calling for the strait-waistcoat in the first half-minute.

"You aren't annoyed?" I said.

"Annoyed?" She chuckled happily. "I've never heard such a splendid thing in my life."

I was pleased and relieved. I had hoped the news wouldn't upset her too much, but I had never expected it to go with such a roar as this.

"I'm proud of him," she said.

"That's fine."

"If every young man in England went about hitting policemen in the stomach, it would be a better country to live in."

I couldn't follow her reasoning, but everything seemed to be all right; so after a few more cheery words I said good-bye and legged it.

"Jeeves," I said when I got back to the inn, "everything's fine. But I am far from understanding why."

"What actually occurred when you met Miss Sipperley, sir?"

"I told her Sippy was in the jug for assaulting the police. Upon which she burst into hearty laughter, waved her trowel in a pleased manner and said she was proud of him."

"I think I can explain her apparently eccentric behaviour, sir.

I am informed that Miss Sipperley has had a good deal of annoyance at the hands of the local constable during the past two weeks.
This has doubtless resulted in a prejudice on her part against the
force as a whole."

"Really? How was that?"

"The constable has been somewhat over-zealous in the performance of his duties, sir. On no fewer than three occasions in the
last ten days he has served summonses upon Miss Sipperley—for
exceeding the speed limit in her car; for allowing her dog to appear
in public without a collar; and for failing to abate a smoky chimney.
Being in the nature of an autocrat, if I may use the term, in the
village, Miss Sipperley has been accustomed to do these things
in the past with impunity, and the constable's unexpected zeal has
made her somewhat ill-disposed to policemen as a class and consequently disposed to look upon such assaults as Mr. Sipperley's
in a kindly and broad-minded spirit."

I saw his point.

"What an amazing bit of luck, Jeeves!"

"Yes, sir."

"Where did you hear all this?"

"My informant was the constable himself, sir. He is my cousin."

I gaped at the man. I saw, so to speak, all.

"Good Lord, Jeeves! You didn't bribe him?"

"Oh, no, sir. But it was his birthday last week, and I gave him
a little present. I have always been fond of Egbert, sir."

"How much?"

"A matter of five pounds, sir."

I felt in my pocket.

"Here you are," I said. "And another fiver for luck."

"Thank you very much, sir."

"Jeeves," I said, "you move in a mysterious way your wonders
to perform. You don't mind if I sing a bit, do you?"

"Not at all, sir," said Jeeves.

The Truth about George

————— • —————

Two men were sitting in the bar-parlour of the Anglers' Rest as I entered it; and one of them, I gathered from his low, excited voice and wide gestures, was telling the other a story. I could hear nothing but an occasional "Biggest I ever saw in my life!" and "Fully as large as that!" but in such a place it was not difficult to imagine the rest; and when the second man, catching my eye, winked at me with a sort of humorous misery, I smiled sympathetically back at him.

The action had the effect of establishing a bond between us; and when the storyteller finished his tale and left, he came over to my table as if answering a formal invitation.

"Dreadful liars some men are," he said genially.

"Fishermen," I suggested, "are traditionally careless of the truth."

"He wasn't a fisherman," said my companion. "That was our local doctor. He was telling me about his latest case of dropsy. Besides" —he tapped me earnestly on the knee— "you must not fall into the popular error about fishermen. Tradition has maligned them. I am a fisherman myself, and I have never told a lie in my life."

I could well believe it. He was a short, stout, comfortable man of middle age, and the thing that struck me first about him was the extraordinary childlike candour of his eyes. They were large and round and honest. I would have bought oil stock from him without a tremor.

The door leading into the white dusty road opened, and a small man with rimless pince-nez and an anxious expression shot in like a rabbit and had consumed a gin and ginger-beer almost before we knew he was there. Having thus refreshed himself, he stood looking at us, seemingly ill at ease.

"N-n-n-n-n-n—" he said.

We looked at him inquiringly.

"N-n-n-n-n-n-ice d-d-d-d—"

His nerve appeared to fail him, and he vanished as abruptly as he had come.

"I think he was leading up to telling us that it was a nice day," hazarded my companion.

"It must be very embarrassing," I said, "for a man with such a painful impediment in his speech to open conversation with strangers."

"Probably trying to cure himself. Like my nephew George. Have I ever told you about my nephew George?"

I reminded him that we had only just met, and that this was the first time I had learned that he had a nephew George.

"Young George Mulliner. My name is Mulliner. I will tell you about George's case—in many ways a rather remarkable one."

My nephew George (said Mr. Mulliner) was as nice a young fellow as you would ever wish to meet, but from childhood up he had been cursed with a terrible stammer. If he had had to earn his living, he would undoubtedly have found this affliction a great handicap, but fortunately his father had left him a comfortable income; and George spent a not unhappy life, residing in the village where he had been born and passing his days in the usual country sports and his evenings in doing crossword puzzles. By the time he was thirty he knew more about Eli, the prophet, Ra, the Sun God, and the bird Emu than anybody else in the county except Susan Blake, the vicar's daughter, who had also taken up the solving of crossword puzzles and was the first girl in Worcestershire to find out the meaning of "stearine" and "crepuscular."

It was his association with Miss Blake that first turned George's thoughts to a serious endeavour to cure himself of his stammer. Naturally, with this hobby in common, the young people saw a great deal of one another; for George was always looking in at the vicarage to ask her if she knew a word of seven letters meaning "appertaining to the profession of plumbing," and Susan was just as constant a caller at George's cozy little cottage—being frequently stumped, as girls will be, by words of eight letters signifying "largely used in the manufacture of poppet valves." The consequence was that one evening, just after she had helped him out of a tight place with the word "disestablishmentarianism," the boy suddenly awoke to the truth and realized that she was all the world to him—or, as he put it to himself from force of habit, precious, beloved, darling, much-loved, highly esteemed or valued.

And yet, every time he tried to tell her so, he could get no farther than a sibilant gurgle which was no more practical use than a hiccup.

Something obviously had to be done, and George went to London to see a specialist.

"I-I-I-I-I-I—" said George.

"You were saying—?"

"Woo-woo-woo-woo-woo-woo—"

"Sing it," said the specialist.

"S-s-s-s-s-s-s—?" said George, puzzled.

The specialist explained. He was a kindly man with moth-eaten whiskers and an eye like a meditative codfish.

"Many people," he said, "who are unable to articulate clearly in ordinary speech find themselves lucid and bell-like when they burst into song."

It seemed a good idea to George. He thought for a moment; then threw his head back, shut his eyes, and let it go in a musical baritone.

"I love a lassie, a bonny, bonny lassie," sang George. "She's as pure as the lily in the dell."

"No doubt," said the specialist, wincing a little.

"She's as sweet as the heather, the bonny purple heather—Susan, my Worcestershire bluebell."

"Ah!" said the specialist. "Sounds a nice girl. Is this she?" he asked adjusting his glasses and peering at the photograph which George had extracted from the interior of the left side of his undervest.

George nodded, and drew in breath.

"Yes, sir," he carolled, "that's my baby. No, sir, don't mean maybe. Yes, sir, that's my baby now. And, by the way, by the way, when I meet that preacher I shall say—'Yes, sir, that's my—' "

"Quite," said the specialist hurriedly. He had a sensitive ear. "Quite, quite."

"If you knew Susie like I know Susie," George was beginning, but the other stopped him.

"Quite. Exactly. I shouldn't wonder. And now," said the specialist, "what precisely is the trouble? No," he added hastily, as George inflated his lungs, "don't sing it. Write the particulars on this piece of paper."

George did so.

"H'm!" said the specialist, examining the screed. "You wish to woo, court, and become betrothed, engaged, affianced to this girl, but you find yourself unable, incapable, incompetent, impotent, and powerless. Every time you attempt it, your vocal cords fail, fall short, are insufficient, wanting, deficient, and go blooey."

George nodded.

"A not unusual case. I have had to deal with this sort of thing before. The effect of love on the vocal cords of even a normally eloquent subject is frequently deleterious. As regards the habitual stammerer, tests have shown that in ninety-seven point five six nine recurring of cases the divine passion reduces him to a condition where he sounds like a soda-water siphon trying to recite

'Gunga Din.' There is only one cure."

"W-w-w-w-w—?" asked George.

"I will tell you. Stammering," proceeded the specialist, putting the tips of his fingers together and eying George benevolently, "is mainly mental and is caused by shyness, which is caused by the inferiority complex, which in its turn is caused by suppressed desires or introverted inhibitions or something. The advice I give to all young men who come in here behaving like soda-water siphons is to go out and make a point of speaking to at least three perfect strangers every day. Engage these strangers in conversation, persevering no matter how priceless a chump you may feel, and before many weeks are out you will find that the little daily dose has had its effect. Shyness will wear off, and with it the stammer."

And, having requested the young man—in a voice of the clearest timbre, free from all trace of impediment—to hand over a fee of five guineas, the specialist sent George out into the world.

The more George thought about the advice he had been given, the less he liked it. He shivered in the cab that took him to the station to catch the train back to East Wobsley. Like all shy young men, he had never hitherto looked upon himself as shy—preferring to attribute his distaste for the society of his fellows to some subtle rareness of soul. But now that the thing had been put squarely up to him, he was compelled to realise that in all essentials he was a perfect rabbit. The thought of accosting perfect strangers and forcing his conversation upon them sickened him.

But no Mulliner has ever shirked an unpleasant duty. As he reached the platform and strode along it to the train, his teeth were set, his eyes shone with an almost fanatical light of determination, and he intended before his journey was over to conduct three heart-to-heart chats if he had to sing every bar of them.

The compartment into which he had made his way was empty

at the moment, but just before the train started a very large, fierce-looking man got in. George would have preferred somebody a little less formidable for his first subject, but he braced himself and bent forward. And, as he did so, the man spoke.

"The wur-wur-wur-wur-weather," he said, "sus-sus-seems to be ter-ter-taking a tur-tur-turn for the ber-ber-better, der-doesn't it?"

George sank back as if he had been hit between the eyes. The train had moved out of the dimness of the station by now, and the sun was shining brightly on the speaker, illuminating his knobbly shoulders, his craggy jaw, and above all, the shockingly choleric look in his eyes. To reply "Y-y-y-y-y-y-y-yes" to such a man would obviously be madness.

But to abstain from speech did not seem to be much better as a policy. George's silence appeared to arouse this man's worst passions. His face had turned purple and he glared painfully.

"I uk-uk-asked you a sus-sus-civil quk-quk-quk," he said irascibly. "Are you d-d-d-d-deaf?"

All we Mulliners have been noted for our presence of mind. To open his mouth, point to his tonsils, and utter a strangled gurgle was with George the work of a moment.

The tension relaxed. The man's annoyance abated.

"D-d-d-dumb?" he said commiseratingly. "I beg your p-p-p-p-pup. I t-t-trust I have not caused you p-p-p-p-pup. It m-must be tut-tut-tut-tut-tut not to be able to sus-sus-speak fuf-fuf-fuf-fuf-fluently."

He then buried himself in his paper, and George sank back in his corner, quivering in every limb.

To get to East Wobsley, as you doubtless know, you have to change at Ippleton and take the branch line. By the time the train reached this junction, George's composure was somewhat restored. He deposited his belongings in a compartment of the East Wobsley train, which was waiting in a glued manner on the other side of the platform, and, finding that it would not start for some ten minutes, decided to pass the time by strolling up and down in the pleasant air.

It was a lovely afternoon. The sun was gilding the platform with its rays, and a gentle breeze blew from the west. A little brook ran tinkling at the side of the road; birds were singing in the hedge-rows; and through the trees could be discerned dimly the noble facade of the County Lunatic Asylum. Soothed by his surroundings, George began to feel so refreshed that he regretted that in this wayside station there was no one present whom he could engage in talk.

It was at this moment that the distinguished-looking stranger entered the platform.

The newcomer was a man of imposing physique, simply dressed in pajamas, brown boots, and a mackintosh. In his hand he carried a top hat, and into this he was dipping his fingers, taking them out, and then waving them in a curious manner to right and left. He nodded so affably to George that the latter, though a little surprised at the other's costume, decided to speak. After all, he reflected, clothes do not make the man, and, judging from the other's smile, a warm heart appeared to beat beneath that orange-and-mauve striped pajama jacket.

"N-n-n-n-nice weather," he said.

"Glad you like it," said the stranger. "I ordered it specially."

George was a little puzzled by this remark, but he persevered.

"M-might I ask wur-wur-what you are dud-doing?"

"Doing?"

"With that her-her-her-her-hat?"

"Oh, with this hat? I see what you mean. Just scattering largess to the multitude," replied the stranger, dipping his fingers once more and waving them with a generous gesture. "Devil of a bore, but it's expected of a man in my position. The fact is," he said,

linking his arm in George's and speaking in a confidential undertone, "I'm the Emperor of Abyssinia. That's my palace over there,"
he said, pointing through the trees. "Don't let it go any farther.
It's not supposed to be generally known."

It was with a rather sickly smile that George now endeavoured
to withdraw his arm from that of his companion, but the other
would have none of this aloofness. He seemed to be in complete
agreement with Shakespeare's dictum that a friend, when found,
should be grappled to you with hoops of steel. He looked about
him and seem satisfied.

"We are alone at last," he said.

This fact had already impressed itself with sickening clearness
on the young man. There are few spots in the civilised world more
deserted than the platform of a small country station. The sun
shone on the smooth asphalt, on the gleaming rails, and on the
machine which, in exchange for a penny placed in the slot marked
"Matches," would supply a package of wholesome butterscotch
—but on nothing else.

What George could have done with at the moment was a posse
of police armed with stout clubs, and there was not even a dog
in sight.

"I've been wanting to talk to you for a long time," said the
stranger genially.

"Huh-huh-have you?" said George.

"Yes. I want your opinion of human sacrifices."

George said he didn't like them.

"Why not?" asked the other, suprised.

George said it was hard to explain. He just didn't.

"Well, I think you're wrong," said the Emperor. "I know there's
a school of thought growing up that holds your views, but I disapprove of it. I hate all this modern advanced thought. Human
sacrifices have always been good enough for the Emperors of Abyssinia, and they're good enough for me. Kindly step in here, if you

please."

He indicated the lamp-and-mop room, at which they had now arrived. It was a dark and sinister apartment, smelling strongly of oil and porters, and was probably the last place on earth in which George would have wished to be closeted with a man of such peculiar views. He shrank back.

"You go in first," he said.

"No larks," said the other suspiciously.

"L-l-l-l-larks?"

"Yes. No pushing a fellow in and locking the door and squirting water at him through the window. I've had that happen to me before."

"Sus-certainly not."

"Right!" said the Emperor. "You're a gentleman and I'm a gentleman. Both gentlemen. Have you a knife, by the way? We shall need a knife."

"No. No knife."

"Ah, well," said the Emperor, "then we'll have to look about for something else. No doubt we shall manage somehow."

And with the debonair manner which so became him, he scattered another handful of largess and walked into the lamp room.

It was not the fact that he had given his word as a gentleman that kept George from locking the door. There is probably no family on earth more nicely scrupulous as regards keeping its promises than the Mulliners, but I am compelled to admit that, had George been able to find the key, he would have locked the door without hesitaion. Not being able to find the key, he had to be satisfied with banging it. This done, he leaped back and raced away down the platform. A confused noise within seemed to indicate that the Emperor had become involved with some lamps.

George made the best of the respite. Covering the ground at a high rate of speed, he flung himself into the train and took refuge under the seat.

There he remained, quaking. At one time he thought that his uncongenial acquaintance had got upon his track, for the door of the compartment opened and a cool wind blew in upon him. Then, glancing along the floor, he perceived feminine ankles. The relief was enormous, but even in his relief George, who was the soul of modesty, did not forget his manners. He closed his eyes.

A voice spoke.

"Porter!"

"Yes, ma'am?"

"What was all that disturbance as I came into the station?"

"Patient escaped from the asylum, ma'am."

"Good gracious!"

The voice would undoubtedly have spoken further, but at this moment the train began to move. There came the sound of a body descending upon a cushioned seat, and some little time later the rustling of a paper.

George had never before traveled under the seat of a railway carriage; and, though he belonged to the younger generation, which is supposed to be so avid of new experiences, he had no desire to do so now. He decided to emerge, and, if possible, to emerge with the minimum of ostentation. Little as he knew of women, he was aware that as a sex they are apt to be startled by the sight of men crawling out from under the seats of compartments. He began his manoeuvers by poking out his head and surveying the terrain.

All was well. The woman, in her seat across the way, was engrossed in her paper. Moving in a series of noiseless wriggles, George extricated himself from his hiding place and, with a twist which would have been impossible to a man not in the habit of doing Swedish exercises daily before breakfast, heaved himself into the corner seat. The woman continued reading her paper.

The events of the past quarter of an hour had tended rather to drive from George's mind the mission which he had undertaken on leaving the specialist's office. But now, having leisure for reflection, he realised that, if he meant to complete his first day of the cure, he was allowing himself to run sadly behind schedule. Speak to three strangers, the specialist had told him, and up to the present he had spoken to only one. True, this one had been a pretty considerable stranger, and a less conscientious young man than George Mulliner might have considered himself justified in chalking him up on the scoreboard as one and a half or even two. But George had the dogged, honest Mulliner streak in him, and he refused to quibble.

He nerved himself for action and cleared his throat.

"Ah-h'rm!" said George.

And, having opened the ball, he smiled a winning smile and waited for his companion to make the next move.

The move which his companion made was in an upwards direction, and measured from six to eight inches. She dropped her paper and regarded George with a pale-eyed horror. One pictures her a little in the position of Robinson Crusoe when he saw the footprint in the sand. She had been convinced that she was completely alone, and lo! out of space a voice had spoken to her. Her face worked, but she made no remark.

George, on his side, was also feeling a little ill at ease. Women always increased his natural shyness. He never knew what to say to them.

Then a happy thought struck him. He had just glanced at his watch and found the hour to be nearly four-thirty. Women, he knew, loved a drop of tea at about this time, and fortunately there was in his suitcase a full thermos flask.

"Pardon me, but I wonder if you would care for a cup of tea?" was what he wanted to say, but, as so often happened with him when in the presence of the opposite sex, he could get no farther than a sort of sizzling sound like a cockroach calling to its young.

The woman continued to stare at him. Her eyes were now about the size of regulation standard golf balls, and her breathing suggested the last stages of asthma. And it was at this point that George, struggling for speech, had one of those inspirations which frequently came to Mulliners. There flashed into his mind what the specialist had told him about singing. Say it with music—that was the thing to do.

He delayed no longer.

"Tea for two and two for tea and me for you and you for me—"

He was shocked to observe his companion turning Nile green. He decided to make his meaning clearer.

"I have a nice thermos. I have a full thermos. Won't you share my thermos, too? When skies are grey and you feel you are blue, tea sends the sun smiling through. I have a nice thermos. I have a full thermos. May I pour out some for you?"

You will agree with me, I think, that no invitation could have been more happily put, but his companion was not responsive. With one last agonised look at him, she closed her eyes and sank back in her seat. Her lips had now turned a curious grey-blue color, and they were moving feebly. She reminded George, who, like myself, was a keen fisherman, of a newly gaffed salmon.

George sat back in his corner, brooding. Rack his brain as he might, he could think of no topic which could be guaranteed to interest, elevate, and amuse. He looked out of the window with a sigh.

The train was now approaching the dear old familiar East Wobsley country. He began to recognise landmarks. A wave of sentiment poured over George as he thought of Susan, and he reached for the bag of buns which he had bought at the refreshment room at Ippleton. Sentiment always made him hungry.

He took his thermos out of the suitcase, and, unscrewing the top, poured himself out a cup of tea. Then, placing the thermos in the seat, he drank.

He looked across at his companion. Her eyes were still closed, and she uttered little sighing noises. George was half inclined to renew his offer of tea, but the only tune he could remember was "Hard-Hearted Hannah, the Vamp from Savannah," and it was difficult to fit suitable words to it. He ate his bun and gazed out at the familiar scenery.

Now, as you approach East Wobsley, the train, I must mention, has to pass over some points; and so violent is the sudden jerking that strong men have been known to spill their beer. George, forgetting this in his preoccupation, had placed the thermos only a few inches from the edge of the seat. The result was that, as the train reached the points, the flask leaped like a live thing, dived to the floor, and exploded.

Even George was distinctly upset by the sudden sharpness of the report. His bun sprang from his hand and was dashed to fragments. He blinked thrice in rapid succession. His heart tried to jump out of his mouth and loosened a front tooth.

But on the woman opposite the effect of the untoward occurrence was still more marked. With a single piercing shriek, she rose from her seat straight into the air like a rocketing pheasant; and, having clutched the communication cord, fell back again. Impressive as her previous leap had been, she excelled it now by several inches. I do not know what the existing record for the Sitting High-Jump is, but she undoubtedly lowered it; and if George had been a member of the Olympic Games Selection Committee, he would have signed this woman up immediately.

It is a curious thing that, in spite of the railway companies' sporting willingness to let their patrons have a tug at the extremely moderate price of five pounds a go, very few people have ever either pulled a communication cord or seen one pulled. There is, thus, a widespread ignorance as to what precisely happens on such occasions.

The procedure, George tells me, is as follows: First there comes a grinding noise, as the brakes are applied. Then the train stops.

And finally, from every point of the compass, a seething mob of interested onlookers begins to appear.

It was about a mile and a half from East Wobsley that the affair had taken place, and as far as the eye could reach the countryside was totally devoid of humanity. A moment before nothing had been visible but smiling cornfields and broad pasturelands; but now from east, west, north, and south running figures began to appear. We must remember that George at the time was in a somewhat over-wrought frame of mind, and his statements should therefore be accepted with caution; but he tells me that out of the middle of a single empty meadow, entirely devoid of cover, no fewer than twenty-seven distinct rustics suddenly appeared, having undoubtedly shot up through the ground.

The rails, which had been completely unoccupied, were now thronged with so dense a crowd of navvies that it seemed to George absurd to pretend that there was any unemployment in England. Every member of the labouring classes throughout the country was so palpably present. Moreover, the train, which at Ippleton had seemed sparsely occupied, was disgorging passengers from every door. It was the sort of mob scene which would have made David W. Griffith scream with delight; and it looked, George says, like Guest Night at the Royal Automobile Club. But, as I say, we must remember that he was overwrought.

It is difficult to say what precisely would have been the correct behaviour of your polished man of the world in such a situation. I think myself that a great deal of sang-froid and address would be required even by the most self-possessed in order to pass off such a contretemps. To George, I may say at once, the crisis revealed itself immediately as one which he was totally incapable of handling. The one clear thought that stood out from the welter of his emotions was the reflection that it was advisable to remove himself, and to do so without delay. Drawing a deep breath, he shot swiftly off the mark.

All we Mulliners have been athletes; and George, when at the University, had been noted for his speed of foot. He ran now as he had never run before. His statement, however, that as he sprinted across the first field he distinctly saw a rabbit shoot an envious glance at him as he passed and shrug its shoulders hopelessly, I am inclined to discount. George, as I have said before, was a little overexcited.

Nevertheless, it is not to be questioned that he made good going. And he had need to, for after the first instant of surprise, which had enabled him to secure a lead, the whole mob was pouring across country after him; and dimly, as he ran, he could hear voices in the throng informally discussing the advisability of lynching him. Moreover, the field through which he was running, a moment before a bare expanse of green, was now black with figures, headed by a man with a beard who carried a pitchfork. George swerved sharply to the right, casting a swift glance over his shoulder at his pursuers. He disliked them all, but especially the man with the pitchfork.

It is impossible for one who was not an eye-witness to say how long the chase continued and how much ground was covered by the interested parties. I know the East Wobsley country well, and I have checked George's statements; and, if it is true that he traveled east as far as Little-Wigmarsh-in-the-Dell and as far west as Higgleford-cum-Wortlebury-beneath-the-Hill, he must undoubtedly have done a lot of running.

But a point which must not be forgotten is that, to a man not in condition to observe closely, the village of Higgleford-cum-Wortlebury-beneath-the-Hill might easily not have been Higgleford-cum-Wortlebury-beneath-the-Hill at all, but another hamlet which in many respects closely resembles it. I need scarcely say that I allude to Lesser-Snodsbury-in-the-Vale.

Let us assume, therefore, that George, having touched Little-

Wigmarsh-in-the-Dell, shot off at a tangent and reached Lesser-Snodsbury-in-the-Vale. This would be a considerable run. And, as he remembers flitting past Farmer Higgins's pigsty and the Dog and Duck at Pondlebury Parva and splashing through the brook Wipple at the point where it joins the River Wopple, we can safely assume that, wherever else he went, he got plenty of exercise.

But the pleasantest of functions must end, and, just as the setting sun was gilding the spire of the ivy-covered church of St. Barnabas the Resilient, where George as a child had sat so often, enlivening the tedium of the sermon by making faces at the choirboys, a damp and bedraggled figure might have been observed crawling painfully along the High Street of East Wobsley in the direction of the cozy little cottage known to its builder as Chatsworth and to the village tradesmen as "Mulliner's."

It was George, home from the hunting field.

Slowly George Mulliner made his way to the familiar door, and, passing through it, flung himself into his favorite chair. But a moment later a more imperious need than the desire to rest forced itself upon his attention. Rising stiffly, he tottered to the kitchen and mixed himself a revivifying whisky-and-soda. Then, refilling his glass, he returned to the sitting room, to find that it was no longer empty. A slim, fair girl, tastefully attired in tailor-made tweeds, was leaning over the desk on which he kept his Dictionary of English Synonyms.

She looked up as he entered, startled.

"Why, Mr. Mulliner!" she exclaimed. "What has been happening? Your clothes are torn, rent, ragged, tattered, and your hair is all dishevelled, untrimmed, hanging loose or negligently, at loose ends!"

George smiled a wan smile.

"You are right," he said. "And, what is more, I am suffering from extreme fatigue, weariness, lassitude, exhaustion, prostration, and languor."

The girl gazed at him, a divine pity in her soft eyes.

"I'm so sorry," she murmured. "So very sorry, grieved, distressed, afflicted, pained, mortified, dejected, and upset."

George took her hand. Her sweet sympathy had effected the cure for which he had been seeking so long. Coming on top of the violent emotions through which he had been passing all day, it seemed to work on him like some healing spell, charm, or incantation. Suddenly, in a flash, he realized that he was no longer a stammerer. Had he wished at that moment to say, "Peter Piper picked a peck of pickled peppers," he could have done it without a second thought.

But he had better things to say than that.

"Miss Blake—Susan—Susie." He took her other hand in his. His voice rang out clear and unimpeded. It seemed to him incredible that he had ever yammered at this girl like an overheated steam radiator. "It cannot have escaped your notice that I have long entertained toward you sentiments warmer and deeper than those of ordinary friendship. It is love, Susan, that has been animating my bosom. Love, first a tiny seed, has burgeoned in my heart till, blazing into flame, it has swept away on the crest of its wave my diffidence, my doubt, my fears, and my foreboding, and now, like the topmost topaz of some ancient tower, it cries to all the world in a voice of thunder: 'You are mine! My mate! Predestined to me since Time first began!' As the star guides the mariner when, battered by boiling billows, he hies him home to the haven of hope and happiness, so do you gleam upon me along life's rough road and seem to say, 'Have courage, George! I am here!' Susan, I am not an eloquent man—I cannot speak fluently as I could wish —but these simple words which you have just heard came from the heart, from the unspotted heart of an English gentleman. Susan, I love you. Will you be my wife, married woman, matron, spouse, helpmeet, consort, partner or better half?"

"Oh, George!" said Susan. "Yes, yea, ay, aye! Decidedly, unquestionably, indubitably, incontrovertibly, and past all dispute!"

He folded her in his arms. And, as he did so, there came from the street outside—faintly, as from a distance—the sound of feet and voices. George leaped to the window. Rounding the corner, just by the Cow and Wheelbarrow public house, licensed to sell ales, wines, and spirits, was the man with the pitchfork, and behind him followed a vast crowd.

"My darling," said George. "For purely personal and private reasons, into which I need not enter, I must now leave you. Will you join me later?"

"I will follow you to the ends of the earth," replied Susan passionately.

"It will not be necessary," said George. "I am only going down to the coal cellar. I shall spend the next half-hour or so there. If anybody calls and asks for me, perhaps you would not mind telling them that I am out."

"I will, I will," said Susan. "And, George, by the way. What I really came here for was to ask you if you knew a word of nine letters, ending in k and signifying an implement employed in the pursuit of agriculture."

"Pitchfork, sweetheart," said George. "But you may take it from me, as one who knows, that agriculture isn't the only thing it is used in pursuit of."

And since that day (concluded Mr. Mulliner) George, believe me or believe me not, has not had the slightest trace of an impediment in his speech. He is now the chosen orator at all political rallies for miles around; and so offensively self-confident has his manner become that only last Friday he had his eye blacked by a hay-corn-and-feed merchant of the name of Stubbs. It just shows you, doesn't it?

The Fat of the Land

———— • ————

Although he had never mentioned it to anybody, feeling that it was but an idle daydream and not within the sphere of practical politics, the idea of having a Fat Uncles sweepstake at the Drones Club had long been in Freddie Widgeon's mind, such as it was. Himself the possessor of one of the fattest uncles in London —Rodney, Lord Blicester—he had noticed how many of his fellow members had fat uncles too, and he felt it a sad waste of good material not to make these the basis of a sporting contest similar, though on a smaller scale, to those in operation in Ireland and Calcutta.

Perfectly simple, the mechanics of the thing. Put the names of the uncles in a hat, put the names of the punters in another hat, draw a name from the first hat, draw a name from the second hat, and the holder of the fattest uncle scooped the jackpot. No difficulty there.

But there was a catch, and a very serious one, to wit, the problem of how to do the weighing. He could not, for instance, go to Lord Blicester and say, "Would you mind just stepping on this try-your-weight machine for a moment, Uncle Rodney? It is essential to satisfy the judges that you are fatter than the Duke of Dunstable." At least, he could, but there would be questions asked, and explanations would lead to pique, bad feeling and possibly the stopping of a much-needed allowance. It was, in short, an impasse, and he had come to look on the scheme as just another of those things which, though good, cannot be pushed along, when, coming into the bar one morning, he found an animated group assembled there and as he entered heard McGarry, the man behind the counter, say, "Ten stone three." Upon which, there was a burst of hearty cheering and, inquiring the reason for this enthusiasm, he was informed that McGarry had revealed an unsuspected talent. He was able to tell the weight of anything from a vegetable marrow to a Covent Garden tenor just by looking at it.

"Never misses by more than half an ounce," said an Egg. "In his circle of friends he is known as the Human Scales. A great gift, don't you think?"

"I'll say it is," said Freddie. "It removes the one obstacle to this project of mine."

And in a few well-chosen words he placed his proposition before the meeting.

It caught on immediately, as he had been confident that it would, and a committee, with a prominent Crumpet at its head, was formed to rough out the details of the venture. It was decided that the deadline should be one o'clock on the opening day of the Eton and Harrow match, when all the uncles would be rolling up and having lunch at the Drones with their nephews. To parade them before McGarry, his decision to be final, would be a simple task, for the first thing they always did was to head for the bar like bisons for a water hole. The price of tickets was put at a somewhat higher figure than suited the purse of many members, but it was pointed out to these that they could club together and form syndicates, and so few had failed to chip in by the time the day of the drawing arrived that the Crumpet was able to announce that the contents of the kitty amounted to well over a hundred pounds. And it was generally recognized that this impressive sum must inevitably go to the lucky stiff who drew the name of Lord Blicester, for while all the starters were portly, having long let their waistlines go, not one of them could be considered in the class of Freddie's outsize uncle. Others, as a well-read Bean put it, abided their question, he was free.

And, of course, as always seemed to happen on these occasions, it was Oofy Prosser, the club millionaire, the one human soul, if you could call him a human soul, not in need of the money, who drew the Blicester ticket. Freddie himself got Oofy's Uncle Horace, and at the conclusion of the drawing he went over to where the plutocrat was sitting reading his morning's mail, to make inquiries.

"Who is this uncle of yours I've drawn, Oofy?" he asked. "I didn't know you had an uncle."

"Nor did I," said Oofy, "till I got a letter from him the other day, signed 'Uncle Horace.' It's rather odd. I could have sworn that my uncles were Hildebrand, who had an apoplectic stroke in 1947, and Stanley, who died of cirrhosis of the liver in 1949, but apparently this is one I overlooked, no doubt because he has been in the Argentine for the last twenty years. He returned to England last week and is staying at a place called Hollrock Manor in Hertfordshire. I haven't seen him yet, but he will be lunching with me here on the big day."

"I wonder if he's fat."

"I shouldn't think so. Warm climate, the Argentine. Keeps the weight down. And isn't that the place where you spend your whole time riding over pampas? No, I wouldn't build any hopes, Freddie. Not a chance of him nosing out your Uncle Rodney. But excuse me, old man, I must be catching up with my reading."

Freddie drifted away disconsolately, and Oofy returned to his letters. One of these bore the address of Hollrock Manor. He read it without any great interest, but was mildly intrigued by the postscript.

"P.S.," his uncle wrote. "You must be wondering what I look like these days, not having seen me since you were a child. I enclose a snapshot, taken in the garden the other morning."

Oofy examined the envelope, but could find no snapshot. Then, looking down, he saw that it had fallen to the floor. He picked it up, and the next moment had sagged back in his chair with a stifled cry.

It was the photograph of an elderly man in a bathing suit; an elderly man who, a glance was enough to tell, had been overdoing it on the starchy foods since early childhood; an elderly man so rotund, so obese, so bulging in every direction that Shakespeare, had he beheld him, would have muttered to himself, "Upon what meat doth this our Horace feed, that he is grown so great?" One wondered how any bathing suit built by human hands could contain so stupendous an amount of uncle without parting at the seams. In the letter he had written to Oofy announcing his arrival in England Horace Prosser had spoken of coming home to lay his bones in the old country. There was nothing in the snapshot to suggest that he had any bones.

Little wonder, then, that as he ran his eye over the man, reading from left to right, Oofy should have been feeling the same sort of stunned breathless feeling he would have felt had this uncle fallen on him from the top of a high building. With pitiless clarity it was borne in on him that the Blicester ticket over which he had been gloating was not worth the paper it was written on. Compared with this mastodon, Lord Blicester was slim to the point of emaciation and hadn't a hope, and the thought that Freddie Widgeon and not he would win all that lovely money was like a dagger in Oofy's bosom. We said earlier that he did not need the cash, but it was we who said it, not Oofy. His views on the matter were sharply divergent. Whenever there was cash around, he wanted to get it. It was well said of him at the Drones that despite his revolting wealth he would always willingly walk ten miles in tight boots to pick up twopence. Many put the figure even lower.

How long he sat there motionless, he could not have said, but after a while his subtle and scheming brain, temporarily numbed, began to function again, and he perceived that all was not yet lost. There was, he saw, a way of achieving the happy ending. It called for the co-operation of a party of the second part of an innocent and unsuspicious nature, and no one could have filled the bill more adequately than Frederick Widgeon, a man whose trust in his fellow men was a byword. Frederick Widgeon, he knew for a fact, believed everything he read in *Time*. He sought him out and laid a gentle hand on his sleeve.

"Freddie, old man," he said, "can you spare me a moment of your valuable time?"

Freddie said he could.

"I don't know," said Oofy, "if you were glancing in my direction just now?"

Freddie said he wasn't.

"Well, if you had been, you would have noticed that I was plunged in meditation, and I'll tell you why. Have you ever been a Boy Scout?"

Freddie said he hadn't.

"I was one at one time, and I have never forgotten the lessons I learned in those knickerbocker and spooring days."

"Tying knots, do you mean, and lighting fires by rubbing sticks together?"

"Not so much that as the doing-one's-daily-good-deed routine. Boy Scouts, as you probably know, are supposed to perform at least one act of kindness every twenty-four hours, and a very good thing, too. Keeps them up on their toes."

"Yes, I can see that. It would, of course."

"Now, one rather tends, as one grows older, to give the daily good deed a miss, and it's all wrong, one shouldn't. There is no reason whatever why, just because one no longer goes about in a khaki shirt with a whistle attached to it, one should omit those little acts of kindness which sweeten life for all and sundry. One ought to keep plugging away. This came to me very forcibly just now, as I sat thinking about this sweepstake thing we're having. Is it right, is it fair, I asked myself, that I, to whom money means nothing, should have drawn the favourite, while somebody who really needs the stuff, like my old friend Freddie Widgeon, gets stuck with a rank outsider? There could be but one answer. It was not right. It was not fair. It was something that had to be adjusted."

"How do you mean, adjusted?"

"Quite simple. We must swap tickets, I taking my uncle's and you yours. Yes, yes," said Oofy, seeing that his old friend was gaping at him like a bewildered codfish, "you are naturally surprised. It seems to you bizarre that I should be doing myself out of a hundred quid or whatever it is. But what you overlook is that I shall be getting the glow that comes from feeling that one has done an act of kindness and helped a fellow human being on the road to happiness. What is a hundred quid compared with that?"

"But—"

"Don't say 'But,' Freddie. I insist on this. No, no, don't thank me. My motives are purely selfish. I want to glow."

And Oofy went off to tell the Crumpet to record the change of tickets in the official notebook in which the names of the ticket holders were listed. He was glowing.

It is a very incurious and phlegmatic nephew who, when he has an uncle whose adiposity is going to net him more than a hundred pounds, does not hasten to go and take a look at that uncle, if only to assure himself that the latter is wading into the mashed potatoes in a satisfactory manner and getting his full supply of bread, butter, beer, roly-poly pudding and pastries. On the following morning, preceded by a telegram saying that he was coming to lunch, Oofy started out in his car for Hollrock Manor. He pictured a fine old house with spacious grounds, and found on arrival that his imagination had not let him astray. Hollrock Manor was plainly a place where the moneyed did themselves well and, always of a greedy nature, he found his mouth watering at the prospect of the lavish luncheon of which he would shortly be partaking. His drive had given him a rare appetite.

He inquired for Mr. Horace Prosser, and presently the other

came wheezing along, and after a certain amount of Well-well-welling and So-here-you-are-at-last-ing, inevitable in the circumstances, they went into the dining room and seated themselves at a table. It gratified Oofy to note that as his relative lowered himself into his chair, the chair visibly quivered beneath him and gave out a protesting squeal. On his journey down he had from time to time had an uneasy feeling that that snapshot might have exaggerated the other's proportions, but one glance had been enough to tell him that these were idle fears. Now that he saw the man in the flesh, he felt, like the Queen of Sheba, that the half had not been told unto him.

The only thing that disturbed him was that, no doubt in a moment of absent-mindedness, his host had not suggested the pre-luncheon martini, in anticipation of which he had been licking his lips for the last hour. And as the waiter presented the bill of fare, it seemed to occur to Mr. Prosser that he had been remiss. He hastened to explain his eccentric behaviour.

"Sorry I couldn't offer you a cocktail, my boy. We don't have them here. But they serve an excellent glass of parsnip juice, if you would care for it. No? Then suppose we order. Will you have stewed lettuce, or would you prefer an orange? Ah, but wait, I see we are in luck. This is grated carrot day. How about starting with potassium broth, going on to grated carrots and winding up with a refreshing cup of dandelion coffee?"

At an early point in these remarks Oofy's lower jaw had drooped like a tired lily. He hitched it up in order to ask a question.

"I say, what *is* this place?"

"It used to belong to Lord Somebody or Sir Somebody Something, I forget which. Like so many landowners, he had to sell after the war. Impossible to keep the old home up. Sad, very sad."

"Sadder than potassium broth?"

"Don't you like potassium broth? You can have seaweed soup, if you wish."

"But I don't understand. Is this a hotel?"

"Well, more a clinic, I suppose you would call it. We come here to reduce."

It is not easy to totter when seated in a chair, but Oofy managed it. He goggled at his companion, the potassium broth falling from his nerveless spoon.

"Did you say 'reduce'?"

"That's right. Doctor Hailsham, who runs the place, guarantees to take a pound a day off you, if you follow his regimen faithfully. I expect to lose three stone before I leave."

Oofy tottered again, and the room seemed to swim about him. He scarcely recognized the hollow croak that proceeded from his lips as his own voice.

"Three *stone?*"

"If not more."

"You're crazy!"

"Who's crazy?"

"You are. What do you want to lose three stone for?"

"You don't think I'm a little overweight?"

"Certainly not. Just pleasantly plump."

Horace Prosser gave a rich chuckle, seeming entertained by some amusing recollection.

"Pleasantly plump, eh? You are more flattering than Loretta was."

"Than who was?"

"A Mrs. Delancy I met on the boat, coming over. She called me a hippopotamus."

"A vulgar ill-bred female bounder!"

"Please! You are speaking of the woman I love."

"I'm what-ing of the what you *what?*"

It was impossible to ascertain whether a blush mantled Horace Prosser's cheek, for in its normal state it was ruddier than a cherry, but he unquestionably looked coy. It would not be too much to say that he simpered. He murmured something about Ah, those moonlight nights, and when Oofy said Ah, what moonlight nights, explained that he was alluding to the moonlight nights when he and this Mrs. Delancy—a widow of some years' standing—had walked together on the boat deck. It was at the conclusion of one of these promenades, he added, that he had asked her to be his wife, and she had replied that the only obstacle standing in the way of the suggested merger was his adipose deposit. She refused, she said, to walk up the aisle with a human hippopotamus.

Horace Prosser chuckled again.

"The whimsical way she put it was that a woman who married a man my size ran a serious risk of being arrested for bigamy. She confessed that she had often yearned for someone like me, but was opposed to the idea of getting twice as much as she had yearned for. Very bright, amusing woman. She comes from Pittsburgh."

Oofy choked on a spoonful of the yellow mess which had been placed before him.

"I still consider her a cad and a bounder."

"So we left it that I would go off somewhere and diet, and if some day I came to her with thirty pounds or so removed from my holdings, our talks would be resumed in what politicians call an atmosphere of the utmost cordiality. She is coming to see me soon, and I don't think she will be disappointed. Have some more of these carrots, my boy. Apart from acting directly on the fatty corpuscles, they are rich in Vitamins A, B, C, D, E, G, and K."

Mr. Prosser went off to have a massage after he had digested his lunch, and Oofy, as he drove back to London, was still shuddering at the recollection of what the other had said about the *effleurage*, stroking, friction, kneading, pétrissage, *tapotement* and vibration which massage at Hollrock Manor involved. He was appalled. With that sort of thing going on in conjunction with the potassium broth and dandelion coffee, it was plain that the man would come to the post a mere shadow. Lord Blicester, if in anything like midseason form, would make rings round him.

Many young men in such a situation would have thrown in the towel and admitted defeat, but Oofy kept his head.

"I must be calm, calm," he was saying to himself as he went to the Drones next day, and it was with outward calmness that he approached Freddie Widgeon, who was having a ham sandwich at the bar.

"Gosh, Freddie," he said, after they had pip-pipped, "I'm glad I ran into you. Do you notice that I am quivering like an aspen?"

"No," said Freddie. "Are you quivering like an aspen?"

"You bet I'm quivering like an aspen."

"Why are you quivering like an aspen?"

"Well, wouldn't any man of good will be quivering like an aspen if he had had the narrowest of escapes from letting an old friend down? Here are the facts in a nutshell. With the best of motives, if you remember, I persuaded you to exchange your Lord Blicester ticket for my Uncle Horace. You recall that?"

"Oh, rather. You wanted to do your Boy Scout act of kindness for the day."

"Exactly. And now what do I find?"

"What do you find?"

"I'll tell you what I find. I find that in comparison with my uncle your uncle is slender. I had a letter from Uncle Horace this morning, enclosing a snapshot of himself. Take a look at it."

Freddie examined the snapshot, and such was his emotion that the ham sandwich flew from his grasp.

"Crumbs!"

"You may well say 'Crumbs'!"

"Golly!"

"And also 'Golly.' I said the same thing myself. It is pretty obvious, I think you will agree with me, that Blicester hasn't a chance. A good selling-plater, I admit, but this time he has come up against a classic yearling."

"You told me your uncle had been perspiring for years in the hot sun of the Argentine."

"No doubt the sun was not as hot as I have always supposed, or possibly his pores do not work freely. I also said, I recall, that he did a lot of riding over pampas. I was wrong. On the evidence of this photograph he can't have ridden over a pampa in his life. Well, fortunately I discovered this in time. There is only one thing to do, Freddie. We must change tickets again."

Freddie gaped.

"You really . . . Oh, thanks," he said, as a passing Bean picked up the ham sandwich and returned it to him. "You really mean that?"

"I certainly do."

"I call it pretty noble of you."

"Oh, well, you know how it is. Once a Boy Scout, always a Boy Scout," said Oofy, and a few moments later he was informing the Crumpet that the list in his notebook must once more be revised.

It was Oofy's practice, whenever life in London seemed to him to be losing its savor and the conversation of his fellow members of the Drones to be devoid of its customary sparkle, to pop over to Paris and get a nice change, and shortly after his chat with Freddie he made another of his trips to the French capital. And as he sat sipping an *apéritif* one morning at a cafe on the Champs Elysées, his thoughts turned to his Uncle Horace, and not for the first time he found himself marveling that the love of a woman could have made that dedicated man mortify the flesh as he was doing. Himself, Oofy would not have forgone the simplest pat of butter to win the hand of Helen of Troy, and had marriage with Cleopatra involved the daily drinking of potassium broth and seaweed soup, there would have been no question of proceeding with the ceremony. "I am sorry," he would have said to Egypt's queen, "but if those are your ideas, I have no option but to cancel the order for the wedding cake and see that work is stopped on the bridesmaid's dresses."

He looked at his watch. About now his uncle, in Hollrock Manor's picturesque little bar, would be ordering his glass of parsnip juice preparatory to tackling whatever garbage the bill of fare was offering that day, perfectly contented because love conquered all and so forth. Ah, well, he felt, it takes all sorts to make a world.

At this point in his reverie his meditations were interrupted by a splintering crash in his rear and, turning, he perceived that a chair at a nearby table had disintegrated beneath the weight of a very stout man in a tweed suit. And he was just chuckling heartily at the amusing incident, when the laughter died on his lips. The well-nourished body extricating itself from the debris was that of his Uncle Horace—that selfsame Uncle Horace whom he had just been picturing among the parsnip juices and seaweed soups of Hollrock Manor, Herts.

"Uncle!" he cried, hastening to the spot.

"Oh, hullo, my boy," said Mr. Prosser, starting to dust himself off. "You here? They seem to make these chairs very flimsy nowadays," he muttered with a touch of peevishness. "Or it may be," he went on in more charitable vein, "that I have put on a little weight these last weeks. This French cooking. Difficult always to resist those sauces. What are you doing in La Ville Lumière?"

"What are *you* doing in La Ville Lumière?" demanded Oofy. "Why aren't you at that frightful place in Hertfordshire?"

"I left there ages ago."

"But how about the woman you love?"

"What woman I love?"

"The one who called you a hippopotamus."

"Oh, Loretta Delancy. That's all over. It turned out to be just one of those fleeting shipboard romances. You know how they all look good to you at sea and fade out with pop when you get ashore.

She came to Hollrock Manor one afternoon, and the scales fell from my eyes. Couldn't imagine what I had ever seen in the woman. The idea of going through all that dieting and massage for her sake seemed so damn silly that next day I wrote her a civil note telling her to take a running jump into the nearest lake and packed up and left. Well, it's nice to run into you like this, my dear boy. We must have some big dinners together. Are you staying long in Paris?"

"I'm leaving today," said Oofy. "I have to see a man named Widgeon on business."

But he did not see Freddie. Though he haunted the club day and night, yearning for a sight of that familiar face, not a glimpse of it did he get. He saw Bingo Little, he saw Catsmeat Potter-Pirbright, he saw Barmy Phipps, Percy Wimbush, Nelson Cork, Archibald Mulliner and all the other pillars of the Drones who lunched there daily, but always there was this extraordinary shortage of Widgeons. It was as though the young man had vanished from human ken like the captain and crew of the *Mary Céleste*.

It was only when he happened to be having a quick one with an Egg who was Freddie's closest friend that the mystery of his disappearance was explained. At the mention of the absent one's name, the Egg sighed a little.

"Oh, Freddie," he said. "Yes, I can tell you about him. At the moment he is rather unfortunately situated. He owes a bookie fifty quid, and is temporarily unable to settle."

"Silly ass."

"Silly, unquestionably, ass, but there it is. What happened was that he drew an uncle in this sweep whom nobody had ever heard of, and blow me tight if he hadn't unexpectedly hit the jackpot. He showed me a snapshot of the man, and I was amazed. I could see at a glance that here was the winner, so far ahead of the field that there could be no competition. Blicester would be an honorable runner-up, but nothing more. Extraordinary how often in these big events you find a dark horse popping up and upsetting all calculations. Well, with the sweepstake money as good as in his pocket, as you might say, poor old Freddie lost his head and put his shirt on a horse at Kempton Park which finished fourth, with the result, as I have indicated, that he owes this bookie fifty quid, and no means of paying him till he collects on the sweep. And the bookie, when informed that he wasn't going to collect, advised him in a fatherly way to be very careful of himself from now on, for though he knew that it was silly to be superstitious, he—the bookie —couldn't help remembering that every time people did him down for money some unpleasant accident always happened to them. Time after time he had noticed it, and it could not be mere coincidence. More like some sort of fate, the bookie said. So Freddie is lying low, disguised in a beard."

"Where?"

"In East Dulwich."

"Whereabouts in East Dulwich?"

"Ah," said the Egg, "that's what the bookie would like to know."

The trouble about East Dulwich, from the point of view of a clean-shaven man trying to find a bearded man there, is that it is rather densely populated, rendering his chances of success slim. Right up to the day before the Eton and Harrow match Oofy prowled to and fro in its streets, hoping for the best, but East Dulwich held its secret well. The opening day of the match found him on the steps of the Drones Club, scanning the horizon like Sister Anne in the Bluebeard story. Surely, he felt, Freddie could not stay away from the premises on this morning of mornings.

Member after member entered the building as he stood there, accompanied by uncles of varying stoutness, but not one of those members was Freddie Widgeon, and Oofy's blood pressure had just reached a new high and looked like going to par, when a cab drew up and something bearded, shooting from its interior, shot past him, shot through the entrance hall and disappeared down the steps leading to the washroom. The eleventh hour had produced the man.

Freddie, when Oofy burst into the washroom some moments later with a "Tally-ho" on his lips, was staring at himself in the mirror, a thing not many would have cared to do when looking as he did. A weaker man than Oofy would have recoiled at the frightful sight that met his eyes. Freddie, when making his purchase, had evidently preferred quantity to quality. The salesman, no doubt, had recommended something in neat Vandykes as worn by the better class of ambassador, but Freddie was a hunted stag, and when hunted stages buy beards, they want something big and bushy as worn by Victorian novelists. The man whom Oofy had been seeking so long could at this moment of their meeting have stepped into the Garrick Club of the sixties, and Wilkie Collins and the rest of the boys would have welcomed him as a brother, supposing him to be Walt Whitman.

"Freddie!" cried Oofy.

"Oh, hullo, Oofy," said Freddie. He was pulling at the beard in a gingerly manner, as if the process hurt him. "You are doubtless surprised—"

"No, I'm not. I was warned of this. Why don't you take the damned thing off?"

"I can't."

"Give it a tug."

"I have given it a tug, and the agony was excruciating. It's stuck on with spirit gum or something."

"Well, never mind your beard. We have no time to talk of beards. Freddie, thank heaven I have found you. Another quarter of an hour, and it would have been too late."

"What would have been too late?"

"It. We've got to change those tickets."

"What, again?"

"Immediately. You remember me saying that my Uncle Horace was staying at a place called Hollrock Manor in Hertfordshire? Well, naturally, I supposed that it was one of those luxury country hotels where he would be having twice of everything and filling up with beer, champagne, liqueurs and what not. But was it?"

"Wasn't it? What was it if it wasn't?"

"It was what they call a clinic, run by some foul doctor, where the superfatted go to reduce. He had gone there to please a woman who had told him he looked like a hippopotamus."

"He does look rather like a hippopotamus."

"He does in that snapshot, I grant you, but that was taken weeks and weeks ago, and during those weeks he has been living on apple juice, tomato juice, orange juice, pineapple juice, parsnip juice, grated carrots, potassium broth, and seaweed soup. He has also been having daily massage, the term massage embracing *effleurage*, stroking, kneading, pétrissage, *tapotement* and vibration."

"Lord love a duck!"

"Lord love a duck is right. I needn't tell you what happens when that sort of thing is going on. Something has to give. By now he must have lost at least a couple of stone and be utterly incapable of giving old Blicester a race. So slip me the Uncle Horace ticket, and I will slip you the Blicester, and the situation will be stabilized once more. Gosh, Freddie, old man, when I think how near I came to letting you down, thinking I was acting in your best interests, I shudder."

Freddie stroked his beard. To Oofy's dismay, he seemed hesitant, dubious.

"Well, I'm not so sure about this," he said. "You say your Uncle Horace has lost a couple of stone. I am strongly of the opinion that he could lose three and still be fatter than my Uncle Rodney, and I'm wondering if I ought to take a chance. You see, a great deal hangs on my winning this tourney. I owe fifty quid to a clairvoyant bookie, who, looking in his crystal ball, has predicted that if I don't brass up, some nasty accident will happen to me, and from what he tells me that crystal ball of his is to be relied on. I should feel an awful ass if I gave up the Uncle Horace ticket and took the Uncle Rodney ticket and Uncle Horace won and I found myself in a hospital with surgeons doing crochet work all over me."

"I only want to help."

"I know you do, but the question is, are you helping?"

Oofy was unable to stroke his beard, for he had not got one, but he fingered his chin. He was thinking with the rapidity with which he always thought when there was money floating around to be picked up. It did not take him long to reach a decision. Agony though it was to part with fifty pounds, winning the sweep would leave him with a nice profit. There was nothing for it but to make the great sacrifice. If you do not speculate, you cannot accumulate.

"I'll tell you what I'll do," he said, producing his wallet and extracting the bank notes with which it always bulged. "I'll give you fifty quid. That will take care of the bookie, and you'll be all right, whatever happens."

As much as was visible of Freddie's face between the crevices of the beard lit up. He looked like someone staring incredulously at someone through a hay stack.

"Golly, Oofy! Will you really do that?"

"It's not much to do for an old friend."

"But what is there in it for you?"

"Just that glow, old man, just that glow," said Oofy.

Going upstairs, he found the Crumpet in the hall, studying the list in his notebook, and broke the news that a little further pencilwork would be required of him. It brought a frown to the other's face.

"I disapprove of all this chopping and changing," he said, though agreeing that there was nothing in the rules against it. "Let's get this straight. Freddie Widgeon now has the Blicester ticket and you have the Horace Prosser ticket. Right?"

"Yes, that's right."

"Not vice versa?"

"No, not vice versa."

"Good. I'm glad that's settled. I've worn out one piece of india-rubber already."

It was at this moment that the hall porter, who for some little time had been trying to attract Oofy's attention, spoke.

"There's a gentleman asking for you, Mr. Prosser. Name of Prosser, same as yours."

"Ah, yes, my uncle. Where is he?"

"He stepped into the bar."

"He would. Will you go and give him a cocktail," said Oofy to the Crumpet. "I'll be with you in a minute, after I've booked a table in the dining room."

It was with the feeling that all was for the best in this best of all possible worlds that he entered the dining room. Like the Battle of Waterloo, it had been a devilish close-run thing, but he had won through, and his morale was high. He did not actually say "Tra-la" as he ordered his table, but the ejaculation was implicit in the sunniness of his smile and the sparkle in his eyes. Coming out again into the hall with a gay air on his lips, he was surprised to find the Crumpet there.

"Hullo," he said. "Didn't you go to the bar?"

"I went."

"Didn't you find the old boy?"

"I found him." The Crumpet's manner seemed strange to Oofy. He was looking grave and reproachful, like a Crumpet who considers that he has been played fast and loose with. "Oofy," he said, "fun's fun, and no one's fonder of a joke than I am, but there are limits. I can see no excuse for a fellow pulling a gag in connection with a race meeting as important as this one. Only genuine uncles were eligible. I suppose you thought it would be humorous to ring in a non-uncle."

"Do what?"

"It's as bad as entering a greyhound for the Grand National."

Oofy could make nothing of this. The thought flitted through his mind that the other had been lunching.

"What on earth are you talking about?"

"I'm talking about that bloke in there with the billowy curves. You said he was your uncle."

"He is my uncle."

"He is nothing of the bally sort."

"His name's Prosser."

"No doubt."

"He signed his letter 'Uncle Horace.' "

"Very possibly. But that doesn't alter the stark fact that he's a sort of distant cousin. He was telling me about it while we quaffed. It appears that as a child you used to call him Uncle Horace but, stripped of his mask, he is, as I say, merely a distant cousin. If you didn't know this and were not just trying to be funny when you entered him, I apologize for my recent remarks. You are more to be pitied than censured, it would seem, for the blighter is, of course, disqualified and the stakes go to Frederick Fortescue Widgeon, holder of the Blicester ticket."

To think simultaneously of what might have been and what is going to be is not an easy task, but Oofy, as he heard these words of doom, found himself doing it. For even as his mind dwelled on the thought that he had paid Freddie Widgeon fifty pounds to deprive himself of the sweepstake money, he was also vividly aware that in a brace of shakes he would be standing his distant cousin Horace a lunch which, Horace being the man he was, could put him in the hole for scarcely less than a fiver. His whole soul seethed like a cistern struck by a thunderbolt, and everything seemed to go black.

The Crumpet was regarding him with concern.

"Don't gulp like that, Oofy," he said. "You can't be sick here."

Oofy was not so sure. He was feeling as if he could be sick anywhere.

Mr. Potter Takes a Rest Cure

———— • ————

Mr. John Hamilton Potter, founder and proprietor of the well-known New York publishing house of J. H. Potter, Inc., laid down the typescript which had been engaging his leisurely attention, and from the depths of his basket-chair gazed dreamily across the green lawns and gleaming flower-beds to where Skeldings Hall basked in the pleasant June sunshine. He was feeling quietly happy. The waters of the moat glittered like liquid silver; a gentle breeze brought to his nostrils the scent of newly-cut grass; the doves in the elms cooed with precisely the right gentlemanly intonation; and he had not seen Clifford Gandle since luncheon. God, it seemed to Mr. Potter, was in His heaven and all was right with the world.

And how near, he reflected, he had come to missing all this delightful old-world peace. When, shortly after his arrival in England, he had met Lady Wickham at a Pen and Ink Club dinner and she had invited him to pay a visit to Skeldings, his first impulse had been to decline. His hostess was a woman of rather markedly overwhelming personality; and, inasmuch as he had only recently recovered from a nervous breakdown and had been ordered by his doctor complete rest and tranquillity, it had seemed to him that at close range and over an extended period of time she might be a little too much for the old system. Furthermore, she wrote novels: and that instinct of self-preservation which lurks in every publisher had suggested to him that behind her invitation lay a sinister desire to read these to him one by one with a view to getting him to produce them in America. Only the fact that he was a lover of the old and picturesque, coupled with the fact that Skeldings Hall dated back to the time of the Tudors, had caused him to accept.

Not once, however—not even when Clifford Gandle was expressing to him with a politician's trained verbosity his views on the Gold Standard and other weighty matters—had he regretted his decision. When he looked back on his life of the past eighteen months—a life spent in an inferno of shrilling telephones and authors, many of them female, popping in to abuse him for not advertising their books better—he could almost fancy that he had been translated to Paradise.

A Paradise, moreover, which was not without its Peri. For at this moment there approached Mr. Potter across the lawn, walking springily as if she were constructed of whalebone and india-rubber, a girl. She was a boyish-looking girl, slim and graceful, and the red hair on her bare head glowed pleasingly in the sun.

"Hullo, Mr. Potter!" she said.

The publisher beamed upon her. This was Roberta Wickham, his hostess's daughter, who had returned to her ancestral home two days ago from a visit to friends in the North. A friendly young thing, she had appealed to Mr. Potter from the first.

"Well, well, well!" said Mr. Potter.

"Don't get up. What are you reading?" Bobbie Wickham picked up the manuscript. "*Ethics of Suicide*," she read. "Cheery!"

Mr. Potter laughed indulgently. "No doubt it seems an odd thing to be reading on such a day and in such surroundings. But a publisher is never free. This was sent over for my decision from my New York office. They won't leave me alone when I am on vacation."

Bobbie Wickham's hazel eyes clouded pensively.

"There's a lot to be said for suicide," she murmured. "If I had to see much of Clifford Gandle, I'd commit suicide myself."

Mr. Potter started. He had always liked this child, but he had never dreamed that she was such a completely kindred soul.

"Don't you like Mr. Gandle?"

"No."

"Nor do I."

"Nor does anyone," said Bobbie, "except mother." Her eyes clouded again. "Mother thinks he's wonderful."

"She does?"

"Yes."

"Well, well!" said Mr. Potter.

Bobbie brooded. "He's a Member of Parliament, you know."

"Yes."

"And they say he may be in the Cabinet any day."

"So he gave me to understand."

"And all that sort of thing is very bad for a man, don't you think? I mean, it seems to make him so starchy."

"The very word."

"And pompous."

"The exact adjective I would have selected," agreed Mr. Potter. "In our frequent conversations, before you arrived, he addressed me as if I were a half-witted deputation of his constituents."

"Did you see much of him before I came?"

"A great deal, though I did my best to avoid him."

"He's a difficult man to avoid."

"Yes." Mr. Potter chuckled sheepishly. "Shall I tell you something that happened a day or two ago? You must not let it go any farther, of course. I was coming out of the smoking-room one morning, and I saw him approaching me along the passage. So —so I jumped back and—ha, ha!—hid in a small cupboard."

"Jolly sensible."

"Yes. But unfortunately he opened the cupboard door and discovered me. It was exceedingly embarrassing."

"What did you say?"

"There was nothing much I could say. I'm afraid he must have thought me out of my senses."

"Well, I—All right, mother. Coming."

The rich contralto of a female novelist calling to its young had broken the stillness of the summer afternoon. Mr. Potter looked up with a start. Lady Wickham was on the lawn. It seemed to Mr. Potter that, as his friend moved towards her, something of the springiness had gone out of her. It was as if she moved reluctantly.

"Where have you been, Roberta?" asked Lady Wickham, as her daughter came within earshot of the normal tone of voice. "I have been looking everywhere for you."

"Anything special, mother?"

"Mr. Gandle wants to go to Hertford. He has to get some books. I think you had better drive him in your car."

"Oh, mother!"

Mr. Potter, watching from his chair, observed a peculiar expression flit into Lady Wickham's face. Had he been her English publisher, instead of merely her prospective American publisher, he would have been familiar with that look. It meant that Lady Wickham was preparing to excercise her celebrated will-power.

"Roberta," she said, with dangerous quiet, "I particularly wish you to drive Mr. Gandle to Hertford."

"But I had promised to go over and play tennis at the Crufts'."

"Mr. Gandle is a much better companion for you than a young waster like Algy Crufts. You must run over and tell him that you cannot play today."

A few minutes later a natty two-seater drew up at the front door of the Crufts' residence down the road; and Bobbie Wickham, seated at the wheel, gave tongue.

"Algy!"

The flannel-clad form of Algernon Crufts appeared at a window. "Hullo! Down in a jiffy."

There was an interval. Then Mr. Crufts joined her. "Hullo! I say, you haven't brought your racket, you poor chump," he said.

"Tennis is off," announced Bobbie briefly. "I've got to drive

Clifford Gandle in to Hertford." She paused. "I say, Algy, shall I tell you something?"

"What?"

"Between ourselves."

"Absolutely."

"Mother wants me to marry Clifford Gandle."

Algy Crufts uttered a strangled exclamation. Such was his emotion he nearly swallowed eight inches of his cigarette-holder.

"Marry Clifford Gandle!"

"Yes. She's all for it. She says he would have a steadying influence on me."

"Ghastly! Take my advice and give the project the most absolute go-by. I was up at Oxford with the man. A blighter, if ever there was one. He was President of the Union and all sorts of frightful things."

"It's all very awkward. I don't know what to do."

"Kick him and tell him to go to blazes. That's the procedure."

"But it's so hard not to do anything mother wants you to do. You know mother."

"I do," said Mr. Crufts, who did.

"Oh, well," said Bobbie, "you never know. There's always the chance that she may take a sudden dislike to him for some reason or other. She does take sudden dislikes to people."

"She does," said Mr. Crufts. Lady Wickham had disliked him at first sight.

"Well, let's hope she will suddenly dislike Clifford Gandle. But I don't mind telling you, Algy, things are looking pretty black."

"Keep smiling," urged Mr. Crufts.

"What's the good of smiling, fathead?" said Bobbie morosely.

Night had fallen on Skeldings Hall. Lady Wickham was in her study, thinking those great thoughts which would subsequently be copyrighted in all languages, including the Scandinavian. Bobbie was strolling somewhere in the grounds, having eluded Mr. Gandle after dinner. And Mr. Gandle, baffled but not defeated, had donned a light overcoat and gone out to try to find Bobbie.

As for Mr. Potter, he was luxuriating in restful solitude in a punt under a willow by the bank of the moat.

From the first moment he had set eyes on it, Hamilton Potter had loved the moat at Skeldings Hall. Here, by the willow, it broadened out almost into the dimensions of a lake; and there was in the glitter of stars on its surface and the sleepy rustling of birds in the trees along its bank something infinitely soothing. The healing darkness wrapped the publisher about like a blanket; the cool night-wind fanned caressingly a forehead a little heated by Lady Wickham's fine old port; and gradually, lulled by the beauty of the scene, Mr. Potter allowed himself to float into one of those reveries which come to publishers at moments such as this.

He mused on jackets and remainders and modes of distribution; on royalties and advertisements and spring lists and booksellers' discounts. And his random thoughts, like fleeting thistledown, had just drifted to the question of the growing price of pulp-paper, when from somewhere near by there came the sound of a voice, jerking him back to the world again.

"Oh, let the solid ground not fail beneath my feet before that I have found what some have found so sweet," said the voice.

A moderate request, one would have supposed; and yet it irritated Mr. Potter like the bite of a mosquito. For the voice was the voice of Clifford Gandle.

"Robertah," proceeded the voice, and Mr. Potter breathed again. He had taken it for granted the man had perceived and was addressing him. He gathered his presence had not been discovered.

"Robertah," said Mr. Gandle, "surely you cannot have been blind to the na-chah of my feelings? Surely you must have guessed that it was love that—"

Hamilton Potter congealed into a solid mass of frozen horror.

He was listening-in on a proposal of marriage.

The emotions of any delicate-minded man who finds himself in such a position cannot fail to be uncomfortable; and the greater his delicacy of mind the more acute must the discomfort be. Mr. Potter, being, as are all publishers, more like a shrinking violet than anything else in the world, nearly swooned. His scalp tingled; his jaw fell; and his toes began to open and shut like poppet-valves.

"Heart of my heart—" said Mr. Gandle.

Mr. Potter gave a convulsive shudder. And the punt-pole, which had been resting on the edge of the boat, clattered down with a noise like a machine-gun.

There was a throbbing silence. Then Mr. Gandle spoke sharply.

"Is anybody they-ah?"

There are situations in which a publisher can do only one thing. Raising himself noiselessly, Mr. Potter wriggled to the side of the punt and lowered himself into the water.

"Who is they-ah?"

Mr. Potter with a strong effort shut his mouth, which was trying to emit a howl of anguish. He had never supposed that water could be so cold. Silently he waded out towards the opposite bank. The only thing that offered any balm in this black moment was the recollection that his hostess had informed him that the moat was not more than four feet deep.

But what Lady Wickham had omitted to inform him was that in one or two places there were ten-foot holes. It came, therefore, as a suprise to Mr. Potter, when, after he had travelled some six yards, there happened to him that precise disaster which Mr. Gandle, in his recent remarks, had expressed himself as so desirous of avoiding. As the publisher took his next step forward, the solid ground failed beneath his feet.

"Oosh!" ejaculated Mr. Potter.

Clifford Gandle was a man of swift intuition. Hearing the cry and becoming aware at the same time of loud splashing noises, he guessed in one masterly flash of inductive reasoning that someone had fallen in. He charged down the bank and perceived the punt. He got into the punt. Bobbie Wickham got into the punt. Mr. Gandle seized the pole and propelled the punt out into the waters.

"Are you they-ah?" inquired Mr. Gandle.

"Glub!" exclaimed Mr. Potter.

"I see him," said Bobbie. "More to the left."

Clifford Gandle drove the rescuing craft more to the left, and was just digging the pole into the water when Mr. Potter, coming up for the third time, found it within his reach. The partiality of drowning men for straws is proverbial; but, as a class, they are broad-minded and will clutch at punt-poles with equal readiness. Mr. Potter seized the pole and pulled strongly; and Clifford Gandle, who happened to be leaning his whole weight on it at the moment, was not proof against what practically amounted to a formal invitation. A moment later he had joined Mr. Potter in the depths.

Bobbie Wickham rescued the punt-pole, which was floating away on the tide, and peered down through the darkness. Stirring things were happening below. Clifford Gandle had grasped Mr. Potter. Mr. Potter had grasped Clifford Gandle. And Bobbie, watching from above, was irresistibly reminded of a picture she had seen in her childhood of alligators fighting in the River Hooghly. She raised the pole, and, with the best intentions, prodded at the tangled mass.

The treatment proved effective. The pole, taking Clifford Gandle shrewdly in the stomach, caused him to release his grip on Mr. Potter; and Mr. Potter, suddenly discovering that he was in shallow water again, did not hesitate. By the time Clifford Gandle had scrambled into the punt he was on dry land, squelching rapidly towards the house.

A silence followed his departure. Then Mr. Gandle, expelling the last pint of water from his mouth, gave judgment.

"The man must be mad!"

He found more water he had overlooked, and replaced it.

"Stark, staring mad!" he repeated. "He must have deliberately flung himself in."

Bobbie Wickham was gazing out into the night; and, had the visibility been better, her companion might have observed in her expression the raptness of inspiration.

"There is no other explanation. The punt was they-ah, by the bank, and he was hee-yah, right out in the middle of the moat. I've suspected for days that he was unbalanced. Once I found him hiding in a cupboard. Crouching there with a wild gleam in his eyes. And that brooding look of his. That strange brooding look. I've noticed it every time I've been talking to him."

Bobbie broke the silence, speaking in a low, grave voice.

"Didn't you know about poor Mr. Potter?"

"Eh?"

"That he had suicidal mania?"

Clifford Gandle drew in his breath sharply.

"You can't blame him," said Bobbie. "How would you feel if you came home one day and found your wife and your two brothers and a cousin sitting round the dinner-table stone dead?"

"What!"

"Poisoned. Something in the curry." She shivered. "This morning I found him gloating over a book called *Ethics of Suicide*."

Clifford Gandle ran his fingers through his dripping hair.

"Something ought to be done!"

"What can you do? The thing isn't supposed to be known. If you mention it to him, he will simply go away; and then mother will be furious, because she wants him to publish her books in America."

"I shall keep the closest watch on the man."

"Yes, that's the thing to do," agreed Bobbie.

She pushed the punt to the shore. Mr. Gandle, who had begun

to feel chilly, leaped out and sped to the house to change his clothes. Bobbie, following at a more leisurely pace, found her mother standing outside her study. Lady Wickham's manner was perturbed.

"Roberta!"

"Yes, mother?"

"What in the world had been happening? A few moments ago Mr. Potter ran past my door, dripping wet. And now Clifford Gandle has just gone by, also soaked. What have they been doing?"

"Fighting in the moat, mother."

"Fighting in the moat? What do you mean?"

"Mr. Potter jumped in to try and get away from Mr. Gandle, and then Mr. Gandle went in after him and seized him round the neck, and they grappled together for quite a long time, struggling furiously. I think they must have had a quarrel."

"What on earth would they quarrel about?"

"Well, you know what a violent man Clifford Gandle is."

This was an aspect of Mr. Gandle's character which Lady Wickham had not perceived. She opened her penetrating eyes.

"Clifford Gandle violent?"

"I think he's the sort who takes sudden dislikes to people."

"Nonsense!"

"Well, it all seems very queer to me," said Bobbie.

She passed on her way upstairs; and, reaching the first landing, turned down the corridor till she came to the principal guest-room. She knocked delicately. There were movements, and the door opened, revealing Hamilton Potter in a flowered dressing-gown.

"Thank Heaven you're safe!" said Bobbie.

The fervour of her tone touched Mr. Potter. His heart warmed to the child.

"If I hadn't been there when Mr. Gandle was trying to drown you—"

Mr. Potter started violently.

"Trying to drown me?" he gasped.

Bobbie's eyebrows rose.

"Hasn't anybody told you about Mr. Gandle—warned you? Didn't you know he was one of the mad Gandles?"

"The—the—"

"Mad Gandles. You know what some of these very old English families are like. All Gandles have been mad for generations back."

"You don't mean—you can't mean—" Mr. Potter gulped. "You can't mean that Mr. Gandle is homicidal?"

"Not normally. But he takes sudden dislikes to people."

"I think he likes me," said Mr. Potter with a certain nervous satisfaction. "He has made a point of seeking me out and giving me his views on—er—various matters."

"Did you ever yawn while he was doing it?"

Mr. Potter blenched.

"Would—would he mind that very much?"

"Mind it! You lock your door at night, don't you, Mr. Potter?"

"But this is terrible."

"He sleeps in this corridor."

"But why is the man at large?"

"He hasn't done anything yet. You can't shut a man up till he had done something."

"Does Lady Wickham know of this?"

"For goodness' sake don't say a word to mother. It would only make her nervous. Everything will be quite all right, if you're only careful. You had better try not to let him get you alone."

"Yes," said Mr. Potter.

The last of the mad Gandles, meanwhile, having peeled off the dress-clothes moistened during the recent water-carnival, had draped his bony form in a suit of orange-coloured pyjamas, and was now devoting the full force of a legislator's mind to the situation which had arisen.

He was a long, thin young man with a curved nose which even in his lighter moments gave him the appearance of disapproving things in general; and there had been nothing in the events of the last hour to cause any diminution of this look of disapproval. For we cannot in fairness but admit that, if ever a mad Gandle had good reason to be mad, Clifford Gandle had at this juncture. He had been interrupted at the crucial point of proposal of marriage. He had been plunged into water and prodded with a punt-pole. He had sown the seeds of a cold in the head. And he fancied he had swallowed a newt. These things do not conduce to sunniness in a man.

Nor did an inspection of the future do anything to remove his gloom. He had come to Skeldings for rest and recuperation after the labours of an exhausting Session, and now it seemed that, instead of passing his time pleasantly in the society of Roberta Wickham, he would be compelled to devote himself to acting as a guardian to a misguided publisher.

It was not as if he liked publishers, either. His relations with Prodder and Wiggs, who had sold forty-three copies of his book of political essays—*Watchman, What of the Night?*—had not been agreeable.

Nevertheless, this last of the Gandles was a conscientious man. He had no intention of shirking the call of duty. The question of whether it was worth while preventing a publisher committing suicide did not present itself to him.

That was why Bobbie's note, when he read it, produced such immediate results.

Exactly when the missive had been delivered, Clifford Gandle could not say. Much thought had rendered him distrait, and the rustle of the paper as it was thrust under his door did not reach his consciousness. It was only when, after a considerable time, he rose with the intention of going to bed that he perceived lying on the floor an envelope.

He stooped and picked it up. He examined it with a thoughtful stare. He opened it.

The letter was brief. It ran as follows:—

"What about his razors?"

A thrill of dismay shot though him.

Razors! He had forgotten them.

Clifford Gandle did not delay. Already it might be he was too late. He hurried down the passage and tapped at Mr. Potter's door.

"Who's there?"

Clifford Gandle was relieved. He was in time.

"Can I come in?"

"Who is that?"

"Gandle."

"What do you want?"

"Can you—er—lend me a razah?"

"A what?"

"A razah."

There followed a complete silence from within. Mr. Gandle tapped again.

"Are you they-ah?"

The silence was broken by an odd rumbling sound. Something heavy knocked against the woodwork. But that the explanation seemed so improbable, Mr. Gandle would have said that this peculiar publisher had pushed a chest of drawers against the door.

"Mr. Pottah!"

More silence.

"Are you they-ah, Mr. Pottah?"

Additional stillness. Mr. Gandle, wearying of a profitless vigil, gave the thing up and returned to his room.

The task that lay before him, he now realized, was to wait awhile and then make his way along the balcony which joined the windows of the two rooms; enter while the other slept, and abstract his weapon or weapons.

He looked at his watch. The hour was close on midnight. He decided to give Mr. Potter till two o'clock.

Clifford Gandle sat down to wait.

Mr. Potter's first action, after the retreating footsteps had told him that his visitor had gone, was to extract a couple of nerve pills from the box by his bed and swallow them. This was a rite which, by the orders of his medical adviser, he had performed thrice a day since leaving America—once half an hour before breakfast, once an hour before luncheon, and again on retiring to rest.

In spite of the fact that he now consumed these pills, it seemed to Mr. Potter that he could scarcely be described as retiring to rest. After the recent ghastly proof of Clifford Gandle's insane malevolence, he could not bring himself to hope that even the most fitful slumber would come to him this night. The horror of the thought of that awful man padding softly to his door and asking for razors chilled Hamilton Potter to the bone.

Nevertheless, he did his best. He switched off the light and, closing his eyes, began to repeat in a soft undertone a formula which he had often found efficacious.

"Day by day," murmured Mr. Potter, "in every way, I am getting better and better. Day by day, in every way, I am getting better and better."

It would have astonished Clifford Gandle, yawning in his room down the corridor, if he could have heard such optimistic sentiments proceeding from those lips.

"Day by day, in every way, I am getting better and better."

Mr. Potter's mind performed an unfortunate sideslip. He lay there tingling. Suppose he *was* getting better and better, what of it? What was the use of getting better and better if at any moment a mad Gandle might spring out with a razor and end it all?

He forced his thoughts away from these uncomfortable channels. He clenched his teeth and whispered through them with a touch of defiance.

"Day by day, in every way, I am getting better and better. Day by day, in every way—"

A pleasant drowsiness stole over Mr. Potter.

"Day by day, in every way," he murmured, "I am getting better and better. Day by day, in every way, I am betting getter and getter. Bay by day, in every way, I am betting getter and wetter. Way by day—"

Mr. Potter slept.

Over the stables the clock chimed the hour of two, and Clifford Gandle stepped out onto the balcony.

It had been well said by many thinkers that in human affairs you can never be certain that some little trifling obstacle will not undo the best-laid of schemes. It was the sunken road at Hougomont that undid the French cavalry at Waterloo, and it was something very similar that caused Clifford Gandle's plan of action to go wrong now—a jug of water, to wit, which the maid who had brought Mr. Potter's hot-water can before dinner had placed immediately beneath the window.

Clifford Gandle, insinuating himself with the extreme of caution through the window and finding his foot resting on something hard, assumed that he was touching the floor, and permitted his full weight to rest upon that foot. Almost immediately afterwards the world collapsed with a crash and a deluge of water; and light, flooding the room, showed Mr. Potter sitting up in bed, blinking.

Mr. Potter stared at Gandle. Clifford Gandle stared at Potter.

"Er—hullo!" said Clifford Gandle.

Mr. Potter uttered a low, curious sound like a cat with a fish-bone in its throat.

"I—er—just looked in," said Clifford Gandle.

Mr. Potter made a noise like a second and slightly larger cat with another fish-bone in its throat.

"I've come for the razah," said Clifford Gandle. "Ah, there it is," he said, and, moving towards the dressing-table, secured it.

Mr. Potter leaped from his bed. He looked about him for a weapon. The only one appeared to be the typescript of *Ethics of Suicide*, and that, while it would have made an admirable instrument for swatting flies, was far too flimsy for the present crisis. All in all, it began to look to Mr. Potter like a sticky evening.

"Good night," said Clifford Gandle.

Mr. Potter was amazed to see that his visitor was withdrawing towards the window. It seemed incredible. He wondered whether Bobbie Wickham had not made some mistake about this man. Nothing could be more temperate than his behaviour at the moment.

And then, as he reached the window, Clifford Gandle smiled, and all Mr. Potter's fears leaped into being again.

The opinion of Clifford Gandle regarding this smile was that it was one of those kindly, reassuring smiles—the sort of smile to put the most nervous melancholiac at his ease. To Mr. Potter it seemed precisely the kind of maniac grin which he would have expected from such a source.

"Good night," said Clifford Gandle.

He smiled again, and was gone. And Mr. Potter, having stood rooted to the spot for some minutes, crossed the floor and closed the window. He then bolted the window. He perceived a pair of shutters, and shut them. He moved the washhand-stand till it rested against the shutters. He placed two chairs and a small bookcase against the washhand-stand. Then he went to bed, leaving the light burning.

"Day by day, in every way," said Mr. Potter, "I am getting better and better."

But his voice lacked the ring of true conviction.

Sunshine filtering in through the shutters, and the song of birds busy in the ivy outside his window, woke Mr. Potter at an early hour next morning; but it was some time before he could bring himself to spring from his bed to greet another day. His disturbed night had left him heavy and lethargic. When finally he had summoned up the energy to rise and remove the zareba in front of the window and open the shutters, he became aware that a glorious morning was upon the world. The samples of sunlight that had crept into the room had indicated only feebly the golden wealth without.

But there was no corresponding sunshine in Mr. Potter's heart. Spiritually as well as physically he was at a low ebb. The more he examined the position of affairs, the less he liked it. He went down to breakfast in pensive mood.

Breakfast at Skeldings was an informal meal, and visitors were expected to take it when they pleased, irrespective of the movements of their hostess, who was a late riser. In the dining-room, when Mr. Potter entered it, only the daughter of the house was present.

Bobbie was reading the morning paper. She nodded cheerfully to him over its top.

"Good morning, Mr. Potter. I hope you slept well."

Mr. Potter winced. "Miss Wickham," he said, "last night an appalling thing occurred."

A startled look came into Bobbie's eyes.

"You don't mean—Mr. Gandle?"

"Yes."

"Oh, Mr. Potter, what?"

"Just as I was going to bed, the man knocked at my door and asked if he could borrow my razah—I mean my razor."

"You didn't lend it to him?"

"No, I did not," replied Mr. Potter, with a touch of asperity. "I barricaded the door."

"How wise of you!"

"And at two in the morning he came in through the window!"

"How horrible!"

"He took my razor. Why he did not attack me, I cannot say. But, having obtained it, he grinned at me in a ghastly way and went out."

There was silence.

"Have an egg or something," said Bobbie, in a hushed voice.

"Thank you, I will take a little ham," whispered Mr. Potter.

There was another silence.

"I'm afraid," said Bobbie at length, "you will have to go."

"That is what I think."

"It is quite evident that Mr. Gandle has taken one of his uncontrollable dislikes to you."

"Yes."

"What I think you ought to do is to leave quite quietly, without saying good-bye or anything, so that he won't know where you've gone and won't be able to follow you. You could write mother a letter, saying you had to go because of Mr. Gandle's persecution."

"Exactly."

"You needn't say anything about his being mad. She knows. Just say that he ducked you in the moat and came into your room at two in the morning and made faces at you. She will understand."

"Yes. I—"

"Hush!"

Clifford Gandle came into the room.

"Good morning," said Bobbie.

"Good morning," said Mr. Gandle.

He helped himself to poached egg; and, glancing across the table at the publisher, was concerned to note how wan and sombre was his aspect. If ever a man looked as if he were on the verge of putting an end to everything, that man was John Hamilton Potter.

Clifford Gandle was not feeling particularly festive himself at the moment, for he was a man who depended greatly for his well-being on a placid eight hours of sleep; but he exerted himself to be bright and optimistic.

"What a lovely morning!" he trilled.

"Yes," said Mr. Potter.

"Surely such weather is enough to make any man happy and satisfied with life."

"Yes," said Mr. Potter doubtfully.

"Who, with all Na-chah smiling, could seriously contemplate removing himself from so bright a world?"

"George Philibert, of 32, Acacia Road, Cricklewood, did," said Bobbie, who had resumed her study of the paper.

"Eh?" said Mr. Gandle.

"George Philibert, of 32, Acacia Road, Cricklewood, was had up before the beak yesterday, charged with attempted suicide. He stated that—"

Mr. Gandle cast a reproachful look at her. He had always supposed Roberta Wickham to be a girl of fair intelligence, as women go; and it seemed to him that he had over-estimated her good sense. He did his best to cover up her blunder.

"Possibly," he said, "with some really definite and serious reason—"

"I can never understand," said Mr. Potter, coming out of what had all the outward appearance of a trance, "why the idea arose that suicide is wrong."

He spoke with a curious intensity. The author of *Ethics of Suicide* had wielded a plausible pen, and the subject was one on which he now held strong views. And, even if he had not already held them, his mood was of a kind to breed them in his bosom.

"The author of a very interesting book which I intend to publish shortly," he said, "points out that none but the votaries of the monotheistic religions look upon suicide as a crime."

"Yes, said Mr. Gandle, "but—"

"If, he goes on to say, the criminal law forbids suicide, that is not an argument valid in the Church. And, besides, the prohibition is ridiculous, for what penalty can frighten a man who is not afraid of death itself?"

"George Philibert got fourteen days," said Bobbie.

"Yes, but—" said Mr. Gandle.

"The ancients were very far from regarding the matter in the modern light. Indeed, in Massilia and on the island of Cos, the man who could give valid reasons for relinquishing his life was handed the cup of hemlock by the magistrate, and that, too, in public."

"Yes, but—"

"And why," said Mr. Potter, "suicide should be regarded as cowardly is beyond me. Surely no man who had not an iron nerve—"

He broke off. The last two words had tapped a chord in his memory. Abruptly it occurred to him that here he was, half-way through breakfast, and he had not taken those iron nerve-pills which his doctor had so strictly ordered him to swallow thirty minutes before the morning meal.

"Yes," said Mr. Gandle. He lowered his cup, and looked across the table. "But—"

His voice died away. He sat staring before him in horror-struck silence. Mr. Potter, with a strange, wild look in his eyes, was in the act of raising to his lips a sinister-looking white pellet. And, as Mr. Gandle gazed, the wretched man's lips closed over the horrid thing and a movement of his Adam's apple showed the deed was done.

"Surely," said Mr. Potter, "no man who—"

It seemed that Fate was inflexibly bent on preventing him from finishing that particular sentence this morning. For he had got thus far when Clifford Gandle, seizing the mustard-pot, rose with a maniac screech and bounded, wild-eyed, round the table at him.

Lady Wickham came downstairs and made her way like a stately galleon under sail towards the dining-room. Unlike others of the household, she was feeling particularly cheerful this morning. She liked fine weather, and the day was unusually fine. Also, she had resolved that after breakfast she would take Mr. Potter aside and use the full force of her commanding personality to extract from him something in the nature of an informal contract.

She would not, she decided, demand too much at first. If he would consent to undertake the American publication of *Agatha's Vow, A Strong Man's Love,* and—possibly—*A Man for A' That,* she would be willing to postpone discussion of *Meadowsweet, Fetters of Fate,* and the rest of her works. But if he thought he could eat her bread and salt and sidestep *Agatha's Vow,* he had grievously under-estimated the power of her cold grey eye when it came to sub-duing such members of the animal kingdom as publishers.

There was a happy smile, therefore, on Lady Wickham's face as she entered the room. She was not actually singing, but she stopped only just short of it.

She was surprised to find that, except for her daughter Roberta, the dining-room was empty.

"Good morning, mother," said Bobbie.

"Good morning. Has Mr. Potter finished his breakfast?"

Bobbie considered the question.

"I don't know if he had actually finished," she said. "But he didn't seem to want any more."

"Where is he?"

"I don't know, mother."

"When did he go?"

"He's only just left."

"I didn't meet him."

"He went out of the window."

The sunshine faded from Lady Wickham's face.

"Out of the window? Why?"

"I think because Clifford Gandle was between him and the door."

"What do you mean? Where is Clifford Gandle?"

"I don't know, mother. He went out of the window, too. They were both running down the drive when I last saw them." Bobbie's face grew pensive. "Mother, I've been thinking," she said. "Are you really sure that Clifford Gandle would be such a steadying influence for me? He seems to me rather eccentric."

"I cannot understand a word of what you are saying."

"Well, he is eccentric. At two o'clock this morning, Mr. Potter told me, he climbed in through Mr. Potter's window, made faces at him, and climbed out again. And just now—"

"Made faces at Mr. Potter?"

"Yes, mother. And just now Mr. Potter was peacefully eating his breakfast, when Clifford Gandle suddenly uttered a loud cry and sprang at him. Mr. Potter jumped out of the window and Clifford Gandle jumped out after him and chased him down the drive. I thought Mr. Potter ran awfully well for an elderly man, but that sort of thing can't be good for him in the middle of breakfast."

Lady Wickham subsided into a chair. "Is everybody mad?"

"I think Clifford Gandle must be. You know, these men who do wonderful things at the University often do crack up suddenly. I was reading a case only yesterday about a man in America. He took every possible prize at Harvard or wherever it was, and then, just as everybody was predicting the most splendid future for him, he bit his aunt. He—"

"Go and find Mr. Potter," cried Lady Wickham. "I must speak to him."

"I'll try. But it won't be easy. I think he's gone for good."

Lady Wickham uttered a bereaved cry, such as a tigress might who sees its prey snatched from it.

"Gone!"

"He told me he was thinking of going. He said he couldn't stand

Clifford Gandle's persecution any longer. And that was before breakfast, so I don't suppose he has changed his mind. I think he means to go on running."

A sigh like the whistling of the wind through the cracks in a broken heart escaped Lady Wickham.

"Mother," said Bobbie, "I've something to tell you. Last night Clifford Gandle asked me to marry him. I hadn't time to answer one way or the other, because just after he had proposed he jumped into the moat and tried to drown Mr. Potter; but if you really think he would be a steadying influence for me—"

Lady Wickham uttered a snort of agony.

"I forbid you to dream of marrying this man!"

"Very well, mother," said Bobbie dutifully. She rose and moved to the sideboard. "Would you like an egg, mother?"

"No!"

"Some ham?"

"No!"

"Very well." Bobbie paused at the door. "Don't you think it would be a good idea," she said, "if I were to go and find Clifford Gandle and tell him to pack up and go away? I'm sure you won't like having him about after this."

Lady Wickham's eyes flashed fire.

"If that man dares come back, I'll—I'll—Yes. Tell him to go. Tell him to go away and never let me set eyes on him again."

"Very well, mother," said Bobbie.

The Medicine Girl

————— • —————

The eighteenth hole at Bingley-on-Sea, that golfers' mecca on the south coast of England, is one of those freak holes—a very short mashie shot up a very steep hill off a tee screened from the clubhouse by a belt of trees. From the terrace, where the stout man in the vivid plus fours stood waiting for his partner to arrive for the morning round, only the green was visible.

On this green, falling from the sky in a perfect arc, there suddenly descended a white ball. It struck the ground, took a backspin, and rolled to within a foot of the hole.

The stout man congealed like one who has seen a vision. So might a knight of the Middle Ages have looked, on beholding the Holy Grail. He had been at Bingley only two days, and so had played this hole only six times; but he knew that if he played it for the rest of his life he would never get a two on it, as this unseen expert was so obviously about to do. Four was Sir Hugo Drake's best —his worst twenty-seven, on the occasion when he overran the green and got imbedded in a sort of Sahara which lay beyond it.

A player like this, he decided, demanded inspection at close range. Possibly it was the pro, taking a little practice; but even the pro might reasonably expect homage after such a shot. Sir Hugo toddled over to the green; and, having reached it and peered into the depths, stood stunned with amazement.

It was not the pro. It was not a man at all. It was a girl—and a small girl, at that. That she was also extremely pretty seemed of slight importance to Sir Hugo. He was not a man who paid much attention to a woman's looks. What mattered to him was that he stood in the presence of a female who could handle a mashie like

225

that. And being a man who liked to give credit where credit is due, he said so.

"My dear young lady," puffed Sir Hugo, "that was an extraordinarily fine stroke."

"Thank you."

"Where on earth did you learn to play like that?" asked Sir Hugo reverently.

"At Garden City, mostly."

The name was new to Sir Hugo.

"Garden City?"

"It's outside New York."

"Oh?" Sir Hugo was enlightened. He had a deep respect for transatlantic golf. "You come from America?"

"Yes. I've been in London about two years. I'm surprised my game hasn't gone off more. I don't get much time for playing."

Sir Hugo sighed.

"Nor do I," he replied sadly. "A busy specialist, you know... They keep one's nose pretty tightly to the grindstone."

"A specialist?" The girl seemed suddenly interested. "What sort of specialist?"

"Nerves."

"Really?"

"Drake's my name: Sir Hugo Drake."

The girl's interest was now unmistakable. She beamed.

"Fancy!" she said. "I thought your last book was wonderful. This is a proud moment for a mere general practitioner, Sir Hugo."

"A what?"

"A general practitioner. I'm one."

Sir Hugo gaped.

"Good God! You're not a doctor?"

"Yes, I am. Smith. Sally Smith. Doctor Sally Smith."

"Good God!" exclaimed Sir Hugo again.

The suspicion of a shadow passed over the girl's face. She was

always meeting men who exclaimed "Good God!" or its equivalent when informed of her profession, and she disliked it. It seemed
to her that they said it in the voice a small boy would use on being
introduced to a circus freak. The male mind did not appear to be
able to grasp immediately the fact that a woman doctor need not
of necessity be a gargoyle with steel-rimmed spectacles and a wash-
leather complexion.

However, this was a nice old man, so she decided not to bite
his head off.

"I suppose it does seem funny," she said. "But there it is."

"Funny?" said Sir Hugo, recovering. "Not at all. Certainly not.
Quite the contrary."

"I like being a doctor, and it doesn't do anybody any harm—at
least, I've never killed a patient yet—so what I say to myself is,
why not?"

"Quite," said Sir Hugo. "Why not? Precisely. Very sensible."

The girl tapped her ball into the hole and picked it up.

"Nice course, this," she said.

"Very," said Sir Hugo. "Are you making a long stay?"

"Just a two weeks' vacation. Are you here for long?"

Sir Hugo Drake had now come to look upon this girl as a soul
mate. A member of his own profession and a golfer capable of a
two on the eighteenth, she deserved, he felt, his full confidence.
He was not a man who, as a rule, discussed his private affairs with
strangers, but he could not bring himself to regard as a stranger
a girl so outstanding at the short mashie shot.

"I don't know how long I'm going to be here," he confided. "The
fact is, I'm looking for my nephew."

"Have you lost him?" Sally asked, surprised.

"He's given me the slip," said Sir Hugo, turning a deeper mauve,
for the affair had caused him much annoyance. "He was living
quietly in the country, down in Hampshire, and he came up to
London, and suddenly he disappeared from London, and I met

a man who said he had seen him down here—in company," said Sir Hugo, lowering his voice to a portentous whisper, "with a female of flashy appearance."

Sally smiled.

"Not me," she said.

"I wish it had been you," said Sir Hugo devoutly. "If he would only have the sense to fall in love with a nice girl like you, I could be easier in my mind."

"You shouldn't worry."

"But I do worry," said Sir Hugo vehemently. "His poor mother was my sister, and since her death I have regarded myself *in loco parentis* to the boy. Causes me a great deal of anxiety. Too much money, that's what he's got, and too much time on his hands. When he was at Cambridge, he came within an ace," said Sir Hugo, fixing his companion with a gaze calculated to make the flesh creep, "of marrying a girl in a tobacco shop!"

"Boys will be boys."

"Not while I'm *in loco parentis* to them, they won't," said Sir Hugo stoutly. "The trouble with William is that he's impulsive. Got a habit of falling in love at first sight. I don't know who this flashy female is, but I've come down here to break the thing up and take him back to Woollam Chersey, where he belongs."

"Is that the name of his place in the country?"

"Yes."

"I should have thought he would be safe, living in the country."

"He is. He is safe, while living in the country. But he keeps dashing away from the country and losing his head. Oh well, I mustn't bother you with my troubles. I see my partner looking for me."

He whooped and waved his hand at the terrace. A long, thin man, clad like himself in plus fours of a regrettable pattern, whooped and waved back.

"Hope we shall meet again," he said.

"I hope so," said Sally.

"Give me a lesson, perhaps?"

"I should be delighted."

"Good!" said Sir Hugo, and strode off to the first tee.

On the front—or esplanade—of Bingley-on-Sea stands the Hotel Superba; and at twenty minutes past four the thin mist which had been hanging over the resort since lunchtime disappeared, and there filtered through the windows of Suite Number Seven on the second floor that curious, faint gamboge light which passes for sunshine in England. Its mild rays shone deprecatingly on one of those many-colored carpets peculiar to suites at south-coast hotels; on the engraving of "The Stag at Bay" over the mantelpiece; on the table set for tea; and on Marie, maid to Mrs. Higginbotham, who had just deposited on the table a plate of sandwiches.

In addition to the sunshine, there entered also the strains of a jazz band, presumably from the winter garden below, where Swiss waiters prowled among potted palms, and such of the Superba's guests as wished to do so were encouraged to dance. Carried away by the melody Marie went so far as to dance a step or two herself. And so absorbed was she in this pursuit that a knocking on the outer door did not penetrate to her consciousness.

It got through, however, to Mrs. Higginbotham in the bedroom, and she gave tongue.

"Marie!"

The maid ceased to pirouette. Her employer's voice was one of those which impress themselves on the most preoccupied.

"Yes, moddom?"

"Are you deaf, you poor fish? Somebody at the door."

"Very good, moddom."

Marie opened the door. There was nothing much to reward her for the effort. Merely a man in spats.

"Mrs. Higginbotham in?" asked this individual.

"Yes, sir."

The visitor crossed the threshold. He was an immaculate and yet somehow subtly battered person in the early thirties. He wore a suit of gray material and unimpeachable cut and—until he removed it—a white derby hat. In his right eye there was a monocle, and through this he inspected the tea table. With a slight diminution of what appeared to be a constitutional gloom, he moved towards it and picked up a sandwich.

Mrs. Higginbotham, still a disembodied voice, continued to interest herself in the proceedings.

"Is that you, Bill?"

"It is not Mr. Bannister, moddom. It is—"

Marie looked at the feaster inquiringly. He was now well into his second sandwich, but he could still speak, and did so.

"Lord Tidmouth."

"It is Lord Tidmouth, moddom."

"Who the dickens is Lord Tidmouth?"

The newcomer seemed to feel that he ought to enter into the spirit of this long-distance conversation. He approached the bedroom door.

"What ho within there! Is that Lottie?"

"Who are you?"

"Tidmouth's the name at the present. It was Bixby till I hooked the old title. I don't know if you remember me. We used to be married once."

Evidently Mrs. Higginbotham possessed one of those highly trained memories from which no fact, however trivial, escapes. She uttered a pleased screech.

"Squiffy!"

"That's right."

"Well, I'm blowed! Where did you spring from?"

"Oh, various parts. I've been traveling a lot. Not been in England for some years. I happened to blow down here and saw you going up in the lift—yesterday, that was—and I asked your name and they told me you were staying here. So at the earliest opportunity up I popped."

"Splendid! I'll be out in a minute."

"Right ho. I say, when did you acquire the Higginbotham?"

"About two years ago."

"Is he here?"

"No. Kensal Green Cemetery."

"Oh? Well, see you soon."

Lord Tidmouth wandered back to the table and started on another sandwich.

"I shan't be long now," Mrs. Higginbotham assured him. "I'm just shaving."

"What!"

"My neck, you silly ass."

"Oh!"

"Have a sandwich."

"I am."

"You're what?"

"A sandwich. I mean, I'm having one. And most extraordinarily good they are. Sardine, or my trained senses deceive me."

He tested this theory by taking another, and all doubts were removed.

"Yes," he continued. "Absolutely sardine. Lottie!"

"Hullo?"

"I read an interesting thing in the paper the other day," said Lord Tidmouth. "It appears that the sardine's worst enemy is the halibut, and I give you my word that until I read it I didn't know the sardine *had* an enemy. And I don't mind telling you that my opinion of the halibut has gone down considerably. Very considerably. Fancy anything wanting to bully a sardine. I mean to say. . . ."

He would have proceeded further, but at this moment there was a flash of light in the doorway of the bedroom, and he found himself blinking at one of the most vivid suits of pajamas ever conceived by the diseased mind of a fashionable haberdasher.

"Holy smoke!" he exclaimed. "I mean—well, well, well!"

"Well, well, well!" said Lottie.

"Well, well, well, *well!*" said Lord Tidmouth.

He took her hand in a sort of trance. He was visibly affected. The thought that he had been married to this and had allowed it to get away from him was evidently moving him powerfully. His monocle slipped from his eye and danced madly on the end of its string.

"My gosh!" he said. "Is that how you look?"

"That's how."

"Well, well, well, well, well, *well!*" said Lord Tidmouth.

Lottie moved to the mirror and scrutinised herself in it. She was pleased that her very considerable beauty had won this striking tribute.

"Sit down," she said.

Lord Tidmouth sat down.

"Tell me all," he said.

"All what?"

"All about yourself. Who was the recent Higginbotham?"

"Oh, a man. Very rich, from up north. I met him when I was in *Follow the Girl.* I went back to the stage after you and I parted brass rags. He passed on last July."

"Marry again?"

"Ass! If I had, would my name still be Higginbotham?"

"Something in that," agreed his lordship.

"I mean, a girl doesn't call herself Higginbotham unless she has to."

"Absolutely not."

"Still, I *am* sort of engaged."

"Oh?"

"To a man named Bannister. Bill Bannister. Country squire sort of chap. Has a big place in Hampshire. Woollam Chersey it's called."

"What!" Lord Tidmouth's manner became almost animated. "Bill Bannister? One of my oldest pals. I'd like to see old Bill again."

"Well, you will, if you stick around. He's calling soon to take me to dance. Tell me about yourself."

"Oh, I've just been mooching round."

"Did *you* marry again?"

"Oh, yes, here and there. My second wife ran away with a Frenchman."

"Did you get a divorce?"

"Yes, and married again. My third wife ran away with a Spaniard."

"Too bad."

"When I married my fourth wife..."

"Who did she run away with?"

"A Brazilian."

"Your home during the last few years seems to have been a sort of meeting place of the nations."

"Yes."

"How many wives have you got now?"

"None at the moment. The supply has sort of petered out. By the way, talking of wives, how do you feel on the subject of rocking horses?"

"What on earth are you talking about?"

"You see, tomorrow is my second wife's first son's third birthday, and I've just bought him a rocking horse."

"You still keep up with them, then?"

"Oh, a fellow has to be civil. Anyway, I've just bought this rocking horse, and I told the man to send it round here till my train went. You don't mind?"

"Of course not."

"Thanks."

There was a pause. The jazz band below had now begun to play a waltz of a singularly glutinous nature. Its effect on the pair in the sitting room seemed to be to induce a certain sentimentality.

"Odd," said Lord Tidmouth.

"What's odd?"

"Meeting again like this after all these years."

"Yes."

There was another pause.

"Dancing much these days?" asked Lord Tidmouth.

"Quite a lot."

"Why not a spot now? Music and everything."

"That's an idea."

They started to dance, and Lord Tidmouth's emotion appeared to deepen. He sighed once or twice.

"Good tune."

"Topping."

Into the rather fishlike eyes of Lord Tidmouth there had begun to creep a strange light, indicative of a brain at work. He was not a man who often thought, but he was thinking now. And what he was thinking was that, conditions having placed such an action within the sphere of practical politics, it would be silly not to kiss this girl. Here she was, he meant to say, within range, as it were, and...well, to put it in a nutshell, how about it?

He kissed her.

And, as he did so, the door opened and there appeared on the threshold a large young man in a flannel suit. His agreeable face, at the moment of his entry, had been wearing a rather preoccupied look. This, as he observed the entwined couple before him, changed to one of disapproval. He eyed them in silence for a space, then in a cold voice he said:

"Good afternoon!"

The effect of these words on the tender scene was immediate. It broke it up like a bomb. Lord Tidmouth released his erstwhile helpmeet and straightened his tie. Lottie bit her tongue.

There was one of those embarrassing pauses.

"I didn't hear you come in," said Lottie.

"So I imagined," said Bill Bannister.

Silence fell again. It was not one of those episodes about which there is much to be said. It impeded rather than inspired conversation.

"Well, I'll go and get dressed," said Lottie.

"I should," said Bill.

Lord Tidmouth, during these exchanges, had been directing at his long-lost friend a look in which remorse and brotherly love were nicely blended. Remorse now faded, and brotherly love had the field to itself. Bill, turning to deal with this cuckoo in the nest, was surprised to observe him advancing with outstretched hand.

"Bill, old man!" said Lord Tidmouth emotionally.

"Eh?" said Bill, at a loss.

Lord Tidmouth sighed.

"Have you really forgotten me, Bill?" he said sadly. "Your ancient pal? Well, well, well! Name of Tidmouth. Used to be Bixby."

Bill stared.

"It isn't Squiffy?"

"It *is* Squiffy."

"For heaven's sake!"

Complete amiability appeared to reign in young Mr. Bannister's bosom once more. He gripped the outstretched hand warmly.

"Well, I'm dashed."

"Me, too, old boy."

"I haven't seen you for years."

"I haven't seen *you* for years."

They talked for a while of the dear old days, as friends reunited will do.

"I hear you're still living at the old address, Bill," said Lord Tidmouth. "If I hadn't run into you like this, I was going to drop you a line."

"Why not come down there for a bit?" said Bill hospitably.

Lord Tidmouth looked doubtful.

"Well, I'd love to, Bill, old man," he said, "but the fact is—been having domestic troubles of late, and all that—left me a bit on the moody side. I'm more or less of a broken man these days, and don't feel quite up to country-house parties."

"It won't be a country-house party. Just you and me and my uncle."

"Which uncle is that?"

"I've only one. Sir Hugo Drake, the nerve specialist."

"I never met him. Nice chap?"

"Oh, not so bad. He'd be all right if he could get it into his head that I'm a grown-up man and not still a kid in knickerbockers. He will fuss over me like a hen, and it drives me crazy. He has a fit every time I look at a girl. He'd die if he ever saw Lottie."

Lord Tidmouth's manner betrayed a certain embarrassment.

"I say, Bill, old man."

"Hullo?"

Lord Tidmouth coughed.

"Touching on that little contretemps, if I may so express it, which occurred just now, I should like to offer a few simple, manly explanations."

"Oh, don't apologise."

"Carried away, don't you know. What with the music and the sardine sandwiches..."

"That's all right."

"Furthermore, Lottie and I used to be married once, and that forms a sort of bond, if you follow me."

Bill's eyebrows shot up.

"Married?"

"Absolutely married. Long time ago, of course, but somehow the taste still lingered. And when I found her supple form nestling in my arms..."

"Squiffy," said Bill earnestly, "kindly stop apologising. Nothing could have been more fortunate. It gives me a decent excuse for getting out of an entanglement which has been getting on my nerves for weeks. Lottie's a good sort, but she's too—what's the word?"

"Jumpy?"

"Jumpy is right. When you were married to her, Squiffy, did she ever give you the devil?"

"Frequently."

"For no reason?"

"For no reason whatever."

Bill sighed.

"You know how it is, Squiffy."

"How what is, old boy?"

"Well, you meet a girl like Lottie and she sweeps you off your feet. And then...well, then you begin to think a bit."

"I see what you mean."

"Besides..."

Bill paused. He, like Squiffy a short while before, seemed embarrassed. He went to the table and drank cold tea.

"Squiffy..."

"Hullo?"

Bill mused for a moment.

"Squiffy..."

"Yes, old man?"

"Squiffy, have you ever felt a sort of strange emptiness in the heart? A sort of aching void of the soul?"

"Oh, rather."

"What do you do about it?"

"I generally take a couple of cocktails."

Bill shook his head.

"Cocktails aren't any good. Nothing's any good. I've read books, gone in for sport, tried work. No use whatever."

"What sort of work?"

"Stock farming. And what's the result? I have a thousand pigs, and my heart is empty."

"What you want is a tonic."

"No. I know what I want, Squiffy. I want love." Lord Tidmouth, that expert, viewed his friend with concern.

"Don't you believe it! Love? Listen, old boy. The amount of love I've had in the last few years, if placed end to end, would reach from London to Paris. And look at me! Besides, I thought you said you had decided to edge away from Lottie."

"Lottie isn't the right girl for me. A good sort, yes. But not the right girl for me. Now, this other girl..."

"What other girl?"

"This girl I'm telling you about."

"You haven't been telling me about any girl. You haven't so much as mentioned a girl. Do you mean to say..."

Bill nodded.

"Yes, I've found the real thing at last."

Lord Tidmouth was interested. He went to the table and selected a sardine sandwich with quivering fingers.

"Who is she?" he asked.

"I don't know. I've only seen her out on the links. She's a poem, Squiffy—all health and fresh air and wholesomeness."

"Ever spoken to her?"

"No. I hadn't the nerve. She's so far above me."

"Tall girl, eh?"

"Spiritually, you ass."

"Oh, I see."

There was a pause.

"I'm going to get to know her somehow," said Bill at length.

"How?"

"I don't know. But I shall."

"And then?"

"I shall marry her."

Lord Tidmouth breathed reflectively.

"Shortly after my arrival in this room," he said, "Lottie gave me to understand that you were practically engaged to marry *her.*"

"Yes," said Bill unhappily.

"Then, obviously, what you want to do first," said Lord Tidmouth, "is to get it well into Lottie's mind that it's all off."

"I know. But how?"

"It should be done tactfully."

"Of course."

"Gracefully... kindly...leaving no hard feelings. But, nevertheless, quite definitely."

"Yes."

Lord Tidmouth pondered.

"Your best plan, old boy," he said, "is to leave the whole thing to me. I understand women. I know exactly the right things to say. Leave the whole thing absolutely and entirely to me, contenting yourself with just murmuring the necessary responses."

Bill brightened.

"You're sure you can manage it?"

"My dear chap!"

"You'll be tactful?"

"Tactful as dammit. All my wives always raved about my tact. They legged it away from me like rabbits, one after the other, but they always admitted that in the matter of tact I stood alone."

"Well, I'm trusting you."

"And so you may, old boy."

The bedroom door opened, and Lottie appeared, dressed for the dance.

Bill Bannister looked at Lord Tidmouth. He looked appealingly, as a young soldier in a tight place might have looked at Napoleon.

Lord Tidmouth returned the gaze with a reassuring nod and a leave-it-to-me wave of the hand.

"I'm ready," said Lottie.

Lord Tidmouth eyed her owlishly.

"Ready for what, old thing?"

"To dance."

"With Bill?"

"With Bill."

Tact gleamed from Lord Tidmouth's monocle.

"Bill isn't going to dance."

"But he said he would."

"He's made up his mind to stay in."

"Well, I've made up my face to go out."

"Shall I tell you something, Lottie?" said Lord Tidmouth.

"Go ahead."

"Bill's never going to dance with you again. Never, never again. He's going home. Back to Happy Hampshire."

A dangerous gleam appeared in Lottie's beautiful, but formidable eyes. She directed it at her shrinking playmate.

"Is this true, Bill?"

Bill Bannister er-yessed in a small voice. It was not for him to question the methods of a master of tact like Tidmouth, but he could not restrain a feeling that the news might have been broken a little more gently.

"You see," said Bill, "I simply must go home. There's the estate to look after and... Well, that's all there is to it, I think it's time I went home."

"A thousand pigs are pining for him," said Tidmouth.

"Let me get this straight," said Lottie in a strange, tense voice, not unlike that of a tigress from whom some practical joker is endeavouring to steal the daily ration of meat. "Are you leaving me flat?"

Lord Tidmouth was delighted at his former helpmeet's ready

intelligence. Of all his wives, he reflected, Lottie had always been the quickest at the uptake.

"That's right," he said. "You've put the thing in a nutshell. It's all off, and so is he."

Ignoring a sharp, whistling, sighing noise which proceeded from the lips which had once promised to love, honor and obey him, he resumed his discourse.

"You see, Bill's a country gentleman, old girl...lives in the wilds, half-a-dozen miles from anywhere...and he doesn't think you would quite fit into the picture."

"Oh? I'm not fit to associate with his beastly vicars and plowboys, eh?" asked Lottie with ominous calm.

"He doesn't say that," urged Lord Tidmouth. "What he means is that you wouldn't be happy in a small village. He's doing you a kindness, really. Why, dash it, if you got fed up with me in the middle of London, how much fedder-up you would be in a place like Woollam Chersey with a bird like Bill. Good heavens, there's nothing offensive in the man's attitude. He admires and respects you, but he feels that Woollam Chersey is not for you. Lots of the world's most wonderful women would be out of place in Woollam Chersey. Queen Elizabeth...Catherine of Russia ...Cleopatra...dozens of them."

He paused, with the complacency of an orator who is conscious of having struck the right note.

"Besides," said Bill, who was not so sure that his collaborator was putting this thing across so well as he thought he was, "if I can't come in without finding you kissing..."

"Old boy!" murmured Lord Tidmouth reproachfully. "Bygones be bygones. 'Let the dead past bury its dead.'"

Lottie sniffed.

"So that's the trouble? You know as well as I do that Squiffy means nothing to me any longer. There's no need for you to be jealous."

"I'm not jealous."

"Oh?" said Lottie sharply. "And *why* aren't you, may I ask? I see it all now. There's somebody else."

"No, no," said Lord Tidmouth. "Quite wrong. Absolutely not so."

"There is! Some woman is stealing him away from me." Her voice rose. "Who is she? What's her name? Tell me her name? Who is she?"

She rested her hands on her hips, and from beneath lowering eyebrows glared militantly. Her manner interested Lord Tidmouth, and caused him to advance a theory to explain it.

"I say, Lottie, old girl," asked his lordship, "have you any Spanish blood in you?"

"Now listen, Lottie..."

This from Bill, who was not enjoying the glare.

"I won't listen!"

"My second wife was half Spanish," proceeded Lord Tidmouth chattily. "How well I remember..."

"Shut up!"

"Oh, rather," said his lordship. "I merely spoke."

Lottie turned to Bill again.

"So," she said, "you want to get rid of me, do you? You want to throw me aside like a—like a—"

"Worn-out glove," prompted Lord Tidmouth.

"Like a worn-out glove. You think you're going to abandon me like an—"

"Old tube of toothpaste."

"Shut up!"

"Oh, rather."

Lottie's eyes flashed.

"Let me tell you, you're mistaken if you think you can get rid of *me* so easily."

"Lottie," said Bill, "please!"

"Lottie, please!" said Lord Tidmouth.

"Lottie, please! Lottie, please! Lottie, please!" cried the injured woman in the tones which had intimidated a hundred theatrical dressing rooms and which, when heard during the course of their brief married life by the late Mr. Higginbotham, had always been enough to send that pusillanimous cotton magnate shooting off to his club for refuge.

She ran to the tea table and snatched up a cup.

"There!"

She hurled the cup down with a crash.

"Did you ring, sir?"

It was a bellboy who spoke. He had appeared in the doorway with a smooth promptness which spoke well for the efficiency of the service at the Superba. This was due partly to long training and partly to the fact that for some moments back he had been standing with his ear glued to the keyhole.

"And there!" cried Lottie, demolishing a second cup.

This one produced Marie.

"Did you call, moddom?"

"And there!" said Lottie. "And there! And there!"

Another cup, saucer and the teapot joined the ruins on the floor.

"Lottie," said Bill urgently, "pull yourself together."

"Absolutely," agreed Lord Tidmouth. "Cups cost money, what?"

A piercing scream from the sufferer nearly broke the remaining cup on the table. Marie, advancing solicitously, was just in time to catch her employer as she fell. There was general consternation. All those present were disturbed and distressed, except the bellboy, who had not had such an enjoyable time since the day, six months ago, when the couple in Suite Ten had settled a lovers' tiff in his presence with chairs, the leg of a table, and a series of small china ornaments from the mantelpiece.

As always on occasions such as this, the air became full of a babble of words.

"Water," cried Marie.

"Vinegar!" recommended the bellboy.

"Eau de cologne!" said Bill.

"Pepper!" said Lord Tidmouth.

Marie had another suggestion.

"Give her air!"

So had the bellboy.

"Slap her hands!"

Lord Tidmouth went further.

"Sit on her head!" he advised.

The clamour was affecting Bill Bannister's nervous system.

"Will you be quiet!" he roared.

The noise subsided.

"Now, then," said Bill, taking command. He turned to the bellboy. "Go for a doctor."

"Yes sir."

"And you," continued Bill, addressing Marie, "take her into the bedroom."

"Yes sir."

The mob scene diminished. Bill, mopping his forehead, was aware of his old friend, Lord Tidmouth, hovering to and fro. He eyed him sourly.

"What are you hanging about for?" he demanded.

Lord Tidmouth reflected.

"Well, honestly, old chap, I don't quite know. Just lending sympathy and moral support, as it were."

"Get a doctor."

"But the boy's getting one."

"Well, get another. Get a dozen."

Lord Tidmouth patted his shoulder with infinite gentleness and understanding.

"I know just how you're feeling, old boy," he said. "You've never seen Lottie in quite this frame of mind before, and you find it upsetting. To me, of course, all this is old stuff. How well I remember," said Lord Tidmouth, beginning to dictate his autobiography, "how clearly it all comes back—that second week of our honeymoon when, in a spirit of kindly criticism, I told her that her new hat looked like nothing on earth. People talk about the San Francisco earthquake. . ."

"Get *out!*"

"Just as you say, old boy."

"And don't come back without a doctor."

"I won't," Lord Tidmouth assured him. "I'll get one if I have to rob a hospital. For the moment, then, laddie, tinkerty-tonk!"

The room now empty, Bill felt more composed. He called sharply to Marie, who popped out of the bedroom like a cuckoo from a clock.

"Marie!"

"Sir?"

"How is she?"

"Still unconscious, sir. And I don't like her breathing. If you ask me, it's storterous."

" 'Storterous'?"

"Sort of puffy. Like this."

Taking in a supply of air, Marie emitted it in a series of moaning gasps. It was not an inartistic performance, but Bill did not like it.

"Marie!" he said.

"Sir?"

"When I want any farmyard imitations, I'll ask for them."

"Very good, sir."

Hurt by destructive criticism, the maid withdrew into the bedroom. The door had scarcely closed behind her when the bellboy appeared. He had the unmistakable look of a bellboy who is about to deliver the goods.

"The doctor, sir," he announced with modest pride.

Bill heaved a relieved sigh.

"Send him in," he said.

And having said it, he stood gaping. Framed in the doorway was a young and becomingly dressed girl. She carried a small black bag, and at the sight of her Bill Bannister's eyes widened to an incredulous stare and his jaw drooped like a lily. Then there swept over him so tumultuous a rush of ecstasy that his vocal cords seemed tangled in a knot.

He swallowed convulsively, and realised despairingly that speech for the moment was entirely beyond him.

Sally eyed him composedly. She had been going out for a walk when the bellboy found her, and she was anxious to finish the task before her and resume that walk as quickly as possible. Of the emotions surging in Bill's soul she had no inkling. And certainly she did not share them. Bill meant nothing to her. She had never seen him before in her life, and was not excited by the sight of him now. She had set him down at a glance as one of those typical, pleasant, idle young men whose charm made so slight an impression on her. Only workers interested Sally Smith.

She was on the point of coming briskly to business, when the extraordinary popeyed nature of his stare forced itself on her attention. A moment later, he advanced a step towards her, still looking like a prawn, and in an odd, strangled voice emitted the single word, "Guk!"

That, at least, was how it sounded to Sally. She raised her eyebrows.

"I beg your pardon?" she said.

Bill Bannister, with a supreme effort, had now got his Adam's apple back into position and regained control of his vocal cords. But even now the sight of this girl rendered speaking difficult. At close range, he found himself observing things about her which had escaped him at a distance. Her nose, which he had supposed straight, turned up at the tip. He had never seen her teeth before. He liked them.

"It can't be!" he said.

"I don't quite understand," said Sally.

"I—er—mean," said Bill. "What I mean is...I've seen you before."

"Really? Where?"

"Out on the links."

"Yes? I've been playing quite a lot."

"Yes," said Bill. "I saw you there... Out on the links... I saw you several times out on the links."

He paused a moment, wishing to make his meaning clearer.

"You were out on the links," he said, "and I saw you."

"I see," said Sally. "And now, where is my patient?"

"Patient?"

"I was told that someone here wanted a doctor."

"Yes. A—sort of friend of mine has had a kind of nervous breakdown."

"A female friend, I suppose?"

"Er—yes."

"Well, hadn't I better see her?"

A bright light shone upon Bill.

"You don't mean to say you're a doctor?"

"I do."

"Gosh! I mean...I say, *do* sit down, won't you?"

"I really can't waste time like this," said Sally coldly. "If you don't want me to attend the patient, I'll go."

"But...she can't see a doctor now."

"Why not?"

"She isn't well."

Sally's momentary pique faded. This extraordinary young man amused her.

"My dear good man," she said, "are you always like this, or have I just struck one of your bad days?"

Bill writhed.

"I know I'm an idiot..."

"Ah! A lucid moment."

"It's the shock of seeing you walk in like this."

"Why shouldn't I walk in? You sent for me."

"Yes, but you don't understand. I mean, I've seen you out on the golf links."

"So you said before."

"You see—Mrs. . . ."

"Miss."

"Thank God!"

"I beg your pardon?"

"Nothing, nothing. I—er—that is to say—or, putting it rather differently. . .Oh, my goodness!"

"What's the matter?"

"You take my breath away."

"For shortness of breath try a jujube. And now, please, my patient."

"Oh yes. . ."

Bill went to the door of the bedroom and called softly:

"Marie!"

Marie appeared in the doorway.

"Yes sir?"

"How is she?"

"Asleep, sir."

"Fine!" said Bill, brightening. "See that she doesn't wake up." He came back to Sally. "The maid says the patient has fallen asleep."

Sally nodded.

"Quite natural. Sleep often follows violent hysteria."

"But, I say, how do you know it was hysteria?"

"By the broken china. Long-distance diagnosis. Well, let her have her sleep-out."

"I will."

There was a pause.

"Tea," said Bill, at length desperately. "Won't you have some tea?"

"Where is it?"

Bill looked about him.

"Well, on the floor, mostly," he admitted. "But I could ring for some more."

"Don't bother. I don't like tea much, anyway."

"You're American, aren't you?"

"I am."

"It's a rummy thing, Americans never seem very keen on tea."

"No."

There was another pause.

"I say," said Bill, "I didn't get your name."

"Doctor Sally Smith. What's yours?"

"Bannister. William Bannister."

"You live here?"

"Certainly not," said Bill, shocked. "I'm staying at the Majestic. I live down in Hampshire."

"One of those big country houses, I suppose?"

"Pretty big."

"I thought so. You look opulent," said Sally, pleased that her original opinion had been confirmed. A rich idler, this man, she felt. Not unpleasant, it was true—she liked his face and was amused by him—but nevertheless idle and rich.

Bill, by this time, had gradually become something more nearly resembling a sentient being. Indeed, he was now quite at his ease again and feeling extraordinarily happy. That this girl and he should be sitting chatting together like this was so wonderful that it put him right on top of his form. He straightened his tie and threw his whole soul into one devoted gaze.

Sally got the gaze and did not like it. For some moments now she had been wishing that this perfect stranger would either make his eyes rather less soulful or else refrain from directing them at her. She was a liberal-minded girl and did not disapprove of admiration from the other sex—indeed, she had grown accustomed to exciting it—but something seemed to whisper to her that this William Bannister could do with a little womanly quelling.

"Would you mind not looking at me like that?" she said coolly.

The soulful look faded out of Bill's eyes as if he had been hit between them with a brick. He felt disconcerted and annoyed. He disliked being snubbed, even by a girl for whom his whole being yearned.

"I'm *not* looking at you like that," he replied with spirit. "At least, I'm not trying to."

Sally nodded tolerantly.

"I see," she said. "Automatic, eh? Very interesting, from a medical point of view. Unconscious reaction of the facial and labial muscles at sight of a pretty woman."

Bill's pique increased. He resented this calm treating of himself as something odd on a microscopic slide.

"I am sorry," he said haughtily, "if I embarrassed you."

Sally laughed.

"You didn't embarrass me," she said. "Did I seem to you to show embarrassment? I thought I had my vascular motors under much better control."

"Your—What did you say?"

"Vascular motors. They regulate the paling and flushing of the skin. In other words, I didn't blush."

"Oh, ah! I see."

The conversation flagged again.

"Do you know," said Bill, hoisting it to its legs again, "I was most awfully surprised when you said you were a doctor."

"Most men seem to be."

"I mean, you don't look like a doctor."

"How ought a doctor to look?"

Bill reflected.

"Well, most of them seem sort of fagged and overworked. Haggard chaps. I mean, it must be an awful strain."

Sally laughed.

"Oh, it's not so bad. You needn't waste your pity on me, Mr. Bannister. I'm as fit as a fiddle, thank heaven, and enjoy every minute of my life. I have a good practice and quite enough money. I go to theatres and concerts. I play games. I spend my vacations travelling. I love my work. I love my recreations. I love life."

"You're wonderful!"

"And why shouldn't I be? I earn every bit of pleasure that I get. I like nice clothes, nice shoes, nice stockings—because I buy them myself. I'm like the Village Blacksmith—I owe not any man. I wonder if you've the remotest idea how happy it can make a woman feel just to be a worker and *alive*—with good nerves, good circulation and good muscles. Feel my arm. Like iron."

"Wonderful!"

"And my legs. Hard as a rock. Prod 'em."

"No, really."

"Go on."

She looked at him with amusement.

"You're blushing!"

Bill was unable to deny the charge.

"Yes," he said. "I'm afraid my vascular motors aren't as well controlled as yours."

"Can't you admire a well-rounded, highly perfected leg in a purely detached spirit as a noble work of nature?"

"Sorry—no. I'm afraid I've never quite managed to do that."

"Why, in some countries the women go swimming with nothing on."

"And the men buy telescopes."

"Don't snigger."

"Forgive me," said Bill. "I laugh, like Figaro, that I may not weep."

She regarded him curiously.

"What do you want to weep about?"

Bill sighed.

"I'm feeling a little depressed," he said. "In the life you have outlined—this hard, tense, independent, self-sufficing life with its good nerves and good circulation and muscles of the brawny arm as strong as iron bands—don't you think—it's just a suggestion —don't you think there's something a little *bleak?*"

" 'Bleak' ?"

Bill nodded.

"Well, frankly... "

"Always be frank."

"Frankly, then,," said Bill, "it reminds me of the sort of nightmare H. G. Wells would have after cold pork. It seems to leave out the one thing that makes life worth living."

"You mean love?"

"Exactly. I grant you one hundred per cent on nerves and circulation and general fitness; I admire your biceps; I'm sure your leg muscle is all it should be; and I take off my hat to your vascular motors ... but doesn't it strike you that you're just the merest trifle lacking in *sentiment?*"

She frowned.

"Nothing of the kind. All I'm lacking in is sentimentality. I don't droop and blush and giggle... "

"No, I noticed that."

" ...But naturally I don't intend to exclude love from my life. I'm not such a fool."

"Ah!"

"Why do you say 'Ah' ?"

A touch of dignity came into Bill's manner.

"Listen!" he said. "You're the loveliest girl I ever met, but you've got to stop bullying me. I shall say 'Ah' just as often as I please."

"I merely asked because most people, when they stand in front of me and say 'Ah,' expect me to examine their throats."

She paused.

"Why are you so interested in my views on love, Mr. Bannister?" she asked casually.

Even Bill, quick worker though he had been from boyhood, would have shrunk—had the conditions been other than they were—from laying bare his soul at this extremely early point in his association with this girl. Emotion might have urged him to do so, but Prudence would have plucked at his sleeve. So intense, however, was his desire to shatter his companion's maddening aloofness... at least, was aloofness exactly the word?... dispassionate friendliness described it better... no, *detached*... that was the word he wanted... she was so cool and detached and seemed so utterly oblivious to the importance of a Bannister's yearning that he let Emotion have its way. And if Prudence did any plucking, he failed to notice it.

"I'll tell you why," he said explosively. "Because, the moment I saw you out there on the links, I knew you were the one girl..."

"You mean you've fallen in love with me?"

"I have.... The news doesn't seem to surprise you," said Bill resentfully.

Sally laughed.

"Oh, it's not such a terrible shock."

"You've heard the same sort of thing before, from other men, I suppose?"

"Dozens of times."

"I might have known it," said Bill gloomily. "Just my luck. And I suppose— "

"No. You're wrong."

Bill became animated again.

"You mean there's nobody else?"

"Nobody."

Bill's animation approached fever point.

"Then do you think... do you suppose... might it happen... would it be... or, putting it another way, is it possible..."

"Crisper, crisper. And simpler: What you're trying to suggest now is that perhaps I might one day love you. Am I right?"

"You take the words out of my mouth."

"I had to, or they would never have emerged at all. Well, if I ever love a man, I shall inform him of the fact, simply and naturally, as if I were saying, 'Good morning.'"

Bill hesitated.

"Tell me," he said, "have you ever—er—wished a man good morning?"

"No. That experience has yet to come."

"Wonderful!"

"Not so very wonderful. It simply means I haven't met the right man."

Bill could not allow a totally false statement like this to pass uncorrected.

"Yes, you have," he assured her. "You don't know it yet, but you have." He advanced towards her, full of his theme. "You have, really."

"Oh?"

"Yes," said Bill. He drew a deep breath. "Gosh!" he exclaimed. "I feel as if a great weight had rolled off me. I had always hoped in my heart that women like you existed, and now it's all come true. Don't laugh at me. It's come upon me like a whirlwind. I never expected it. I never guessed. I never..."

"Excuse me, sir," said Marie, appearing at the bedroom door.

Bill regarded her with marked displeasure. In the past, Marie had always seemed to him rather a nice girl, but now he felt he had seldom encountered a more pronounced pest.

"Well," he said irritably, "what is it?"

"If you please, sir, she's awake now."

Bill could make nothing of this. The girl appeared to him to be

Bill could make nothing of this. The girl appeared to him to be babbling. Sheer gossip from the padded cell.

"Awake?" he said. "What on earth are you talking about? Who's awake?"

"Why, moddom, sir."

Bill blinked like an awakened somnambulist.

"Moddom?"

Sally laughed.

"I think you had forgotten our patient, hadn't you?"

She turned briskly to Marie.

"Ask her to come in, please. I will examine her at once."

It was a calmer and more subdued Lottie who emerged from the bedroom. But it was plain that the volcano was not altogether extinct. In her manner, as she suddenly beheld a charming and attractive girl in Bill's society in her sitting room, there were obvious indications that something of the old fire still lingered. She stiffened. She glared in hostile fashion. Bill, watching, was disturbed to see her hands go to her hips in a well-remembered gesture.

"Oh?" said Lottie. "And who may this be?"

"I'm the doctor," said Sally.

"You think I'm going to swallow that?"

Sally sighed resignedly.

"Can you read?"

"Of course I can read."

"Then read that," said Sally, producing a card.

Lottie scrutinised it doubtfully. Then her manner changed.

"Doctor Sally Smith," she said. "Well, I suppose that's all right. Still, it looks funny to me. And let me tell you that if there is any funny business going on between you two, I'll very soon..."

"Quiet, please," said Sally.

She spoke calmly, but the speaker stopped as if she had run into a brick wall.

"Perhaps I'd better leave you?" said Bill.

"Just as you like."

"I'll go for a stroll on the front."

"All right," said Sally. "I shan't be long."

She put her stethoscope together as the door closed. Lottie, having recovered, felt disposed for conversation.

"You'll forgive me, I'm sure, Doctor..." She paused. "Isn't that too silly of me, I've forgotten your damned name."

"It's quite an easy one to remember," said Sally, busy with her stethoscope. "Smith."

Lottie beamed.

"Oh, thank you. I was saying, Doctor, that I was sure you'd forgive me for flying off the handle a little just now. The fact is, I've just been having a bit of a row with Mr. Bannister, and coming in and finding you two together like that, naturally I said to myself..."

"Take off that bathrobe."

"Eh? Oh, all right. Let me see, where was I? What started it all was him saying to me—or, rather, Squiffy did, and he didn't contradict it—that he wasn't ever going to take me dancing again. 'Oh,' I said, 'and why not, may I ask?' 'I'm going home,' he said. 'Going home?' I said. 'Yes,' he said, 'going home.' So naturally I said, 'I know what the trouble with *you* is,' I said, 'you want to cast me off like a worn-out glove. But if you think for one moment that I'm going to stand anything like that...' "

"The lungs appear sound," said Sally.

" 'You're mistaken,' I said..."

"Take a deep breath. Well, the heart seems all right. Now for the reflexes. Cross your legs... Nothing the matter with them. All right, that's all."

"Examination over?"

"Yes."

Lottie became interested.

"What's wrong with me?"

"Nothing much. You need a rest."

"Aren't you going to look at my tongue?"

"I can tell, without looking at it, that that needs a rest, too. What you want is a few weeks in a nice quiet sanitarium."

"You're going to send me to a sanitarium?"

"Well, I'm advising you to go. You need a place where there are cold baths and plain food and no cigarettes and no cocktails."

Lottie shuddered.

"It sounds like hell," she said. She frowned. "I believe it's a trick."

"A trick?"

"I believe you're just trying to get me out of the way so that you can have him to yourself."

"Him?" Sally stared. "You can't mean—Do you really imagine for one moment that I'm in love with Mr. Bannister?"

"You aren't?"

"Of course not."

"And you want me to go to a sanitarium?"

"I think you ought to."

"Well," said Lottie, "it all looks funny to *me!*"

The door opened and Lord Tidmouth appeared. He seemed pleased with himself.

"Hullo!" said Lord Tidmouth. "I say, I've snaffled a medicine man." His eye rested on Sally. He stared. "Hullo!"

Sally returned his gaze composedly.

"I have already examined the patient," she said.

"*You* have?" said Lord Tidmouth, perplexed.

"Yes. My name is Doctor Smith."

"*Doctor* Smith?"

"Doctor Smith."

Lord Tidmouth's was not a very agile brain, but it was capable of flashes of intuition.

"You mean *you're* a doctor?" he said, brightly.

"Yes."

"I see. Of course," said Lord Tidmouth, with the air of a man who is always prepared to listen to reason, "there *are* lady doctors."

"Yes. I'm one of them."

"Absolutely. Yes, I see your point. I say," said Lord Tidmouth, "this is rather awkward. Old Bill sent me to get a doctor, and I grabbed one in the lobby."

"I'm afraid there's nothing for him to do here."

"Not a thing," agreed Lottie. "What do you think I'm doing here, Squiffy, you poor nut—holding a medical convention?"

Lord Tidmouth rubbed his chin.

"But he's apt to be a bit shirty, isn't he, if he finds I've lugged him up here for nothing? He wasn't any too pleased at having to come at all. He was on his way to the links."

"Oh well," said Sally, sympathizing with his concern, "as you've called him in, we can have a consultation, if he likes. Where is he?"

"Navigating the stairs. Stout old boy, not very quick on his pins." He went to the door. "This way, Doc," he called.

A puffing noise without announced that the medicine man was nearing journey's end. The next moment he had entered, and Sally, turning to the door, was surprised to find that this was no stranger in their midst but an old acquaintance.

"Why, Sir Hugo!" she said.

Sir Hugo Drake had just enough breath left to say, "God bless my soul! You here?" After that, he resumed his puffing.

Lord Tidmouth became apologetic.

"I'm awfully sorry," he said, addressing his panting captive. "I'm afraid there's been a misunderstanding."

"Lord Tidmouth," explained Sally, "didn't know that I was here."

"No," said his lordship. "The whole trouble was, you see, old Bill got the wind up and sent the entire strength of the company out scouring the town for medicos. It begins to look like a full house."

Sir Hugo realised the position.

"No need for me at all, eh? Well, I'm just as pleased. I've an appointment on the links. Of course, if you'd like a consultation... "

"Could you spare the time?" asked Sally.

"Certainly, if you wish it. Mustn't take too long, though."

"Oh, of course not. Only a few minutes."

"Very well, then. This young lady the patient?"

"Yes."

"Well, step into the bedroom, young lady, and we'll go into your case."

Lottie rose obediently. She was feeling a little flattered at this inrush of doctors on her behalf.

"She says I ought to go into a sanitarium," she said, indicating Sally.

"Subject to Sir Hugo's opinion," said Sally.

Sir Hugo nodded.

"Oh, we'll thresh the whole thing out, never fear. We'll go into your case minutely. Run along, my dear."

"Well, I ought to be all right between the two of you," said Lottie, and closed the bedroom door behind her.

Lord Tidmouth seemed relieved that matters had reached such an amicable settlement. He had had visions of this red-faced bird setting about him with a niblick.

"Then I'll leave you to it, what? I've often wondered," he said meditatively, "what you doctors talk about when you hold consultations. Lots of deep stuff, I expect."

For a moment after the departure of Lord Tidmouth there was silence in the room. Sir Hugo was still engaged in recovering his full supply of breath. This done, he looked at Sally inquiringly.

"What's the trouble?"

"Oh, nothing," said Sally. "Just a little nerves."

Sir Hugo cocked an eye at the debris on the floor.

"Seems to have been violent."

"Yes. That type. Too many cocktails and cigarettes, and no self-restraint. I thought she ought to have a few weeks' rest."

Sir Hugo snorted.

"I imagined from the way that young fellow snatched me up and carried me off that it was a matter of life and death. Silly idiot! Now I shall be late for my golf match."

"How did you get on this morning after you left me?" asked Sally.

Sir Hugo sighed, as Napoleon might have sighed if somebody had met him after the battle of Waterloo and asked, "Well, how did it all come out?"

"He beat me four and three."

"What a shame!"

"I didn't seem able to do anything right," said Sir Hugo, wallowing in this womanly sympathy. "If I didn't hook, I sliced. And if I didn't slice, I topped."

"That's too bad."

"I only needed a nine to win the fourteenth, and I ought to have got it easily. But I blew up on the green."

"That's often the way, isn't it?"

"Mark you," said Sir Hugo, "I wasn't so bad off the tee. Some of my drives were extremely good. It was the short shots that beat me. Just the ones you are so wonderful at. If I could play my mashie as you do, my handicap would be down below twenty before I knew where I was."

"What do you find is the trouble? Shanking?"

"No, topping, principally."

"You oughtn't to look up."

"I know I oughtn't, but I do."

"Do you think you are gripping right?" asked Sally.

"Well, I'm *gripping*," said Sir Hugo. "I don't know if I'm doing it right."

"Would you like me to show you?"

"My dear young lady, I should like it above all things!"

A monocled head appeared round the edge of the door. Curiosity had been too much for Lord Tidmouth.

"How are you getting on?" he inquired.

"Kindly leave us alone, young man," said Sir Hugo testily. "We are at a very difficult point in the diagnosis."

"Oh, right ho. Poo-boop-a-doop," said Lord Tidmouth amiably, and vanished again.

Sir Hugo turned to Sally.

"You were saying you would show me..."

Sally stretched out a hand towards the golf bag.

"May I borrow one of your clubs?" she said. "Now, then. So much depends on the right grip. Do you use the Vardon?"

"I used to, but lately I've gone back to the double-V."

"Well, the great thing is not to grip too tight. Grip firmly but lightly."

"Firmly but lightly. I see."

"The hands should be kept low, and, above all, should finish low. So many people finish their iron shots with the hands up as if they were driving."

"True," said Sir Hugo. "True."

"At the finish of the chip shot the club should be very little above the horizontal. Not like in the drive."

Sir Hugo nodded.

"I see. Talking of driving, it may interest you to hear of a little experience I had the other day. I had made my drive..."

"A rather similar thing once happened to me," said Sally. "It was this way..."

"I went to play my second," proceeded Sir Hugo, who may not have been much good as a golfer, but stood almost alone as a golf bore. A man who had outtalked tough, forceful men in clubs, he was not going to let himself be silenced by a mere girl. "I went to play my second, and, believe me or believe me not..."

"What do you think?" said Sally. "I found..."

"I just..."

"I simply..."

The bedroom door opened abruptly.

"Haven't you two finished yet?" asked Lottie peevishly.

Sir Hugo started like one awakened from a beautiful dream.

"Oh, quite, quite," he said, embarrassed. "We were just about to call you. We've examined your case from every angle..."

"And Sir Hugo agrees with me..." said Sally.

"Exactly. That your trouble..."

" ... Is a slight matter of nerves..."

" ...Nothing of any consequence, though disagreeable..."

"And you must be kept in a sanitarium..."

"Firmly but lightly," said Sir Hugo. "I mean—ah—just so."

Lord Tidmouth manifested himself again.

"Hullo," he said. "Consultation over?"

"Yes," said Lottie. "They say I ought to go to a sanitarium."

"I can recommend this one," said Sir Hugo. "I will write down the address."

"Oh, all right," said Lottie. "Leave it on the table. I'm going out."

"To find Bill?" said Lord Tidmouth. "He's probably on the front somewhere."

Lottie laughed a bitter laugh.

"Bill? I don't want Bill. I've nothing to say to Mr. Bannister. If I'm to be dumped in a sanitarium, I'm going to get in a bit of dancing first. Come along and shake them up, Squiffy?"

"Absolutely," agreed Lord Tidmouth. "Just what the old system needs. Well, toodle-oo, everybody."

Sir Hugo was staring openmouthed at the closed door. He had the air of a man who has received an unpleasant shock.

"*Bannister*, did she say?"

"Yes. Mr. Bannister was here when I came. He went out."

Sir Hugo snorted powerfully.

"So this is the woman he's been fooling around! I might have guessed it would be some peroxide blonde."

Sally saw daylight.

"Is Mr. Bannister the nephew you were telling me about?"

"He is. And that is the woman! Of all the maddening, worthless nephews a man was ever cursed with..." He paused, and seemed to ponder. "Just show me that grip once more, will you?" he said, coming out of his reverie.

"All right," said Sally agreeably. "But don't you want to worry about your nephew?"

"He can wait," said Sir Hugo grimly.

"I see. Well, give me your hands—" She took his hands and clasped them round the club. And it was in this attitude that Bill, returning for the latest bulletin, found them.

Bill's first emotion was one of excusable wrath at the spectacle. Here was the only girl he had ever really loved, and he had no sooner left her than she started holding hands with a man of advanced years in a suit of plus fours of the kind that makes horses shy. He cleared his throat austerely, and was about to speak when the plus-foured one turned:

"William!" he said, and Bill wilted.

If one of the more austere of the minor prophets had worn plus fours, he would have looked just as Sir Hugo Drake was looking now. The great specialist had drawn himself up, and he could not have regarded Bill more sternly if the latter had been a germ.

"So I've found you, have I!"

"Oh—hullo, Uncle!" said Bill.

"Don't say 'Hullo, Uncle!' to me," boomed Sir Hugo. "This is a pleasant surprise for a man who stands *in loco parentis*, is it not! I come down here to this place, to this Bingley-on-Sea, and before I've hardly had time to put a ball down on the first tee, I am called in to attend to your female associates!"

"Uncle, please!"

Sir Hugo strode to the door.

"I am returning to Woollam Chersey tonight, William," he said. "I shall expect you to accompany me."

"I can't!"

"Why not?"

Bill looked helplessly at Sally.

"I'll be back in a day or two," he said.

"Then I shall remain till you leave," said Sir Hugo. "And let me tell you I shall watch this suite like a hawk."

"There's no *need* for you to watch this suite..."

"There is every need for me to watch this suite. Good God, boy! I've seen the female! If you imagine that I'm going to stand idly by and see you get yourself inextricably entangled with a woman who dyes her hair and throws teacups about hotels, you are vastly mistaken." He looked at his watch. "Great heavens! Is that the time? I must fly. I'll remember what you told me about that grip. Firmly but lightly. Hands not too much over. William, I shall be seeing you again. We will discuss this affair then."

Although his uncle—corporeally considered—had now left him, his aura or influence seemed still to oppress William Bannister. He gulped once or twice before speaking.

"How on earth did he get here?" he gasped.

Lord Tidmouth found him in the lobby and dragged him up," said Sally. "Poor Mr. Bannister, you don't have much luck with your medical advisers, do you?" She moved towards the door. "Well, good-bye."

Bill quivered.

"You're not going?"

"Yes, I am. Will you give me your address?"

"Woollam Chersey, Hampshire, finds me." He drew a deep breath. "How wonderful! You want to write to me?"

"No. I just want to know where to send my bill."

"Good heavens!"

"What's the matter?"

Bill walked across to the sofa and kicked it violently.

"It's enough to drive a man mad," he said. "Whenever I say anything—anything with any sentiment in it—you immediately become the doctor again."

"What do you expect me to do—swoon in your arms?"

"You haven't an atom of feeling in you."

"Oh yes, I have. And someday the right man will bring it out. Cheer up, Mr. Bannister. You look like a sulky baby that's been refused its bottle." She laughed. "I think your uncle's quite right, and you're still a small boy."

Bill scowled.

"Oh? I'll prove to you someday that I'm grown up."

Sally laughed again.

"Oh, I'm not saying you may not grow up someday. But at present you're just a child."

"I'm not."

"You are."

"I'm not."

"Yes, you are."

There was a knock at the door. The bellboy entered.

"Please, sir," said the bellboy, "your rocking horse has arrived."

"What!" cried Bill.

"There!" cried Sally.

Bill passed a hand through his disordered hair.

"My rocking horse? What do you mean, my rocking horse?"

"Well, all I know is, there's a rocking horse outside. Shall they bring it in?"

"No!" cried Bill.

"Yes," said Sally. "Good-bye, Mr. Bannister. Naturally you will want to be alone. You don't want grown-ups around at a moment like this. Good-bye."

"Come back!" shouted Bill. But Sally had gone.

If there was a thought in the mind of Lord Tidmouth, as he sat, some two weeks after his visit to Bingley-on-Sea, playing solitaire in the living hall of his friend Bill Bannister's country seat at Woollam Chersey, in the county of Hampshire, it was a vaguely formulated feeling that life was extremely pleasant and that there was no getting away from it that these all-male parties were the best. He had had an excellent dinner, the lamps were lighted, and it seemed to him that there was nothing whatever to worry about in the world.

Lord Tidmouth liked peace and quiet. Women, in his experience, militated against an atmosphere of quiet peace. Look at his second wife, for instance. For the matter of that, look at his third and fourth. He was placidly content that the Manor, Woollam Chersey, harboured, besides himself, only William, his host, inert now in a neighbouring armchair, and William's uncle, Sir Hugo Drake, at present occupied in the passage without, practising putts into a tumbler.

The room in which Bill and Lord Tidmouth sat was old and panelled. Its furniture was masculine and solid. From the walls portraits of dead and gone Bannisters gazed down, and in one corner there was a suit of armour, which it was Lord Tidmouth's practice to tap smartly whenever he passed it. He liked the ringing sound it gave out. What with an occasional tap on this suit of armour, plenty to eat and drink, and sufficient opportunities for playing solitaire, Lord Tidmouth found life at Woollam Chersey satisfactory.

A kindly soul, he wished he could have thought that his host was in a similar frame of mind. As far as he allowed himself to worry about anything, he was a little worried about good old Bill. The man seemed on edge. Very far from his merry self he had been since that afternoon at Bingley. This troubled Lord Tidmouth at times.

It did not, however, trouble him to the extent of spoiling his enjoyment in his game of solitaire. With pursed lips he uncovered a card, held it in air, put it on one of the piles, removed a second card from another pile and put it on a third pile—in fact, went through all the movements peculiar to those addicted to this strange game.

It is almost inevitable that a man who is playing solitaire will sooner or later sing. Lord Tidmouth, who had for some little time been humming in an undertone, now came boldly into the open and committed himself to the rendition of a popular ballad.

> *I fee-ar naw faw in shee-ining arr-mour,*
> *Though his lance be swift and—er—keen ...*

In his armchair Bill stirred uneasily.

> *But I fee-ar, I fee-ar the glarr-moor*
> *Ther-oo thy der-ooping larr-shes seen,*
> *I fee-ar, I fee-ar the GLAR-moor ...*

"Oh, shut up!" said Bill.

Lord Tidmouth, ceasing to sing, turned amiably.

"Sorry, old top," he said. "I thought you were dead."

"What are you doing?"

"Playing solitaire, laddie." He fiddled with the cards, and absently burst into song once more. "Just playing SOL-i-taire ... "

"Stop it!"

"Stop playing?"

"Stop yowling."

"Oh, right ho."

Bill rose and surveyed the card-strewn table with an unfriendly eye.

"Do you mean to say you really get any pleasure out of that

rotten game?"

"Darned good game," protested Lord Tidmouth. He manipulated the cards. "Did you ever hear the story of the ventriloquist who played solitaire? He used to annoy his wife by holding long conversations with himself in his sleep. It became such a trial to the poor woman that she had serious thoughts of getting a divorce. And then one evening, by the greatest good luck, he caught himself cheating at solitaire and never spoke to himself again."

"Silly idiot!"

"Harsh words, old man, from host to guest. Nice place you've got here, Bill."

"Glad you like it."

"Been in the family quite a time, I take it?"

"A few centuries."

Bill's manner became furtive. He glanced to and fro in a conspiratorial fashion. It seemed that whatever had been on his mind all evening was coming to a head.

"Squiffy!"

"Hullo?"

"Where's my uncle?"

"Out in the corridor putting vigorously. What a man!"

"Thank God that'll keep him occupied for awhile. Squiffy, there's something I want to tell you."

"Carry on, old boy."

"Tonight I . . . "

He broke off. A stout figure, swathed in a mauve smoking jacket and carrying a putter, had entered.

"It's coming!" said Sir Hugo Drake joyfully. "The knack is coming. I'm getting it. Four out of my last seven shots straight into the glass."

"I think I'll take a shot in a glass myself," said Lord Tidmouth, rising and making for the table where the decanter and siphon so invitingly stood.

"I fancy I have at last found out what has been wrong with my putting... William!"

"Hullo?"

"I say I think I have at last found out what has been wrong with my putting."

"Oh?"

"I've been gripping too tight. How right that girl was. Grip firmly but lightly, she said, that's the secret. It stands to reason..."

"Excuse me," said Bill, and removed himself with the smooth swiftness of a family ghost.

Sir Hugo stood staring after him. This was not the first time activity of this sort had suddenly descended upon his nephew in the middle of a conversation. He did not like it. Apart from the incivility of it, it seemed to him ominous. He confided this fear to Lord Tidmouth, who was still occupied with his spot.

"Lord Tidmouth!"

His companion lowered his glass courteously.

"Present!" he said. "Here in person."

Sir Hugo jerked a thumb towards the door.

"Did you see that?"

"What?"

"Did you see the curious, sudden way that boy left the room?"

"He did move fairly nippily," agreed Lord Tidmouth. "Now you saw him and now you didn't, as it were."

"He has been like that ever since he got home—nervous, rude, jumpy, abrupt."

"Yes, I've noticed he's been a bit jumpy."

"What do you suppose is the matter with him?"

"Not been eating enough yeast," said Lord Tidmouth confidently.

"No! He's in love."

"You think so?"

"I'm sure of it. I noticed it the day I arrived here. I had begun to tell him about the long brassie shot I made at the sixteenth hole, and he gave a sort of hollow gasp and walked away."

"Walked away?"

"Walked away in the middle of a sentence. The boy's in love. There can be no other explanation."

Lord Tidmouth considered.

"Now I come to remember it, he did say something to me down at that seaside place about being in love."

"I was sure of it. William is pining for that peroxide woman."

"You mean Lottie?"

"The flashy young person I sent to the sanitarium."

Lord Tidmouth shook his head.

"I don't think so. I have an idea he told me he was in love with someone else."

Sir Hugo was not a man who took kindly to having his diagnoses questioned.

"Absurd! Nothing of the kind. Do you think I don't know what I'm talking about? He was infatuated with that young woman then, and he's still infatuated with her. Possibly we ought not to be surprised. After all, they parted only a mere two weeks ago. But I confess I am much disturbed."

"What are you going to do about it?"

A senile cunning gleamed from Sir Hugo's eyes.

"Rather ask what *have* I done about it."

"All right. What *have* you done about it?"

"Never mind."

"Then why did you tell me to ask?" said Lord Tidmouth, justly aggrieved.

He went to the table and mixed himself another whisky and soda with an injured air. Sir Hugo was far too occupied to observe it.

"Young man," he said, "have you ever studied psychology?"

"Psy—"

" —chology."

Lord Tidmouth shook his head.

"Well, no," he said, "not to any great extent. They didn't teach me much at school except the difference between right and wrong. There *is* some difference, but I've forgotten what."

"Have you ever asked yourself what is the secret of the glamour which this young woman exercises over William?"

"I suppose it's the same she used to exercise over *me*. Used to be married to her once, don't you know."

"What!"

"Oh yes. But it blew over."

Sir Hugo considered this unforeseen piece of information. He seemed to be turning it over in his mind.

"I cannot decide whether that is good or bad."

"Bit of both, I found out."

"I mean, whether it helps my plan or not."

"What plan?"

"It is based on psychology. I ask myself, What is this young person's attraction for William based on?"

"Psychology?" asked Lord Tidmouth, who was becoming fogged.

"It is due to the fact that he has encountered her so far only in the gaudy atmosphere of hotels and dance halls—her natural setting. But suppose he should see her in the home of his ancestors, where every stick and stone breathes of family traditions, beneath the eyes of the family portraits? What then?"

"I'll bite. What?"

"She would disgust him. His self-respect would awaken. The scales would fall from his eyes, and his infatuation would wither and decay. Whatever his faults, William is a Bannister."

"In that case, it might be a sound scheme to invite her down here for a visit."

Sir Hugo chuckled.

"Ha, ha! Young man, can you keep a secret?"

"I don't know. I've never tried."

"Well, let me tell you this, Lord Tidmouth. I have the situation well in hand. Youth," said Sir Hugo, "may fancy it can control its own destiny, but Age, with its riper wisdom, is generally able, should the occasion arise, to lay it a stymie. Excuse me, I must go and putt."

Lord Tidmouth resumed his solitaire. He was glad Sir Hugo had left him. He had nothing specific against the old buster, but it was pleasanter to be alone. Presently he was deep in his game once more, and singing like a nightingale.

"My strength's something—something..." sang Lord Tidmouth. And then, more confidently, as one feeling himself on secure ground:

And a right good shield of hides untanned...

He put a red five on a black six.

And a right good shield of hides untanned...

A four of clubs went on the red five.

Which on my arm I ber-huckle...

A slight but definite sound as of one in pain, coming from his immediate rear, aroused him, and he turned. He perceived his friend William Bannister.

"Hullo, Bill, old man. You back?"

Bill was looking cautiously about him.

"Where's my uncle?"

"Just oozed off. Want me to call him?"

"Good heavens, no. Squiffy..."

"Hullo?"

Bill did not reply for a few moments. These moments he occupied in wandering in a rather feverish manner about the room, fiddling with various objects that came in his path. He halted at the mantelpiece, gazed for a while at the portrait of his great-grandfather which hung above it, quickly wearied of the spectacle and resumed his prowling. Lord Tidmouth watched him with growing disapproval. Between Sir Hugo Drake and this William, his quiet, peaceful evening was being entirely disorganised.

"Squiffy!" said Bill, halting suddenly.

"Still here," replied Lord Tidmouth plaintively. "What's the idea? Training for a marathon?"

"Squiffy," said Bill, "listen to me. We're pals, aren't we?"

"Absolutely. Bosom is the way I should put it."

"Very well, then. I want you to do me a great service."

"What?"

"Get my uncle out of the way tonight."

"Murder him?"

"If you like. Anyway, go to his room with me and see that he gets to sleep. Tonight I want to be alone."

Lord Tidmouth had listened so far, but he refused to listen any further without lodging a definite protest. It was not so much the fact that, having been invited down to this place for a restful visit, he found himself requested by his host to go and tell his uncle bedtime stories. What was jarring his sensitive soul was the sinister atmosphere his old friend had begun to create.

"Bill, old man," he said, "you're being very mysterious this P.M. You shimmer about and dash in and out of rooms and make dark, significant speeches. All you need is a mask and false whiskers and you could step into any mystery play and no questions asked. What's up?"

"I'll tell you."

"You forgot to say 'Hist'!"

Bill drew up a chair and sank his voice to a whisper.

"I've got a big thing on tonight and I must not be interrupted."

The pained look on Lord Tidmouth's face deepened. Of course, he supposed, it didn't really matter, seeing that they were alone, but he did wish that Bill could conduct a chat with an old crony without converting it into something that suggested an executive session of the Black Hand or a conference between apaches in some underground den in Montmartre.

"Old egg," he said, "do stop being mysterious. A big thing, you say? Well, tell me in a frank, manly way what it is. Get it right off the chest, and we'll both feel easier."

Bill mused, as if seeking words.

"Well, if you want the thing in a nutshell, tonight, Squiffy, I put my fate to the test—to win or lose it all, as the poet says."

"What poet?"

"What the devil does it matter what poet?"

"I merely asked."

"Montrose, if you really want to know."

"I don't."

Bill rose and resumed his pacing.

"Squiffy, do you know what it is to be in love?"

"Do I!" Lord Tidmouth spoke with a specialist's briskness. "My dear chap, except for an occasional rainy Monday, I don't suppose I've been out of love in the last six years. If you think a man can accumulate four wives without knowing what it is to be in love, try it and see."

"Well, I'm in love. So much in love that I could howl like a dog." He broke off and regarded his companion sharply. "I suppose," he said, "you're going to ask 'What dog?' "

"No, no," Lord Tidmouth assured him. He knew—no man better—that there were all sorts of dogs. Mastiffs, Pekes, Alsatians, Aberdeen terriers ... scores of them. He had had no intention of saying, "What dog?"

Bill clenched his hands.

"It's awful. It's killing me."

Lord Tidmouth was impressed.

"Bill, old man," he said, "this is serious news. We all thought you had got over it. So your old uncle was actually right! Well, well!"

"What do you mean?"

"I felt all along," proceeded Lord Tidmouth, "that something like this would happen. I wanted to warn you at the time. You see, having been married to her myself, I know her fascination. Yes, I nearly warned you at the time. 'Bill, old bird,' I came within a toucher of saying, 'pause before it is too late!' And now she's in a sanitarium, and you're pining for her. 'Oh, for the touch of a vanished hand...' "

Bill stared an unfriendly stare.

"What on earth are you talking about? Who's in a sanitarium?"

"Lottie, of course."

"Lottie? Are you really idiot enough to suppose I'm in love with Lottie?"

His tone stung Lord Tidmouth.

"Better men than you have been, Bill," he said. "Myself, for one. The recent Higginbotham, presumably, for another. Let me tell you that there are many more difficult things in this world than falling in love with Lottie. Whom are you in love with, then?"

Bill breathed rapturously.

"Sally!"

"Who's Sally?"

"Sally Smith."

Lord Tidmouth made a great mental effort.

"You don't mean the lady doctor down at Bingley?"

"Yes, I do."

"And you're in love with her?"

"Yes."

"Well," said Lord Tidmouth, bewildered, "this is all new stuff to me." He reflected. "But, if you miss her so much, why did you come down here, miles away from her?"

"I couldn't stay near her. It was driving me mad."

"Why?"

"She wouldn't let me tell her how much I loved her."

"I see."

Bill sprang up.

"Shall I tell you something, Squiffy?"

"By all means, old boy. I'm here to listen."

"I went to see her just before I left Bingley. I was absolutely determined that this time I would ask her to marry me. And do you know what happened?"

"What?"

A bitter laugh escaped Bill Bannister. At least, Lord Tidmouth presumed that it was a bitter laugh. It had sounded more like a death rattle.

"The moment I appeared—before I could even speak—she said: 'Put out your tongue!' "

"What did you do?"

"I put it out. 'Coated,' she said, and prescribed a mild tonic. Now, could I have followed that up by asking her to be my wife?"

"It wasn't what you would call a good cue," admitted Lord Tidmouth.

"I left," said Bill. "I came away, cursing. Cursing everything —myself, my luck and the fate that ever brought us together. I came down here, hoping that I would get over it. Not a chance. I'm worse than ever. But today, thank heaven, I got an idea."

"What was that?"

Bill looked about the room warily, as if suspecting the presence of Hugo Drakes in every nook and cranny. Relieved to see not even one, he resumed.

"I said to myself—she's a doctor. If I were ill, she would fly to my side. I looked her up in the telephone book. I found her name. I sat staring at that telephone book most of the afternoon, and it stared back at me. At five o'clock I gave in and... "

"Good Lord! Telephoned?"

"Yes. I pretended to be my man. I said that Mr. Bannister was seriously ill. We were sending the car and would she come at once."

Lord Tidmouth whistled.

"You certainly don't mind taking a chance."

"Not when there's something worth taking a chance for. It's a two hours' ride in the car. The chauffeur left at half-past six. He should have reached her between half-past eight and nine. She ought to get here just about eleven."

"It's nearly eleven now."

"Yes. So can you wonder I'm a little jumpy?"

"Do you think she'll come?"

Bill quivered.

"She *must* come. She must. And I shall have it out with her fairly and squarely. No more dodging and evasion. She shan't put me off this time... So now perhaps you'll understand why you've got to keep my infernal, snooping, blundering, fussing busybody of an uncle out of the way."

"But he'll hear her drive up in the car."

"Why? The car's almost noiseless."

Lord Tidmouth pondered.

"Well," he said at length, "I'm glad I'm not you."

"Why?"

"Because it is my firm and settled belief, old top, that, when she gets here and finds it was all a put-up job, this female is going to cut up rough."

"Don't call her a female."

"Well, she *is*, isn't she? I mean, that's rather what you might call the idea, I should have thought."

"She won't suspect. I shall convince her that I'm a sick man."

"By the time she has done with you you probably will be. Hell hath no fury like a woman who's come eighty miles to be made a fool of."

"Don't be such a pessimist."

"Oh, all right. Have it your own way. All I can say is, may the Lord have mercy on your soul. I mean..."

"Sh!" whispered Bill sharply. He turned to the door. "Hullo, Uncle, how's the putting coming along?"

Sir Hugo Drake was in spacious mood. He beamed cordially. "A very marked and sustained improvement."

"That's good. Off to bed now?"

"Yes. Off to bed now. Early to bed, early to rise, nothing like it for keeping the eye clear and the hand steady."

"Tidmouth wants to come up with you and have a chat."

"Delighted."

"Tell him that excellent story of yours about the caddie and the indiarubber tee."

"Certainly. Well, come along, my boy. You coming, William?"

"No, I think I'll sit up a little longer."

"Good night, then. See you in the morning."

He wandered out. Lord Tidmouth lingered. He seemed a little anxious.

"Is that a long story, Bill?"

"Longish," admitted Bill. "But to help a pal, Squiffy..."

"Oh, all right," said Lord Tidmouth resignedly. "We Tidmouths never desert a friend. Well, honk honk!"

He smiled bravely, and followed Sir Hugo.

The summons to William Bannister's sickbed had come to Sally, oddly enough, at a moment when she had just been thinking of that sufferer. For it is a curious fact that, busy woman though she was, she had found herself thinking quite a good deal about Bill in these last two weeks. And, if excuses must be made for her, let these meditations be set down to the quality in him that made him different from other men—his naive directness.

Sally, both in her native America and during her stay in England, had been called upon at fairly frequent intervals to reject the proffered hands and hearts of many men. These had conducted the negotiations in a variety of ways, but none, not even the most forceful, had affected her quite like William Bannister. There was a childlike earnestness about his wooing which she found engaging.

It seemed a pity to her that with the admirable quality of directness he should combine that other quality which above all others in this world she despised and disliked—the quality of being content to sit down and loaf his life away on inherited money. She had seen so many of these good-looking, amiable, feckless Englishmen of private means, and all her instincts rose against them. Except as a joke, they were impossible. With so much to be done in life, they did nothing.

And Bill Bannister was one of them. She liked his looks and that easy, athletic swing of his body. She found him pleasant and agreeable. But he was also bone-idle, a well-bred waster, a drone who had nothing better to do with his time than hang about seashore resorts, dangling after perfumed and peroxided females of doubtful character.

For Sally's verdict on Lottie, pieced together from a brief acquaintance and a review of the dubious circumstances in which he had found her, was not a flattering one. She ignored the "Higginbotham" which should have been such a hallmark of respectability. She thoroughly disbelieved in the Higginbotham. Her views on the late Mr. Higginbotham were identical with those of Betsy Prigg on her friend Sairey Gamp's friend Mrs. Harris. Firmly and decisively, Sally had set Lottie down in the ranks of those who are so well described as "no better than they should be."

Sometimes Sally wondered a little why it was that she should feel this odd indignation against a woman who was virtually a complete stranger. It could not be because the other had ensnared William Bannister. William Bannister and his affairs were, of course, nothing to her. So what might have seemed to a superficial investigator a straight case of jealousy was nothing of the kind.

It did not matter to her a row of pins who entrapped William Bannister.

Nevertheless, every time she thought of Lottie, an odd thrill of indignation passed through Sally.

And every time she thought of William Bannister wasting his time on such a woman, she felt another thrill of indignation.

The whole thing was perplexing.

Her feelings, as she bowled along the Hampshire roads in Bill's car tonight, were mixed. She was sorry he was not feeling well, though she much doubted whether his ailment were as severe as she had been given to understand. Men were all alike—men of Bill Bannister's kind especially so. A pain in the toe and they thought they were dying.

Of the chance of visiting the home of Bill's ancestors she was glad. With her American love of the practical she combined that other American love for old houses and historic associations. She had read up The Manor, Woollam Chersey, in *Stately Homes of England*, and was intrigued to find that parts of it dated back to the thirteenth century, while even the more modern portions were at least Elizabethan. She looked forward to seeing on the morrow its park, its messuages, its pleasances and the record-breaking oak planted by the actual hand of King Charles the First.

Tonight, as she passed through the great gateway and bowled up the drive, there was little to be seen. Dark trees and banks of shrubs blocked what little would have been visible in the darkness. It was only when the car stopped that she realised that she had reached the house.

Sally got out and dismissed the chauffeur. She could find her way in. There was an open french window at the end of the lawn on her left, from which light proceeded. She made her way thither, and on the threshold stopped. A rather remarkable sight had met her eyes. Inside, walking with the brisk step of a man in perfect health up and down a cosily furnished room, was her patient.

Anyone less wasted with sickness she had never seen.

Up and down the floor paced Bill. He was smoking a cigarette. A thrill of honest indignation shot through Sally. She saw all. And in the darkness her teeth came together with a little click.

Somewhere in the room a telephone tinkled. Bill moved beyond her range of vision. But his voice came to her clearly.

"Hullo?... Grosvenor 7525?... Doctor Smith's house?... This is Mr. Bannister's valet speaking. Can you tell me if the doctor has left?... Just before nine?... Thank you... Hullo... The doctor will not be returning tonight... Yes, very serious. She will have to sit up with the patient... Yes... Good night."

There came the click of the receiver being replaced, and then for some moments silence. But a few moments later there was something for Sally to see again. Her patient had apparently left the room during this interval, for he now reappeared wearing a dark silk dressing gown. He then proceeded to arrange a pillow and lie down on the sofa. And after that he seemed to be of the opinion that the stage was adequately set, for he remained there without moving.

Sally waited no longer. Outwardly calm, but seething within with what Lord Tidmouth had called the fury of a woman who has driven eighty miles to be made a fool of, she walked briskly into the room.

"Good evening!" she said suddenly and sharply, and Bill Bannister shot up from the sofa as though compelled by an explosive.

Bill stood staring. His nervous system, in its highly strung condition, was not proof against this entirely unexpected greeting. The Manor was not haunted, but if it had been and if the family spectre had suddenly presented itself at his elbow and barked at him, he would have reacted in a very similar way. He gulped, and fingered his collar.

"You made me jump!" he said plaintively.

Sally was cool and hostile.

"Weren't you expecting me?"

"Er—yes. Yes. Of course."

"Well, here I am."

This was undeniable, and Bill should have accepted it as such. He should also have sunk back on the sofa, thus indicating that the effort he had just made had been too much for his frail strength. Instead, he became gushingly hospitable.

"I say, do sit down, won't you? Won't you have something to eat —something to drink?"

Sally raised her eyebrows.

"I must say," she observed, "that for a man who has brought a doctor a night journey of eighty miles you look surprisingly well."

Bill rejected the idea passionately.

"I'm not," he cried. "I'm desperately ill."

"Oh?" said Sally.

Bill's manner became defiant, almost sullen.

"You can't tell how a man's feeling just by looking at him," he said.

"I don't intend to. We'll have a thorough examination."

A devout look came into Bill's eyes.

"It's like a dream," he said.

"What is?"

"Your being here... in my home... "

"Tell me your symptoms," said Sally.

Bill blinked.

"Did you say symptoms?"

"I did."

"Well... I say, do let me help you off with your coat."

"I can manage," said Sally. She removed her wraps and threw them on a chair. "Now, then... Hello! You're shivering!"

"Am I," said Bill.

"Do you feel chilly?"

"No. Hot all over."

"Let me feel your pulse... H'm! A hundred and ten. Very

interesting. And yet you haven't a temperature. A pulse of a hundred and ten without fever. Quite remarkable. Do you feel dizzy?"

"Yes," said Bill truthfully.

"Then sit down."

"Thanks," said Bill, doing so. "Won't you?"

Sally opened her bag, and from it removed an odd something, at which her patient gazed with unconcealed apprehension.

"What's that?" he asked.

"Stethoscope," said Sally briefly. "Now we can get on."

"Yes," said Bill doubtfully. He had heard of stethoscopes and knew them to be comparatively harmless, but he was still uneasy. In his visions of this moment, he had always seen this girl bending over him with a divine sympathy in her lovely eyes—trembling a little perhaps—possibly passing a cool hand over his forehead. Up to the present, she had done none of these things. Instead, she seemed to him—though this, he forced himself to feel, was merely due to his guilty conscience—annoyed about something.

A simple solution of the mystery came to him. In spite of the fact that she had ignored his previous offer of refreshment, she really needed some. She had had a tiring journey, and tiring journeys always affected women like this. He recalled an aunt of his, who, until you shot a cup of tea into her, always became —even after the simplest trip—a menace to man and beast.

"I say, do have something to eat and drink," he urged.

Sally frowned.

"Later," she said. "Now, then—the symptoms, please."

Bill made a last effort to stem the tide.

"Must we talk about my symptoms?" he asked plaintively.

"Might I mention," retorted Sally, "that I've driven eighty miles simply in order to talk about them."

"But surely there's not such a desperate hurry as all that? I mean, can't we have just five minutes' conversation. . . . " Her eye was not encouraging, but he persevered. "You don't seem to understand how tremendously happy it makes me—to see you sitting there..."

Sally cut into his rambling discourse like an east wind.

"It may seem eccentric to you, Mr. Bannister," she said frigidly, "but when I get an urgent call to visit an invalid I find my thoughts straying in the direction of his health. It's a foolish habit we doctors have. So may I repeat—the symptoms?" She fixed him with a compelling glance. "When," she asked, "did you first notice that there was anything wrong with you?"

Bill could answer that.

"Three weeks ago."

"About the time you first met me."

"Yes."

"An odd coincidence. What happened?"

"My heart stood still."

"It couldn't."

"It did."

"Hearts don't stand still."

"Mine did," insisted Bill stoutly. "It then had strong palpitations. They've been getting worse ever since. Sometimes," he proceeded, beginning to get into his stride, "I feel as if I were going to suffocate. It is as if I were being choked inside by an iron hand."

"Probably dyspepsia. Go on."

"My hands tremble. My head aches. My feet feel like lead. I have floating spots before the eyes and I can't sleep."

"No?"

"Not a wink. I toss on my pillow. I turn feverishly from side to side. But it's all no good. Dawn comes and finds me still awake. I stare before me hopelessly. Another night," concluded Bill with fine pathos, "has passed, and in the garden outside the roosters are crowing."

"Anything connected with roosters," said Sally, "you had better tell to a vet."

A man in a sitting position finds it difficult to draw himself up indignantly, but Bill did his best.

"Is that all you can do to a patient—laugh at him?"

"If you think I am finding this a laughing matter," said Sally grimly, "you're wrong. Undress, please."

Bill started violently.

"What... what did you say?" he quavered.

"Undress," Sally repeated.

"But... but I can't."

"Would you like me to help you?"

"I mean—is it necessary?"

"Quite."

"But..."

Sally surveyed him coolly.

"I notice the vascular motors are still under poor control," she said. "Why do you blush?"

"What do you expect me to do—cheer?" Bill's voice shook. The prude in him had been deeply stirred. "Look here," he demanded, "do you mean to tell me this is the first time any of your male patients has jibbed at undressing in front of you?"

"Oh no. I had a case last week."

"I'm glad," said Bill primly, "that somebody has a little delicacy besides myself."

"It wasn't delicacy. He didn't want me to see that he was wearing detachable cuffs. You know the kind? They fasten on with a clip, and are generally made of celluloid. Like motion-picture films."

"Er—do you go much to the pictures?" asked Bill.

Sally refused to allow the conversation to be diverted.

"Never mind whether I go to the pictures," she said. "Please undress."

Bill gave up the struggle. He threw off his dressing gown.

"That'll do for the present," said Sally. "I can't think what you were making such a fuss about. Your cuffs aren't detachable... Now, please."

She placed the stethoscope against his chest, and applied her ear to it. Bill gazed down upon the top of her head emotionally.

"I wonder," he said, "if you realise what this means to me—to see you here—in my home—to feel that we two are alone together at last..."

"Did you ever have any children's diseases?"

"No... Alone together at last..."

"Mumps?" said Sally.

Bill gulped.

"No!"

"Measles?"

"No!" shouted Bill.

Sally looked up.

"I merely asked," she said.

Bill was quivering with self-pity.

"It's too bad," he said. "Here I am, trying to pour out my soul to you, and you keep interrupting with questions about mumps and measles."

"My dear Mr. Bannister," said Sally, "I'm not interested in your soul. My job has to do with what the hymnbook calls your 'vile body.'"

There was a pause. She put her ear to the stethoscope again.

"Can't you understand," cried Bill, breaking into eloquence once more, "that the mere sight of you sets every nerve in my body tingling? When you came in I felt like a traveller in the desert who is dying of thirst and suddenly comes upon an oasis. I felt..."

"Any retching or nausea?"

"Oh, my God!"

"Now tell me about your sex life," said Sally.

Bill recoiled.

"Stand still."

"I won't stand still," said Bill explosively.

"Then move about," said Sally equably. "But give me the information I asked for."

Bill eyed her austerely.

"Don't you know the meaning of the word 'reticence'?" he asked.

"Of course not. I'm a doctor."

Bill took a turn up and down the room.

"Well, naturally," he said with dignity, halting once more, "I have had—er—experiences—like other men."

Sally was at the stethoscope again.

"Um-hum?" she said.

"I admit it. There *have* been women in my life."

"Say ninety-nine."

"Not half as many as that!"

"Say ninety-nine, please."

"Oh?" Bill became calmer. "I didn't... I thought... I imagined that you were referring... Well, in short, ninety-nine."

Sally straightened herself. She put the stethoscope away.

"Thank you," she said. "Your lungs appear to be all right. Remove the rest of your clothes, please."

"What!"

"You heard."

"I won't do it," cried Bill pinkly.

Sally shrugged her shoulders.

"Just as you like," she said. "Then the examination is finished." She paused. "Tell me, Mr. Bannister," she asked, "just to satisfy my curiosity, what sort of a fool did you think I was?"

Bill gaped.

"I beg your pardon?"

"I'm glad you have the grace to. Did you imagine that this was the first time I had ever been called out into the country?"

"I..."

"Let me tell you it is not. And do you know what usually happens when I am called to the country? I see you don't," she said, as Bill choked wordlessly. "Well, when I am sent for to visit a patient in the country, Mr. Bannister, the road is lined with anxious relatives, waiting for the car. They help me out and bustle me into the house. They run around like chickens with their heads cut off —and everybody who isn't having hysterics on the stairs is in the kitchen brewing camomile tea."

"Camomile tea?"

"People who get sick in the country are always given camomile tea."

"I never knew that before."

"You'll learn a lot of things," said Sally, "if you stick around with me. And one of them, Mr. Bannister, is that I'm not a complete idiot. You'll excuse my slight warmth. I've driven eighty miles on a fool's errand, and somehow I find it a little irritating."

Bill waved his hands agitatedly.

"But I tell you you're wrong."

"What! Have you the nerve to pretend there's anything whatever the matter with you?"

"Certainly there is. I—I'm not myself."

"I congratulate you."

"I'm a very sick man."

"And I'm a very angry woman."

Bill coughed an injured cough.

"Of course, if you don't believe me, there's nothing more to say."

"Oh, isn't there?" said Sally. "I'll find plenty more to say, trust *me*. I may as well tell you, Mr. Bannister, that when I arrived I looked in at the window and saw you striding about, the picture of health. A moment later, the telephone rang and you went to it and said you were your valet..."

Bill flushed darkly. He moved to the window and stood there, looking out with his back turned. Sally watched him with satisfaction. Her outburst had left her feeling more amiable.

Bill wheeled round. His face was set. He spoke through clenched teeth.

"I see," he said. "So you knew all along, and you've been amusing yourself at my expense?"

"You might say—getting a little of my own back."

"You've had a lot of fun with me, haven't you?"

"Quite a good deal, since you mention it."

"And now, I suppose, you're going?"

"Going?" said Sally. "Of course I'm not. I shall sleep here. You don't expect me to drive all night, do you?"

"I beg your pardon," said Bill. He pointed to the gallery that ran round two sides of the room. "You'll be up there."

"Thank you."

Bill laughed shortly.

"Well, it's something, I suppose, that you have consented to sleep under my roof."

"You could hardly have expected me to go to the garage."

"No. I suppose you would like to be turning in, then?"

"Yes, please."

"I'll show you to your room."

"You have already."

"Well... good night," said Bill.

"Good night," said Sally.

He stood without moving, watching her as she went up the stairs. She reached the door, opened it, and was gone. Bill turned sharply and flung himself into a chair.

He had been sitting for some minutes, with only his thoughts for unpleasant company, when there was the sound of a footstep on the stairs, and he sprang up as though electrified.

But it was not Sally. It was only Lord Tidmouth. That ill-used gentleman was looking rather weary, and his eyes, as he reached the foot of the stairs, were fixed purposefully on the decanter on the table. He moved towards it with a stealthy rapidity, like a leopard; and only when he had poured into a glass a generous measure of the life-restoring fluid did he turn to his host.

"Hullo, Bill, old man," said his lordship.

Bill regarded him sourly.

"Oh, it's you, is it?" he said.

Lord Tidmouth sighed.

"What's left of me after an hour's tête-à-tête with the old relative," he said. "Bill, that uncle of yours waggles a wicked jawbone!"

"Does he?"

"He talked and talked and talked. And then he talked some more. Mostly about his mashie shots. I got him off to bye-bye at last, and I've tottered down to restore the tissues with a spot of alcohol. They say," continued Lord Tidmouth earnestly, "that strong drink biteth like a serpent and—if I remember correctly—stingeth like a jolly old adder. Well, all I have to say is—let it! That's what I say, Bill—*let* it! It's what it's there for. Excuse me for a moment, old man, while I mix myself a stiffish serpent and soda."

He turned to the table again.

"So you got him off to sleep?" said Bill.

Lord Tidmouth's fingers had been closing about the siphon, but he courteously suspended operations in order to reply to his host's question.

"Yes," he said, "I got him off to sleep. But at infinite cost to life and limb. I feel a perfect wreck. However, I've left him slumbering like a little child, one hand still clutching James Braid's *Advanced Golf*. So that's that."

"Much obliged. Well, I'll be turning in."

"Half a moment," said Lord Tidmouth. "Isn't it about time that lady doctor of yours rolled up? Allowing two hours for the journey—that is, assuming she had no puncture or blowout or engine trouble or lost the way or..."

"Oh, go to blazes!" said Bill.

Lord Tidmouth watched his disappearing back with rather an aggrieved air.

"Not one of our good listeners!" he murmured.

Then, having sterner work before him than the consideration of a host's brusqueness, he addressed himself once more to the siphon.

Lord Tidmouth was a careful man with siphons. Experience had taught him that a too vehement pressing of the trigger led to disaster. Strong drink might bite like an adder, but soda water could spout like a geyser. He knew the perils perfectly, and it was, therefore, all the more annoying that a moment later a hissing stream should have shot up between his cuff and his skin.

This happened because, as he was in the very act of working the trigger arrangement, a loud and breezy voice in his immediate rear spoke.

"Hullo!" it said.

Voices speaking to Lord Tidmouth where no voice should have been always affected him powerfully. He became involved in a Niagara of seltzer, from which he emerged to gaze censoriously at the intruder.

"If you know me a thousand years," he was beginning, as he turned, "never do that again!" Then he saw the newcomer steadily and saw her whole. For it was a she. It was, as a matter of fact, none other than the first of his battalion of wives—the exuberant Lottie Higginbotham. And he stared at her as at a vision.

"Great God of Battles!" said Lord Tidmouth. "You!"

Lottie was completely at her ease. She placed on the floor the suitcase which she was carrying, and with a dexterous hand removed the whisky and soda from her companion's grasp. She drank deeply and, having done so, sighed with satisfaction.

"You always did know how to mix them, Squiffy," she said.

It was a handsome compliment—and rather touching, in its way, as giving evidence that the memory of the dear old days still lingered. But Lord Tidmouth paid no attention to it. He was still goggling.

"What on earth are you doing here?" he asked blankly.

"Who, me?" said Lottie.

"Yes, you."

"I was sent for."

"How do you mean, sent for?"

"I got a telegram from Bill's uncle asking me to come."

A blinding flash of light illuminated Lord Tidmouth's darkness. He recalled the veiled hints the old boy had dropped earlier in the evening. So this was what he had been hinting at!

"Did he specify that you were to come beetling in at midnight?" he inquired.

"I came directly I got the telegram. It sounded interesting."

"Oh?" Lord Tidmouth pondered for awhile. "Well, welcome to the manor and all that sort of rot," he said.

Lottie was very bright and animated. She flitted about the room like a hummingbird.

"This looks a pretty good sort of place," she said. "I can see myself in a place like this. Who are all these?" she asked, indicating the portraits.

"Just ancestors," said Lord Tidmouth. "Bill's. Bill's ancestors."

"No beauty chorus," was Lottie's comment, after she had made her round of inspection. "Talking of Bill, is he expecting me?"

"No, he's not!"

"Oh? Then I shall come on him as a surprise."

"Surprise," said Lord Tidmouth, with feeling, "is *right!*"

"Listen," said Lottie. Do you know why Sir Hugo wanted me to come here?"

Lord Tidmouth was embarrassed. He did know, but he could hardly impart the information.

"I couldn't tell you."

"I'm telling *you*," said Lottie brightly. "I thought it all out on the train. Bill has discovered that he can't get on without me. I knew it would happen. He's pining for me. Yessir, that's what that boy's doing—pining for me."

"Well..."

"It stands to reason," argued Lottie, "he must be pretty crazy about me to make his old uncle wire for me in such a hurry."

Lord Tidmouth closed his eyes. He seemed to be praying.

"Full information," he said, "will no doubt be supplied tomorrow by the aged relative. But, if you'll take a pal's advice—if you'll be guided by one to whom you once stood in a sacred and tender relationship, viz., marriage," explained Lord Tidmouth, "you will biff off at the earliest opportunity."

"What!"

"At the very earliest opp."

"What are you talking about?"

Lord Tidmouth groaned in spirit. He was feeling unequal to the situation. At any moment now, he told himself, that lady doctor of old Bill's would be breezing in, and naturally the last thing the dear old boy would wish was to have the place congested with extraneous females. Sir Hugo Drake, the pre-eminent dodderer, had made a proper mess of things.

"You just tuck yourself away somewhere till tomorrow morning," he urged, "and then we'll smuggle you off."

Lottie stared. She had never had a very high opinion of her former husband's intelligence, but she had never known him to descend into such abysses of lunacy as this.

"I think you're cuckoo," she said. "What do I want to go away for? Bill's in love with me and can't live without me."

"Absolutely," said Lord Tidmouth. "Of course. Quite so. Yes. Beyond a question. Indubitably. Only..."

"Well?"

"Nothing, nothing. You see that room on top of the stairs? Technically, it's mine, but you can have it for tonight. Not the one to the right. That's Bill's. The one to the left. Accept it with my hearty good wishes."

"What'll you do?"

"Oh, I'll doss somewhere. And in the morning..."

Lottie eyed him sharply.

"Listen!" she said.

"Hullo?"

"Is anything the matter?"

"The matter?"

"You're acting sort of mysterious, it seems to me, and I'm wondering if there's any funny business going on. Are you trying to keep Bill and me apart?"

"No, no."

"Well, you better hadn't, that's all," said Lottie decidedly. "If I find you're pulling any smooth stuff, I'll murder you. Nothing could be fairer than that, could it?"

"Absolutely not."

"Well, good night, then."

"Good night!" said Lord Tidmouth.

Alone at last, he found in the confused welter of his thoughts one thing clear—that he had not yet had that drink and that he wanted it now more than ever. He moved to the table, and began the ritual again. He had barely completed it when once more a voice spoke behind him.

"You still up?" It was his old friend, Bill Bannister. There was surprise in Bill's voice. Also irritation and peevishness. "Why the devil don't you go to bed?"

"Why don't *you?*" rejoined Lord Tidmouth, not unreasonably.

"I'm restless," said Bill. "I can't sleep."

Lord Tidmouth eyed him pityingly. The nonsleeping his old friend had done so far would, he felt, be a mere nothing compared to the nonsleeping he would do when he heard the latest.

"Bill," he said, and his tone was the unmistakable tone of a man who is going to break something gently. "I've a piece of information to impart."

"Keep it for the morning."

"But it's serious. Bill, we have a little visitor!"

"I know. I know."

Lord Tidmouth was relieved.

"Oh, you *know*? I thought you didn't. But how do you know?" he went on, puzzled. "She only just..."

"Stop babbling and go to bed."

"Yes, but, Bill..."

"Shut up."

"Lottie..."

"Don't talk to me about Lottie."

"I was only saying that Lottie..."

"Stop it."

"I just wanted to mention that Lottie..."

"Will you get out!"

Lord Tidmouth gave it up.

"Oh, all right," he said resignedly. "I think I'll take a stroll in the garden. Well, bung-oh! And I came down here for a rest cure!"

Bill ran quickly up the stairs and knocked at Sally's door. The conclusion of their recent conversation had left him in a nervous and disordered frame of mind. Though she had plainly shown herself of the opinion that all had been said that needed to be said, he was unable to adopt this view. He was full of talk, and considered that in their late interview he had but scratched the surface.

"Sally!" he said in a choking voice.

A voice from within answered.

"What is it? Who's there?"

"Come out. I want to talk to you."

Sally emerged. She was wearing a pale green wrap.

"Well?" she said.

Bill did not answer immediately. The sight of the wrap had had a stunning effect. He had not supposed that it was possible that this girl could look prettier than when he had seen her last, but she had accomplished this stupendous feat with ease. His legs shook, and he leaned against the banisters.

"Have you got everything you want?" he managed to ask at length.

"Yes, thank you. I find that you have given me your room."

"Yes."

"Where are you going to sleep?"

"I shall manage."

"Oh? Well, it's very kind of you." She paused. "Was that all you wanted to say to me?"

"No," said Bill urgently.

"Well?"

"Don't stand in that doorway. Come out here."

"Just as you like. Well?"

Bill gulped.

"I've been walking about in the garden," he said.

"Yes?"

"Thinking."

"Yes?"

"Trying to get a grip on myself."

"I hope you were successful," said Sally politely.

"I wasn't."

Sally smiled indulgently.

"Too bad," she said. "Well, good night."

"Come back."

"Sorry," said Sally, returning. "I thought you had finished."

"I haven't begun." He moved to the head of the stairs. "Come on down. We can't talk here."

"Do we want to talk?"

"I do."

"Oh, very well."

She followed him down the stairs.

"Now," said Bill, "we can begin."

Sally had perched herself on the arm of a chair. She eyed him coolly.

"Don't you country folk ever go to bed?" she asked. "I had no idea you wandered about the house all night, knocking at people's doors and dragging them out for cosy talks."

Bill scowled.

"You seem amused."

"I am," said Sally.

"Oh? Well, let me tell you," said Bill, "that we have now finished with the amusing part of this business. I now propose to call your attention to the fact that this little farce, which seems to entertain you so much, has a serious side. I'm going to have it out with you here and now."

"Proceed. You interest me strangely."

"Don't laugh at me!"

"What else do you expect me to do?"

Bill ground his heel into the carpet.

"In the first place," he said, "I admit that I did get you down here by a trick."

"A contemptible trick."

"That's as it may be. Anyway, you're here, and you've got to listen to me."

Sally yawned.

"And to cut a long story short..."

"I'll make it short enough. Three words will be sufficient. I love you."

"This is wonderful news."

"That's right. Laugh! Listen. You think you can play the fool with a man as much as you please—hold him off with a raised eyebrow when he becomes too pressing—keep him under control with a laugh..."

"Why, this is eloquence! The Boy Orator!"

"Oh, you may sneer, but you know in your heart you're afraid."

Sally stiffened. The smile faded from her lips. She froze.

"Afraid? You flatter yourself."

"I may not be your match at fencing," said Bill, "but the bludgeon is quite as handy a weapon as the rapier."

"From the insight you have given me into your character tonight," said Sally, "I should have thought your favourite weapon would have been the blackjack."

"You and I are going to settle things tonight. You have known right from the start that I loved you, and from our first meeting you have fought me. All right! Tonight shall decide which of us two is the strongest."

"*Stronger.* Didn't they teach you that at school? Even when insulting a woman, always be grammatical."

Bill glowered.

"So I'm insulting you? By offering you my love?"

"No," said Sally. "By suggesting that, if I refuse it, you will employ force. For that is what you are suggesting, is it not?"

"Yes. It is."

"Good," said Sally. "Then excuse me for a moment."

She got up.

"What are you doing?"

"I was merely going to fetch my bag and prepare a soothing injection. I should think two centigrams of morphia would be sufficient."

Bill seized her wrist.

"Stop fooling!"

"Oh!" Sally could not restrain a gasp. "You're very strong."

"I'm glad you're beginning to realise it."

"Let me go."

"I won't!" said Bill. "Never again. Well?" he said. "Here you are, in my arms. How do you like it? Now try to be aloof and superior. Now try to hold me off with your matter-of-factness."

"You beast!"

"Beast, eh?" Bill laughed. "I'm improving. Just now I was only a poor fool—just something to laugh at. Laugh at me now—if you can."

Sally suddenly ceased to struggle.

"Oh well!" she said. "They always warned me it was dangerous to be a doctor. Do you know, the last man who treated me like this was a lunatic. In the violent ward of an asylum. But he was more decent than you. He merely wanted to murder me."

She felt the arms that were holding her unclasp. She sank onto the sofa. Bill was looking away from her, out of the window. After a moment, he spoke.

"All right," he said. "You win. I beg your pardon," he said formally.

Sally was herself again.

"Don't mention it," she said. "You might just as well apologise for having rheumatism."

"What!"

"It wasn't your fault. The thing was purely pathological. But I shall have to cure you... I'll write you a little prescription."

Bill started.

"For God's sake!"

Sally went to the desk, and took up a pencil.

"Kalii bromati..." he heard her murmur. "Natrii bromati.. Grammata quinque..." She got up. "Here you are," she said amiably. "One powder three times a day after meals. Any druggist will make that up for you."

"You're very kind!"

"In addition there will be hygienic regulation of your mode of living. Avoid excitement and mental strain."

"Thanks," said Bill. "That's a great help."

"Take plenty of fresh air, do physical jerks every morning, and eat plenty of vegetables. Good night!"

She stroked his face softly, and he quivered. He looked up amazed.

"Sally!"

"What's the matter?"

"You stroked my face."

"Yes."

"Gently."

"Yes."

"Almost—lovingly."

"Yes."

Bill blinked.

"Then..."

"Oh, don't jump to conclusions," said Sally. "The gesture was purely automatic. We doctors often stroke our patients' faces when they have passed the crisis."

"Oh? So you think I have passed the crisis?"

"I think so. You see, you had the sense to call in a good doctor. Good night."

She walked composedly up the stairs. And, as she did so, the door of Lottie's room opened, and its occupant came yawning into view.

"Squiffy!" called Lottie, who, thinking things over in bed, had decided that what was needed to induce sleep was another of her erstwhile mate's scientifically blended glassfuls.

Her eye fell on Bill, gaping below, and she gave tongue cheerily.

"Hullo, Bill!"

She perceived Sally.

"Hul-*lo!*" she said.

Sally said nothing. She walked into her room, and Bill, standing as in a trance, heard the key click in the lock.

Bill came to life. Dashing past Lottie, he rushed at the door. He shook the handle.

"Sally!" he cried. "Sally!"

There was no answer.

Sir Hugo Drake had passed a restful night, undisturbed by dreams of foozled mashie shots. Morning found him sleeping like the little child of Lord Tidmouth's description. Waking as the sun crept over his pillow, he yawned, sat up, and perceived that another day, with all its possibilities for improving a man's putting, had arrived. He donned his favourite suit of plus fours, and, taking putter and ball, went down to the hall.

He had just grounded the ball and was taking careful aim at the leg of the sofa when from the recesses of that sofa two clenched fists suddenly rose in air and an unseen someone uttered the gasping sigh of the newly awakened.

"God bless my soul!" said Sir Hugo.

It was his nephew William. That much was plain from the tousled head which now appeared. Sir Hugo drew nearer to observe this strange phenomenon.

"Oh, hullo, Uncle," said Bill drowsily.

Sir Hugo was a man who always went to the root of a problem.

"William!" he cried. "What are you doing there?"

"Eugh!" replied Bill, stretching. He blinked. "What?" he asked sleepily.

Sir Hugo was not to be diverted from his theme.

"That's what *I* said—'What?'"

"What?"

"Yes, what?"

Bill rubbed his eyes.

"What what?" he asked.

Sir Hugo became impatient.

"Good God, boy, wake up!"

Bill rose to his feet. He inspected his uncle uncertainly.

"What did you ask me?" he said.

"Have you been sleeping there all night?"

"Yes," said Bill. "Oo, I'm stiff!"

"But why?"

"Well, wouldn't *you* be stiff if you had slept all night on a hardish sofa?"

"I'm not asking you why you're stiff. I'm asking you why you slept on that sofa."

Bill was awake now.

"I gave up my room to a lady."

"You gave up your room to a lady?"

"Yes. I... Oh, heavens!" said Bill peevishly. "Need we do this vaudeville cross-talk stuff so early in the morning?"

"But I don't understand. Did a lady arrive last night?"

"Yes. Soon after eleven."

"Good God!" Like Lord Tidmouth, he felt that Lottie had not wasted time. "Did you see her?"

"Of course I saw her."

"I mean—you spoke to her? You had a talk—a conversation—an interview with her?"

"Yes."

Sir Hugo probed delicately for information.

"What occurred?"

"How do you mean, what occurred?"

"Well—er—did you come to an understanding?"

"No!" said Bill.

"Did you—ah—how shall I put it?—did you shower her face with kisses?"

"No, I did not!"

Sir Hugo looked like a minor prophet receiving good news about the latest battle with the Philistines.

"Capital! Excellent! Precisely as I foresaw. When the test came, you found you were a Bannister, after all. I knew it. I knew it."

Bill regarded his rejoicing relative sourly.

"Uncle," he said, "you're gibbering."

He spoke with feeling. The one thing a man does not want to meet, when he has slept all night on a sofa and has not had breakfast, is a gibbering uncle.

"I'm not gibbering," said Sir Hugo. "I repeat that you have proved yourself a true Bannister. You have come nobly out of the ordeal. I foresaw the whole thing. Directly you saw this woman in the home of your ancestors, beneath the gaze of the family portraits, the scales fell from your eyes, and your infatuation withered and died."

Bill would have none of this.

"It did not wither," he said emphatically.

Sir Hugo stared.

"It did not wither?"

"It did not wither."

"You say it did not wither?"

Bill gave him a nasty look.

"Damn it, Uncle, you're back to the cross-talk stuff again."

"You mean to tell me," cried Sir Hugo, "that, even after you have seen this woman in your ancestral home, you are still infatuated with her?"

"More than ever."

"Good God!"

"And I'm not going to rest," said Bill, "till I have made her my wife."

"Your wife?"

"My wife."

"Your—"

Bill held up a warning hand.

"Uncle!"

"You want to *marry* her?"

"Yes."

"But... Good heavens, boy! Have you reflected?"

"Yes."

"Have you considered?"

"Yes."

"Have you gone off your head?"

"Yes. No," said Bill quickly. "What do you mean?"

"You—a Bannister—want to marry this woman?"

"Yes. And I'm going to find her now and tell her so."

Sir Hugo gazed after him blankly. He mopped his forehead and stared gloomily into the future. He was feeling that this was going to put him right off his game. He doubted if he would break a hundred today—after this.

He was still brooding bleakly on this lamentable state of affairs when the door of the room to the left of the stairs opened and Lottie came out, all brightness and camaraderie. Her air of sparkling-eyed cheerfulness smote Sir Hugo like a blow, even before she had come within speaking range.

"Hello, Doc," said Lottie amiably.

"Good morning," said Sir Hugo.

"You don't seem surprised to see me."

"No. I heard that you had arrived. I have just been talking to William, and he has told me the appalling news."

Lottie was puzzled.

"What news?"

"He is resolved to marry you."

A slight but distinct cloud marred Lottie's shining morning face. She looked at her companion narrowly, and her hands began to steal towards her hips.

"Just what," she asked "do you mean by 'appalling news'?"

"It is appalling," said Sir Hugo stoutly.

Lottie breathed softly through her nose.

"You think I'm not good enough for him?"

"Precisely."

"Listen," said Lottie, in a spirit of enquiry, "what's the earliest in the morning you ever got a sock right on the side of the head?"

For the first time Sir Hugo became aware that something he had said—he could not think what—had apparently disturbed and annoyed this woman before him. He did not like the way she was advancing upon him. He had seen tigresses in the zoo walk just like that.

A swift thinker, he took refuge behind a chair and held up a deprecating hand.

"Now, now, my good girl..."

"Don't you call me a good girl!"

"No, no," said Sir Hugo hastily. "You're not, you're not. But, my dear Miss..."

"Mrs."

"My dear Mrs...."

"Higginbotham is the name."

"My dear Mrs. Higginbotham, cannot you see for yourself how impossible this match is?"

Lottie drew in her breath sharply.

"Honest," she said, "I owe it to my womanly feelings to paste you one."

"No, no, be reasonable."

"How do you mean it's impossible?" demanded Lottie warmly. "If Bill's so crazy about me..."

"But William is a Bannister."

"What of it?"

"And you..." Sir Hugo paused carefully. He realised that infinite tact was required. "After all—in the kindliest spirit of academic enquiry—who *are* you?"

"Née Burke. Relict of the late Edward Higginbotham," said Lottie briefly.

"I mean, what is your family?"

"If anybody's been telling you I've a family, it's not true."

"You misunderstand me. But the whole thing is impossible, quite impossible."

"How do you mean?"

Sir Hugo drew a deep breath, and eyed Mr. Higginbotham's widow severely.

"My dear young lady," said Sir Hugo, "have you really reflected what marriage to William would be like? My nephew, you must remember, my dear Mrs. Higginbotham, is a Bannister. And without meaning to be in any way offensive, I think you will admit that your social position is scarcely equal to that of a Bannister. I fear the county would resent it bitterly if William should be considered to have married beneath him. Cannot you see how unpleasant it would be for you, received by nobody, ignored by all? Your proud, generous spirit would never endure it. And, believe me," said Sir Hugo feelingly, "this damned out-of-the-way place is quite dull enough even when you have got a neighbour or two to talk to. My dear girl, you would be bored stiff in a week."

Lottie frowned thoughtfully. Hers was a mind that could face facts, and she had to admit that she had never considered this aspect of the matter before.

"I never thought of that," she said.

"Think of it now," urged Sir Hugo. "Think of it very carefully. In fact, in order to enable you to think the better, I will leave you. Just sit quietly in one of these chairs, and try to picture to yourself what it would be like for you here during—say—the months of January and February, with no amusements, no friends—in short, nothing to entertain you but William. Think it over, Mrs. Higginbotham," said Sir Hugo. "And, if you wish to secure me for a further consultation, you will find me walking in the raspberry bushes."

He bustled out, and Lottie, taking his advice, sat down in a chair and began to think. He had opened up a new line of thought.

Presently, there was a sound behind her, the sound of one meditatively singing, "I fear no foe in shining armour," and she was aware that she had been joined by Lord Tidmouth.

"Hullo, old egg," said Lord Tidmouth.

"Hullo, Squiffy," said Lottie.

She was pleased to see him. Although, some years earlier, she had been compelled to sever the matrimonial bond that linked them, she had always thought kindly of dear old Squiffy. He was her sort. He liked dancing and noisy parties and going to the races and breezing to and fro about London. Theirs, in short, was a spiritual affinity.

"Squiffy," she said, "I've just been having a talk with old what's-his-name."

"Sir Hugo?"

"Yes. Do you know what he said?"

"I can tell you *verbatim*," replied Lord Tidmouth confidently. "He said that, while fair off the tee, he had a lot of trouble with his mashie shots, and this he attributed to..."

"No. He was talking about Bill."

"What about Bill?"

"Well, what would happen if I married Bill."

"What did the old boy predict?"

"He said I would be bored stiff."

Lord Tidmouth considered.

"Well," he said, "I'm not saying he wasn't right. Bill is a stout fellow, one of the best, but you can't get away from the fact that he insists on spending most of his life in this rather mouldy spot."

"Is it mouldy?"

"Pretty mouldy, from what I have seen of it. All right if you care for being buried in the country..."

"It's a pretty place. As far as I've seen—from my window."

"It *is* pretty," agreed Lord Tidmouth. "Very pretty. You might call it picturesque. Have you seen the river?"

"No."

"It lies at the bottom of the garden. Except during the winter months, when—they tell me—the garden lies at the bottom of the river."

Lottie shivered.

"It wouldn't be a very lively place in winter, would it?"

"Not compared with some such spot as London."

"Are you living in London now, Squiffy?"

Lord Tidmouth nodded.

"Yes," he said, "I've come back to lay my old bones in the metrop, when I've done with them, that's to say. I've got a rather sweetish little flat in the Albany."

"The Albany!" breathed Lottie wistfully.

"Right in the centre of things and handy for the theatres, opera houses and places of amusement. All the liveliest joints within a mere biscuit throw."

"Yes."

"Wasted on me, of course, because I never throw biscuits," said Lord Tidmouth. "You must come and see my little nest."

"I will."

"Do."

"Have you plenty of room there?"

"Eh? Oh yes, lots of room."

Lottie paused.

"Room for me?"

"Oh yes."

"I mean—what's the word I want?"

"I don't know, old thing. Where did you see it last?"

"Permanently," said Lottie. "That's it." She came to him and grasped the lapels of his coat. She looked up at him invitingly. "How would you like to have me running round the place, Squiffy?"

Lord Tidmouth wrinkled his forehead.

"I don't think I'm quite getting this," he said. "It seems to be sort of floating past me. If it wasn't for the fact that you're so keen on Bill, I should say you were..."

"I'm going to give Bill up."

"No, really?"

"Yes. I couldn't stick it here. The old boy was quite right. It would give me the willies in a week."

"Something in that."

"And the thought crossed my mind..."

"Well?"

"It just occurred to me as a passing idea..."

"What?"

"Well, you and me..."

"What about us?"

Lottie pulled at his coat.

"We always suited each other, Squiffy," she said. "I'm not denying we had our rows, but we're older now, and I think we should hit it off. We both like the same things. I think we should be awfully happy if we had another try at it."

Lord Tidmouth stared at her, impressed.

"Perfectly amazing you should say that," he said. "The very same thought occurred to me the moment I saw you at Bingley. I remember saying to myself, 'Squiffy, old man' I said, 'haven't you rather, as it were, let a dashed good thing slip from your grasp?' And I replied to myself, 'Yes, old man, I have.'"

Lottie beamed at this twin soul.

"I'm awfully fond of you, Squiffy."

"Awfully nice of you to say so."

"After all, what are brains?"

"Quite."

"Or looks?"

"Exactly."

"Kiss me."

"Right ho."

"Nice?"

"Fine."

"Have another."

"Thanks."

"Once again?"

"In one moment, old thing," said Lord Tidmouth. "We will go into this matter later, when we have a spot more privacy. I observe our genial host approaching."

He waved his hand at the Last of the Bannisters, who was coming in through the french windows from the lawn.

Bill was peevish.

"Oh, there you are!" he said, sighting Lottie.

"Yes, here I am."

"'Morning, Bill," said Lord Tidmouth agreeably."

"Go to hell!" said Bill.

"Right ho," said his lordship.

Bill turned to Lottie.

"Are you proposing to stay here long?" he asked.

"No," said Lottie. "I'm going off to London with my future husband."

"Your—who?"

"Me," said Lord Tidmouth.

Bill digested the news. It did not seem to relieve his gloom.

"Oh?" he said. "Well, a fat lot of use that is—now."

Lottie looked hurt.

"Bill! I believe you're cross with me."

"Cross!"

"Isn't he cross?" asked Lottie, turning to her betrothed for support.

Lord Tidmouth adjusted his monocle and surveyed Bill keenly.

"Yes," he said, "I think he's cross."

Bill quivered with righteous wrath.

"You've only ruined my life, that's all."

"Oh, don't say that, old top."

"I just met her in the garden." Bill's face twisted. "She wouldn't look at me."

"Who wouldn't?" asked Lord Tidmouth.

Bill brooded a moment. Then he turned to Lottie.

"Breakfast is ready in the morning room," he said. "I should be much obliged if you would get yours quick—and go."

"Well, I must say you're a darned fine host!"

"Oh, get along."

"All right," said Lottie proudly. "I'm going."

"Save the brown egg for me," said Lord Tidmouth. "I must remain here awhile and reason with this bird. Bill," he said reproachfully, as Lottie left the room, "you're very hard on that poor little girl, Bill. You show a nasty, domineering, sheik-y spirit which I don't like to see."

"I could wring her neck. What did she want to come here for —and last night of all nights?"

"But be fair, old man. She was sent for. Telegrams were dispatched."

"Sent for?"

"Yes. By the aged relative. He wired to her to come."

Bill stared.

"My uncle did?"

"Yes."

"Why on earth?"

"Well, it was like this. . . ."

Bill blazed into fury.

"I'd like to wring *his* neck. Where is he? I'll go and have a heart-to-heart talk with the old fool. What the devil does he mean by it? *I'll* talk to him."

Lord Tidmouth followed him to the door.

"Steady, old man. Be judicious. Exercise discretion."

He realised that his audience had walked out on him and was now beyond earshot. He came back into the room, and was debating within himself whether it were best to breakfast now, or to postpone that feast till after one or two of the murders which seemed imminent had taken place, when Sally came in from the garden.

"Oh, hullo," he said. "So you got here?"

"Yes," said Sally shortly.

"Well—er—good morning and so forth."

"Good morning."

Lord Tidmouth may not have been one of the world's great thinkers, but he could put two and two together. This female, he reasoned, had turned up, after all, last night, and had presumably seen instantly through poor old Bill's pretence of illness. This would account, in his opinion, for her air of pronounced shirtiness.

"Nice day," he said, for want of a better remark.

"Is it?"

"If you're looking for Bill," said Lord Tidmouth perseveringly, "he's gone out to murder his uncle."

"I am not looking for Mr. Bannister."

"Oh?" said Lord Tidmouth. "Oh? Well, in that case, right ho. Coming in to breakfast?"

"No."

"Oh?"

There was a silence. Lord Tidmouth was not equal to breaking it. Conversationally, he had shot his bolt.

It was Sally who finally spoke.

"Lord Tidmouth."

"On the spot."

Sally choked.

"That woman... that—that woman... how long has she been here?"

"Lottie?" said Lord Tidmouth.

"I don't know her name."

"Well, it's Lottie," he assured her. "Short for Charlotte, I believe. Though you never know."

"Has she been living here?"

"Absolutely not. She arrived last night, round about midnight."

"What! Is that true?"

"Oh, rather. The old uncle sent for her."

"Sir Hugo? Sir *Hugo* sent for her?"

"That's right."

"But why?"

"Well, as far as I could follow him, it was something to do with psychology and all that sort of rot."

"I don't understand you."

"Well, it was this way: I gather that he thought old Bill was pining for her, and he fancied it would cure him if he saw her in the old ancestral home. Old Bill had nothing to do with it. He got the shock of his life when he saw her."

Sally drew a deep breath.

"Oh! Well, that's a relief."

"Glad you're pleased," said Lord Tidmouth politely.

"I thought my patient had had a relapse. Which, after I had been working on him for three weeks, would have been too bad."

Lord Tidmouth was seeing deeper and deeper into this business every moment.

"Old Bill's potty about you," he said.

"Indeed?"

"Absolutely potty. Many's the time he's raved about you to me. He says he could howl like a dog."

"Really?"

"And, as for Lottie, if that's the trouble, don't give her another thought. If it's of any interest, she's going to marry *me*."

Sally was surprised.

"You? But that's very rapid, isn't it?"

"Rapid?"

"I mean, you've only seen her about twice, haven't you?"

Lord Tidmouth laughed indulgently.

"My dear old soul," he said, "the above and self were man and wife for years and years and years... Well, at least eighteen months. I am speaking now of some time ago, when I was in my prime."

"You mean, you used to be married to—her?"

"Absolutely. And we've decided to give it another try. You never know but what these things will take better a second time. I think we'll be like the paper on the wall. Great Lovers of History, if you know what I mean. I can honestly say I've never married a woman I felt more pally towards than Lottie."

Sally held out her hand.

"I hope you'll be very happy, Lord Tidmouth," she said.

"Thanks," said his lordship. "Thanks frightfully. And you?"

"What do you mean?"

"Well, my dear old thing... I mean, now that you know that Bill's relations with Lottie were strictly on the up-and-up, and realising, as you must do, that he's perfectly goofy about you, what I'm driving at is, why don't you marry the poor old blighter and put him out of his misery?"

"Lord Tidmouth, mind your own business!"

Lord Tidmouth winced beneath the harsh words.

"I say," he said plaintively, "you needn't bite a fellow's head off like that."

Sally laughed.

"Poor Lord Tidmouth! I oughtn't to have snubbed you, ought I?"

"Don't apologise. I'm used to it. My third wife was a great snubber."

"I was only annoyed for a moment that you should think I could possibly be in love with Mr. Bannister."

Lord Tidmouth could not follow this.

"Don't see why you shouldn't be," he said. "Bill's an excellent chap."

"A rich waster."

"Handsome..."

"Mere conventional good looks."

"Kind to animals."

"Well, I'm not an animal. If ever I fall in love, Lord Tidmouth, it will be with someone who is some use in the world. Mr. Bannister is not my sort. If he had ever done one decent stroke of work in his life..."

"You're pretty strong on work, aren't you?"

"It's my gospel. A man who doesn't work is simply an excrescence on the social fabric."

Lord Tidmouth's monocle fell from its resting place.

"Pardon me while I wince once more," he said. "That one found a chink in the Tidmouth armour."

"Oh, you!" said Sally, smiling. "One doesn't expect you to work. You're a mere butterfly."

"Pardon me. I may be a butterfly, but I am not mere."

"You're not a bad sort, anyway."

"Dear lady, your words are as music to my ears. Exit rapidly before you change your mind. Teuf-teuf!" said Lord Tidmouth, disappearing in the direction of the breakfast room.

Sir Hugo came bustling in from the garden. A recent glance at his watch, taken in conjunction with a sense of emptiness, had told him that it was time he breakfasted.

At the sight of Sally, he stopped, astonished.

He peered at her, blinking. He seemed to be wondering whether much anxiety of mind had affected his eyesight.

"Doctor Smith!"

"Good morning, Sir Hugo."

"I had no notion you were here."

"I was sent for—last night—professionally."

"Somebody ill?"

"Not now."

"Are you making a long stay?"

"No. I shall leave almost immediately. I have to be in London for my hospital rounds."

"Oh? Have you seen my nephew William?"

"Not since last night. Lord Tidmouth says he went out to look for you."

"I am most anxious to find him. I have something of the most vital importance to say to him."

"Yes?" said Sally indifferently.

"I am endeavouring to save him from making a ghastly blunder and ruining his whole life. He is on the very verge of taking a step which can only result in the most terrible disaster... By the way, I knew there was something I wanted to ask you. When you putt, which leg do you rest the weight on?"

"I always putt off the left leg."

"Indeed? Now, that's most interesting. The left, eh?"

"Yes."

"Some people say the right."

"Yes. J. H. Taylor says the right."

"Still, Walter Hagen prefers the left."

"He ought to know."

"Yes. I remember seeing Walter Hagen hole a most remarkable putt. He was fully thirty feet from the hole on an undulating green. He..." Sir Hugo broke off. Something with the general aspect of a thundercloud had loomed through the french windows. "Ah, William," he said, "I was looking for you."

Bill gazed at him blackly.

"Oh, you were?" he said. "Well, I was looking for *you*. What's all this Tidmouth tells me?"

"Tidmouth tells you?"

"Yes, Tidmouth tells me."

"Tidmouth tells you?"

A spasm shook Bill.

"Will you stop that cross-talk stuff!" he cried. "What Tidmouth told me was that you had got hold of some asinine idea that I'm in love with Lottie Higginbotham."

"Quite correct. And what I say, William—and I say this very seriously—"

Bill cut in on his oration.

"There's only one woman in the world that I love or ever shall love," he said, "and that's Sally."

"Sally?" said Sir Hugo, blinking.

"I'm Sally," said Sally.

Sir Hugo looked from one to the other. He seemed stunned.

"You love this girl?" he gasped at length.

"Yes."

Sir Hugo raised both hands, like a minor prophet blessing the people. His mauve face was lit up with a happiness which, as a rule, was only to be found there on the rare occasions when he laid an approach putt dead.

"My dear boy!" he boomed. "My dear young lady! This is the most wonderful news I have ever had. Bless you, bless you. My dear Doctor, take him! Take him, I say, and may he be as happy as I should be in his place. I'll leave you. Naturally you wish to be alone. Dear me, this is splendid news. William, you have made me a very happy man. What did you say your handicap was, my dear?"

"Six—at Garden City."

"Six at Garden City! Wonderful! What the Bannisters need," said Sir Hugo, "is a golfer like you in the family."

He toddled off, rejoicing, to his breakfast.

Bill laughed nervously.

"I'm afraid," he said, "Uncle was a little premature."

"A little, perhaps."

"But don't you think..."

"No, I'm afraid not."

"I had nothing to do with Lottie's being here last night."

"I know that."

"And doesn't it make any difference."

"No."

"But, Sally..."

"No. I'm afraid you're not my sort of man."

"I love you."

"Is love everything?"

"Yes."

"No," said Sally. "Respect matters, too."

"I see. You despise me?"

"Not despise. But I can't take you seriously."

"I see."

She thought that he was going to say more, but he stopped there. He walked to the desk and sat down.

"I'm sorry," said Sally.

"Don't mention it," said Bill coldly. "Have you had breakfast?"

"Not yet."

"You'd better go along and have it, then. It's in the morning room."

"Aren't you having any?"

"I had a cup of coffee just now in the kitchen. I don't want any more."

"Have I spoiled your appetite?" asked Sally demurely.

"Not at all," said Bill with dignity. "I very seldom eat much breakfast."

"Nor do I. A very healthful plan."

Bill had opened the drawer of the desk, and was pulling papers out of it. He spoke without looking up, and his tone was frigid.

"You will excuse me, won't you?" he said formally.

Sally was curious.

"What are you doing?"

"I thought of doing a little work."

Sally gasped.

"Work?" she cried, astounded.

She drew a step nearer, her eyes round.

"Yes," said Bill aloofly. "Business connected with the estate. I've been neglecting it."

"Work!" said Sally, in a whisper.

Bill regarded her coldly.

"You won't think me rude? I've got rather behind-hand. I've been a little worried lately."

"I didn't know you ever did any work!"

"Oh? Well, I do. A considerable amount of work. Do you suppose a place like this runs itself?"

"But I never dreamed of this," said Sally, still in the same hushed voice. "Do you mind if I sit here? I won't disturb you."

"Please do," said Bill indifferently.

She settled herself into a chair, and sat watching him. Ostentatiously ignoring her presence, he started to busy himself with the papers.

Some moments passed.

"How are you getting on?" she asked.

"All right, thanks."

"I won't disturb you."

"That's all right."

There was another silence.

"You don't mind my sitting here?" said Sally.

"Not at all."

"Just go on as if I were not here."

"Very well."

"I would hate to feel I was disturbing you."

"Kind of you."

"So I won't say another word."

"All right."

There was a brief interval of silence. Then Sally got up and stood behind him.

"What are you working at?" she asked.

Bill looked up and answered distantly.

"Well, if the information conveys anything to you, I am writing out an order for some new Alpha separators."

"Alpha... what?"

"Separators. They are machines you use to separate the cream from the milk."

"How interesting!" She came closer. "Why do you want Alpha separators?"

"Because I happen to own a dairy farm."

"You do? Tell me more."

"More what?"

"More about your dairy farm."

Bill raised his eyebrows.

"Why? Does it interest you?"

"Tremendously," said Sally. "Anything to do with work interests me.... An Alpha separator—it sounds complicated."

"Why?"

"Well, it does."

"It isn't. If you're really interested..."

"Oh, I am."

Bill's manner lost something of its frigidity. His dairy farm was very near to his heart. He had fussed over it for years, as if it had been a baby sister, and he welcomed the chance of holding forth on the subject. So few people ever allowed him to do so.

"It's based on centrifugal force," he said.

"Yes?"

"Here's a diagram." An ardent note came into his voice. "That thing there is the reservoir."

"I see."

"Below it," proceeded Bill emotionally, "is the regulator with a float valve... "

"Go on," said Sally, thrilled.

All the coldness had now left Bill Bannister's demeanour and speech. An almost fanatical note had replaced it. He spoke with a loving warmth which would have excited the respectful envy of the author of the Song of Solomon.

"As soon as the regulator is full," he said, his eyes shining with a strange light, "the float valve shuts off the influx."

Sally was all enthusiasm.

"How frightfully clever of it!"

"Shall I tell you something?" said Bill, growing still more ardent.

"Do!"

"That machine," said Bill devoutly, "can separate two thousand seven hundred and twenty-four quarts of milk an hour!"

Sally closed her eyes ecstatically.

"Two thousand... "

" ... seven hundred and twenty-four."

They looked at each other in silence.

"It's the most wonderful thing I ever heard," whispered Sally.

Bill beamed.

"I thought you'd be pleased."

"Oh, I *am!*" She pointed. "And what's that little ninctobinkus?"

"That?" Bill paused, the better to prepare her for the big news. "That," he said passionately, "is the Holstein butter churner."

"O-o-oh!" breathed Sally.

He looked at her anxiously.

"Is anything the matter?"

"No, no. Go on talking."

"About milk?"

Sally nodded.

"Yes," she said. "I never knew it could be so exciting. Do you get your milk from contented cows?"

"They've never complained to me yet," said Bill. He placed his finger on the paper. "See that thing? The sterilizer!"

"Wonderful!" said Sally.

"That's the boiler there. At seventy degrees centigrade the obligatory and optional bacteria are destroyed."

"Serve them right!" said Sally. She looked at him with almost uncontrollable excitement. "Do you mean seriously to tell me," she asked, "that you are familiar with the bacteria of milk?"

"Of course I am."

Sally's eyes danced delightedly.

"But this is extraordinary!" she cried. "The cavillus acidi lactici..."

"The bacillus lactis acidi..."

"The bactorium koli..."

"The bacillus erogenes..."

"The proteus vulgaris..."

"The streptococci..."

"The colosiridium butiricum..."

"The bacillus butiricus," cried Bill, rolling the words round his tongue in an ecstasy. "The bacillus sluorovenus. *And* the penicilium glaucum!"

Sally leaned on the desk. She felt weak.

"Great heavens!"

"What's the matter?"

"It can't be possible!"

"What?"

"That you actually do know something about something, after all," said Sally, staring at him. "You really do do work—decent, honest, respectable work!"

The fanatic milk gleam died out of Bill's eyes. Her words had reminded him that this was no congenial crony who stood before him, but the girl who had flouted his deepest feelings; who had laughed and mocked at his protestations of love; who had told him in so many words that he was not a person to be taken seriously.

He stiffened. His manner took on a cold hostility once more.

"I do," he said. "And from now on I'm going to work harder than ever. Don't you imagine," he went on, his eyes stony and forbidding, "that just because you've turned me down, I'm going to sit moaning and fussing over my broken heart. I'm going to *work*, and not think about you any more."

Sally beamed.

"That's the stuff!"

"I shall forget you."

"Fine!"

"Completely."

"Splendid!"

"Put you right out of my mind forever."

"Magnificent!"

Bill thumped the desk with a hamlike fist.

"As soon as you have left this house," he said, "I shall order new tractors."

"Yes, do," said Sally.

"New harrows," said Bill remorselessly.

"Bravo!"

"And fertilizers."

Sally's eyes were shining.

"Fertilizers, too!"

"Also," thundered Bill, "Chili saltpetre and Thomas tap cinders."

"*Not* Thomas tap cinders?"

"Yes. Thomas tap cinders," said Bill uncompromisingly.

"I never heard anything so absolutely glorious in my life," said Sally.

The telephone rang sharply. Bill took up the receiver.

"Hullo? This is Mr. Bannister... For you," he said, handing her the instrument.

Sally sat on the desk.

"Hello?" she said. "Yes, speaking... Now?... Quite impossible, I'm afraid... You might try Doctor Borstal. He substitutes for me... I can't possibly leave here now. The case I am attending is very serious. Much more serious than I thought... Good-bye."

The interruption had caused another radical alteration in Bill Bannister's feelings. Forgotten were the stouthearted words of a moment ago. Looking hungrily at Sally, as she sat swinging her feet from the desk, he melted again. Forget her? Put her right out of his mind? He couldn't do it in a million years.

"Sally..." he cried.

She had jumped off the desk and was fumbling in her bag.

"One moment," she said. "I'm looking for my thermometer."

"Are you feverish?"

"That's just what I want to find out."

"Sally..."

"Go on," she said. "I'm listening."

She put the thermometer in her mouth. Bill stood over her, though every instinct urged him to grovel on the floor. He was desperate now. The thought that soon she would be gone—right out of his life—lent him an unusual eloquence. Words poured from him like ashes from a Thomas tap cinder.

"Sally... Sally... Sally... I love you. I know you're sick of hearing me say it, but I can't help myself. I love you. I love you."

Sally nodded encouragingly.

"M'hm," she said.

"I never knew how much I loved you till I saw you here—among my things—sitting on my desk—Won't you marry me, Sally? Think of all the fun we'd have. You would love this place. We would ride every morning through the fields, with the clean, fresh wind blowing in our faces."

"M'hm."

"And all around us there would be life and movement... things growing... human beings like carved statues against the morning sky... The good smell of the earth... animals... benzine and crude oil... benzine and crude oil, Sally!"

"M'hm!"

"It's summer. The fields would be like gold in the morning. Sparkling in the sun. Harvest time. Ripe wheat. Do you hear, Sally? Ripe wheat shining in the summer sun, and you and I riding together... oh, Sally!"

She drew the thermometer from her mouth.

"I have no fever," she said.

"Sally..."

"But I'm trembling, and my pulse is a hundred and ten. And —do you know—"

"What?"

"I've lost control of my vascular motors."

"Sally!"

"One moment. I am faced with the most difficult diagnosis of my career. I ascertain the following: The organs are intact. I have no pain. No fever. But the pulse is a hundred and ten. The reflexes are heightened. On the periphery of the skin I note a strong radiation of warmth. A slight twitching in the nape of the neck. The hands tremble. The heart action is quickened. Every symptom points to something serious... something very serious indeed."

"You're ill!"

"I'm not. I'm in love. Yes, that is what I diagnose—acute love!"

She looked at him.

"Do you remember what I said to you that day we met? If ever I found a man I could love I would tell him so as frankly as if I were saying good morning."

She came towards him, holding out her hands.

"Good morning, Bill!"

"I say," said Lord Tidmouth, manifesting himself suddenly in the doorway, "do you two know that breakfast..." He broke off.

His educated eye, trained by many years of marrying one woman after another with scarcely a breathing space in between, had taken in the situation at a glance. "Sorry!" he said. "Excuse it, please!"

The door closed. From the passage beyond they heard his voice announcing that he feared no foe in shining armour.